WEBLEY AND
THE WORLD MACHINE

ZACHARY PAUL CHOPCHINSKI

ILLUSTRATED BY: MICHAELA HELÍKOVÁ

WEBLEY AND

THE WORLD MACHINE

ZACHARY PAUL CHOPCHINSKI

WEBLEY AND THE WORLD MACHINE

For information address Books & Bow Ties Publishing, 4844 E. Michigan st, Orlando, FL. 32812
www.zachchop.com
Webley and The World Machine/Zachary P. Chopchinski—1st ed. Printed in the United States of America.
January 2018
Published by Books & Bow Ties Publishing
Orlando, FL.
ISBN-10: 1981268502
ISBN-13:978-1981268504

Edited by Plot2Published
Cover design by Deranged Doctors Designs
Author photo by Jessica Verge Photography
Formatting by Layla Venturini

Praise For

Webley and

The World Machine

"It's Bioshock meets Sucker Punch with a side of Wild Wild West"

-**Kacey Abels,** *The Reading Tree Book Blog*

"I'm completely lost in the World Machine. It's my new happy place!"

-S.J's Book Blog

Acknowledgements

There are so many things that I owe to so many people for all the help that they generously gave to help me make this book all that it became. To my lovely wife, never forget that I see you, and always know all that you do for me. I will never be able to pay you back for everything, but if it helps, I will give you all the love, fur-babies, and cookie cake that you could ever ask for. As long as I can have your love and all the tacos!

I would also like to thank Bridgette O'Hare for dealing with my ADHD and lack of ability to keep solid schedules. I love you to pieces and appreciate the fantastic job you did editing this book. Also thank you to Martina for dealing with me for nearly twenty hours in a car. Though the smells and laughs only lasted until we blacked out from exhaustion, I know that our friendship will last forever. Or, at least, until the next road trip and you end up killing me. Either way, good times. A huge thank you to The Hellgnome for making the coin that started the whole story! Check out his work on Instagram (@ocu_lar). I really need to give a big thank you to my illustrator Michaela Helíková! Thank you for seeing what is inside my head and making it a reality!

Thank you to all of my Beta readers. You guys got the rough job, but I tell you what, you made this book that much more of a polished product for all of the readers. I don't want to name you, because my gift to you is that if the book flops, you have no official attachment to it. If this book reaches a best seller, this part will be edited out...POSSIBLY...

Thank you to all of my friends that stood by me while I wrote this. All of those lovely authors, readers, bloggers, and stalkers that supported me through this book and grew just as excited as I did as it grew and grew. In this world, with Indie Authors, it really does take a village. All of my friends that I have met along my journey, and those from before it began, I wouldn't change my village for the world.

Lastly, I would like to thank my doctor, who told me just after I finished writing this book that the amount of caffeine that I was consuming in the end would likely kill me if I didn't stop. Good looking out, Doc. Then he told me that I had to give up caffeine to recoup. In that sense, shove-off! I am sipping coffee as I write this. It's my body, I'll do what I want!

Anyway, I love you all dearly, and here is to many more adventures.

DEDICATION

To my best friend and love of my life; my wife.

Layla, you started this adventure for me. As I grow and develop, it is only due to the support and nurturing that you give me. All that I am as a man and an author is thanks to you. You make me better, and I will always love and cherish you for all that you have done. Until the day the world ceases to turn, and forever past. The world for you, Mama Bear.

"Get action. Seize the moment. Man was never intended to become an oyster."

–Theodore Roosevelt

MORE FROM ZACH

The Gabrielle Series:
The Curious Tale of Gabrielle
Curiosity and The Hounds of Arawn
Curiosity and The Sentient's Oblation
Curiosity and Arawn's Penance

From Now On: The Last Words Anthology

PROLOGUE

2,400,000 B.C, The World Machine

Cog rolled end over end across the platform, tumbling like a rag doll. The brass surface was slick with oil and gears from fallen soldiers from both sides.

His brother had gone too far this time. Those damn machines he'd built were proving a little too difficult to kill. Though Cog had always considered himself a master of inventions and a skilled warrior, the winged pack he'd designed was still scarcely a match for the mechanical monstrosities his traitorous brother had created.

The world exploded around him as airships and mechanical creatures circled overhead. The smell of gunpowder and copper filled the air as brother fought brother and friend fought friend. All for what? Power? Freedom? Greed?

One of his fellow soldiers flew into a massive girder, spinning and colliding with a brass beam. The force of the explosion pushed Cog to the ground. Remnants of the battleship dropped from the sky and landed amongst a giant set of gears, slowly rotating in a feeble attempt to power the furnace that kept them all alive.

His brother had orchestrated this attack, and the boss had said to protect the furnaces at all costs. The thought of failing tore at Cog as he collected himself and drew his trusty pistols, firing wildly into the air at any mechanism that flew past.

As he swatted one of the insect-like mechanical creatures from the sky, several more took notice of his attack. They turned their attention from an airship and swooped down, their bladed appendages nearly missing Cog's head. He ducked, unleashing another barrage of shots from his weapons.

The cold chill of fear rippled through Cog as something told him he needed to get to the furnace. He sprinted the length of the platform, the metallic surface clinking beneath his feet with every step. As he neared the giant turning gears that powered The World Machine, towers of fire and smoke billowed from its gargantuan pipes. The same winged monstrosities that had nearly gotten the best of him were doing their worst on the exterior of the furnace.

An airship thundered overhead. One of his. Captain Silny shouted to his men as the ship's guns fired upon the attackers of the furnace. A litany of small explosions scattered the onslaught of enemy soldiers. At that moment, Cog realized what would happen if the airship continued to shoot at the creatures.

He opened his mouth to protest, but another explosion floored him as shrapnel projected into the sky above. Sheer terror caused Cog to briefly lose himself to the blackness. When he pushed the sludge from his brain, he saw the great ship had vanished into a cloud of fire and smoke, and the furnace's warmth and light had extinguished.

Cog looked at the silent heart of the Machine in disbelief. In the deep crimson smoke, the outlines of those damn flying things still whizzed about with triumphant victory. They didn't even know the depth of what they'd done. With a scowl, Cog retrieved his pistols from the platform near his feet. He couldn't let those bastards win.

Without the radiant heat and power from the furnaces, the Machine would suffer, and all the Dwellers would die. His friends. His family. His love. They would all perish unless he did something. Even if he had to kill thousands of these monsters himself, he had to save the Machine.

1

MR. SMOOTH

PRESENT DAY, GERMANY

Adal shot up from his bed and looked around the room as sweat trickled down his forehead. Too often he awoke in the middle of the night, sweating and kicking his blankets off. It didn't help that his father refused to drop the central air lower than seventy-nine degrees. It also didn't help that when the hot morning sun peeked over the horizon, it poured right through his window.

"Damn!" Adal shot his panic filled eyes at his alarm clock. He was running late. Today was the day he was presenting his Grandfather's story and family history to his senior class. He hopped from his bed. As he did, his foot tangled in his sheet causing him to fall face first to the floor.

A loud 'thud' was followed by him placing his arms outward like he was doing pushups and leveraging himself to stand again. He paused for a moment and looked around his room as though assuring that no one had seen him take the tumble.

Coming back to reality, he scoffed and rolled his eyes before darting to his bathroom.

He stumbled about his morning ritual as quickly as he could, taking only a few minutes to stare at himself in the mirror. Adal made it a point to look as good as he could before he left his room. He had long worked on his stylish reputation and wouldn't let something as trivial as being late jeopardize it.

Once prepared for the day, Adal took a moment to appreciate his appearance before leaving the mirror. His low-cut white t-shirt dipped just far enough to show the crease between his pecs that he'd spent months chiseling with track and field. His hair and fade lined up perfectly, and he ran his hand over his neck. Smooth as ever.

After giving himself a wink in the mirror, Adal slipped his sneakers on and hastened for his bedroom door. As he grabbed the handle, he froze in place and smiled. He turned around and grabbed his notebook off the desk near the door. In all the morning rush, he nearly forgot the reason for his hurrying.

Swinging his bedroom door open, he ran through the hall and hopped down the stairs to the first landing. Collecting himself, he walked down the last three stairs and then made a dash for the front door.

"Adalwolf Stein. You get your butt over here right now," his father's voice bellowed from the dining room. When his father used his full name, Adal knew he was in it deep. Everyone knew him as Adal. Few people knew his whole name, and he would only answer to it for his parents, mostly because he didn't have a choice.

Adal rolled his eyes and turned around, walking into the dining room. His father and grandfather were seated at the table eating. Grandpa Lawrence was reading the paper, as he did every morning, while his mother poured coffee and beckoned Adal to the one empty seat with a plate already set for him. His father sat at the head of the table, a stern look on his face as he peered impatiently over the frame of his glasses at his son.

"Boy, are you running late again?" Adal's father leaned back in his chair, sipping his coffee. Adal reluctantly walked over and plopped down in the empty chair, setting his notebook on the table next to a pitcher of orange juice.

"Well, the boy wouldn't be so late if you didn't stop him from gettin' to school. Pick those fights, Son," his grandfather chimed in, not even lowering the paper that covered his face.

Adal smiled. He knew his grandfather was trying to conceal a laugh as he hid behind his morning paper.

"Dad, now's not the time. The boy is becoming an adult, and he needs to be thinking about his future, about what he wants to do with his life. He has to get himself together and learn to be organized," his father said.

This time, his grandfather remained silent. Adal hated when his grandfather kept quiet, it meant that he agreed with his father.

Adal's father had drilled into his head every day for as long as he could remember the importance of getting into University and getting a good job. Don't follow those lazy friends of yours! Adal's dad had said to him so many times that he could mimic both the tone and inflection of his father's lecture.

"Dad, it's not my fault. I was up all night working on my report for History. I forgot to set my alarm!"

"That's the problem, Adal. You need to listen to your father. We raised you better than that," Adal's mother joined in as she wiped down the counter with a paper towel.

Adal sucked on his teeth and sunk into his chair. They weren't about to hear him. They never did. His parents were always 'A+' parents. You could bring home an A, and they would ask why it wasn't an A+.

He knew they loved him, but he wished they showed it in ways other than riding him all the time. That's why, over the years, Adal had grown so close to his grandfather. Ever since he was little, his grandfather had been the only one with any chill.

The story was always the same when he asked his dad why he was so hard on him all the time. Being raised in Germany, a mixed-race son of a black American and a white German, Adal's father was always the outcast. That drove him to move to Africa where he'd met his mother.

After Grandma Ursula had died and Grandpa Lawrence needed help to get around, they moved back to Germany. That adversity made his dad proud, strong, stubborn, and driven. Adal had inherited his father's strength and pride, but he had a personality to go with it.

"Look, I get it. I screwed up. My bad. Can I go? I really am going to be late for my presentation." Adal stood from his chair and grabbed his notebook before his parents could argue. His mother sighed, and his father sipped his coffee.

"You can go, Adalwolf, but we will talk about this when you get home. Things are going to change around here. I expect a decent grade on that report today, and I want to see your teacher's notes on it too." His father slid his glasses back up his nose to signal that he was done speaking, and Adal turned on his heels to leave.

"Adal," his grandfather spoke up, putting the newspaper down. With age, his grandfather's hair had turned white, giving a sharp contrast to his dark complexion. He never called Adal "Adalwolf"; he was the only one in his family who respected Adal enough to know he hated his full name.

"Are you doing the report on our family? My story and how we got here?" he asked, nodding his head to Adal's notebook.

"You know it!"

"Then let the boy alone. He's got this. Quit being so hard on my grandson all the time." Lawrence nudged his son in the shoulder producing a smile from Adal and a frustrated snort from his son. As a rule, you did not speak to an elder with disrespect in their home. It took Adal a few strikes on the back of the head growing up to learn that lesson, but it took nonetheless.

"Thanks, Gramps." Adal chuckled, pointing to his grandfather and nodding his head up toward the ceiling.

"Damn, I remember that day like it happened this morning." Grandpa Lawrence leaned back in his chair, the familiar memories of war playing across his face. "We arrived at the outskirts of the bunker where that son of a bitch Hitler was holed up just as the sun was peeking its head over the hills. We'd marched all night, and let me tell you, my feet were so blistered I couldn't take a goddamn step without popping one of those bad boys." A guttural laugh escaped the old man's lips, and Adal knew he would really be late.

"The tanks rumbled as I walked with my machine-gun in my hands. Oh lord, that was the most empowering moment of the war. We knew what we were gettin' ourselves into, and we were ready to be heroes. We were the 761st Tank Battalion. Our motto was Come Out Fightin'. Being a mostly Colored unit, we were always given the suicide missions. Damn army didn't care about us. At first, we couldn't believe we survived, but after a while, we liked defying the odds. We liked showing those bastards what we were made of…"

Adal leaned against the wall by the kitchen door, he couldn't interrupt Grandpa Lawrence, so he got comfortable. Adal's father rolled his eyes, no doubt having heard the story a million times.

"...We reached our rally point. The tanks quit rolling, and we all gathered in formation. What we got was a simple plan with high danger and a lot of work. This wasn't anything we weren't used to. We basically came to blow it up, shoot it down, kill them all—a regular day at work. They called my unit the 'Cutters.' We carried the BAR, that was the Browning Automatic Rifle."

"Yeah, we all know that, Dad." Adal's father chimed in as he turned the page of his newspaper and took a sip of his coffee.

"I'm tellin the boy!" Lawrence snapped before continuing his story. "Anyway, we kept those krauts in check with heavy fire while our tanks did what they came to do. We walked a little before we came through a park and the bunker was in sight. Now, usually, we'd wait before we attacked a target. Sort of a 'wait for the best time' kinda thing, you understand that?"

Adal nodded his head, but his grandfather didn't wait for a response.

"We had a little bet going against the Red Army, so we weren't waitin' for anything. You see, sometimes in war, you gotta make a game out of it, you know . . . to keep out the dark thoughts that you killin' a bunch of people. We entered the clearing, and our tanks opened fire. BOOM! We learned early on that the sounds could deafen the poor bastard who shot them off. That's why I got this bad ear, ya' see. Anyway, so we fired, moved, fired, and moved killing as many of those kraut bastards as we could. It was sort of funny seeing all those German faces when they saw our tanks. Hitler's final stand outside his goddamn compound and there we were, a battalion of black men showing those Arian bastards what real warriors were," Lawrence paused to take a sip of his coffee and shovel a piece of Brötchen into his mouth. Crumbs of bread and drops of coffee stuck to the stubble on his face.

"When we got inside the compound, we mopped up what was left of the enemy. I'll admit, the Germans weren't stupid, they had some good defenses once we were inside. I personally fought with three SS soldiers in a hallway for almost five minutes before I remembered I still had a grenade remaining. Like to say they went out with a bang."

Adal laughed. He'd heard the story at least a dozen times, but this part always made him laugh. Grandpa Lawrence was the coolest guy he knew, and Adal had always wanted to be like him.

"...the Russians were already in, working the German's from the other side. Damn, they'd got in there fast. Like a bunch of goddamn magicians. Everything turned into a mad dash to get down to the basement bunker and get to that bastard, Hitler. After I don't even know how long of fighting and moving, we finally made it to the bunker only to find that the coward had killed himself and his wife. Let me tell you, when I say we were hot under the collar about that, I'm not yankin' your chain." Lawrence pounded his fist on the table, the anger resurfacing as he told the story.

"The Russians took credit for the entire raid. Those sons of bitches wouldn't have even made it into the compound if it wasn't for our tanks. Damn, let me tell you what I saw down in that bunker..."

"Gramps, I got to go. I'm really going to be late." Without even waiting for a response, Adal ran to the front door, opened it and slid outside, accidentally slamming it behind him. He flinched at the loud bang and knew he would hear about that when he got home later. Leaping through the air, Adal cleared the steps of his front stoop and landed silently on the sidewalk.

He hurried up the sidewalk toward the school. Adal didn't want to run because that would make him sweat, and he couldn't show up to school looking sloppy. That wasn't his style. Besides, he still had seventeen minutes to get to school according to his watch, and it was only a few blocks away. No worries. He could still make it.

Other teens walked along the sidewalk toward the school, but even though he didn't run, Adal was passing them. At six feet three inches, he had a long stride, and walking as fast as he could, he easily matched the speed of some of his classmates while jogging. A few said 'Hello' as he passed, but Adal was lost in thoughts of his parents from breakfast.

"Why does he have to always be in my business all the time?" Adal mumbled, rounding a corner. The school was almost in view—only five blocks straight ahead, he should be there in a few minutes. Still lost in his thoughts, Adal didn't even notice he had gained a follower. A sharp pinch on his shoulder nearly made him drop his notebook.

Catching the book midair, Adal turned to confront the person who thought it funny to trip him up. He was ready to pour his morning frustrations on the newcomer when he turned and saw who it was. He sighed and shook his head.

"Well, looks like you aren't always as together as you'd like to think," teased Arija as she nudged him in the arm. She tossed her straight raven hair over one shoulder and giggled as she adjusted her backpack. Arija had done these sorts of things to get under his skin ever since they met and became friends ten years ago. As the two had grown, they only became closer friends, and over the last year, they'd become inseparable.

Arija was the smartest girl in their class, but she also had the heart of a fighter. Adal considered her too good for any of the boys at school. She deserved a man. Someone who would take care of her and treat her right. Though they were only friends, Adal had to admit that she looked good.

Adal's other friends made fun of him for not going after Arija, but he was too cool to be considered taken. He liked the attention he got from other girls. A girlfriend would cramp his style. Adal knew Arija liked him, he could see it in the way she'd bat those big hazel eyes at him, but she was his best friend, and he didn't want to do anything to screw that up.

"Girl, you almost messed up my presentation. You do that, don't think I won't make you write me another one!" Adal tugged at his shirt, pulling out the imaginary wrinkles she'd caused. Arija let out an unimpressed laugh at his attempted bravado.

"You act like I don't already do half your homework so you don't flunk out and get kicked off the team! So, the way I figure it, you kinda owe me more favors than you have thoughts in the day." She turned her nose up at him and picked up her pace, gaining several steps ahead.

Arija was cute when she pretended to be mad at him, and Adal let a wide grin crease his face as he picked up speed.

"You know I appreciate that. Besides, you also keep my old man off my back." Adal put his arm around Arija's shoulder and pulled her to his side. She smiled, pushing away from him.

"Don't think just because you're Mr. Smooth that you can butter me up. I only need you to pass so we stand a chance in the competition. I have the girls' team covered, but we need you on the boys' team to keep them in the winning circle. It's strictly business, get yourself together." They always played this game, pretended like they didn't care about each other, but Arija kept him in check, and for that, Adal was grateful.

"Oh, you know you can't resist my charms. No girl can!" Adal ran ahead of Arija and turned to face her, so she couldn't get past him. She stopped. He grinned as he leaned down, touching his forehead against hers so they were nose to nose. Arija may have been several inches shorter than him, but she never let his height intimidate her. Eventually, Arija laughed and pushed him away, but Adal had to admit, he liked messing with her.

A rolling sound came from behind Adal, and before he knew what was happening, his foot landed on something slippery and was sliding out from under him. His feet flew into the air as his back slammed into the hard ground. A chorus of laughter erupted from a gang of boys leaned against the wall of a small coffee shop just next to them.

"Smooth landing, Adal!" one boy cackled, stepping over the fallen Adal. He snatched up his skateboard.

Arija's face flushed with anger as she helped her friend to his feet. The other boys remained with their backs against the wall, but the one that spoke stood next to Adal, holding the skateboard that had put Adal on his back to begin with.

"And to think, they made you team captain? Can't even stay on your feet while walking. Lucky, she was here to help the little boy up. What are you supposed to be again, anyway, his groupie?" the boy teased Arija crudely as rage burned on Adal's face.

"What the hell was that, Elias?" Adal shouted, thrusting both of his hands into the boy's chest and shoving him back into his group of friends. The group gathered their leader and stalked toward Adal, Elias in the lead.

"Just testing your skills, man. I mean, you're supposed to be the best, ain't you?" Elias was so close Adal could smell the bully's rank breath. Arija stood next to her friend as the other boys attempted a half-circle. She clenched her fists and gritted her teeth. Adal's jaw sawed back and forth as Elias spoke.

"You want me to show you the best? Normally, I reserve that for your mother, but if you want a piece too . . ." Adal swelled his chest and pressed it to Elias' nose. When Adal stood straight up, he was four to five inches taller than Elias, and his muscles were much more defined. The smug grin left Elias' face, and his expression went cold.

"Don't think for a moment I'm intimidated by some big golem! Maybe it's time someone taught both you and your girlfriend a lesson," Elias spat on the ground at Arija's feet. She reared back to swung at him, but Adal caught her arm and lowered it, shaking his head at her.

"You see, now that's the problem we have here, Elias. You keep insulting my friend, and she's a much better fighter than all of you put together. I think you owe her an apology." Adal gestured to the group, sliding himself into the limited space between Arija and the rest of the boys. He wasn't worried about her getting hurt, he was more worried about her hurting the rest of them and getting them all expelled.

"An apology? Really? Well, Mr. Captain, I think you're going to be disappointed," Elias snapped, looking over his shoulders to his friends. Adal didn't seem disappointed in his response. Instead, he rubbed his hand over his mouth, producing a wide grin and a single chuckle.

"Well then, looks like I'm just going to have to show you," Adal retorted, looking to Arija. The two shared a knowing smile as if they were having a telepathic conversation.

"Show me what, exactly?" Elias asked, pressing his chest into Adal. Adal leaned in to speak into Elias' ear, adrenaline rushing

"These hands," Adal whispered.
Elias' expression dropped, but it was too late for him to react. In a flash, he threw his open palm upward, hitting Elias in the throat and causing him to stumble back into two of his friends. One of the other boys avoided the impact and moved around Elias, swinging at Adal. Anticipating what the other boy would do, Adal stepped backward, and the hook flew wide. The boy recovered and went for another hook with his other fist.

Arija lunged forward and grabbed the boy's arm. Before he could react, she pulled him to the ground and had her hands and arms wrapped around his upper body in a near textbook armbar. Though she had been on the track and field team for years, Arija had also taken a liking to the wrestling team, presently holding several school records. The boy screamed in pain, and Arija applied just enough pressure to his arm to make him suffer but not enough to break the delicate bones in the wrist and forearm.

Elias was on his knees coughing as the two remaining friends turned their attention from Adal to Arija. The two boys kicked at Arija's back and ribs as they tried to pry their friend loose. Adal grabbed one of them by his collar and yanked him backward. At the same time, he brought one of his feet up and kicked the second boy in the stomach. Adal could hear the air leaving his lungs with the powerful hit.

Elias recovered, hooked his hand upward from his kneeling position, and caught Adal in the side of his ribs. Adal fell backward, and Elias stood with his hands in a fighting pose. Arija held onto her original attacker, still applying pressure, while the second coughed for air on the ground next to her. She kept one foot ready to kick him in case he tried to do anything stupid.

Elias squared off with Adal and threw several punches, faster than Adal would ever give him credit for. Adal dodged the first one, but the second and third caught him in the jaw. He brought one hand up to the spot the punch landed and moved his jaw from side to side, assessing the damage. He then followed with his own barrage of strikes, most of which found their way to Elias' chest and face. The boy he'd pulled off Arija charged at Adal while Elias swung at him.

He collided with Adal's waist and tried to lift him into the air for a body slam, but Adal was too heavy. Adal slammed both fists down into his new attacker's back and kneed him in the chest. Then, he grabbed the boy by both shoulders and rolled him away, turning once more to face Elias.

"Enough!" shouted a voice, coming out of the coffee shop. Elias turned on his heels and looked while Adal kept his pose, looking over Elias' shoulder. An older woman with graying blonde hair came out of the shop and stood just outside of the doorway. She wore a black apron, and her face was splotchy and red.

"I cannot believe you would fight in front of the family shop, Elias! What's come over you!" the woman shook her finger at the pile of boys on the ground. Elias scoffed at her, and she appeared next to him, slapping him in the back of the head like Adal's father often did him.

"Ey! Sorry, Mama! They started it!" Elias flinched under the second slap that popped his hair up in the air.

"I do not care! How dare you embarrass us like this! Wait until I tell your father!" the woman looked from Elias to Adal, then to Arija on the ground. Adal had to stifle his laughter. Arija still had the boy in her grasp, and the look of pain on his face was truly priceless. Elias' mother walked over to her, waving her hands in the air. "Girl! Let him go! That isn't necessary!" she snapped at Arija.

Arija looked at Adal and waited for his cue. When he nodded, she sighed, released her grip on the teen and kicked him away from her. She hopped to her feet and brushed her legs off. The boy rolled away and slowly stood, groaning and rubbing his arm.

"You two, go to school!" Elias' mother barked at Adal and Arija. "The lot of you, in the shop NOW! I want a few words with all of you!" The boys looked at one another and groaned as they lined up and marched their way into the shop. As Elias reached the door, he turned to face Adal.

"Next time, you're mine!" he snarled and spat at the ground before walking into the shop.

"Next time, don't bring your mom to a fist fight!" Adal shot back.

"How about next time he actually gives us a fight and not a little slap fest?" Arija added, laughing.

Adal and Arija stood and looked at one another for a moment. Then they both smiled and brushed themselves off as they laughed. "Thanks for having my back. Oh, and thanks for not snapping off that guy's arm." Adal picked up his notebook and brushed the street soot from its cover. He then looked at his reflection in the shop's window and adjusted his shirt. He reached out his knuckles toward Arija, and the two bumped fists.

"Anytime," Arija replied, punching Adal in the shoulder. "Just so you know, you fight like a girl."

"Hey, if fighting like a girl means fighting like you, I'll take that compliment all day long." With that, Adal flinched as he looked at his watch.

"Shit, girl, we're way late for first class!" Adal's confident pose was replaced by teen panic making Arija giggle.

"Well then, let's see why they made you captain of the boys' team," Arija teased as she bolted from where she stood. Arija was nearly half a block away before Adal even registered that she had started running.

2

THE SEAL

The first two hours of school went by in a blur. Adal's thoughts were caught up in the fight he'd gotten in that morning and his need to excel at his History presentation.

He sat in History class and ran his tongue over the inside of his split lip. Most of the soreness had gone, but it would take a few days for his lip to heal. He would never admit it aloud, but Elias had gotten a nice punch in.

He peered over his shoulder toward the windows that looked out over the quad. Arija sat perched on the top of her chair with her feet on the desk drawing in her notebook, as usual. Adal couldn't help but smile as he watched her black pen glide across the page like an ice-skater. Of all her strengths and hobbies, Arija fancied herself an artist most of all.

Arija seemed unfazed by the morning's events. She was always up for making a guy look weaker than she was. She had always needed to be the toughest person in the room.

In Israel, women were required to serve in the military, and Arija's mother had been no exception. But, the once fierce and proud warrior began to look at life a little differently when Arija was born. Aliza Rapp wanted more for her daughter than constant war and battle, so when Arija was two years old, they left Israel and moved to Germany. Arija idolized her mother's strength, a resolve which hardened after her mother died of a brain tumor. Adal knew he was lucky to be her friend. He never wanted to know what it felt like to be on the receiving end of her wrath.

A violent mash of scribbling sounds erupted from the back of the class. Arija, unhappy with her renderings of the tree that grew in the center of the quad, had scribbled over the failed attempt. It was so intrusive that the student presenting his family history report paused for a moment and waited for her to stop. Arija was usually polite in class, but when she was engulfed in the worlds she created with charcoal and ink, the real world slipped away.

Adal's vision blurred as he stared at the board behind his classmate at the front of the room. The text written on the whiteboard appeared as colored waves over white. His mind wandered over the morning and his father getting on him as always. Then, his thoughts turned to his grandfather who always had his back. He broke his stare from the board and looked down at his notebook. He needed to get this right if for nothing more than for Grandpa Lawrence. Adal's grandfather's voice drifted into his mind as he read over the story of his family history.

We'd heard the rumors of the Nazi treasures, but I was a little disappointed when I saw the room. What he had in there were cases upon cases of old crap…

As we checked out everything, one thing stuck out—a coin on one of the old cabinets. When I picked it up, I found the coin was brass. It was big and heavy, almost half the size of my palm. It had gears on one side, and on the other were a wrench, hammer, and an anvil.

Something about it was mesmerizing. I twisted it through my fingers. The day's spoils were still up for grabs, so I slid the coin into my pocket. The way I looked at it was the Reds owed us for gettin' them into the bunker.

We never did get any credit for that raid. We didn't kill Hitler, and the Russians had the jump on communication, so there was no need to give any credit to a bunch of black men, apparently. Even after all we did, we got to return to a world where we were lower than the goddamn dog.

It was at that point I thought to myself, "Why the hell should I go back?" It wasn't like I had anything to go back to...

A round of clapping pulled Adal from his thoughts and forced him to sit up and offer three light claps. The presenter wrapped up, and the look on his face washed with relief. Adal drew a deep breath through his nose as the teacher moved down the row and locked eyes with him. As the clapping subsided, the student took his seat next to Adal.

"Next presenter is Adal. Let's hear some encouragement for him," the teacher announced, lazily clapping his hands. Adal sighed and momentarily slouched in his chair before scooping up his notebook and standing. He walked past the row of desks and stood in front of the board facing the class. Adal tugged at his shirt and adjusted his pants.

He looked and noticed that Arija had stopped drawing. She'd settled into her desk and closed her book. Her full attention was on Adal, and she was smiling at him with her hazel eyes. Adal smiled back and looked down at his paper. Finding the first line, he glimpsed at the teacher from the side of his eye and then opened his mouth for the first word.

"CkhmhpwaWERFERmhmhrcm!" a forced cough interrupted with a not-so-hidden insult buried in the middle. Adal's blood boiled as he looked to the back corner of class and saw Elias and one of his friends from the morning. As their eyes locked, Elias smiled widely at Adal. The glare was disconnected when a piece of paper thwacked Elias in the corner of his eye, causing him to wince. Adal traced its origin to see Arija closing her notebook once more.

"Enough horseplay!" the teacher interjected, addressing the entire class. The room turned deathly silent, the air thick and uncomfortable. Adal glared at Elias for a moment before looking back to his page and finding his place again.

"You need this grade. Don't let him trip you up," Adal whispered to himself before clearing his throat.

"For my family history, the person I interviewed was my grandfather. His name was . . ."

"cuhDICKcuhcuh!" came another taunting cough from the corner of the room. Adal's concentration snapped, he looked up from his book, and in one motion he tossed it to the floor and charged at Elias, but Arija was one step ahead of him. She wasn't about to let Adal ruin their chances at the championship.

Arija leaped from her seat and climbed over the desk next to her to get at Elias. Adal was rushing past two rows of awestruck students who had slid themselves out of the way of the oncoming train. Had

40

it been at any other moment, he would have likely only responded with his own snide retort. Possibly, something along the lines of "your mother's favorite pastime?" Elias, however, was talking shit about his grandfather, and that was not going to fly. Not today.

Elias had an ear-to-ear grin on his face as he and his associate rose from their seats, hands in the air. Just as Adal was reaching out to grab Elias by the collar and teach him the lesson he'd missed that morning, Arija broke his stride.

She placed the heel of her foot against the second boy's desk and shoved hard. The desk slid into the one beside it, tripping Elias and making him fall back into his own chair. In the same movement, she stepped in front of Adal, and he collided with her chest. Arija grunted from the pressure of his body against hers. She grabbed both of Adal's wrists and clenched as hard as she could, pushing him back from the fight.

"Chill out, Adal! He isn't worth it! Not here, anyway!" Arija let out a grunt as she fought against him to prevent him from getting past her and snapping Elias in two.

"No, screw that. He wants a piece, he can have the whole thing!" Adal pressed harder against Arija. Elias leaned back in his chair and crossed his arms over his chest.

The students in the room morphed from shocked silence to cheering the fight on. Several stood on desks and yelled taunts while others gathered in a circle around them, pumping their fists in the air. Adal felt the heat radiating from his face. Tension built in his fists as he tried to push past Arija to get to Elias.

Adal had lived his life relying on his words to get him out of situations like this. He had even tried to use sarcasm to get him out of the confrontation this morning after Elias made the first move to fight, but today . . . today, Adal had been pushed past that point. His grandfather always taught him to never start a confrontation but always finish it.

Just when Arija thought she wouldn't be able to hold her friend back any longer, a voice called out over the students. It was a firm and authoritative tone, not the meek and lazy drawl of the history teacher. As the voice echoed from the concrete walls of the classroom, the students fell silent, and Adal backed away from Arija. Even Elias sat up in his chair, the smile gone from his face.

"Adalwolf Stein!" shouted a deep and raspy voice from behind them. Adal and Arija turned to see the headmaster, Mr. Muller, standing in the doorway.

Mr. Muller had proven over the years to be a stern but fair man. He had a soft spot for the athletic teams and their members. Adal always found this ironic as he was a large man and could hardly walk from one end of the school to another without stopping to catch his breath.

Adal pulled his hands from Arija's grasp and huffed out a sigh then looked at the headmaster in silence and waited for Muller to say something. He'd been caught trying to start a fight on school grounds, and Adal knew the headmaster would call his father. He ran through the scenarios of the different lectures he was bound to hear when he got home.

The class had all turned their attention from the fight and Mr. Muller to their own books. They didn't want any part of the discipline that would follow. Muller had made a name for himself with strict and unique punishments. He once made a student work as a janitor for a week after being caught smoking on the grounds. Rumor was that he even gave the regular janitor the week off to really set the tone.

"That's quite enough of that! Step away from that boy and come here!" Muller pointed to Adal and then to the floor at his own feet. Adal huffed loudly and turned to Elias, glaring at him and gritting his teeth. He was so close. Arija tugged at his sleeve, making Adal turn to her. She shook her head and motioned to the headmaster.

"As in today, Mr. Stein!" barked the headmaster. Adal lowered his head and started toward the doorway with Arija right behind him.

"Can I help you, young lady? I don't think I asked for you to join him, did I?" Muller snapped at Arija, pointing over her shoulder to her empty seat by the window. Arija looked at Adal, then at Mr. Muller, and then slowly turned and walked back to her desk, taking a seat. As Adal reached the headmaster, the large man turned and motioned for him to continue into the hallway.

The door closed with a metallic slam as Muller followed Adal into the hall. As soon as the two were alone, Adal turned and tried to reason with him.

"Mr. Muller, Elias started that mess! I wasn't doing anything wrong! He was egging me on, and the teacher wasn't about to do anything, so I just—" Adal trailed off as he looked at the expression the headmaster wore. It was not the stern glare that had previously covered his chubby face, nor was his face particularly red anymore. Rather, Muller now looked like he might throw up.

"What . . . what's wrong? Aren't you supposed to be drilling me about fighting on school property, disrespecting my class, calling my parents, and so on?" Adal didn't mean to come off sarcastically, but the expression from the ordinarily prickly headmaster made him uncomfortable.

"Son, perhaps we should take this to my office," Muller interjected, motioning for Adal to turn, and he continued walking. A sinking sensation formed in the pit of Adal's gut as the headmaster shoved his nail-bitten hands into his pockets and walked toward his office.

"Why? What's wrong? This isn't about the fighting, is it? You aren't about to kick me out of school, are you?" Adal called after Mr. Muller, panic and confusion laced with his words. Adal rubbed his hand across his forehead. If he got expelled, he'd be kicked off the team, his old man would kill him, and Arija would never forgive him. The more he thought about it, the more the sinking feeling in his stomach churned. Adal rubbed his sweaty palms together for a moment before he shot off down the hall after the headmaster.

"Son, please. This isn't the place for it," Muller continued, not bothering to look back over his shoulder at the sound of approaching footsteps.

"Look, please don't call my parents. The fight was my bad. I need this grade, Mr. Muller. My old man will kill me! Please don't call my parents . . . please," Adal pled as he sped up to walk next to the headmaster. Adal had never in his life begged for anything. His grandfather had taught him better than that. But now, as he walked next to the hulking headmaster, facing the consequences of the longest lecture of his life, followed by his old man riding his case until he died, Adal had no other option.

"Adalwolf, stop. I'm not going to call your parents. Your parents called me!" Muller interrupted, putting his hands on each of Adal's shoulders. The headmaster pulled a loop of keys from the badge reel clipped to his pants and shoved one into the lock on his office door. "Please come in, Adal, we need to talk." Adal looked from the headmaster to the brightly lit office.

"My folks called you? Why would they do that?" he asked, stepping away from the headmaster and into the office. The man frowned and turned his head from Adal. He shut the door and shuffled over to the large wooden desk that seemed out of place in his unusually small space.

"Mr. Muller, why did they call you?" Adal commanded, raising his voice and stepping toward Muller's desk. Adal's heart pounded in his chest like it was trying to force its way out. Muller shuffled papers on his desk as he tried to avoid eye contact with the frantic teen. After a few moments, the headmaster brought his eyes up to meet Adal's and reached out one shaky hand toward the chair that faced his desk.

"Please, Adal, sit down. We need to talk."

"No! Not 'til you tell me what's going on. Why did my parents call you?" Adal's jaw tightened, and he clenched his fist as if he were preparing to beat the truth out of the headmaster. Adal didn't know why but he had the heart stopping feeling that something was really, really wrong. Muller sighed and clasped his hands on the desk in front of him.

"Your parents called because they are at the hospital. Shortly after you left for school, your grandfather collapsed. It was his heart." Muller swallowed as a bead of sweat plummeted from the tip of his nose. "He didn't make it, son. I'm sorry." Adal stumbled back knocking over a potted plant near the wall.

"That shit ain't funny, man! Don't say that to me! Don't you tell me he's dead! Don't you do that!" Adal yelled, not caring who could hear or what they would think.

"Now, calm down, please. There isn't any reason for that language." Muller pulled himself up from his desk and walked over to where Adal still stood stunned. He placed a hand on Adal's shoulder and squeezed.

"Don't touch me!" Adal shouted, shoving the old man back. Adal didn't care how much trouble he would be in. Rage, grief, and confusion had taken over like a tidal wave. Heat engulfed Adal's face at the thought of his grandfather, the one person who understood him, the person who taught him to be strong. He would never see Grandpa Lawrence again, would never hear another of the old man's war stories or stay up late eating ice cream and playing poker. Who would defend him to his parents now? Muller stumbled back into the chair in front of his desk, not sure how to handle the situation.

The room was closing in, and Adal was suddenly so hot he wanted to peel his skin off his flesh. Adal slammed his fist into the side table next to him leaving a small crater in the cheap wood. Muller let out a surprised shout as he moved out of the way of the monstrous teen.

The wood of the side table split and cracked as Adal repeatedly slammed his fists into it until his knuckles were bare and bloody. With every strike, pain shot from his fist up his arms. Tears ran down Adal's face and stung the gashes on his lips.

As Adal reared back for yet another hit, two arms wrapped around him and squeezed. He continued to strike at the wooden table as Arija spun him around to face her. Adal didn't even know she'd come into the office, but the office door was wide open, and dozens of eyes peered back at him with confusion, fear, and sadness. Elias tried to push his way through the crowd to see but was muscled back by a few of the boys on the track and field team.

"Adal, stop it," Arija whispered in his ear as he flailed his arms. "Adal talk to me!" she commanded as she released him and cupped his cheeks with her hands.

"He's gone, and I wasn't there!" Adal shouted, still not caring how loud he was. His eyes welled with tears. Sure, Adal expected that one day his grandfather would pass, but he thought he'd have more time.

Arija looked from his glistening eyes and dripping cheeks to his battered hands. Droplets of blood fell from the tips of his knuckles to the floor. A swell of anger and sadness overcame Arija, and she ground her teeth as she forced it back down. The bell had rung, and now the hallway was filled with students and teachers.

As if just waking up from a long sleep, Muller straightened his suit jacket, wrung his hands together, and turned to face the hallway full of people. As he scanned his wide eyes across the group that had formed, he threw his hands up in the air and let out an exasperated sigh.

"That's enough! Nothing to see! Back to your studies . . . Now!" The headmaster made a shooing motion with his hands toward the onlookers. In unison, the teachers ushered their pupils to their classrooms, and the chorus of heavy doors closing rumbled down the hall. Arija and Adal stared at one another for a moment, an entire conversation happening in utter silence.

Adal was suddenly overcome with an urge to run. Something awoke inside him, and he knew he needed to get out of Mr. Muller's office. Like an accident on the highway, he'd become a spectacle. The thought of it made him want to punch every student and teacher in their stupid, curious faces. Adal pulled away from Arija, turned on his heels, and sprinted out of the office and down the hall. Each step echoed in the corridor, and by the time the headmaster had the chance to call after Adal, he was rounding a corner and disappearing from sight.

Adal wasn't sure how he got home. He remembered nothing after Arija tried to calm him down. Now, he sat in silence in his grandfather's room, clutching a picture of Grandpa Lawrence from his time in the war. His parents weren't home yet from the hospital. They probably couldn't bring themselves to come back to where it all happened.

Adal knew his dad didn't do well with death. When Adal's grandmother died, his dad didn't speak for weeks.

The grim silence of the house rang in Adal's ears as he cried. His eyes danced back and forth over the texture of the wall searching for answers. He didn't know how long he'd been home, but he wished he had never left that morning. Grandpa Lawrence's words from that morning danced at the forefront of Adal's mind, *Are you doing the report on our family? My story and how we got here?* Adal squeezed the picture in his hands until the glass of the frame groaned and threatened to shatter. *Quit being so hard on my grandson all the time.*

Adal tossed the picture on the bed as he damned himself for being in such a rush this morning. He was in such a hurry to get out of the house and avoid his father's droning lecture that he hadn't really had the chance to say goodbye. He couldn't tell the man he appreciated how he backed him up when his father rode his case. Adal slammed his fist into the soft bed, leaving a smudge of blood from his knuckles.

"Couldn't have stayed, could you?" he sneered to himself, pressing his eyes closed. Two more tears escaped. "You could have done something. You know CPR. You left him, and he probably died while you fought that asshole . . ."

The phone rang in the distance, causing Adal to flinch and stand. He wasn't going to answer it, but he looked through the open doorway and listened to it ring. As he glared into the empty hallway, something caught his eye. On the dresser next to the door was an envelope with a crudely tied bow around it. Adal looked at the package for a few minutes before he walked over and picked it up. Snooping through his grandfather's things was wrong, and on a normal day Adal would have let the man have his privacy, but this was no normal day, and something about this package called to him.

There was a little weight to the envelope telling Adal something was inside. Turning it over, he noticed just behind the bow was a neatly printed name: *ADAL*. His heart sank as he recognized his grandfather's handwriting, and he immediately ripped the bow away and opened the envelope, pouring the contents into his hand.

A folded letter slid from the envelope along with his grandfather's lucky coin, the one he'd found during the war. Adal rolled the large metal piece in his fingers and admired the carved hammer and gears before putting it into his pocket and opening the letter. The fresh pain of sadness flowed through his chest as he read the simple note.

Adal,

Sometimes in life, we lose track of the big picture because we are looking too closely at the small things. I want you to have my lucky coin as you prepare for your next adventure in life. May it bring you all the clarity it has brought me over the years. Oh, and no matter how today turned out, I'm proud of you.

Adal crumpled the piece of paper in his hand as hot angry tears welled in his eyes and spilled onto his cheeks. How the hell did he know to write this letter? Why was he always there when Adal needed him, and yet Adal could never return the favor? Why didn't he get to say goodbye?

The questions burned in his thoughts for a few moments until another sound from the other side of the house caught his attention. This time, it wasn't the phone ringing but the doorbell. Adal sucked in a breath and waited. Again, someone rang the bell and knocked on the door.

He gritted his teeth and marched down the hall taking the stairs one at a time, stopping with each step as he slowly made his way to the front door. The frosted glass offered a vague outline of a person broken up by the intricate etchings, but Adal couldn't tell who it was. With the bell still ringing and the unknown person now pounding on the door too, Adal grabbed the handle and yanked the heavy door open, prepared to unleash a flurry of verbal insults at the person interrupting his grief.

"There you are! Don't you know I've been trying to get ahold of you? Adal, what the hell is your problem?" Arija barked at him as she stepped through the doorway. Her verbal assault was immediately followed by her rushing him and throwing her arms around him as tight as she could. Adal stood with his hands in the air for a moment, but as the warmth and familiarity of her body pressed against him, the ice that covered Adal's heart began to melt. He lowered one arm and placed it across her back and ever-so-gently squeezed.

"I am so sorry about what happened," she breathed into his chest, the warmth running up his torso. Adal squeezed tighter, closed his eyes, and finally allowed his body to relax. Arija pulled her face away from his chest and began drilling him once more.

"Do you know what's happening? The headmaster called your parents and a truancy officer. I think your parents arrived at the school a little more than an hour ago. I had to wait for class to end before I could find you. The school is throwing all sorts of shade about you having a breakdown."

"I don't care! They can all kiss my ass as far as I'm concerned. Who cares what they think!" Adal had grown tired of constantly being judged by everyone he met—his parents, his teachers, the track team, Elias. He was in the middle of dealing with his own shit, and everyone else could just fuck off. Except for Arija. She was now the only person left that accepted him without judgment.

"I know. Hey, I came here to help you, remember? So, you can yell all you want, but how about you calm that down a little when talking to me?" Arija's sass made Adal smile. She wasn't a pushover, and she could throw back whatever was thrown at her. She was stronger in that way than anybody he had ever met.

"All right. My bad." Adal threw his hands in the air. He looked down the vacant street and then back to the open door that led into a house now full of emptiness and forgotten memories. He thought of his parents and the truancy officer and how he had no intentions of dealing with any of that mess when it came home for him.

"You know what?" Adal asked, turning and closing the door behind him. "Let's get the hell out of here." He turned, walked past Arija and down the steps of his stoop. Without thought, Arija turned on her heels and followed.

Part I:

The Machine

3

Into the Dark

The two friends walked down the street in silence. When they reached the end, they turned the corner and just continued walking. For a long while, neither of them exchanged any words. Adal remained lost in his thoughts about his life, his grandfather, and what he was going to do. He sure as hell wasn't about to go home to the storm waiting for him.

Arija walked silently next to him giving Adal all the time he needed to reflect on what had happened. She thought back on her own experiences when her mother had died. How everything hurt, and there wasn't any combination of words or sentiments in the world able to take that pain away. She decided it was best to give Adal the space he needed. After nearly an hour of walking the city streets in silence, Adal cleared his throat.

"You know what the worst thing is? At first, I didn't even think about the fact that he's dead. I wasn't sad about that at all. I was pissed he left me all alone. He was the one who had my back, and I was too busy worrying about myself to even acknowledge that he's gone." Adal maintained a distant stare at the horizon, not even looking at Arija when he spoke.

She let his words settle as she considered the best response. "Well, that's because you have an ego the size of a small bus. I'm surprised you can even fit it through a door." Arija let the joke hang in the air for a while before she continued. "It's not your fault, I just haven't been keeping you in check enough lately," she went on, trying to keep a straight face.

When Arija's mother died, Adal was the one person able to make her laugh, the only person who could make her feel like a human. It was her turn to bring him back to the world of the living. Through the corner of his eye, Adal shot a glance at her and caught the slight, sarcastic smile she had given up trying to hide. A warm sensation tickled his throat, and he couldn't help but smile back.

"Girl, you know you love it. Just admit it." Adal laughed, pushing on Arija's shoulder and causing her to stumble a half step.

"Keep dreaming. I only keep you around because, next to you, I look like the Virgin May and my R.B.F isn't as obvious," Arija laughed and slugged him in the shoulder as hard as she could.

"Damn, kid! Watch the guns!" Adal rubbed his shoulder, his face scrunched in mock pain, but he was smiling.

Arija fluttered her eyes and looked away. "Look, I know this sucks. The world feels like its crumbling around you, and you think you're all alone. I've been there, remember? Things will get better. They did for me, and they will for you. Just remember that your grandfather wouldn't want you to be down about it, would he? I know that old salty bastard, and I guarantee he would crack a joke or throw in one of his depressing war stories because that's what 'men' do. So, quit thinking about yourself and man up!"

Arija's words rang in Adal's ear for a moment. He never admitted when he was wrong, it made him look weak, but she had a point. Gramps always liked Arija. He often said when they were younger that Arija was the only one of his friends that actually had her head not firmly seated 'somewhere you might sit on.' That always made Adal giggle as a kid, and the thought made him smile now.

Adal remembered vividly when Arija's mother died. She'd visit her mom in the hospital every day, and even though the end was rolling in, she never seemed to let it show. Sure, she vented her anger in the girl's wrestling ring, but outside, she kept drawing and appreciating life. *Man up, right,* he thought and let out a chuckle.

"Damn, my hand is killing me!" Adal changed the subject, shaking his hand like it was on fire. As the two walked, the pain had increased as the adrenaline had worn off, but the subject was mostly because he wanted to avoid the emotions the conversation had brought up.

"Didn't we just have a conversation about 'manning up'? Jeez, no wonder you're failing half your classes," Arija teased as she snatched Adal's injured hand and examined it.

"Yeah, this looks pretty swollen. The cuts aren't deep. Not sure if you broke anything or not though. Note to self, if I ever get into a fight with a wooden desk, you're the guy to call." She slapped the top of his hand, making him wince.

"Girl, one day I'll get you into the ring, and we'll see what's up." Adal examined the injured hand for a moment before dropping it back to his side.

He shifted his blurred focus from the horizon in front of him to the surrounding area. Adal recognized where they were in an instant. As the cobblestone roads faded away, the buildings became fewer, and more plants appeared around them.

Adal and Arija had come to these woods just outside of town often when they were younger. They'd played hide and seek and made a secret fort out of bushes and sticks. Adal still remembered the first time Arija had followed him out there as a kid. She'd managed to shadow him all the way to his secret hideout without him knowing. He was inside the fort, drawing up a 'No Girls Allowed' sign before he realized she'd followed him in. Adal still came to the woods almost every day. They housed his favorite running path, and somehow, he had reflexively made his way there once more.

The blue sky around them was morphing to a pink and orange hue. Adal figured they'd been walking for a couple hours because the day seemed to have gotten away from them. He still wasn't ready to go home, so he made his way toward the start of the running path.

Arija had known where they were going from their first turn off the street Adal's house was on. Sometimes she thought she knew Adal better than he knew himself. This was the only place he would go when he needed time to himself, but Arija also loved these woods. Her favorite part was the small area in the center of the park's trail that had a running brook and several small caves they had played in when they were younger.

The entire area was riddled with underground caves, and when they were kids, Arija and Adal had set out to explore them all. Of course, that didn't happen. Many of the caves were so deep they couldn't reach the end. If she knew Adal—and she did—he would find his way to that area whether or not he consciously meant to.

Within a few minutes, the two had made their way to the opening of the wooded path that started the trail. The sun was cresting over the tops of the trees, and the warm summer air was giving way to the chill of the night. Just as they started on the trail, the light at the entrance to the path flickered on. A few seconds later, the other lights that lined the trail blinked on. Adal paused and turned to Arija.

"I just want to say two things. First, I appreciate you having my back and all. I know sometimes I'm not the easiest, but then again you sure aren't either, so there's that . . ." Adal gave a toothy grin, his first real smile since school that morning.

"Yeah, OK. What's the second thing?" Arija tried to hide the smile that threatened to push its way across her face.

"I still owe you from this morning . . ." Adal trailed off, and before she knew what he meant, he was off and down the trail ahead of her. Arija hopped forward and threw herself into a full sprint after him. The two had raced this path many times, but they often were evenly matched. With his head start, Arija would have to teach him a lesson in fairness.

The trees whispered past the two as they ran, hinting at secrets they couldn't tell. Adal pumped his arms by his side, laughing as he thought he had the upper hand, but after only a minute or two, Arija had covered the distance between them and was gaining on him. He tucked his head down and rolled up as far on the balls of his feet as he could with every stride, but this only bought him time as Arija soon closed the gap.

"I . . . thought . . . you . . . owed me . . . one." Arija panted as she strode up alongside Adal. The air stung at their lungs as they ran like their lives depended on it. Adal looked from the path ahead of them to the slapping sound coming from beside him. He looked down to see that not only had Arija caught up with him, but she still held on to the school satchel she kept her drawing supplies in. Adal's ego dropped. There's no way she could beat him on *his* trail while also carrying her bag.

The trail curved ahead, and Adal knew the bend hooked around a large chunk of woods then opened into a small park area where he liked to hang out. He looked over at Arija who was slowly making her way ahead of him. *Not today!*

"Think . . . you have . . . me beat?" Adal forced out as he swung his arms as hard as he could. He looked at the wood line on his right. A few feet from the edge of the trail, the woods dipped down a relatively steep slope to a small ravine the path wrapped around. All things considered, it had to be maybe one and a half football pitches or so. Even with the fading light, he could do this.

"Well . . . how . . . about . . . a shortcut?" Adal threw his weight to the side and veered off the path. At first, he stumbled as he met the slope covered in fallen branches and dead leaves. Throwing his arms out, Adal regained his balance and sprinted down the hill.

"Oh, what the—?" Arija shouted behind him. Adal heard the distinct crunch of leaves and twigs behind him as Arija left the path and pursued him. These woods were dense, with low branches and fallen limbs. It made the run both difficult and dangerous. Arija had never been into this part of the woods, and she was fairly certain Adal hadn't either. She knew what he was trying to do, he was trying to cut off the path on the other side. Arija jumped over a felled tree and stumbled a few steps as she tried to regain her balance.

The two slid and stumbled as they made their way over stumps and rocks. Adal managed to maintain his lead as he used his leg strength to project himself over many of the smaller obstacles in his path. Arija took the opposite approach and slid under the branches she could and jetted around those she couldn't. Her bag slapped at the back of her hip as she ran. It dug into her side, but she refused to take it off. Her drawings were her life.

"What's the matter? Can't hang?" Adal teased as he put one foot on a stump and leaped into the air. He grabbed a tree branch in front of him and swung forward. Free running got him interested in track and field a couple of years ago. The exhilaration of constantly maneuvering around obstacles that could change around every turn created a unique challenge and a rush that Adal lived for.

"What's the matter? Can't beat me in a fair race?" Arija replied as she slapped a branch away from her face. Adal could barely hear her. He laughed and turned his head to admire how much farther ahead he was.

"You think . . ."

"Adal look out!" Arija's eyes widened, and she pointed in front of him. Adal turned to look, but it was too late. A low-hanging branch from a tilted tree created a perfect bar at shin level. He didn't have time to react before both of his shins slid straight into the obstacle. His view flashed from the sights ahead of him, to the ground, to Arija's inverted face behind him as he tumbled end over end. Adal tumbled down the hill, his body painfully colliding with sticks and rocks as he rolled and bounced all the way down.

He skidded to an agonizing stop at the edge of a small creek that flowed into one of the many small caves in the area. A glint of light flickered off of something in the opening of the cave. Adal glanced at it for a moment before he dropped his head to the soft ground and groaned. The smell of earth and wet leaves filled his nostrils, and he wished more than anything he could just hop up and play the fall off, but that wasn't going to happen.

"Adal! Are you all right?" Arija shouted, coming to a sliding stop near to him.

"I'm good," Adal coughed into the ground. He groaned again as he rolled to his side and looked up at Arija. She stared down at him with concern and amusement. Arija had seen some crazy falls, but she'd never seen anyone bounce down a hill like that.

"Can you move? Is anything broken?" She made her way to his side and put her hand on his shoulder, examining him.

Adal swatted her hand away, a little embarrassed, and forced himself into a sitting position. He looked to his once pearly-white shirt that was now covered in dirt and grass stains. Hissing, he brushed his chest and lap off and examined his clothes.

"I'm good. Other than ruining my outfit," Adal insisted, picking a small twig out of his hair.

"Way to stick the landing!" Arija laughed and stood, realizing he wasn't hurt. She lowered her hand to help him up with a smirk on her face. The image of Adal bouncing like a ball down the hill flashed in her mind. He looked up at her and ignored the gesture. Embarrassed, he pushed himself to his feet. The earth around him wobbled a bit. He was slightly dizzy from the fall. He looked at Arija and scoffed.

"Hey, it will take a lot more than some fall to put me out. Besides, you distracted me! I had this race won until you messed me up." Adal's excuse was almost comical, and Arija rolled her eyes at him and shook her head.

"Whatever helps you sleep at night, Adal." She pursed her lips and pinched his chin like a mother cooing at an infant. He turned his head away and adjusted his clothes once more. As he tugged at his shirt and patted his pockets down, Adal's heart sank as he realized something was missing.

"Where is it?" he shouted, frantically looking on the ground around him. The fading light was making it difficult to see, and the leaf covered ground was a blur of dark browns and blacks as the sun disappeared over the trees.

"What are you talking about?" Arija asked impatiently as Adal crawled on his hands and knees around her feet, brushing leaves away.

"My grandfather's coin! I had it in my pocket! It has to be here somewhere!" He looked from the ground to the small creek to the massive hill he'd just rolled down.

"Calm down. We'll find it. It couldn't have gone too far." Arija pulled a small flashlight key-chain from her bag and turned its head, emitting a faded beam of light. She fanned it back and forth around the ground at their feet.

"Damn it. I will not calm down. This will take forever. I'm not going to stop until I check this entire hill. I can't believe this is happening, it's the only thing I have left of him." Adal threw a pile of sticks and leaves as hard as he could, but they only gingerly floated back down to the ground. "Idiot!" he cursed at himself before standing to his feet. Seconds later, he was sprinting away from Arija again.

"Wait, where are you going? What about the coin?" she yelled as she took off after him.
Adal leaped over a small body of stagnant water and landed on the muddy banks on the other side. He stopped in his tracks and looked at the small cave ahead of him just as something collided into his back and sent him stumbling forward. Adal fell to his hands and knees at the mouth of the cavern with Arija lying on top of him.

"What did you stop for?" she barked as she pushed off Adal's back and pulled herself up. As she stood, her head spun, and she almost fell right back down onto him. A sweet, metallic taste trickled into her mouth, and she brought her hand up to feel the place on her lip where she'd bitten down as her chin collided with Adal's shoulder.

"I remembered that I saw the coin flash in the light right after I hit the ground. I think it rolled into this cave," Adal said over his shoulder, pushing off the ground and bringing himself up. His normally pristine clothes were muddy, and blood and dirt were smeared across his face. With the panic that shone on his features, he looked like a raging lunatic that had escaped from an asylum.

Adal squinted in the dim light. What remained of the sun peeked over the hill, and the mouth of the cave seemed like a black void. Slowly, he made his way over to the opening. If the sun had been shining brighter, he would have run immediately into the cave after the coin, but in the dark, he didn't know what would be waiting for him on the other side. Wild dogs lived in some of the caves and there were many rumors of people going in and never coming out. Adal was already nursing an injured hand, sore body, and bruised ego, he wasn't about to become dog chow too.

"Let me see your flashlight," Adal said, walking over to Arija and snatching it from her hands.

"Sure thing. Anything else?" sarcasm dripped from Arija's words, but she understood why this was so important to Adal. When her mother died, Arija had been crying in the study when she found her mother's sketch pad. The first drawing inside was one of Arija playing in the grass. That sketch pad had never left Arija's side since that day. She kept it in her bag, right next to her own. She felt if she could draw the beautiful things in life, her mother would somehow be able to see them.

Adal focused the beam and passed it over the cave. After a pause to check for movement, he ducked his head and slowly made his way into the opening. Arija scoffed and followed her friend, placing her hand on his hip to avoid slipping on the damp stones.

The dull light from the tiny flashlight danced over the stone surfaces and dull-green foliage that crept over the opening to the cave and ran several feet into the dark. Adal kept the beam focused on the ground so they wouldn't slip and fall, but occasionally the light reflected from small puddles of water and illuminated the area above their heads. The salty fragrance of wet rocks was overwhelming as the two made their way further into the cave. Arija thought she might choke to death on the thickness of the air.

The rock ceiling was only about an inch over Adal's head and a few inches over Arija's. A wave of panicked claustrophobia took hold of Arija, making little beads of sweat form at her hairline.

"There it is!" Adal shouted, pointing the beam at the base of the wall several feet away. A glint of gold and bronze shone back at them as the light moved over it. Adal leaped forward and ran the several steps to the coin, scooping it up and squeezing it in his hands.

"There, you have it. Can we get the hell out of here now?" Arija prodded. She wasn't sure if he knew, or even if he could tell, that she wasn't a fan of small places.

"Yeah yeah, we're good. Let's . . . wait what?" Adal took the light from under his arm and focused it on the coin in the palm of his hand. He brought it close to his face. "Hey, look at this."

"What?" Arija took a step closer, peering around Adal to see the coin in his hand. The once beautifully etched gears on the back of the coin now seemed to be moving and turning as if the coin was an old machine coming to life.

"Man, I must have hit my head harder than I thought." Adal squeezed his eyes closed and then opened them, blinking several times to clear his vision.

"I don't think so, because I can see it too," Arija interjected, reaching out and touching the cold metal with her finger. Adal brought the coin closer to his face, jabbing it with one outstretched finger. The second his finger touched the coin he yelped and jumped into the air, letting the coin fall back to the ground. A sharp ping rang out as the metal struck the stone floor and rolled away from them.

"What was that?" Arija grasped unsuccessfully at the stagnant air as she tried to grab the coin as it fell.

"I don't . . . I don't know. I think the damn gears pinched my finger! Shit!" Adal waived the light around the pitch-black cave, trying to catch sight of the bronze once more. Out of the corner of his eye, Adal noticed the glint of metal as it rolled down a corridor, deeper into the cave. Adal kept his light shining on the coin as they ran down the tunnel after it.

4

CANNONBALL

The high-pitched ringing of the coin as it rolled down the tunnel of the cave was joined by the slapping echo of their feet as Adal and Arija ran after the only thing they had left of Adal's grandfather. With the light trained on the small object, Adal was able to catch up to it and quickly scooped it up into his hands, turning to Arija and smiling. They both panted heavily for a moment as they tried to catch their breath.

"I got this," Adal huffed between gasps of air, flicking the coin into the air. Arija sighed and rolled her eyes. As the coin came back down, Adal took a step backward to make sure he caught it, but the ground was uneven in this part of the cave. As he stepped backward, his heel found a downward incline, and he lost his footing. Adal tried to shift his weight, but it was too late.

He wind-milled his arms in an attempt to regain his balance, but before he could get control of the situation, his back hit hard on a rock wall and he began sliding down a stone slope. The flashlight flew into the air and came crashing down at Arija's feet.

Descending head first down the natural ramp, eventually the light from Arija's flashlight grew smaller and smaller until it disappeared from Adal's view altogether. He kicked his feet and flailed his arms trying to snag something in the abyss, but there was nothing to grab. Smooth rock walls followed him down the slope. As Adal slid in the dark, his clothing became soaked as it collected water that hid in little pockets along the slope.

Suddenly, a chill filled the air around him, and he was no longer sliding. The rock ledge separated from his back and he was in free fall. His stomach felt like it would rip its way out of his mouth. Every muscle in his body clenched in anticipation of the impact. He imagined he was going to die a splatted mess on a stone floor in the eternal darkness of an unexplored cave. Something strange took over and Adal felt a calm set in. If this was how he was going out, he could at least enjoy the fall.

"CANNON BALL!" The words ripped past Adal's lips as he hurled through the darkness. Even if no one else ever heard his last words, he wanted them to be epic. Just as the thought occurred to him, a cold shock washed over him as he crashed into a massive body of water. His head plunged under the liquid, and his lungs with water.

Bursting back to the surface, he coughed to clear his lungs of the liquid fire that burned his insides. The strange coincidence of him falling into a body of water after yelling "cannon ball" made him laugh, and he was soon taken over by a laughing, coughing fit. As he rubbed his eyes, calming himself down and trying to figure out where he was, Adal heard a distant sound, almost like a plane taking off. The sound quickly grew louder and louder until he realized it wasn't a plane, it was someone screaming.

"Oh no!" Adal pushed himself through the water, to get away from the place he'd landed. "HOLD YOUR BREATH!" Adal yelled up toward the falling Arija. As he swam toward uncertainty, the screaming stopped and Arija's voice took its place.

"ADAL! I'M GOING TO KILL YOU IF I DON'T DIE FIRST!" Arija shouted as she crashed into the water in virtually the exact same spot Adal had landed moments before.

Panic took over when he didn't immediately hear her return to the surface, and Adal swam over to the area where he thought he heard her hit. He was floating around in the dark, desperately splashing at the water when he saw a small light bubble up from under the water. Arija came crashing up to the surface coughing and wheezing.

"Arija, are you all right?" Adal asked as he swam toward her. She splashed in place for a moment until she got her bearings and searched for Adal with the light. She turned around in the water and shone the light directly into Adal's eyes. With fear and relief fighting for control of her features, Arija swam over to Adal and threw her arms around him. He squeezed her back, happy to be alive just before the palm of Arija's hand slapped at the back of his head, sending a sharp pain down his neck.

"What mess have you gotten us into now? I swear to God, Adal, if you get us killed I'm resurrecting your ass so I can kill you again," she coughed.

"Ow! Hey, I wasn't shooting for this place, you know?" Adal splashed in the water and tried to get a little distance between them. "I can't believe you followed me down here! What were you thinking?" he barked back at her, bobbing in place.

"Oh, yeah, like I was going to just let you slip away into some unknown cavern and disappear. First off, I have no idea how to explain that one to anybody. Second, and most importantly, I have told you before that I am not about to let you have all the fun!"

Adal laughed at her and splashed a little water in her direction. As Arija bobbed in the water next to him, the flashlight's beam washed over her features and made her look like a demon with a wicked grin.

"Can I ask why we are still floating in this dark pool when we have no idea what's in it?" Arija asked as she moved the flashlight to point down into the water.

"Actually, good point. Let's see if we can get out of this stuff. I've seen that horror movie, and I'm not about to be the brother that dies first." Adal sloshed in place and looked around suspiciously. Arija scanned the light around the cave and saw what appeared to be a walkway and an embankment a few feet away.

They splashed and kicked toward it and were crawling on the cold stone shore and out of the water in less than a minute. Adal flopped to his side and coughed the remaining water out of his lungs while Arija crawled a little further past him and continued to shine the light around to see if she could find a way out.

"Well, I'm not seeing any way to get out of here. What are we going to do?" Arija was trying to put up a good front, like they could find a way out and be home in time for them to get their asses chewed out by their parents, but inside, Arija fought the urge to cry. They were deep inside a cave that no one ever went into and no one knew they were there. She didn't see them getting out.

"My Bag!" Arija's voice had taken on an extra octave. "Adal! My bag is soaked, and my sketchpads are ruined!" Arija dropped the flashlight and took her dripping drawings out of her bag and laying them flat on the ground. The half-erased image of the tree she'd been drawing earlier that day was folding in on itself, the pencil marks were smeared over the soggy pages. Arija dropped her head and the tears she'd held back took over as she pulled out the ripped pages of her mother's sketchpad. The ink from the images running and bleeding as they soaked up the moisture from the page. Arija laid the pads out on the ground and dumped the rest of the contents of her bag onto the stone floor. She shook the water from her bag and tried to dry the various pens and pencils as best she could.

"I'm sorry . . ." Adal spoke softly, looking off into the abyss from where he lay on his back. The burn in his lungs and the freshly forming bruises on his back had sobered him, somewhat. His head had cleared from the emotional storm of the day in facing their new reality. Adal had gotten them into plenty of trouble in the past, but nothing like this. He grunted as he rolled to his side and stood.

"I'm so sorry about your drawings. This is my bad, but we aren't going out like this. Let's look around and see what we can find. Stick close, though. Not about to have to look for you in the dark," he tried his best at humor, but his heart wasn't in it. Arija picked up the flashlight, rotated, and shone the light in his eyes, but he could see the slight smirk on her face.

"Sure. Like it's my fault we ended up down here? You and that coin of yours." Arija didn't blame Adal for where they were. She wouldn't be there if she didn't choose to follow him, she just liked giving him a hard time. It was familiar and comfortable to joke with Adal, and for a moment she'd forgotten about just how screwed they really were.

Arija's mother had always taught her that "life is full of choices. If you choose to stand and act on your own accord, then your successes are entirely yours, but your failures are yours to own as well." Arija lived by this. She stacked the still dripping sketch pads on top of each other, placed all the contents back into her bag and stood. There was nothing she could do about them now, she might as well take them with her and see if she could find a way to salvage them.

"Speaking of the coin, where is it? Hand it over." Adal said as he held out his hand.

"I don't have it. I thought you had it."

"You have got to be kidding me!" Adal shouted as he searched the ground around him for his grandfather's coin. "I don't see it! Is it in the water?" Adal ran over to the pool of dark liquid and pawed at it like a kitten. His grandfather had told Adal this was his lucky coin, but he'd had nothing but bad luck since he got the unique hunk of metal.

"Adal, there is no way either of us is getting back into that water! Think about it." Arija walked over to him, placing her hand on his shoulder.

"You don't understand, I need to find it. I can't lose . . ." Adal's words fell away as a ping emitted from behind them. It sounded like something bouncing off a metal beam.

Arija whipped around and shone her light in the general direction of the sound. What else was down here in the dark with them? Images of rabid wolves and demonic, blind cave dwellers filled Arija's mind as she swayed the weak beam of light from side to side.

Adal stepped around her, and the two stood shoulder to shoulder frozen in place, waiting for something to happen. Adal reached out and grabbed Arija's hand, squeezing it so hard he almost expected to hear her bones snap. A second ping came from beyond the reach of the shaky beam of light, and Adal shot a glance to Arija only to find her looking back at him.

"What is that?" Arija asked in an exhaled whisper.

"I don't know. I can't see anything with this piece of shit flashlight."

Arija rotated the light again, but all they could see was the stone wall and a bunch of stones and boulders that littered the area in front of them. A third ping sounded, and Adal decided that he couldn't wait any longer for something to happen. That sound wasn't natural for a place like this. He had to find out what was making the noise.

"What are you doing?" Arija snapped as he released the vice grip on her hand and took several steps toward the sound.

"Just keep the light steady. I'm going to figure out what that sound is," Adal said over his shoulder, continuing to walk toward the sound. Arija wasn't about to let him get himself killed while she stood there and watched. She scoffed and jogged up next to him.

"Stick together, remember? Let's not let this situation get any worse than it already is," she said.

The two made another couple of cautious steps before another ping sounded. They stopped and looked at one another. The sound was coming from directly in front of them, but they were standing less than twenty feet from the smooth stone wall.

Arija moved the light over the wall and a small glint of gold flickered back at them from the base of the wall. Adal inhaled so deeply that Arija thought he'd seen something other than what she did. He darted forward to the old coin and snatched it up once more.

"That's what's up!" Adal yelled, a large smile on his face as he looked at the coin in his hands. "Man, I have to quit dropping this! Hey, what's wrong with you?" he laughed, bringing his attention back to Arija. Arija stood in silence and held the light on the coin.

"Adal . . . how did that get over here?" A chill ran the length of Arija's spine like the boney fingers of death. They had landed in the middle of what she could only say was an underground lake. The coin managed to end up over one hundred yards away against a wall.

"Chill. It must have flown out of my hand as I fell." Adal leaned against the stone wall and tossed the coin into the air. A deafening sound like gears turning echoed through the chamber and, in an instant, Adal disappeared in a cloak of smoke.

5

THE LIFT THAT FALLS

Arija dropped her flashlight and ran toward where Adal had been standing.

"Adal!" she shouted, rushing into the cloud of smoke. Immediately overcome with the smell of wet air, she realized the smoke was actually steam. Something rolled before her feet, and Arija toppled forward and landed face first on something soft. It was Adal. He was lying on his back, and he wrapped his arms around her as she fell on him.

"You all right?" Adal squeezed her tightly so she couldn't flail and hit him. Her face was buried in his chest, and for a moment, the sweet scent of musk and deodorant filed her nose. Arija fought the urge to smile and pushed herself upwards, so she was looking into his eyes.

"What was that?" she asked as she searched his face for answers.

"I don't know. The wall suddenly opened, and I fell . . . in—?"

Arija rolled off Adal and looked around the room they had fallen into. As the steam cleared away, Arija could see it was a small, perfectly square room, like a hidden chamber within the cave. The only light was coming from the flashlight that had rolled a few feet away from where they sat. Arija slowly stood with Adal and took a step toward the opening to go for the light.

At that moment, another soft 'click' emerged from the dark. The two froze in place, eyes wide and looking around the dimly lit room. As another 'click' came from the dark, an orange glow formed from around them. Adal and Arija slammed their backs together and looked around the room as if waiting for a fight.

"What is this?" Arija asked, pressing against Adal.

"Yeah, like I know!" Adal shot back. Their hearts pounded in their chests as the orange lights grew brighter and brighter. As the eerie glow illuminated the walls, Arija realized that they weren't the smooth stone of the cave, but bronze or copper. Rivets the size of fists ran in straight lines from floor to ceiling, and huge gears were pressed against all four walls. Only half of the gear was visible with the other half disappearing into the floor.

"It almost looks like we're in a still or something. Or maybe an oven . . ." Arija's curious nature took over, and she inquisitively walked over to one of the walls and ran her hands down its smooth surface.

"Oven? Nope! Time to go!" Adal grabbed Arija's hand and pulled her away from the back of the room toward the doorway. As he neared the inside of the entrance, Adal stopped, and his body went cold. Emblazoned next to the door, into the heavy brass, was a symbol. He slowly reached into his pocket, pulled out his grandfather's coin and held it up to the etching on the wall.

"No way!" he and Arija said in stereo as they looked from the hammer and wrench design on the side of the coin, to the door with the exact same design. The center of the design was an anvil, and in the center of the anvil appeared to be a nut from a piece of machinery.

"How is that possible?" Arija asked.

"I . . . I have no clue. What is that?" Adal reached out a finger and inspected the center of the design. There appeared to be a hole with some small gears turning. "No way . . ." Adal took his coin, looked at the gears on its back that were still turning, and held it up to the hole. It was a perfect fit.

Cautiously, he slid the coin in. Instantly, a small 'click' came from the coin as it seated itself in the middle of the design and a barrage of clicking sounds followed. Adal and Arija stepped away from the design and huddled back in the center of the room when the ground rumbled at their feet.

"So . . . time to go?" Adal turned to Arija. Her mouth was hanging open as she looked around the strange room.

"Yeah. Let's go," she replied, not able to take her eyes off the mesmerizing gears as they turned. Realizing that Arija was too curious about this place, he grabbed her by the hand once more and stepped toward the door. Suddenly, two heavy doors slid into view and slammed closed before them, trapping the two friends in the bronze chamber. As if snapping out of a trance, Arija's heart pounded. She ran to the obstruction and smashed her fists into its metal frame.

"What's happening?" she shouted, stepping back and kicking it as hard as she could. Adal stood stunned in the center of the small room. He always said that Arija could kick like a horse, but her blow was only met by a dull 'thud.' Adal slammed both of his fists against the solid doors in his own final attempt at saving them, but he knew he couldn't punch through metal.

"Damn! What are we going to?" Adal started when another loud bang echoed in the small room as the four giant gears began to turn. The two friends stepped away from the walls and back to the center of the room.

The entire place shook, and Arija squeezed her eyes shut and wrapped both arms around Adal, burying her face in the bend of his shoulder. A sudden weightlessness overcame them like they were falling, and Adal slammed his eyes shut and held onto Arija. The butterflies in his stomach were suddenly in his chest and then almost out of his mouth as the room began its downward descent.

"Are . . . are we in a lift?" Arija asked, opening her eyes and instinctively putting one hand on her stomach as they lurched downward. "Are we going faster?" she continued when Adal didn't answer.

The sensation was growing in Adal's own stomach, and after a few moments, his stomach fluttered more and more until he and Arija were simultaneously lifted from the ground.

"What's happening?" Adal shouted, trying to pull Arija back to him as they drifted up until their backs touched the ceiling.

"Adal, if I die in here, I'm going to haunt the shit out of you!" Arija reached out her hand and intertwined her fingers with Adal's.

After what felt like hours, Adal looked at Arija who was staring at the floor. He tugged at her sleeve, and she motioned for him to look down. The same design that was on the wall and the coin was also etched into the floor.

"What is that? What the hell is this place?" As if it was an answer to his question, they slowly started to drift back down to the floor.

"We're slowing down!" Arija squeezed Adal's hand as the image on the ground got bigger. As if being carefully placed on the ground by an invisible giant, Adal and Arija floated down until their feet were firmly on the metal floor. The ground was still vibrating, so they assumed they were still moving, but they must have slowed enough to allow them to stand.

"Do you think this will ever—" A vibration interrupted Adal as the two were bounced into the air and then slammed back down onto the metal floor. A taste of metal crept into Adal's mouth, and he wasn't sure if he had just tasted the floor or if the impact made him bite his own lip.

". . . stop . . ." he groaned.

"Adal, I think I'll definitely have to kill you for getting me into . . . whatever *this* is." Arija groaned in return as she pushed herself up off the floor. A loud cracking sound made them jump to their feet as the massive doors creaked and squealed open. Arija and Adal stood shoulder to shoulder with their hands out in front of them, ready and waiting for whatever could be coming next.

"Whatever happens, we got this," Adal reassured Arija who scoffed in reply.

"Yeah, I'm sure. We just rode a mysterious elevator to who knows where, and I'm sure we can totally handle what's waiting at the bottom." The doors finished opening and Arija found herself staring at another dark corridor.

After waiting a moment, the two walked over to the doorway and cautiously peered out. Adal couldn't be certain, but he thought something was moving in the darkness. Adal and Arija had both taken up positions on either side of the doorway in the event that something came from the darkness, they could flatten themselves against the wall and be virtually invisible.

As Arija stuck her head out of the door and placed the edge of her foot on the floor, another loud snap made her jump. Lights sprang up from the dark and fully illuminated the space before them. They stood at one end of a long hallway lit by large bulbs with intricate filaments.

Arija was lost in the design of one of the Edison bulbs on the wall next to her when Adal tapped her shoulder. She turned to look and realized that the walls down the length of the hallway were moving. Thousands of gears and pistons of all sizes turned, whirled, and pumped in their places.

"What is this place? Are we inside some sort of machine?" Arija took several steps into the large hall, her curiosity winning over her fear. Adal waited a moment before he followed her, his mouth ajar as he watched the wall of gears turn.

"I don't know, but this place is dope!" Adal said as he spun around and around looking at everything. "Let's keep going and check this place out." He stopped and turned to face Arija who was watching him with a strange look on her face. This was one of the most amazing places she had ever seen, but one of them had to stay collected, or they would both end up in even more of a mess than they already were. Arija tried to hide her excitement and forced a hesitant expression.

"Aww, come on, don't be like that. I *know* you're itching to see what the rest of this place looks like," Adal taunted. Arija couldn't help herself, and she let a wide grin crease her face. "Nice! All right, let's go. Oh, just one thing." Adal ran past Arija and leaned into the lift. He popped his grandfather's coin from the wall and slid it back into his pocket. Hopping from the doorway and jogging up to Arija, a loud slam echoed down the hall as the doors to the lift closed. Adal sank into his shoulders, a sheepish grin visible on his face.

"Well . . . we were going to go deeper anyway." Adal waited for Arija to slug him, but she just scoffed and rolled her eyes.

"Adal, if you don't quit touching things, I'm going to make you walk with your hands in your pockets!" Arija snapped. She wasn't really mad, she just liked giving him a hard time, but at the rate he was going, he was going to get them both killed. Adal laughed, and they were off down the hall. For a while, they moved in silence. The dull hum of machinery lulling them into thoughts about what this place could be. Every so often one of them would pause and run their fingers over a particularly interesting cog or gear, but neither of them could figure out what they were meant to do.

At the end of the hall was another set of large brass doors. Cogs and gears spun in place up the face of the doors, but they didn't seem to actually meet one another or have a purpose. Two large, copper poles ran the height of the doors in the center. Adal reached out and wrapped his hand around one and Arija reflexively slapped it away.

"Seriously?" she shot, glaring at him.

"Hey, I thought you were down for this. Why else are we here?" Adal replied matter-of-factly.

"Yeah, I know, but think before you just do things, please. I can't bail you out of everything."

"Girl, you worry too much!" Adal teased as he looked back at the door. He reached out his hand again to grasp the pole but paused for a moment, swallowing a lump of doubt that had lodged itself in his throat. Arija was right, and he had to get his act together, but this was all just too cool to take slowly. He wanted to know what was beyond the door so badly that he couldn't stand it. He flexed his chest muscles as he gave a mighty tug at the metal handles. To his surprise, the doors didn't budge.

Adal let a nervous chuckle escape his lips as he looked at Arija. He gave several more pulls as best he could, but the heavy metal doors wouldn't budge. Arija looked around the hallway for something she could use to help him. Something caught her eyes just off to the side of the door, and she had to stifle a laugh.

"Psst!" Arija whispered. Adal turned to her as she leaned against the wall. A slight smirk appeared, and she pointed with her thumb above her head. On the wall near the door was a large switch in an up position. Holding her gaze sarcastically, Arija reached above her head and pulled the lever downward. Two loud clanks were followed by two bars over the gap between the doors sliding aside.

"I would ask what you would do without me, but the thought of what would actually happen to you terrifies me." Arija pushed herself from the wall and stood next to Adal. He pursed his lips and rolled his eyes as he grabbed the handle and gave it another hard pull.

6

A World of Metal and Steam

To Adal's surprise, the heavy doors easily gave way, and a warm wave of air washed over them.

"Oh. My. God!" Arija gasped.

Adal said nothing but allowed his mouth to fall open as he stumbled forward. They were standing on a large platform that opened into what looked like a whole other world beneath their own. Drifting off into infinity, were girders, gears, pistons, and all other assorted mechanical oddities. Adal rubbed the palms of his hands into his eyes until he saw spots, but when he released, the strange mechanical world was still there.

Beams crisscrossed throughout the spacious room winding around tall buildings that seemed to be floating in mid-air and as Adal took a step toward the edge of the platform, someone came swooping down along a beam right above their heads. Adal jumped back, grasping his chest and panting as a man holding two metal bars slid down the beam toward the buildings like he was zip lining.

The stranger looked over his shoulder to yell obscenities, and Adal's eyes bulged, and he took a reflexive step back. The zip liner's face was half leathery skin and half bronze. His tan skin too tight like it was stretched over a face too big for its size. A black leather cloak rippled in the air behind the mechanical man as he pulled what looked like a pocket watch out of his burgundy vest pocket and waved it in the air.

Arija and Adal looked at each other wide-eyed and then took another few cautious steps toward the edge of the platform. Arija looked up and then down again, realizing that there seemed to be no end to the world. There was a layer of fog several feet below them that Arija couldn't see past and she thought for a moment that they were above the clouds before she remembered that they were actually underground. The entire area was washed in an orange and yellow hue, almost reminding Adal of the sunset from his bedroom window.

"What. Is. This?" Adal allowed his eyes to dance over everything before him. As he squinted at the mechanical town, he could vaguely make out what looked like people walking along the beams and swinging from them to small platforms just underneath the floating buildings.

Arija opened her mouth to respond when a flock of birds burst from underneath the platform, making both Arija and Adal jump back.

"What was THAT?" they asked in tandem. Adal pointed past Arija to a railing several feet away to where one of the birds had landed and was looking at them inquisitively. They slowly crept toward the mechanical bird, their eyes unable to leave the creature.

The little bird had wings of bronze, and each feather appeared to have been bolted into place by micro-rivets. It had two small rubies where its eyes should have been, and countless small gears turned along its stomach. Arija was a slave to her curiosity and reached her hand out to touch it. The little bird squeaked and fluttered off into the direction that its friends had flown. Arija slammed her eyes shut for a moment to etch its beautiful features into her mind. If she ever got her sketchpad to dry, she was going to capture the bird's mechanical beauty.

The body moves flawlessly.
Seems almost natural.

Rubies for eyes.
Can it see?
Possible camera in eyes?

Internal mechanisms.
what powers it?

Bronze plating
covering the entire body.
including the wings

"Was that even a real animal?" Adal asked.

"I don't know what is real, anymore."

"Yeah, no kidding!" Adal turned, so he was facing the edge of the platform again. "Do you hear that?"

From somewhere beyond the platform, they could hear a distant rumbling, like thunder rolling in off the sea. Arija and Adal stepped away from the railing and looked around for the source of the sound that was growing louder and louder by the second.

"Look! There!" Adal shouted, pointing to the left of the railing. At first, it was difficult to see. It was just a strange shape moving somewhere off in the distance, but after a moment, the object began to take on a recognizable form.

A large antique looking train suspended from a track attached to one of the beams was moving at an incredibly fast speed toward them. Arija and Adal weren't sure where it came from, and it looked vintage, like something out of the 1920s. Arija looked around the platform they were on and realized the train was going to stop where they stood.

"I think it's coming here!" she yelled, looking around for a safe area to hide, but there was nowhere to go. Arija considered running back into the hallway but all that was in there was the elevator, and it didn't have any buttons or anything that they could use to make it go back up. At least if there was a person on the train, maybe they could find a way to get out of the cave.

A loud screeching erupted from the tracks as a large railcar came to a sudden halt right above the edge of the platform. With the train this close, Adal could see that there were wheels on both the top and the bottom of it. The wheels on the bottom were just touching the edge of the platform and with a loud '*thunk*' and a plumb of steam the wheels on the top of the train, connected to the beam, released.

The train, now sitting on the platform in front of Adal and Arija, was a deep black in color with copper rivets covering its ancient back. Windows adorned one entire side of the car, and by the looks of it, there was no one inside. With a jolt, the two sliding doors on the side threw themselves open.

"All right, now I know what you're gonna say, but—" Adal began as he craned his neck to see inside the elaborate train car.

"Let's check this thing out!" Arija finished his sentence realizing that they really had no other choice. The best thing to do in this situation was to find a person and hope they could help them get back home. After all, a person had to have built all of this.

Adal and Arija ran to the side of the car and peered inside. To their surprise, what was inside was standard as far as trains were concerned. Beautifully polished wooden benches ran along either side of the car. Deep, earthy leather adorned the sitting surfaces and was neatly held in place by polished brass knobs.

They cautiously stepped inside the car, but as Adal looked around, he realized something was off. Everything inside the train car was much larger than what he expected, even for someone his size. Arija walked down the center aisle toward a control panel at the other end.

"Man, this joint keeps getting weirder and weirder." Adal hopped up to sit on the edge of one of the benches that came up to his waist. The hammer and anvil symbol from the coin was carved into the floor, and Adal wracked his brain to figure out what that meant.

"Adal, look," Arija called, walking over to the controls and sitting on the stationary stool that sat in front of them. There were buttons, levers, and gauges completely covering the surface of the control panel, and she delicately ran her hands over each one until she came to one large lever in particular.

"Hey, this lever says 'Home' and 'Away.' I wonder what that means?" Arija examined the ornate calligraphy it was written in.

"Well, let's see what 'Home' looks like then, shall we?" Adal said as he rotated on the bench to look at her. He couldn't have removed the smile from his face even if he needed to. This was the coolest thing that he had ever seen. In the back of his mind Adal thought about his grandfather and what all of this meant, but as the pain of guilt and mourning jabbed at him, he pushed the thought aside.

"All right. Let's see what this is!" Arija grunted, pulling the heavy lever back from the "Away" side to the "Home" side. In a jolt, the two doors slid closed. A loud screech like the sound of hydraulics was followed by a click, and the train was raised up a few inches. Adal grabbed on to the side of the bench to stop himself from falling over at the sudden jerky motion, and then the train sped off in the direction it came. The force of the speed almost tossed Arija from her stool, and it rolled Adal on his side, but when they both regained their composure, the ride was like being on a roller-coaster.

"Where do you think this is going?" Adal asked, hoisting himself up and looking out the window.

"I'm not sure, but we seriously need to be careful. This is like something out of a fairytale, and I'm not sure if you've ever actually read a real one, but they don't usually end well." Arija hopped off the stool, and after steadying herself on the nearest bench, she made her way to Adal and plopped onto the bench next to him.

"Don't worry, girl! I got this. Nothing down here I can't handle," Adal laughed as he looked back out of the window. They sat in silence and watched their surroundings fly past in a blur of copper and steam.

Flocks of what appeared to be more of those mechanical birds fluttered by on several occasions. Every so often, Arija would point to something strange moving in the distance, but before Adal could look, it was gone.

Thousands if not millions of girders the width of tree trunks and walkways the width of streets rolled past them. Occasionally, the car would take a sharp turn around a bend and Arija would be pressed into Adal. She didn't push way immediately, basking in the comforting smell of home.

"Look at that!" Adal shouted, pointing down below them. Arija leaned over him and looked out of the large window. They were flying over a massive farm. Crops appeared to roll on and on as far as they could see. Row after row, the emeralds of the foliage stabbed out from the orange and bronze surroundings. Arija couldn't quite tell, but it looked as though people were working in the fields.

"Is that . . .? Are those . . .?" Arija questioned, leaning closer to the window.

"Man, this place just keeps getting weirder and weirder," Adal responded. Shortly after the large fields had crept into view, they disappeared in the distance, and the train came to another screeching halt. This time, Arija and Adal were caught off-guard and rolled sideways from the bench, hitting the floor. Adal landed on his back with Arija on top of him.

"You know, you keep falling on me like this you're gonna owe me dinner." Adal joked, winking at her. Arija dropped her elbow into his stomach making him cough and rolled off him.

"You wish!" she laughed, extending out her arm to help him stand. Adal pulled his hand from hers and tugged at his shirt, adjusting the wrinkles. In all the excitement, he had forgotten entirely that he was still soaked to the bone.

"Check that out." Arija pointed, walking past Adal to one of the windows on the other side of the car. The train had come to a stop at another platform, only this one opened into a walkway leading to a cottage. The sun glistened off its metallic surface, and steam poured from three chimneys that sat on its roof. Large, circular, frosted glass windows like eyes looked back at them in the train car, and a row of steps led from the platform to the large brass door.

"Maybe whoever lives here can help us get back home?" Arija turned back to look at Adal, and they stared at each other in silence for a moment before they made their way out of the car and toward the house. As they stepped down onto the platform, the doors of the vehicle slammed behind them. Arija let her eyes run over the sleek and polished walls surrounded by running tubes and moving parts. Off to the right of the building was an enclosed spiral staircase that looked like it led to a glass atrium on top of the home.

Adal listened to the best of his abilities for the sounds of any movement inside the home as they reached the front door. Once they were close enough to the house, Adal realized just how large the cottage truly was. The door, like every door he had come in contact with since he'd arrived in this strange place, was over-sized. The windows were too large to be standard windows, and even the strange potted plant that sat on the doorstep was much larger than he would have thought it should have been.

"So, do we knock?" Adal asked, looking at Arija, who only shrugged and put her arms up.

"I got this, but be ready to run if anything happens." He put his hand on the doorknob that looked like it was once a giant bolt of some kind.

"Yeah, and where are we running to, exactly?" Arija replied as she looked back to the train that still sat on the edge of the platform.

Adal shot her a look and turned the knob, slowly pressing the door open. He stopped when he saw that there were lights on inside the home but when he didn't hear any sounds, he pushed the door open and walked inside.

Arija followed him into a large room that looked like it was both a kitchen and dining area combined. Large copper pots and pans hung from the ceiling over a center island that was bigger than Adal's bed, and iron appliances with gold leaflet etchings ran the length of the opposite wall. Centered in the room was a table with four chairs. As Adal and Arija walked over to the table, they were surprised to find that the top was a few inches above his head.

"Ok, I'm just going to say it; since we've gotten here, everything is oversized. I can't be the only one uncomfortable with that." Adal whispered to Arija who just stared, wide-eyed at the table.

"No kidding. It's like all these things were built for a giant. A giant that scares me beyond thought." She finally said. "At least there doesn't seem to be anybody home for now. So, let's figure out what our next move is. Looking at this place, someone definitely lives here."

"So, should we keep going?" Adal asked as he ran his fingers across the smooth metal surface of one of the table chairs.

"I don't see why not. I have to see the rest of this place. I wish I could sketch some of this!" Arija turned her bag upside down and produced the soggy pile of paper. Embarrassment warmed Adal's face. He knew how much those sketch pads meant to Arija and it was his fault they were ruined.

"Let's try that door," he pointed to a partially open door across the room. It was made of similarly fogged glass to that of the observatory above them, but it had designs etched into it. Arija took a step toward the door when movement from the other side made her freeze in place.

"Calm down. I don't hear anything. Besides, if someone were home they would probably have heard us already." Adal's award-winning smile lifted some weight from her chest and Arija let out a low exhale that she didn't know she'd been holding. Just as they started to walk across the room again, the low rumbling sound of voices made them stop and turn toward the front door.

At first, Arija and Adal couldn't make out anything except for a low rumble of sounds, but after a few minutes, they realized that two people were standing just outside the door talking. Arija and Adal looked at one another, fear marring their faces.

". . . don' ye joke with me. I know what's what's in my machine. There are Topsiders here. I can smell 'em! How'd they find their way here in the first place, I cain't say. You send 'em my grip car?" Arija could tell it was a man's voice that spoke, but it was unbelievably loud like she was stuck inside the speaker of a stereo. Arija shot a glance at Adal at the word "Topsiders." She didn't exactly know what it meant, but she knew it referred to them.

"Now don't be silly, Webley! You know right well that I sent the car for them. They are guests and it's best that we treat them as such. Haven't seen a Topsider in these parts in quite some time. Furthermore, don't play surprised. With your mischief, sometimes it's a wonder that you don't have more curious creatures running about." a second, softer voice responded.

As the voices grew louder, Arija looked around the room for a place to hide, or a weapon to fight with. Anything was better than standing in the middle of the kitchen waiting for the voices to come inside.

"Reckon they made their way inte' the 'ouse?" the heavier voice inquired.

Arija and Adal looked at each other. Adal mouthed some expletives while Arija tried to figure out a game plan. Things were about to get a whole lot trickier.

"Well, I suppose the only way to know is to find out." A panic came over Adal, and they both started to pace as they desperately looked for somewhere to hide. Adal snapped his finger and got Arija's attention. He pointed at her, then to behind where the door would open.

She looked at him in curious alarm. He held up his fists in a boxing stance and nodded at her. She bobbed her head in agreement. Springing to her toes, Arija quietly ran over to the wall so that when the door opened, she would be able to get the drop on their visitor. Adal walked to the center of the room in line with the door and waited, fists raised and heart pounding.

At that moment, the door jingled slightly, and they knew it was sure to open, and at least two men were going to enter. Adal hopped up and down on his toes, rolling his shoulders and neck. The small cracks rippled as he circled his shoulders and placed his hands out before him. Whoever was about to enter, he was going to show them he meant business. Adal gave one more fleeting glance to where Arija hid, mentally preparing for whatever was to happen. With a shooting beam of the midday sun, the door opened into the kitchen, and the fight was on.

7

WEBLEY

Adal shouted at the tops of his lungs as he charged at the door. The orange light from outside hit him in the eyes and made it difficult to see. With his eyes closed and moving strictly on instinct, he made his way to the doorway with all the speed that he could muster and began to swing away. As his balled-up fist connected with the fleshy feel of human skin, Adal winced in pain but kept swinging.

He reared his fist back and let loose another bone shattering punch, but the expectant sounds of wailing in pain didn't follow. Instead, all Adal could hear was a deep chuckle, as if his punches did nothing but tickle the intruder. As the man stepped into the doorway, blocking the sun, Adal opened his eyes and looked up at the monstrous beast that stood before him.

"Lively lot, aren't ye?" chuckled the giant as he reached forward for Adal. Thinking quickly, Adal ducked and stepped back, still throwing his rapid punches. "Aha, and a quick one te boot!" the monster stepped toward Adal with his hands out.

"Now Webley, remember they told us there was a second one. Must be around here somewhere . . ." came a second voice from behind the giant. Arija knew this was her chance now that the thing named Webley, was inside and she could get behind him. As quick as she could, she popped around the door in an attempt to surprise them.

Arija faltered a half step when she saw the sheer size of Webley, but Adal needed her to back him up, so she pushed her frozen feet back into motion. She jumped forward and grabbed on to what appeared to be overalls made of a dark, dense leather of some kind. She scaled his muscular back and pulled at his long, hazel hair on the way up. Webley smelt of smoke and oil, but there was a sweet undertone that she couldn't quite put her finger on.

"Careful, Webley. She seems like the one to watch out for," the second man warned. As Webley entered the home, the other man had come into the doorway, but Arija didn't have the chance to steal a look. He didn't appear willing to join the fight, so she didn't see him as a threat. Once she made her way to the top of the giant, Arija swatted and pounded her fists at the top of his massive head. A thick leather strap held what looked like a pair of bronze goggles around Webley's forehead and Arija pulled them up and then let them go, snapping them on his head and causing the giant to wail in pain.

"Thanks, Cog. Kinda figured that one out!" Webley replied, reaching up to address Arija's attack. Adal took the opportunity, jumped up and grabbed ahold of Webley's long beard that hung down to his stomach. He pulled with one hand, and punch the giant in the stomach with the other, but his hits didn't seem to be doing any damage. As he pulled, he noticed two shiny copper buttons holding up Webley's pants. His reflection shot back at him, and he saw the look of fear in his own eyes.

"Not the beard! Tha's just rude!" Webley swung his arms, grasped Adal by the back of his neck and shoulders and shook him. Webley's hands were the size of dinner plates and his arms the size of tree trunks and Adal noticed that on one of his forearms was a bronze plate with four small rivets bolting it to his skin. At the edge of the plate, the skin looked stretched, and several deep scars framed its metallic edges. On the center of the bronze plate was an engraving of his grandfather's coin. Adal squirmed, but couldn't get free. Arija shouted and yanked two full hands of Webley's hazel colored hair.

"OUCH!" the giant bellowed and brought his attention back to the fierce warrior sitting on his shoulders. "Now tha's enough o' tha!" and with another massive swoop, Webley scooped up Arija and brought her down off his shoulders in the same grasp he'd on Adal. Webley held them both out in front of him as they fought and squirmed together trying to get free.

"Let her go!" Adal shouted, pounding his fist into the hand that held him.

"Yeah, let me go so I can keep going at you!" Arija clawed, bit, and kicked at the hand that held her, but the strong fingers wouldn't let go. Webley only responded with a howl of laughter, his arms shaking with his whole body. A figure appeared next to Webley as he held the two in the air, and Adal and Arija quit fighting as they looked down at the thing that Webley had called Cog.

Cog looked to be a little smaller than Adal, and he was shaped like a man, but there was nothing human about him. He wore a black leather vest with small white pinstripes running lengthwise and pressed black slacks, with a white button-up that had the top two buttons open and the sleeves rolled up. What Adal could see of his skin was sleek and bronze, like almost everything else in this strange place. He had small rivets and layers in patches over his body, but his face looked like it was polished from one solid piece of brass. As the strange robot looked up at Adal, he tipped his black leather newsboy cap.

"Hiya there," Cog's voice was soft but demanding, and he stared at Adal for a moment before removing his monocle that looked like half of a set of welding glasses, rubbing the glass on his vest and then replacing it on his face. Adal stared in awe at the strange creature, taking note that his other eye was outlined by a polished gear.

Adal brought his attention back to Webley who also wore a white button-up under his overalls. Two glowing, emerald eyes shot out at them from behind the tangled mess that Arija had left. Adal couldn't help but think the giant's eyes looked soft and coupled with the wide grin and rosy cheeks, Adal almost thought he seemed friendly.

Webley
and
Cog

"Now, do you see why we should have knocked instead of just coming in? Topsiders aren't always the brightest, Webley. You obviously scared them . . ."

"Hey!" Arija interjected, but she didn't have anything else to say.

"Knock on me own 'ouse? Tha'll be the day. Sides tha', wa'nt this a bit-o-fun?" Webley chuckled some more, shaking Arija and Adal as he did so.

"Well, all that aside, the fun is over, and maybe we can go about meeting our guests formally. Besides, it is nearly dinner, and it has been quite a day. I am sure their little heads are buzzing with the new sights."

"O' all right!" The grip on Arija and Adal's neck tightened as Webley brought them closer to him.

"Look 'ere you two. If I let ya down, ya going to stop all this yippin' an fightin'?" Webley's look was stern for a moment as he spoke this time. Adal and Arija looked to one another, then back to Webley and nodded their heads in silence.

"HA! Fantastic! We 'an get ta know one-another!" Webley swung the two about, taking two steps toward the big table in the center of the room. He plopped Arija in one seat and Adal in another before going to his own chair and falling into it. The entire area shook under his weight. Adal and Arija were stunned. Neither of them could think of anything to say or a way of justifying what was happening. Cog walked over to the table but did not sit down.

"Ah, much better. Thank you, Webley. Apologies, fine guests. I am sure this day has proven a bit, well, interesting for the two of you to say the least. Allow me to break some of the tension. My name is Cog." Cog removed his hat and bowed toward the table. Arija let her artistic eye run over Cog as he sat next to her. Cog even had 'hair' that appeared to be small spiral bronze shaving neatly parted and bolted to the side.

Adal looked at Arija and arched one inquisitive eyebrow. Understanding what he was asking her, she gave an ever so slight shrug in response. Arija couldn't find any reason to continue to be scared or fight these things. Fighting hadn't really worked out so far, and besides, there really wasn't anywhere to go. Maybe Webley or Cog could help them get back home.

"Arija," she said softly, looking from Cog to Webley.

"Ah, Arija. Hebrew in origin. Lioness of God. No doubt you surely exude the meaning of your well-deserved name." Arija's face softened in shock.

"Might I inquire as to your last name, Arija?" Cog was very polite and inquisitive.

"Rapp. Arija Rapp."

"Ah, wonderful. Something that is Raven-like. My, what a befitting title of a young Topsider such as yourself. What about you?" Cog turned his attention to Adal.

"Adal . . ." he replied bluntly. Adal still didn't like their situation. He didn't trust these people . . . these . . . things, whatever they were. Adal had gotten used to being in control of most situations, but Webley had made short, effortless work of him, and he didn't like it one bit.

"Adal. Hmmm, not entirely familiar with that title. By chance, is it short for something?" Cog leaned forward slightly, interested.

"Adalwolf Stein . . ." he sighed.

"Ah, wonderful title indeed! Adalwolf, or the 'noble wolf,' and Stein being 'that of stone.' A strong title!" Adal and Arija looked at an excited Cog inquisitively. "My apologies. I like to spin tales and create. A strong name is a pinnacle of every creature destined for greatness. Sort of a hobby of mine."

"Your name is Cog. Like what you find in a machine, right? Because you're a robot or something?" Adal couldn't contain his question.

The corners of Cog's mechanical mouth turned down. "Actually, it is short for Cogsworth, and I am no machine. I am a Dweller just like everyone else here," Cog spoke in a matter-of-fact tone. Arija snorted and shook her head at Adal. She couldn't believe he would ask such a question and was amused by Cog's response. Adal looked at her and shrugged with a "What?" look on his face.

"Well, Arija and Adal, I'm Webley. Name don' really mean much. Jus Webley, I guess. Welcome to The World Machine!" Webley spoke with such excitement and tenacity. It was as though he had been waiting for visitors for his entire life.

"The World Machine? Is that what this place is called?" Arija asked, finding some comfort in the introductions.

"Yes, miss! This is my land, my home, my machine. Built it meself, ya' know." Webley's chest swelled with pride as he spoke.

"Wait, you built this . . . place?" Adal asked in amazement. "How is that even possible?"

"Wha' ye mean? I'm a creator. It's wha' I do. Everything ye see about ye, all that is round here, made it meself." Webley shifted in his seat and interlaced his fingers together on the table.

Arija and Adal looked at one another again in shock. This place was not only real, it was inhabited by mechanical beings, strange machines and technology, and it was all built by Webley, the friendly giant? Any other time Arija would call a bluff, but it was not something she wanted to challenge. This was happening, and she had to go with it. She looked over at Adal again, whose face was lit up like a Christmas tree.

"Pardon my intrusion in the conversation, but it is growing quite late. I am sure that the two of you have so much more to ask, but perhaps dinner could be in order?" Cog asked, turning from the table and making his way over to the kitchen area. It wasn't until that moment that Arija and Adal realized their stomachs actually hurt with hunger.

"So, this is all real, then? We didn't die in that cave or hit our heads. This place is an actual thing, and we are in it?" Arija blurted as she watched Cog filling a large pot with water.

"Can assure ye tha this is all real. Like I said, built it all meself. On tha note, do ye still 'ave it?" Webley asked, holding his large hand out to Adal expectantly.

"Have what?"

"The key. 'Ave ye still got the key?" Webley reiterated, shaking his hand in anticipation.

"Key?" Adal asked, shaking his head.

"The coin, I think," Arija interjected, pointing at Adal's pocket. Adal pulled out the coin from his pocket and held it out.

"This?" he asked. "This isn't a key, this is my grandfather's coin. He gave it to me." Webley's face lit up, and he scooped the coin out of Adal's hands.

"There it is!" Webley shouted, turning to Cog and flicking the coin into the air. Cog merely shook his head without turning to look at Webley. He continued to work over what sort of resembled a stove but with more compartments and knobs than Adal could figure out. There were multiple levers and chambers that resembled pressure cookers. On occasion, the room would sound with the hissing of steam and heat releasing from one of the containers.

"I told you that you had misplaced it. All these years and you insisted you knew exactly where it was. One day you should learn to be more careful . . ." Cog cautioned without looking up from what he was cooking.

"I knew 'xactly where it was! Right where I left it." Webley flicked the coin into the air and snatched it back into his palm before it fell to the table. Arija stared at the coin as Webley flicked it and caught it over and over until her senses were overwhelmed with whatever Cog was cooking. Adal shot a glance to the kitchen as his stomach growled and his mouth began to water.

"If that's a key, then how did Grandpa Lawrence get ahold of it during the war?" Arija asked, trying to slide the heavy chair closer to the table and failing as her legs came nowhere near the floor. Webley spun the coin on the table, it pinged as it hit and hopped all over the intricate, worn surface.

"Not sure 'bout tha'. I tend to misplace things from time to time. Long ago, I spent a lot of time an' energy on a very special bracelet tha' I was gonna use for a bit o' fun. Not sure where that bugger ended up either. Curious tale, tha' thing . . ." the coin still spun and hopped on the table and Arija watched it, mesmerized.

Adal's stomach growled and as if on cue, Cog started plating food next to the stove. Adal was excited to get something in him when an interesting thought crept into his head: What exactly would these people eat down here? He tried to focus on the conversation that Webley and Arija were having, but the thought of food overwhelmed him. Hopefully, whatever Cog dropped on the table wasn't made of machine oil and spare parts.

"So, you're a 'Creator'? What sort of things do you create? How did you make this place?" Arija asked, her curious nature drinking up the situation like it was fresh lemonade on a hot summer day.

"Well, I create anythin' really. Ya name it, I can create it. That's what a creator does, doe'nt he? As for this place an' my story, not gonna bore you lot with that tonight. Ah! Supper!" Webley broke from their conversation as Cog appeared beside the table and slid four plates to each of the four chairs.

8

Dwellers Do Not Consume Other Living Things

Steam and a succulent aroma lunged into Adal's and Arija's faces, and Adal said a silent prayer of thanks that it wasn't a plate full of machine parts.

"This looks wonderful?" Arija posed. Adal knew she didn't mean for it to sound like a question, but neither of them could have ever guessed what would be on the plate in front of them. Adal looked from his plate back to Cog. The platters before them were almost comically large—nearly the size of the top of his bedside table at home. Webley had already begun to wolf down his dinner, but Arija and Adal just stared, dumbfounded.

"What is the matter? Are you not a fan of ratatouille?" Cog asked as he reached out to grab the plate back from Arija. "I can whip you up something else if it isn't to your liking."

"No, not at all! I love this dish. I just haven't had it in years," Arija replied apologetically. She looked at the dish for a moment. Though not something traditional to her family, ratatouille had been her mother's favorite dish. She hadn't had it since her mother had died.

"This smells great," Adal said, picking up his fork.

"Then dig in!" Webley smiled, speaking through a mouth full of food. Adal and Arija exchanged glances, and both took up a fork full.

"To be honest, this wasn't what I was expecting. You eat food like us?" Adal asked. He heard a clank as Arija dropped her fork back down to her plate. She fanned the air under the table with her foot to give Adal a solid kick but couldn't reach.

"What were you expecting, might I ask? Oil soup?" Cog didn't appear to be insulted, but Adal had the sense he'd intended to make him look stupid.

"I mean, kinda . . ."

"Adal!" Arija shot at him.

Adal could almost feel the heat from her glare and her hand itching for the back of his head. He quickly apologized, but that was always his problem—Adal never could let a question just sit in his head. He needed answers, or the questions would drive him mad. Something he no doubt had inherited from his grandfather if such things can be inherited.

Cog and Webley both laughed.

115

"Well, there is oil in this. Vegetable oil, so there is that. Also, you will find that the Dwellers of The World Machine all enjoy their fruits and vegetables. Very healthy and good for us all." Cog took another bite of his dish.

"What about meat? What do the Dwellers eat for meat?" Adal asked as he shoveled another forkful into his mouth.

Webley and Cog both stopped with their forks in mid-air and glared at Adal as if he had just insulted their mothers. Adal froze under their stares, amazed that for a being that appeared to be made of metal somehow Cog managed a full range of facial expressions. Adal hadn't quite figured that out yet.

"Dwellers do not consume other living things. We eat only vegetables and fruits we raise and grow. Consumption or use of a being after death is something forbidden here." Cog held his look for a moment and then smiled. There was something strangely sinister about the mechanical man, but Adal couldn't quite put his finger on it.

"Ah, no need ta get so serious. Cog 'ere is the best cook in the Machine. Ya'd be surprised ta see what he can make!" Webley sucked a lingering vegetable from his fork and then wiped his mouth with the back of his hand.

Adal didn't want to say anything else stupid, and his stomach was nearly screaming at him, so he scooped up a forkful of vegetables and shoveled the hot mixture into his mouth. Arija sat in silence, watching Cog eye Adal, Webley slurped down more veggies, and Adal look shamefully into his bowl. She was taking everything in and wanted to make sure she could bail them out of whatever trouble Adal's mouth got them into.

With a lull in the conversation, Arija scooped some onion and eggplant onto her fork and took her first cautious bite of dinner. As soon as the warm, comforting taste touched her tongue, she closed her eyes. Memories of her mother cooking in the kitchen while she colored at the kitchen table flooded her mind. For the remainder of dinner, the group sat in silence with only the clinking of their forks to break the void.

As Arija licked up the remaining broth from her fork, Cog rose and collected the dishes. Webley stood and stretched, emitting a barrage of exhausted moans and cracks from his joints that sounded like tree limbs breaking.

Adal thought he might explode from all he'd eaten, and as he looked over at Arija, he could tell she felt the same. The orange hue of light that filled the air outside had turned to a navy and purple glow.

"Well, looks to me tha' it's 'bout time te' rest for a bit then be off to bed. Come, ye two an' let's be off to the study. Cog, would ye mind bringin' the coffee?" Webley motioned to Arija and Adal to follow him. He walked past the two and guided them into the next room.

Adal and Arija stopped as they entered a study lit by a large fireplace and accented with dark wood. The study itself almost looked like an antique library. Arija's mouth dropped open and her eyes bulged as she looked around what was possibly the coolest room she'd ever been in.

Built-in bookshelves lined every wall, and an iron ladder on tracks ran along the shelves as thousands of books sat framed in every crevice. Adal gazed up at the vaulted ceilings and thought the room had to be two to three stories tall as it even dwarfed Webley. The sweet smell of old books tickled Arija's nose. She was home. If nothing else came from whatever journey the two had found themselves on, being in this room was enough.

One wall directly across from them was without books. A skeletonized clock the size of a small car was mounted on the wall and ticked away quietly as the huge gears turned. Hanging above the brick fireplace was a large gun and a giant metal tool that had a wrench on one side of the long handle, and a hammer on the other. Adal walked around the room to the large sofa next to the fireplace. He ran his hands across the tough leather fastened in place by small copper rivets. Across from the sofa were two chairs, one significantly bigger than the other which looked to be a perfect fit for Adal.

"Please, 'ave a seat," Webley requested, motioning to the sofa. Adal plopped down on the leather sofa and was immediately sucked into the surprisingly soft cushions. Arija shook her head and walked over to the sofa to join him.

As she settled into the strangely comforting couch, the door from the kitchen burst open and Cog came into the room balancing four huge cups in his hands. The cups may have been normal for Webley, but to Arija and Adal they may as well have been bowls.

Cog sat in the seat next to Webley, taking a huge sip from his cup. Adal picked up one cup and peered at the black liquid inside. For a moment, he worried that it was oil, but he closed his eyes and took a sip of the steaming substance.

"It's coffee!" he said as he turned to Arija. She picked up her cup, holding the large mug with both hands. The steaming hot aroma of roasted beans wafted into her nose and she sank back into the sofa, closing her eyes. This was a perfect day for Arija Rapp, sitting in the most unique and beautiful library she'd ever seen, sipping coffee on one of the most comfortable leather couches she'd ever sat on. The only thing that could make this any better would be to have her sketch pad, so she could document everything she was seeing.

"Hope ye like it. I roast it m'self down in the furnace. Really gives it the ol' smokey and fiery tones." Webley took a large gulp of his coffee. The comment pulled Arija from her thoughts. She had to agree that this was some of the best coffee she'd ever had. Even Adal, who would normally fill his coffee with more cream and sugar than actual coffee, had to agree that the rich black beverage was amazing. If this all kept up, he would never leave.

"I don't want to be that guy, or anything, but can I have my coin back?" Adal asked out of the blue, nodding toward Webley's pocket. When the group had risen from the table, Webley had snatched the coin up and tucked it away. Cog looked from Webley to Adal as if he were waiting to see what Webley's response would be.

Arija smacked Adal's thigh. She knew if he kept this up, their friendly host could crush them with one hit.

"The key? I don' think I can give ye tha', Adal. Kinda important, ya know." Webley took another sip of his coffee. Adal's heart sank. That coin was the last thing his grandfather had given him before he died. He dragged his nails down the palms of his hands as anger started to bubble in his gut.

"Look, that may be your 'key' and all, but my grandfather gave that to me. I want it back!"

"My, ye are a feisty one! I think we can be friends! Well, the both of ye, really. Hasn' been often tha' I get te meet new folks. You two seem like a couple o' decent Topsiders. Tell ye wha', ye stay 'ere with me for a while and let me show ye about my machine, and ye can 'ave it back. How's tha'?"

In all the events of the day, Adal and Arija hadn't even had the chance to consider staying. They had been so focused on getting home, but without saying a word they both knew they couldn't just leave a place like this without exploring.

"You cool with that?" Adal asked Arija, but her ear to ear grin already gave her answer away.

"I suppose we could make that work." Arija took another sip of coffee, trying to play off her excitement. Webley jumped up from his seat and threw his gigantic hands into the air like a little kid who'd been told he could go to the park.

"It's settled then! Ye will stay with me for a time, an' in return, ye get the key back!"

Adal and Arija flinched at his explosion of enthusiasm, but couldn't help but smile. Something about Webley's literal larger-than-life aura was contagious.

"Cog, can ye do me a favor an' prepare the guest rooms? Think our new friends might appreciate a comfy bed after a day like this one!" Cog nodded and downed the last of his coffee.

"All right, then. Just give me a few moments and I will have those ready." Cog stood and disappeared up a spiral staircase hidden in the corner of the room. Adal and Arija both took a double-take. How had they missed that when they first came into the room?

"Well, as much fun as it 'as been ta' meet ye both tonight, I think tha' I will be off for the evenin'. Got to prepare my machine fer visitors an' all. Sleep well an' be ready for a grand time tomorrow." Webley stood, finished the rest of his coffee, and was back out the door to the kitchen. A moment later, they heard the front door open then close.

"What's going on?" Arija blurted as soon as the door closed. She turned to Adal with a concerned look on her face.

"Well, we are staying, aren't we?" Adal asked, confusion wrinkling his face.

"Obviously, we are. This place is amazing, and I have to see it, but what's going on? This can't be real, but it is. We're somewhere underground . . . far underground. There are machines and mechanical 'Dwellers' everywhere, a giant man named Webley . . . I mean, what's going on?"

Arija was battling her true emotions as she spoke. She wanted nothing more than to stay and study the place. She wanted to catalogue, interact, and draw all the amazing creations in The World Machine, but she was also always the responsible one. Adal was usually the one that ran off on crazy ideas, and she was concerned that if she didn't ask these questions, who knew where they would end up.

"Look, this place is dope. There's no way we can't stay for a while and check it out. Especially considering I want my coin back. So, we'll stay, figure out what this place is, get my coin, and return to our boring lives back home when we are done. My old man can give me attitude, and you can go off to rule the world under the fear that you put into . . . well, everyone. Cool?" Adal tried his best at charm, but he was too tired to put much effort into it. In fact, he wanted nothing more than to crawl into bed and figure everything out in the morning.

"Fine. Just, let's be clear, we need to really think about everything we do here. At the first sign of trouble, we are back in that railcar and out of here. Deal?" Arija narrowed her eyes at Adal as if saying "no funny stuff."

"Yeah, yeah. Fine, deal. What's the matter? Think I can't handle things down here?" Adal asked, stretching his arms out and then bringing them into a flex while he yawned. Arija rolled her eyes.

"Sure, you can handle yourself. Until Webley decides that he's tired of playing with you like some giant cat and mouse and pounds you into the ground with one hit."

A sound came from across the room and made both Arija and Adal jump in their seats. They turned to see that Cog was standing at the base of the stairs, looking at them. He had a strange smile on his face, and Arija and Adal both knew he had heard everything.

"I just wanted to let you two know your rooms are ready. If you wouldn't mind following me, I can get you settled in."

Adal and Arija slid from the couch and walked over to Cog. He looked at them for a moment then smiled wider, shaking his head.

"I also want to say, before you turn in, that I can appreciate your caution. I admit if I found myself in the world of Topsiders, I wouldn't be too inclined to trust anyone either. You find safety and security in only what is familiar to you. It is your nature. Believe me when I say, you have nothing to fear here. Especially from Webley or myself. He values life and creation more than anything else. If there is any point when you are uncomfortable, or if there is something I can do to ease your minds, please let me know."

Arija thanked Cog for his kind words while Adal silently nodded his head. Cog, having spoken his peace, turned and walked up the stairs with Arija and Adal in tow.

9

Steam, Showers, and Garter Belts

Adal drifted awake to the sound of soft music playing. He wasn't sure where it was coming from, but he knew the piece by heart. The music was one of his grandfather's favorite works: Bagatelle No. 25 in A minor, or Fur Elise as he would sometimes refer to it. As the beautiful music lulled him in and out of sleep, Adal slowly opened his eyes and looked at the ceiling above him. The entire surface appeared to be a painted mural. Two mighty hands wielded a hammer and tongs over an anvil. The wielder was hidden behind a veil of smoke and fire, but the smith was forging what looked to be a coin.

Adal rubbed his eyes and sat up. The comfort of the bed he slept in was almost coma-inducing. He didn't remember falling asleep, but it was the deepest sleep he could recall having in his life. He hadn't even had the energy or ability to dream. The thought crossed his mind he should be grateful for that. With everything that had happened the last few days, dreams would likely have turned to nightmares.

The music continued to play, and Adal looked about the room for its origin.

Above his head was another large, skeletonized clock that took up half of the wall. Just below the clock was a spinning tube with small notches being plucked by brass bars. It took Adal a moment to realize that the entire wall was a music box and an alarm clock rolled into one. The time on the wall said it was 6 a.m., and Adal scrunched his face in disgust. Next to the rotating drum was a lever. Adal reached up and pulled it, silencing the music.

"Webley wasn't kidding when he said first thing, was he?" he rolled from his comfortable bed and took one last look around the room. It reminded him of a museum. There were glass cases with an assortment of mechanical oddities, and just next to the bed was a large telescope poised out of the window. He wasn't sure the point of this, as they were well underground, but he was sure plenty of things were going to confuse him today.

With a final stretch, Adal stood and walked over to the washroom on the opposite side of the room. The room was not disproportionately sized for Webley. In fact, nothing on this floor of the house was. Other than that, the washroom was relatively standard to what he was used to, though everything in it looked antique—a large claw foot bathtub, a Victorian sink, and a high tank toilet. The reservoir of water for the toilet was near the ceiling and copper piping that bent and twisted into beautiful knotted designs connected it to the actual seat on the floor. Just inside the door sat a small table with a stack of clothing and a small note. Adal walked over and took up the paper.

I took the liberty of fashioning you some new clothing. Judging by the wet and dirty attire you arrived in, I think you will find this helpful. When ready, please come down to the library.

-Cog

Adal looked from the clothing to the shower and shrugged. Upon inspection, it seemed the shower worked the same as his back home, and Adal turned up the hot water and let the room fill with steam.

Arija's eyes fluttered open and then slammed shut again. Her face was swollen, and her eyes stung with exhaustion. As she pulled the heavy comforter back over her head, she silently cursed herself for staying up all night. Arija had examined every square inch of the room she was in. All the strange machines and inventions, pieces of art, and things that would have seemed normal in her life. She was fascinated with it all.

A beautiful song pierced her ears, but Arija was not a morning person and she angrily shoved a pillow over her head. After a few angry minutes where she considered chucking something hard at the alarm, Arija pulled herself up to a sitting position. She forced herself to put down the pillow and slid out of bed, shuffling over to the wall alarm and calmly shut it off. She leaned against the wall and sighed. Life would be better after a shower and some coffee.

Arija had already checked out the bathroom the night before and found that it was fitting for the house she was staying in. Next to the claw-foot tub was a small vanity where an assortment of brushes, combs and containers were neatly lined up. Arija had already found out that the small bronze containers held various bits of makeup, but she wasn't really the makeup wearing type. Seeing the containers again this morning, before she'd had time for coffee, only brought back another bout of anger.

"Even mechanical men think it's all about appearances. If anything, these things should be in Adal's room!" Arija laughed at the thought as she turned up the hot water and stepped into the tub for a much-needed hot shower.

Fifteen minutes later she stepped out of the shower and walked over to the vanity. She inspected the neatly folded pile of clothing as she picked up one of the boar hair brushes. She ran the brush through her hair and left the bathroom with the pile of clothes. Arija fanned the outfit out on the bed and her lip curled up into a scowl.

"Note to self: watch that creepy robot guy," Arija said as she wondered how Cog knew her sizes. She had never seen stitching and designs like these on clothes before other than maybe in pictures in her history textbooks. She picked up a leather corset by one of the straps like it was a piece of garbage. Arija had never worn one before as these sorts of "doll clothing" (as she often called them) weren't her style.

"This will be fun. Take me an hour to buckle this bad boy up," Arija scoffed as she dropped the corset back onto the bed and picked up the skirt. She ran her fingers across the leather and wondered what it was made of. It felt like leather, but it was much lighter and more flowy than any leather she'd ever seen. She shrugged and slid the skirt on before noticing a pair of black leggings sitting on the bed. She put on the leggings and then buckled herself into the corset. As Arija started to walk out of the room, she noticed a pair of tall leather boots sitting next to the door. She grabbed them and sat down on the edge of the bed to put them on. After buckling the boots up to her knees, Arija stood and admired herself in the full-length mirror.

"All right, I guess I don't look too bad in this outfit." Arija grabbed the brush she'd set on the bed, opened the door, and walked out into the hall.

Adal stepped out of the shower and was admiring himself in the fogged mirror as he did every morning. He ran his hand over the stubble on his face and reflexively looked around for his razor before he realized where he was. Next to the sink was a straight razor, but Adal didn't know how to use one. He let his hand hover over the shiny metallic object before he decided he didn't want to cut his throat trying. He got dressed instead.

"Well, there goes that," Adal said, stepping back and looking at his outfit. Adal loved the old-style outfit Cog had left for him. In fact, he would probably make it his new style when he went back home. His favorite part was the leather vest. Adal had never worn a vest before, he'd always thought them to be nerdy, but this vest was dope, and with the chains that ran to the pocket, he thought he looked more like a biker than a nerd. Tugging at the ends of his shirt, and pleased with what he saw, Adal made his way into the hallway.

Unlike when they initially came up last night, the corridor was bright and warm. Adal looked up to find the entire ceiling of the hall was a glass dome like in the train stations back home. Warm, radiant rays of light pierced the glass and washed over Adal's face.

The walls in the hall were lined edge to edge with painted pictures of an assortment of strange things that Adal didn't recognize. Some looked like blueprints, others like paintings of landscapes and Dwellers. As Adal stopped to eye a particularly confusing painting, a door down the hall opened and Arija walked out.

The two stood in silence for a moment, looking at the attire of the other. Adal tried to suppress the grin that spread across his face, but he knew he had been unsuccessful. Arija had on a burgundy lace and leather corset with two large pockets, a black skirt and what appeared to be black pants underneath. His eyes lingered at her neckline where she had what looked like leather shoulder covers and a leather strap around her neck.

"Stop staring," Arija said as she looked Adal up and down. His oversized pinstriped vest covering a white button up sat surprisingly well on him. He had one hand on his thick, brown belt and the other in his long overcoat pocket. A small flutter developed in Arija's stomach, but she didn't need to feed his already huge ego.

"Sleep well?" Adal managed, trying to break the awkward silence.

"Yup. You?"

"Yeah. Deep. So, these clothes?" Adal laughed, pulling his coat open and turning in a circle. Arija sighed and let a small laugh escape her lips.

"Right? Not sure if I can get used to these. I mean, they look good, especially on me, but not the most comfortable. Have you ever seen what passed as Victorian underwear? It's almost like a romper." Arija adjusted her corset and tugged it upward.

"Is that an invitation?" Adal smirked. Arija gasped dramatically and slugged him in the arm.

"In your dreams! In fact, not even there!" she barked, trying not to smile but failing. "Let's get downstairs. I'm sure they're waiting for us by now." Arija turned and walked down the hall with Adal in tow.

"Hey!" Arija called over her shoulder. She paused and tossed Adal the brush she'd grabbed from her room.

"Thanks, girl!" Adal ran the brush over his hair as they continued walking.

"Yeah, I know you have to be the prettiest one in the room, so I figured you'd need that more than I do."

Adal paused his brushing and scowled at her. "Hey, don't hate because I look great all the time. You ever need advice, I got you," Adal said as he continued to run the brush over his thick hair.

"Just keep moving before I bruise that pretty face of yours," Arija sneered. She considered tripping him, but figured he would trip himself eventually.

Once the two got to the library, Cog was waiting for them. He stood in the center of the room and wore the same outfit as the previous day. Arija had a strange thought and wondered if the Dwellers ever had to change their clothes. Thinking to the assortment of odd, and mildly insulting, questions Adal had already asked and would likely ask in the future, she kept the thought to herself.

"Good morning! I hope you slept well. Ah, I see you chose to wear the clothing I made you last night. I hope they fit all right. I did the best I could in assessing your sizes," Cog started, with a smile.

"Actually, these look great and fit me just right," Adal began. "But Arija is having some problems with her unde—" Arija brought her elbow into Adal's stomach, stopping him mid-sentence and making him cough and gasp for air.

"They are perfect. Thank you for the trouble you went through," Arija said, shooting Adal a look from the corner of her eyes.

"Ah, surely, no trouble at all. Now, I think a quick bite is in order before we set out on the day. Webley is waiting out back and is working on a special start to the day. Might I interest the two of you in an apple and some coffee?" Cog motioned to the table between the sofa and two chairs. A small tray sat in the center with two ruby apples and the usual bowls of coffee. Neither of them were particularly hungry, and they were eager to start the day, so they tucked the apples away in their pockets and took several large gulps of coffee.

"Well now, shall we?" Cog asked, waiving for them to follow him. Without wanting to waste another minute, the two were on Cog's tail as he led them into the kitchen, then through another door at the other end. Arija's heart was pounding hard as she thought about what they may do today, so hard she thought it might break out of her chest and make a run for it. Meanwhile, Adal had to battle the urge to run past Cog like a child on holiday.

After walking through the next door, Adal and Arija found themselves standing at the entrance of a greenhouse. The vaulted, fogged glass ceilings had a large, intricate pipe system winding its way across the entire room. Periodic droplets of ice-cold water fell on Adal as he walked underneath; causing him to hold his hands out and look up as if expecting a rainstorm. Rack after iron rack of flowers, herbs, small trees, and even edibles, filed the room, making it feel like a jungle.

Why wouldn't there be a near entire forest in this strange home? Arija thought as she delicately ran her fingers across a strange spiked plant she'd never seen before. It looked like some sort of cross between a cactus and a palm tree.

Arija's eyes dance from one curious plant to another. Some of them had flowers she had never seen before. One, in particular, made both Arija and Adal freeze as they passed. It was the size of a decorative fountain. Emerald greens spun into a cone shape and the large petals tilted just so it could show off its plum-colored interior. As they neared it, Arija closed her eyes and took in a deep breath, filling her lungs with all the plant's marvelous odors, but as soon as her lungs filled with the smells of the air, she was overcome with the urge to vomit. Without turning, Cog's shoulder shook with laughter.

"Careful with some of these, Webley fancies himself a bit of a collector. That particular one is very rare. Even in the realm of the Topsiders. It is called the Corpse Flower. Bloom is very rare, and the smell, well . . ." His chuckles fell away as they put distance between themselves and the foul plant. "There, have a smell of those. It will cleanse that horrible odor. These, I have been told, smell of honey."

Adal didn't even pause to consider as he inhaled so deeply that several of the tiny, white flowers nearly went up his nose. Arija tried to hide her desperate urge to forget the smell, but she too nearly inhaled a small cluster of flowers.

The group rounded the final corner to one last door that led them out of the house and into the openness of the machine. Adal looked around inquisitively at the lush grass. Everything they'd experienced since stepping foot in this place was made of machine and metal, but this was real, healthy, thick grass. He hadn't even noticed that Cog had continued walking, or that Arija was about to run right into him.

Arija was walking blindly, staring up at the sky above them. The sky was a blue hue almost identical to the sky from home although something was slightly off about the color. She ran theories through her head as to how it was even possible, and as she did, she slammed right into Adal and was brought back to reality.

"My bad!" Adal said, adjusting his clothes.

"You're all set," she answered, suddenly aware of all that surrounded them. Webley's back yard was not large. Rather, the area was quaint with luscious grass stretched over the surface, strangely beautiful plants scattered randomly across the yard, and a small but elegant bird bath that sat almost directly in the center of the patch of green. In the bath, several small mechanical birds, like they'd seen on the platform, fluttered and splashed in the water, their movements so perfect and realistic that it was possible to forget they were machines.

On the other side of the lawn was Webley standing on a platform that extended out past the yard. From their vantage point, it looked as though his yard dropped off as sharply into the open abyss as the platform they first came to the day before.

10

PINEAPPLE LEATHER

Off in the distance, Adal and Arija watched the wonderfully blue light that illuminated above them change into the orange hue they had previously seen. The orange coloring reminded Adal of the street lamps that came on after dark by his house, and he wondered how it could be both daylight and sunset at the same time.

"How is this place lit?" Adal asked Cog, squinting at the sky above them.

"Do you like it? Webley insisted on doing something to make the house a bit more to your liking," Cog spoke as though they had simply turned a switch on, but something of this magnitude had to be more complicated than that. Adal looked over his shoulder at Arija who was already shaking her head.

"Yeah, but how though?" he asked again.

Cog paused and turned to them. "Bulbs. A very special type of bulb with filaments hand-forged by Webley. When we can collect certain gases, and fill the bulbs with both the forged filaments and the specific gases, we are able to draw various effects. These bulbs are used to light the entire World Machine. The ones overhead were made last night to give the appearance of a blue sky for your morning. The rest of the machine, however, is still lit with the traditional bulbs. The only other place you will find these will be over the valleys. Fruits and vegetables also prefer this type of light."

Adal took the explanation at its value since he didn't know much about this sort of thing, but Arija wracked her brain trying to figure out if something like that was even possible. She was amazed that the technology here was so simple, yet so vastly different to that from back home, and she wondered if it was possible to bring some of this technology back with them.

"Ah, 'ere ye are! Mornin'! Been wonderin' when ye might get up. Come on over, I got somethin' te show ya." Webley waived them on, almost as excited as they were. He held two large packs in his hands. From where they stood, the two packs looked to be nothing more than leather rucksacks. As Arija followed Adal across the lawn, she was stopped by Cog.

"Please pardon my intrusion, but as we met, I couldn't help but notice your pack. After dinner, you left it at the table and last night I took the liberty to examine it." Cog's words caused a heat of embarrassment mixed with anger to warm Arija's cheeks. Cog had looked through her bag and had found a mess of soaked and ruined half drawings and doodles. Adal was the only person other than her mother who had ever seen Arija's sketches and she'd planned on keeping it that way.

"Excuse me?" she asked, aggravation lacing her words.

"Again, I beg pardon; I too know what it is like to have the urge to make something beautiful. Webley made sure of that . . ." Cog paused for a moment, his last comment confusing Arija. Noting her expression, Cog picked his speech back up.

"Anyway, I made you something and want to give it to you." Cog unslung a beautifully ornate messenger bag. It was burgundy in color and had an etched-lace overlay. Bronze clasps and buckles enclosed the top flap and the emblem of Adal's coin was burned into the center. Arija blinked and shook her head then took the gift into her hand and ran her fingers over the soft fabric. A leather strap bound the flap down and she unbuckled it to examine the contents of the bag.

"I have to ask you something. You said earlier that you don't believe in killing living beings. That it's common practice to admire and appreciate life and its creatures in the Machine. So, why are there so many products made of leather?" Arija asked, pulling a large book from the bag.

"How do you mean? All of our leather is made from pineapple," Cog responded, confused.

"You make your leather from pineapple?" she asked, assuming he was joking.

"Yes. It is a process we discovered long ago. If you take the pineapple leaves, you can make a sort of .

. ." Cog paused, noting the confused look on Arija's face before adding, "It's quite durable and soft."

Arija shrugged and brought her attention back to the large book in her hands. Its cover was dark brown and well worn, yet when she opened it, the blank pages were a perfect ivory—soft and new. It was a sketchbook to replace her own that had been destroyed. A small pouch at the bottom of the bag held charcoal sticks and other sketching tools. She was speechless. After a moment of gawking at the gift, she mustered a soft "Thank you."

Cog nodded and stepped aside, motioning for her to join Adal next to Webley who was explaining something. Arija couldn't concentrate on what was happening around her, her head was buzzing, and she itched to sit down and drawn some things she'd seen.

"Ye two ready te' see the Machine?" Webley's voice was chipper and held hints of a chuckle. He tossed one of the packs he carried to Adal and the other to Arija who had just enough time to sling the satchel Cog had given her over her shoulder before nearly dropping the one that was thrown at her. Adal took only a moment of examining the pack before wanting to dive into it.

"What's in this thing?" he asked, struggling to locate the clasp that would open it.

"Ye will see. It's the way we'll be gettin' about today. Easiest manner o' travel. I wouldn't try te' open it. Jus' put it on. Tell ye 'bout it in a moment." The toothy grin on Webley's face was a little concerning, but Adal took one last look at the bag and threw it over his shoulder. Arija did the same. "Comfortable? Well now, Cog do ye mind showin' 'em wha' these are?"

Adal and Arija shrugged. The satchels were surprisingly light for their size. In fact, their standard haul of school books weighed significantly more than these. Cog walked between them and looked off into the distance. He had donned his own pack similar to theirs, and with a jerk of his arms, the sides of the pack burst open and a set of large, scaled wings expanded into the space between them.

Adal jumped backward and Arija threw her hands up to cover her face. Webley howled with laughter and it looked as though even Cog's shoulders shook with amusement. The wings were gorgeous and reminded Arija of the small mechanical finch from the platform the previous day. Rather than feathers, row upon row of small scales comprised the majority of their mass. Several strips of copper ran the length as bones would support a real wing. All this centered about a small, metal box that sat in the center of Cog's shoulders.

"What the? Wings?" Adal asked, collecting himself and trying to play off his exaggerated flinch.

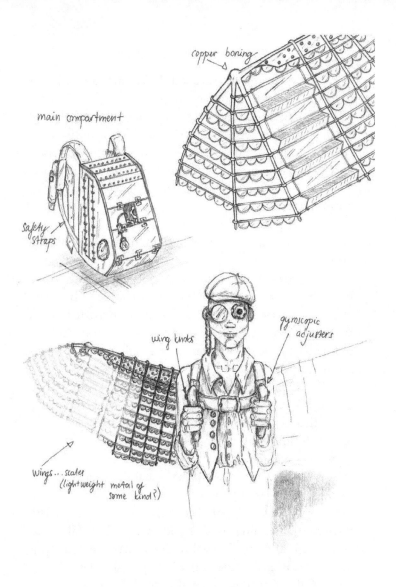

copper boning

main compartment

safety straps

wing knobs

gyroscopic adjusters

wings... scales
(lightweight metal of
some kind?)

He cleared his throat and continued in a lower octave. "I mean, of course wings!"

Arija rolled her eyes but she couldn't help the small smile that formed at the side of her mouth.

Adal looked back and forth over the structure on Cog's back and his expression dropped once more. "Ah, wait! Wings?" the realization of what that mean hitting his mind.

"The fliegensacks are the best way to get around, I promise," Cog chimed in, turning to face the group.

Arija's heart danced in her chest. Adal may have her beat regarding confined spaces, but she wasn't scared of heights, and heights petrified Adal. Watching his seamless bravado falter slightly and his humanistic side show forced a laugh out of Arija's mouth.

"Oh, come on, Adal. You mean to tell me you got us all the way here and you can't even handle a little flying? I thought you were invincible?" she teased, hitting him in the arm.

"I mean, sure, you can be sarcastic, but do you see an engine on those, uhh what are they called? Flyingsacks?" Adal paused for a moment, knowing he butchered the name of the pack on his back before finishing. "Planning on just gliding and then falling to your death? I'm not." Adal didn't appreciate being put on the spot and made fun of. Especially considering he was the one that normally needed to be kept in check. Arija ceased her giggling and then turned and looked at Webley who was shaking his head.

"Still 'avent got the feel fer the Machine. Ye will learn tha' things are vastly different down 'ere than they are from yer home. No need ta fear engines.

It's simple." Webley walked over to Cog and brought their attention to the box in the center of the fliegensack.

"In tha', there's a small fork tha' vibrates at a set frequency once started. This frequency transfers to the small scales on the wings. They vibrate an create their own form o' lift. Like the birds on the surface. There are also calibrated gyroscopic adjusters." Webley stuck his hand between Cog and the back of the pack. "Tha' will turn the whole thing in any direction tha' ye want. Only 'ave te' make the slightest movement. All ye 'ave te' do is . . ." Webley reached over to a small turn-knob on one of the straps and turned it.

Suddenly, the sound of faint vibrations emitted from the wings. Arija and Adal stepped forward and looked closely at each of the scales. They indeed appeared to be vibrating but at such a speed that they could no longer discern where each individual scale began or ended.

"Wait, are you telling me that something straight out of a science fiction book really works and we're about to fly through the air on these things? For one, I don't know how far down the drop is on this place. Oh, and don't forget all the weird machines and structures everywhere! I don't think I'm down for this one," Adal added. He pulled at the straps of his pack, moisture forming in the palm of his hands.

"I think I agree. I mean, well . . ." Arija wanted to agree with Adal. This all sounded like utter madness, but then, "I'm going to do it!" Her heart was pounding. This was something she just couldn't say no to. The science sounded preposterous, but then again so would this place if she hadn't seen it with her own two eyes.

"Ah! Wonderful! 'ats wha' I wanted te' hear!" Webley patted Arija on the shoulder and placed his large arms around the both of them. He led them forward to the edge of the platform. As Adal and Arija stepped to the drop and looked out, the world about them was incredible and rendered them speechless.

There were beams, walkways, indiscernible giant machinery, and an odd assortment of flying "things" off in the distance for what looked to be miles. It was like looking into a dream. Adal and Arija alike couldn't resist and looked down. Sure enough, as they had expected it was a sheer drop without a bottom in sight. The light continued downward, and all that could be seen was exactly the same as what stretched out before them.

"Well, Cog, wha' do ye think? 'ere should we go first?" Webley shouted over his shoulder as Cog appeared at Arija's side.

"I think going into town would be an interesting way of introducing these two to the wonders of the Machine."

"Ahh! Great idea. Te' town then."

Adal looked at his pack, then at Arija's and Cog's, noticing something odd. He looked back to Webley and noticed that he didn't have a pack of his own.

"Not coming with us? Where's your pack?" Adal asked, trying to distract himself from what was below him. A warm breeze drifted upward and blew across Adal's face and he thought he was going to be sick.

"Don't need one. I have me own ways. In fact
. . . Race ya there!" Webley bellowed as he dropped his
arms from their shoulders and leaped forward into the
air. On reflex, Adal tried to grasp for him to keep him
from falling, nearly slipping forward into the open air
himself. Webley continued forward for nearly fifty
feet, until he reached a small beam that ran
horizontally between two other beams that stretched
as far down as they could see. His hand clasped the
metal from underneath and Webley threw himself into
the air with a twist, landing on the flat surface.

"Ye comin' 'er wha'?" he shouted back at the
group, before turning from them and leaping from
surface to surface, scaling everything like some sort of
gigantic primate. Adal and Arija looked at each other
behind Cog's back, eyes wide and glossy.

"Well, I do suppose we should be off after
him. Trust me when I say he is quite fast and literally
knows this machine like the back of his hand. So, for
your first time, I recommend leaping. As you fall, turn
the knob on the straps once to open and twice to
start. These things move quickly and are very
responsive to your own movements. Just trust
yourself and you will be fine. Follow me, and we can
still beat him. Ready?" Cog stepped a half step behind
the two and placed his hands in the center of their
shoulders.

"I . . . uh . . . I . . ." Adal began, looking at the
open space ahead of him. He looked at Arija, pleading
with his eyes for her to stop this. Her face was pale
and a bead of sweat trickled down her cheek. Adal
blinked several times and waited for her response. If
she wasn't going to go, he had a way out of this

insanity. If she jumped, he knew he would never live it down for the rest of his life if he didn't. Even if it was only for a few moments until he hit the ground. Or in this place, would they just fall forever?

Arija knew Adal was terrified. If she was being totally honest with herself, so was she, but she would never let him know that. She had to run the facts through her head in the micro-second she had before needing to make her choice. Her eyes hadn't deceived her, this place was real, the science sounded preposterous, but she made it a point to never fear anything.

"Hey!" she nudged Adal and held her fist out. He looked at it nervously for a moment before extending his own. The two dabbed their fists together and Arija turned to Cog with a smile on her face.

"Once to open, two to start, right?" she asked. Cog smiled and nodded back. Arija let the butterflies in her stomach run wild, turning her head slightly and taking a fleeting glance at Adal. She took a deep breath through her nose, crouched down, bringing her hands up to her face, before executing a textbook backflip over the edge. She had managed to turn herself with enough force to be eye-to-eye with Adal before she disappeared over the edge, and he could have sworn that she winked at him.

To Fly Or Not To Fly

"Oh, hell no!" Adal attempted a reflexive step backward from the edge when he felt Cog's hard metallic hand on his back.

"Sorry, Adal. I think you will thank me later." Before Adal could utter a threat, a powerful shove forced him over the edge.

The air left his lungs as Adal let out the loudest and longest scream of his life. The wind whistled through his ears, and for the first few moments, he flailed his arms and legs as he fell. He made the mistake of looking down, and his stomach flipped but he could see he was gaining on Arija. The more he fell and the closer he got, he noticed that Arija wasn't panicking at all, in fact, she was smiling.

The heart pounding feel of adrenaline and euphoria washed over Arija as she fell. This was the most incredible sensation she had ever felt. Freedom. Skydiving had always piqued her interest, but she'd never had the courage to do it, now she never wanted the feeling to end. Columns and pillars whipped past, and she became hypnotically lost in the moment. Closing her eyes, she let the air rush past her, feeling the pounding of her heart throughout her whole body before throwing her eyes open and remembering that she was falling. Arija grabbed for the knob, holding on to it before giving it the necessary two turns.

A slight jolt threw the pack open, and she was jerked immediately as the wings stopped her from falling. A vibrating hum ran down her back as she hung in the air. Arija's wings shone beautifully in the glimmer of the orange light and for a moment she thought they were on fire.

A laugh escaped her lips as she looked down and the reality of what was happening set in. Her mind was buzzing, and every particle of her body was at full attention. She twisted her body, and the pack jumped into gear and rotated her in three full circles before she stopped. Arija shook the dizziness from her head and looked down, prompting the pack to drop her a few feet before she caught on and looked up again. As the buzzing in her head grew louder,

Arija realized it wasn't buzzing after all. She looked up just in time to see Adal fly past her, still in free fall and yelling at the top of his lungs.

"Turn the knob!" she shouted. Arija turned her body to get a better look at her falling friend, and she began to move in his direction. This would take some getting used to. She tested her bounds and found that if she only turned her head, she didn't move, but if she allowed her body to twist with her, the pack pushed her in that direction. Testing once more, she discovered that the more she twisted, the faster she turned, so she rotated herself in Adal's direction and zipped off after him.

Adal shouted as he flew past Arija. Seeing her suspended in the air with her wings out reminded him about the knob on the strap he clung to for dear life. Wiping sweat from his hand to better grasp the knob, Adal gave it a quick turn. With a jolt, the wings expanded, but he continued to fall. Panicked, Adal flailed his arms once more. His heart jumped into his throat as he realized that he was nearing a large tank that sat atop an iron structure.

He kicked his legs and swatted at the wings in an attempt to start them. The tank and platform grew closer and closer. It figured, falling started him on this trip and now it would end it. At that moment, he heard a voice shouting impatiently.

"Turn it AGAIN!" Arija barked as she flew up next to him. Adal looked up at his friend's scared and frustrated face and then turned the knob again. He stopped mid-fall only a few feet from a tank the size of a small house. Adal ran the palm of his hand across his sweat drenched head and said, "Two turns, you idiot!" He turned to look at Arija and swooped back into the air.

12

A Team Effort

Once the panic subsided, the sensation of flight was amazing. Adal zipped around the immediate area to get a feel for the controls of his new appendages. Arija followed suit, cutting across his path and jetting circles around him when she could. The more they tested out their abilities, the more daring they became. Charging at one another and swooping away just in time, keeping so close they could feel the breeze created by the other.

"This is the most amazing thing I've ever done!" Adal shouted, flying past a wall equipped with large pistons that pumped and ejected steam. He ran his hand across the smooth, cold metal and pushed away, flipping and flying inverted over Arija. She pointed her body and shot upward from under Adal, just missing his head and causing him to tumble in the air.

"What's the matter? Still a bit jumpy?" she teased, spinning and pulling herself into a ball that briefly caused her to drop several feet before she opened herself once more and flew away. Adal gave chase and swung his arms at her feet as the two moved between structure after structure.

"If you two think you are comfortable enough, I'd like to remind you we are still in a race," Cog said standing on top of a small shack bound and fastened to a pillar. He had watched as the two got their bearings and had a little fun, but it was time to get back to business. The shack reminded Adal of a small fishing shack from his grandfather's photo albums. He chuckled to himself thinking about what sorts of odd things that one could "fish" for down here.

Arija slapped her forehead. In all of their excitement, she had completely forgotten about Webley and the race. "Sorry about that. Please, lead on Cog."

Cog shook his head. "It has been quite amusing watching you learn your way around, but now that you have your bearings, I think it is time to catch up to Webley. So, try to keep up." Cog lunged from his perch and was off into the air. Arija straightened her body in his direction and shot off after him with Adal close behind. She watched Cog weave in and out between buildings, railings, and other obstacles, narrowly missing them as he turned and twisted. It was clear that flying to Cog was like breathing to Arija and Adal, and they struggled to keep up.

As Arija took a sharp turn around a tall building made up almost entirely of glass and piping, she caught the corner of a window with her hip and spun face first into the side of the building. Dazed, she shook the shock from her head and reoriented herself in Cog's direction. She pushed off the glass building with her feet and was back in the race.

154

Adal pushed himself to get as close to Cog as possible. The way he saw it, he still had to establish that his skill was better than Arija's. With each turn and twist made by Cog, Adal made it a point to cut the turns even tighter, swoop even closer to each obstacle. He watched as Arija smashed into a building and he couldn't help the laughter that burst out of his mouth. As he shot past a still shaken Arija, he turned back and waved. Arija roll her eyes, extend her middle finger, and then shot off after him.

Passing through a slim gap that scarcely had enough space, a small flutter of birds flew directly in front of the group. Cog spun and missed the flock entirely, but Adal and Arija found themselves swatting at the air to avoid colliding with the small creatures.

"Careful with those. Some of these small ones can fly right in front of you and jam your wings up. Keep a look out!" Cog shouted over his shoulder at them.

Adal's first thought was that regardless of the birds damaging the wings, a metal animal hitting him in the face at this speed likely wouldn't feel great. No sooner had the thought crossed his mind . . .

"Look out!" Cog shouted, pointing off to their right. By the time Adal and Arija had the chance to act, another small flock of birds flew into them. Adal covered his face with one hand and swatted at the air with the other. When he uncovered his face, his eyes bulged as he realized the birds were running from a large winged creature that was now coming straight for them.

Adal stared in shock as what appeared to be a mixture of a large beetle and a mosquito flapping its brass wings in their direction. Long legs hung underneath its metallic body like dead tree limbs. Arija pointed at the creature, but she couldn't bring herself to speak. Adal glanced from her back to the flying monster when he saw what she was pointing at. There wasn't just one beetle flying at them, but a whole fleet of them. Their fat, hefty bodies dropping and raising as they flapped their too small wings and struggled to keep afloat. Light reflected off their black metallic bodies and blinded Adal as he squinted in their general direction.

"Those things are like the size of a house!" he yelled, shielding his eyes from the glare.

Cog swerved downward and barely missed colliding with one of the bugs as it chased several of the birds directly at him. Arija followed suit as she heard the scrape of one of their long legs on the back of her wings.

"Adal!" Arija yelled, but it was too late. Three of the larger insects flew directly into Adal as he twisted to avoid them. He managed to swerve out of the way of the first hit and let out an exhale of relief until another two insects came around a corner. The first insect struck Adal underneath his right wing, spinning him and turning him upside down. Adal reeled, rubbing his hand across his head to steady his mind, but that's when the second beetle hit him so hard the wind was knocked out of him.

Adal bounced over the back of the creature and reflexively threw his arms out to grasp whatever he could. His hands found the edge of an unseen flap and he dug his fingers in. For a brief moment, he saw Arija and Cog still twisting and flipping through the air to avoid the rest of the group as Adal flew away, clinging to the back of a mechanical flying beetle. As the spinning in his head subsided, Adal looked back over his shoulder only to find he couldn't see Arija or Cog anymore.

With all of his remaining strength, Adal pulled himself up higher on the creature. He looked from side to side and could see what was left of his wings flapping limply off the sides of his new transport. With every twist and turn, they would violently flap about and pull at him, nearly knocking him off the beetle to fall to his death. *Fuck!* Adal thought as he looked at his useless wings flapping in the wind.

Pulling himself up, Adal turned over, placing his stomach on the top of the creature and tried to wrap his legs around it. The insect was too wide, but he was able to hook his legs under the shell between its wings, his own now freely flailing behind him. He took the moment to examine his situation. He was riding a giant beetle mosquito as several others flew alongside him. Adal didn't think they knew or cared that he was there, and he took this as a good thing. At least it wasn't trying to shake him off.

With his wings tugging at his back, he squeezed his legs as tight as he could and attempted to remove his pack in its entirety. With several hard tugs at the clasp, Adal released himself and watched the wings flutter off behind him and disappear. As Adal brought his attention forward again, the small triumphant smile was pulled from his face. The insect was flying directly toward a large copper pillar. Adal closed his eyes and flattened himself on the creatures back as he was violently jerked downwards. As the insect plummeted straight down, Adal was jerked up and lost his grip on the bug, sliding up and off the insect's back.

As he slid off the end of the creature, Adal managed to grab one of its long legs. His added weight made the creature swerve and shake about. He had thrown its balance off, and it was having a hard time keeping steady. The creature wailed a mechanical cry as it twisted and turned.

Constantly adjusting his grip and kicking his legs to avoid close obstacles, Adal did all he could not to fall or even look down for that matter. Fighting the driving sensation that he was going to fall at any moment, Adal gave one final tug in an attempt to steady himself. The creature let out another mechanical screech, like grinding gears, and Adal looked up just in time to see yet another beam just as his ride slammed into it.

An explosion of components and metal shavings sent Adal flying forward through the air. The openness around him was possibly the most agonizingly peaceful sensation he had ever experienced. He was spread wide as he flew on his own, and Adal could only close his eyes and wait for the inevitable collision that would cease his existence. A collision that came quicker than he anticipated and wasn't nearly as devastating as he would have thought.

A sharp pain flowed through his entire body shortly after he began to fall followed by continuous jolts of agony as he rolled repeatedly on what felt like a flat surface. After several harsh turns, Adal finally came to a stop on his back and let out a loud groan of pain. A stale, metallic taste filled his mouth, and he coughed loudly, attempting to collect the wind that had been knocked from him.

"Aw . . . shit . . ." Adal slowly opened his eyes and blinked the world back into focus. Remaining still to avoid discovering if anything was truly broken, Adal shot his eyes from side to side. The platform he had landed on was sizable and looked almost identical to the landing platform for the train. Numerous mounds of what could only be described as scrap metal were scattered around reminding Adal of a landfill. Pulling himself slowly to a sitting position, he realized that he still clutched the long leg of the flying insect in his hand.

"Shit!" He yelled as he dropped the severed leg and wiped his hand on his black pants. Squeezing his eyes shut, Adal shook his head to regain his composure. It was then he felt the vibrations. Opening his eyes again, he found that one of the large bugs had also landed on the platform. It was roughly twenty yards away and was staring at him like he'd just killed his brother, which he had. It had glowing blue slitted eyes and a set of large fangs that resembled that of a spider's.

"Good . . . thing. Nice thing . . ." Adal cooed, not taking his eyes off the creature. Adal sat frozen, thinking if he sat still enough the insect wouldn't be able to see him. *Wait, no that's dinosaurs*, Adal chided himself as the creature bared its large fangs and lowered its head like a dog about to strike.

"Damn!" Adal sprang to his feet, adrenaline pumping through his body for not the first time that day. Just as he touched his feet to the metal ground, the insect lunged directly for him. Adal reached down and grabbed the severed leg he'd tossed aside and brought it up into the air.

"I don't think so!" he shouted as the animal lunged at him. Adal took a half-step backward and swung the leg as hard as he could. It collided with the left eye of his attacker and the insect retreated backward, squealing in pain.

Adal brought the improvised club back again and swung. This time the creature maneuvered just at the right moment, and Adal's attack went wide. The creature swiped one of its legs in an outward motion and swept Adal's feet out from under him. He hit the floor with a hard thud. The creature tried for him once more, only this time, Adal plunged the leg right into the gap between the insect's two fangs. The leg went half of its length into the beetle and Adal knew he had managed to force it down the creature's throat.

"Eat this!" Adal yelled, yanking the weapon free and striking again at the bug's face. Another solid hit sent it backward, but only for a moment before it lunged forward with its fangs extended. Adal had just enough time to form a bar and jam it upward, blocking the large spikes just inches from his face. He pressed with all of his remaining strength as the creature lowered its fangs closer and closer to Adal's face until he could feel the tips of them stabbing at his cheeks. Adal gritted his teeth, shouted in anger, and pushed with everything he had.

The creature was then whipped aside, releasing the pressure on Adal and tumbling away. Two separate masses slid across the floor and it was a moment before he realized what had happened. As the insect rolled onto its back, Arija was fast to her feet and tossing aside the wings from her back that were now just as crumpled a mess as Adal's.

"Shit! Arija!" he shouted, jumping up and running to her side. As she brushed away the nerves from the crash, she held a glare both intense and concerned.

"Jesus, Adal! What is that thing?" Arija stepped away from the body as it twitched on its back. Adal knew nothing about the creatures in this world, but it sure looked like it was dying.

"I have no idea. The one I got snagged on collided with something and one of its friends decided I was going to be lunch. Nice hit, by the way! I owe you one." Adal couldn't help himself and he wrapped his arms around Arija and squeezed so hard that he thought he'd break at least one bone.

"Yeah, well you owe me more than one. I nearly broke my neck on that dive. So, is it just the one?" Arija asked, pulling from Adal's grip and looking about.

"I think so. I mean, there were more, but I haven't seen them since I hit the ground. Where's Cog?" Adal brushed imaginary dirt and dust from his shirt and shook out the sides of his long coat.

"Not sure. When we hit that group, Cog flew off to avoid the impact. I turned and went right after you as soon as I could." A clanking sound caught their attention, and they both froze. Adal's heart jumped back into his throat and Arija scanned the area, her eyes narrowed and deadly.

From behind a mound of scrap metal came another one of the mechanical monstrosities. The three stood there, eyes locked for a moment before Arija and Adal slowly took a step back.

"So . . . maybe a team effort on this one?" Adal asked, picking up the leg he had previously used for protection and handing it to Arija. She looked at the crude weapon like she was determining her odds and nodded.

13

THE KLEINMASCH, A.K.A THE BESQUITO

Adal looked around and found another segment of leg from the second creature to use for himself. After scrutinizing his own weapon, Adal looked up to see that the besquito—as he was now calling the strange beetle, mosquito mix—was hunched over its fallen brother and nudging it with one leg. For a confusing moment, Adal felt guilty, and he wondered how a machine could show such convincing emotion.

"These things are no joke. Keep yourself as far away as you can," Adal began, mentally reminding himself that the besquito attacked him first. "Also . . ."

"Adal," Arija interrupted, pointing off to their right. Adal slowly turned and saw that two more of the bugs had landed on the platform. They too made their way toward the inverted machine.

"So . . . this isn't good." Adal pressed his shoulder against Arija's, suddenly needing to be as close to her as he could get.

"I think maybe we should leave," Arija added, motioning off to the side. Adal reached out a hand and squeezed hers as they slowly made their way toward the edge of the platform. A clanking sound jolted their attentions from behind them and as they turned, an ear shattering screech nearly knocking them backward. Another besquito stood on top of the scrap pile behind them. They were boxed in.

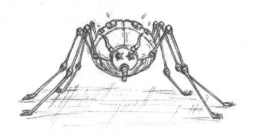

"Run!" Adal shouted, tugging Arija away. The two turned on their heels and ran toward another scrap pile for cover. One shriek was echoed by another and then another as the besquitos sounded the charge. The floor beneath Adal and Arija's feet shook with every step the horde of mechanical creatures took.

Arija's curiosity took over, and she stole a glimpse over her shoulder. Five of the large creatures hopped from pile to pile at an incredible speed. Pain surged through Arija's shoulder as Adal grabbed her, pulling her back into the present.

She stared at him, anger clear on her face when she realized they had reached the edge of the platform and if he hadn't grabbed her, she would have run right off the end. Adal looked over the edge, the distance dizzying and then raised his weapon. Arija watched him, silently pleading with him to find a solution. She raised her severed leg and turned to face the monsters.

"Get ready. If these things want a piece, they're going to get the whole thing!" Adal's chest swelled and the muscles in his arms danced under the thin layer of fabric. Arija let the sweet smell of brisk air fill her lungs as the tingling of nerves took over her body. She was her mother's daughter and would give them all she had.

The ground shook as two more of the creatures landed ahead of them. Adal squeezed his sweat drenched hands along the leg like it was a baseball bat and contemplated just how screwed they were. He couldn't even handle one of these things, and now seven angry, car-sized, mechanical insects looked at them like they were dinner.

"This isn't good!" Arija stated, looking over at Adal and seeing the fight leave his eyes.

"Don't do that! We got this!" Adal flashed a brave glance at Arija, but they both knew he was just as scared as she was. The line of besquitos inched forward, screeching and flapping their wings. Arija swallowed the lump in her throat and tried to concentrate on finding the insects' weak spot. One creature stepped forward from the line, causing the rest of the creatures to stop. An eerie ticking emitted as it rattled its large fangs and stretched its wings out. The group behind it lowered their heads in respect for their alpha and then a chorus of screeches and wails forced Arija and Adal to drop their weapons and cover their ears.

A gust of wind puffed over Arija's head as something flew at her and she instinctively dropped to her knees. She fumbled, reaching for the makeshift weapon. As she wrapped her shaking hands around it, she pushed herself up to her feet, swinging the leg from side to side like she was swatting at a fly. Catching a glimpse of something, Arija stopped and turned to face the line of mechanical insects. Cog was now standing in the space between the creatures and Adal and Arija. He kept his focus on the creatures, not even bothering to glance over his shoulder at them.

The wings from his pack retracted and tucked themselves away neatly in his bag. Arija suddenly wished she'd known she could do that instead of destroying the only thing that could have prevented this situation. Cog carefully took off his newsboy hat and placed it in a side compartment of his pack. Arija nudged Adal and motioned at a small pipe in Cog's right hand. It couldn't have been any larger than the severed legs they had. Arija scrunched her brow in concern as they walked up to stand next to cog. At least now they had a third person to fight with.

"This isn't your fight, Topsiders. Please step back and allow me the opportunity." Cog's words were cold, like a teacher reminding a pupil of his place. Arija and Adal looked at one another. Adal shrugged and took a step back but Arija scrunched her face and shook her head at him. "I meant what I said," Cog continued, as if reading her mind. Arija's shoulders sank and she let out a defeated puff of air. Adal dropped his weapon and put his hands out in front of him, palms up.

"Have at it, boss. They're all yours." Adal walked back over to the edge of the platform, leaving a confused Arija still holding on to her weapon.

Cog waited, giving Arija the chance to leave before he extended his arm outward. He twisted his hand on the small pipe and with a sharp ping, the pipe extended, nearly tripling in length. He lowered his arm and poised the staff behind his arm and shoulder, taking two steps toward the first creature.

"You do not want this fight. I recommend that you leave," Cog insisted, glaring at his foe. The six remaining in line behind it shifted in their positions. It was as though they were considering his commands. Arija didn't know if Cog was talking to the monsters or to her, but she instinctively took a few steps back. She watched as the creatures reacted to Cog's words, seeming to understand them, and she wondered if they had understood everything she and Adal had been saying too.

Cog took another step toward the monster and it followed him with its eyes but didn't back away. Cog spun his staff with such force that the weapon seemed to bend and move in the air, its structure not visible anymore. He pointed the tip of it at the face of the bug and paused, giving another warning.

The mechanical insect shrieked and leaped at Cog, who anticipated the attack and ducked out of the way in perfect timing. The creature took a step toward Arija who now felt foolish holding onto the severed leg. She dropped the leg and backed away toward Adal. The creature looked at them in confusion for a moment, as though trying to decide which of them looked more delicious, when Cog again appeared between them and the insect.

Again, it lunged at him, but Cog brought the edge of the weapon up under the creature's head and sent it tumbling back toward the rest of the swarm. The line of besquitos all jumped back as their leader landed with a loud thud and slid toward them. This time, Cog did not mean to wait for a response. Before the animal could maneuver its way onto its feet, Cog landed on its stomach, driving his weapon through its torso and puncturing the platform on which they stood. The creature cried out in the sort of way a dying machine would before several shudders were followed by a deathly still. The rest of the group

169

roared in a rage and flapped their giant wings, thumping their long legs like they were waiting for revenge. Arija wrapped her long fingers around Adal's, too afraid to take her eyes off the giant insects but needing to know he was there.

Cog jumped off the dead besquito, keeping his weapon pointed toward the swarm. The remaining insects seemed hesitant to attack, like they understood what had just happened and were afraid. A few gnashed their teeth and bared their fangs, and others swiped their long legs at Cog like they intended to trip him.

Cog shrugged his shoulders like he was slightly annoyed that the creatures ruined his day and then he ran at the group, swinging his weapon from side to side. He jumped higher than Arija imagined was possible and buried his weapon in one's eye, then immediately drove the other end through the bottom of another's head. The two besquitos toppled to the platform, twitching and writhing for a moment before falling still.

Arija and Adal watched as the remaining three insects charged at Cog. Just as the first two were approaching him from either side, he twirled his weapon, stabbing one end into the chest of one only to remove it and stab the other end into the chest of the second.

Arija had never seen the polite, quiet robot look so vicious, and she turned a shocked look toward Adal who was pumping his fist in the air and ducking his head like he was directing Cog in the fight. The last creature stared Cog down for a few seconds before thinking better of it and flying away.

"I am so sorry for that! Really, I am. These things would have made short work of you and I had to act in accordance." Cog's stone-cold face came back to life as he approached Adal and Arija, restricting his weapon back into the small, tube form. Cog clicked the tool into a sheath that ran along his lower back and then brought his attention back to Adal and Arija. "They didn't hurt you, did they?"

"No . . . I'm fine," Adal coughed, straightening up and giving an embarrassed glance at Cog's weapon. "I need to get me one of those."

"What were those things?" Arija asked, stepping around Cog and slowly walking toward the lifeless pile of dead machines. One twitched with a final death rattle and both Arija and Adal jumped. Cog looked at the fallen machines and sighed.

"In the Machine, we all have our purposes. These creatures, in particular, are known as the Kleinmasch."

"The Klein what?" Adal interrupted. "I prefer besquito, easier to say."

Arija made a face like she'd just smelled something awful as she turned her head to stare back at Adal.

"Kleinmasch," Cog continued, not even bothering to ask Adal what a besquito was. "They are a breed of Dweller that feasts on others. They live in the darkest parts of the Machine. Often, they reside in areas that only Webley would dare go."

"Why would Webley make something like this?" Arija asked, intrigued by what their purpose could be.

171

"These things were not made by Webley . . ." Cog trailed off, looking away from his companions and back to the dead machines.

"Then who made them?" Arija caught Cog's eye before scrunching her face and turning to look back at the pile of dead machines.

Cog looked at the twisted pile of lifeless scrap. He puffed out a sigh of air as if deciding how to reply. "We have to go. The Dwellers in these parts aren't the friendliest to visitors. Besides, surely, Webley, will be wondering what is taking us. Are you two well enough to fly?" Cog asked, quickly changing the subject and walking over to Adal.

"I, uh, guess we're fine." Adal turned a confused look to Arija who was still examining the Kleinmasch from a distance.

Something had caught her eye, it could have just been an overactive imagination but she could have sworn she saw someone watching them. The hair on the back of her neck stood at attention, confirming what she thought she saw. "What about our wings? Both sets were destroyed" Arija finally said as she turned her attention back to the group.

Adal studied her face as he looked back and forth between her and Cog. Arija had a propensity for looking mad all the time, but Adal could always read her. She was holding something back.

"That isn't a worry. My wings are calibrated for extra weight. Often, I leave on errands that require the ability to move with extra mass. Do you think the two of you can hold on?"

Arija finally brought her gaze to Adal. "Are you sure this is the best way?" she asked.

"I mean, I'm not really feeling like almost dying a third time today," Adal chimed in, still trying to read Arija's expression.

"I could leave the two of you here alone and fly back to collect you each another set of wings, if you would prefer," Cog arched a single metallic eyebrow.

"Nope. We'll hold on." Adal answered for the both of them. Arija was glaring at Cog like she was waiting for him to explode. Cog shot a glance to Arija, and they locked eyes for a moment in a wicked battle of wits before Cog smiled and pulled a handful of extra straps from his pack.

As Arija strapped herself to Cog, she gave a fleeting glance to where the Kleinmasch was and the shadowed area behind it where she'd seen the eyes. Arija knew Cog had seen them too, but he'd kept quiet, and so would she until she could figure out why.

The group finished preparing themselves for flight, and with more grace than Arija could have imagined, they jetted into the air, shooting past their hidden admirer. As the platform grew distant, Arija thought about the eyes she'd seen. These were not the blue eyes of the Kleinmasch, these eyes were a pale green and much smaller than the Kleinmasch's had been. She instinctively reached for the bag still clinging to her hip that Cog had given her. She wanted to draw the eyes before she forgot them. Just as the platform was almost out of view, Arija thought she saw a figure cloaked in black jump from the platform and fall into the never-ending machine.

14

THE ROOST

Fausto's long fall was halted as he reached out and grasped a passing beam. Using his momentum to swing himself, he launched into the air and grabbed hold of another beam. Sliding from that beam to the one below it, Fausto made his way deep into the pits of the World Machine. Waiting in his den, the master would cherish the news his loyal servant would bring him. Fausto brings good news to the master. The excitement of the news he brought, and the anticipation of a big reward caused his cold mechanical heart to flutter.

These parts of the machine were vastly different from those up toward the light. The closer you got to Webley, the brighter and warmer everything around you became, but Fausto knew just how dark and cold the Machine could really be. Fausto let his mind wander back to when he knew the bright parts of the Machine as he flung from one beam to the next like a mechanical Quasimodo.

The warm orange and yellow hue faded to a mixture of greens, blues, and purples as the polished surfaces transformed into wet, rusted, and neglected beams. This was the part of the Machine that Webley had forgotten about. No, not forgotten, abandoned. Webley had failed the Kleinmasch, only caring about the Dwellers that obeyed his every word. Well, Fausto was a free-thinking Dweller. Fausto was meant to be a leader and soon they would see it, they would all see it.

After a time, strands of wire began to appear. Fausto was getting close. It wasn't uncommon to see stray strands of wire hanging from one platform to another, but, the further into the machine you went, the more strands you would see. Fausto grasped a beam and swung himself, maneuvering around the web-like structure. A wicked smile creased his face as he saw his home in the distance.

Fausto scoffed as he thought about the way Cog had described the Kleinmasch as Dwellers. The Kleinmasch were nothing like the Dwellers. They were far superior and vastly more intricate and advanced than any Dweller could ever hope to be.

Dozens of Baeg scuttled about the large webs as Fausto stopped his descent and stood on a beam, looking out over his home. He reached one long, thin hand out and slid it between the wire strands of a web, letting the Baeg crawl over his fingers. Fausto had always had an appreciation for the Baeg. Though their spider-like bodies could fit into the palm of his hand, they could strip prey of every nut and bolt in moments if they had a large-enough horde. Their ability to repair their larger brethren, the Feithidi, also made them extremely useful if you were building an army. It was a shame there weren't any Baeg on the platform earlier. They would have been able to repair the Feithidi that attacked Cog and the Topsiders and make the fight that much more interesting.

Fausto watched as the leather-covered spider jumped from his hand back into its web. The Baeg were the only one of the Kleinmasch made using the leather before the master decided it wasn't worth the extra time.

A rumble came from somewhere overhead as a mass of creatures flew by. Somewhere deep in this web, one of the Kleinmasch made its home. Judging by the look, this was the lair of several Feithidi.

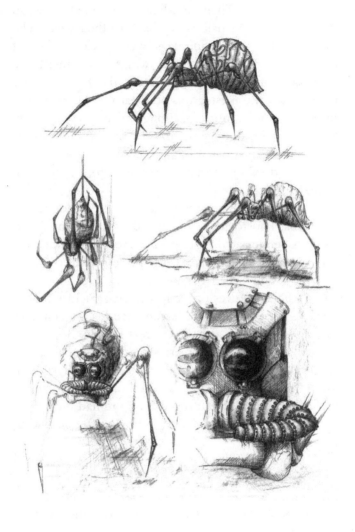

They were out, probably hunting for the rest of the collective. Their tank-like shells were hollow, so they could carry smaller prey back to their webs. The Feithidi's long, dangling legs were useless when it came to jumping, but their wings gave them the advantage of flight. Unfortunately, the Feithidi were made when the master was still learning his craft and their wings were not big enough to carry their hefty bodies leaving them only able to fly short distances. Fausto jumped down from the beam, grabbed a wire strand, and swung around a corner into a long, dark tunnel.

Lost in his thoughts about the intricacies of the webs, Fausto made his way down the tunnel and to the opening at the other end. He looked out over the city full of Kleinmasch, the place he called home, The Roost.

Fausto's eyes danced over the structure before him. Parts of the World Machine had been taken over by the Kleinmasch after The Great Divide. Before the Divide, the Kleinmasch were slaves to Webley, always following *his* rule, never able to think on their own. Then the master rose, and life was better. Fausto looked over the large furnace. The fire had long since cooled since they made it their home after following the master.

Walking through a large set of poles, a small spike fell to the ground ahead of his feet. Casting his eyes upward, Fausto saw he was standing directly under one of the many Cead that guarded the entrance to the city.

He never really understood the full usefulness of the Cead. Just like most of the other Kleinmasch in the city, their spider-like bodies made it easy to climb and jump from beam to beam. Their long legs projected them hundreds of feet into the air, but they were topped with small, orb-like bodies. Their unintimidating statures made them a strange and weak choice to guard the doors. If it hadn't been for the fact that they were able to spit these spikes in rapid succession from their tiny mouths, Fausto would have thought them completely useless. But the master had a soft spot for his first creations, so there they were, guarding the entrance with their tiny spikes.

The city was bustling as it always was. There was scarcely a time in which droves of Kleinmasch were not scuttling about, feasting on their prey, crafting webs and structures, even tearing down the structures of others to make their own. Further into The Roost, the structures became more ornate and organized. The insignia of the master sprawled wide as his intricate web-work stretched across the walkways.

The main chamber to the master's throne was guarded by the brutes of the entire species—The Umar. They were gigantic spider-like creations that struck fear in all the other Kleinmasch with their tendency to eat anything, including their own kind. Every aspect of these guardians was oversized and powerful. Each of their eight legs was wider than Fausto and twice as long, and their clunky round bodies were the size of ten Feithidi. The Umar surely would have been terrifying if they weren't dumb as a bag of bolts. Their only purpose was to defend the master; tearing into anything he deemed a threat with their long, pointed fangs.

The two Umar on guard at the time groaned in deafening tandem as they twisted their bodies to

179

examine the visitor. As they realized it was just Fausto coming home, they snapped back to attention and allowed him to pass. Though the Umar could easily crush Fausto with one stupidly placed foot, they knew not to mess with him. It would be their own deadly mistake.

The royal nest reminded Fausto of a macabre mixture of a mortuary and a laboratory. Walls were lined with Breeders—Dwellers caught over the years and attached to larger machines. The master used the Breeders' internal mechanics to power the pump-like machines that produced small Kleinmasch and spare parts into the nurseries behind them. If there was one fate Fausto would never wish upon himself, it was becoming a Breeder. The Breeders were completely conscious and aware of the internal agony that befell them, but they were paralyzed to do anything about it. Fausto would have almost felt bad for the Breeders, if it weren't for the fact that they were dirty, nasty Dwellers, and their torture was for the greater good. One day all of this would be his. One day, he knew the master would realize just how good Fausto was and give him his own kingdom to rule.

At the end of the chamber, the master of all Kleinmasch sat on his throne, a living, turning creation made of Dwellers, Kleinmasch, and other odd creatures from long ago. It moved and twisted as their mechanical parts still held life. The master was speaking with several Cead, his eyebrows turned in and the corners of his lips turned down in a frown. Likely, the useless creatures had taken their attention away from the gates to feast again. This would either result in their death, or the loss of rations. Fausto silently hoped death would win out.

As the master set his eyes on Fausto, he raised one of his arms and waived the Cead away. Looked like they would be going the next week without food. If you asked some creatures in The Roost, that was a fate worse than death.

As the Cead shambled their way past Fausto, he approached the throne and knelt in front of it.

The master was vastly different from any of his creations. He held the same humanoid body-type as Fausto with arms, legs, hands, and feet. He wore black leather garbs fastened around his body by silver buckles and buttons holding the numerous straps and flaps together. His patchwork robes were made by the Baeg and were some of the most intricate designs Fausto had ever seen. His skin was also very different from all other creatures. Rather than the typical bronze or copper colorations, the master's skin was a high-polished silver. This was a sign that the master was special. He was the chosen one, the one who would bring the Kleinmasch out of oppression and become the new ruler to the Dwellers of the World Machine.

From his back protruded eight long, thin legs that carried the master to any location faster than any of the other Kleinmasch. The master rarely used his own two legs, relying primarily on his arachnid appendages. Fausto brought his eyes up to meet the master's. He was currently in his natural state, but the master had altered his mechanics so he could attach the body of any creature to himself and become them. This gave the master infinite abilities, and infinite power.

181

"Ah, Fausto, welcome home. Been having fun away from the city, playing in the Machine?" the master's voice was calm but held the sharp edge of a knife, able to cut you down as he told you he loved you. The master lifted himself into the air and seated himself upon his throne.

"I come with news, Pajak. Something that will interest you very much, in fact." No other creature in The Roost was permitted to refer to the master by his name. Only Fausto had that ability because Fausto was the master's favorite.

Pajak considered himself a creator, and with his ability to make and take life, he demanded to be treated like the god he knew he was.

"Ah, news. Always something I greatly anticipate. You have the remarkable ability to impress me with the facts you discover on your outings." Fausto winced at the way Pajak emphasized the word outings. He always thought Pajak hated him leaving because he was worried about him reverting to old ways, or maybe because he missed him. If Fausto only knew how far off he really was.

"I was watching a group of Feithidi collect food, when I saw them come across a particularly interesting type of prey," Fausto began, holding pause and weighing Pajak's interest on the subject.

"Oh? What type of prey might that be? Has *HE* been up to making more annoyances we can feast upon?" Pajak laughed as he brought his attention to a twitching eye protruding from a Dweller's skull stuck to the arm of his throne. Pajak lazily flicked the Dweller until the spasm stopped and then gave a deep yawn like this was the most uninteresting thing he had heard in his life.

"No, I highly doubt *HE* had anything to do with these ones. As I watched the Feithidi corner their prey, I realized they were Topsiders." Fausto let a proud smile cross his cold face as words effortlessly slipped through his lips.

Pajak drove the tip of his finger into the section of skull he had been toying with. In that moment, the eyes twitched once more before slowly closing. He looked pensively at the lifeless part of his throne. Pajak's face turned down, like a child that had broken his favorite toy, but Fausto knew it wouldn't last. They would bring him a new Dweller to replace the dead part of his throne by the end of the day.

"You are mistaken," Pajak said coldly, still not looking up at Fausto.

"I assure you, I am not. I saw them myself and close enough to nearly hear their breath. Two Topsiders, a man and woman, and they were with Cog. In fact, had it not been for his wretched meddling, you would have a human head to replace this broken Dweller." Fausto stepped closer to Pajak, idly gesturing toward the motionless skull. Unlike the others, Fausto wasn't scared of the master. Pajak needed Fausto to bring him information about Webley, and Fausto liked to think maybe the master loved him, if only just a little.

"You're saying there are Topsiders in the Machine?" snarled Pajak, looking at Fausto and sitting back in his throne.

"I have witnessed them. Cog destroyed several of our brethren, while saving the Topsiders."

Pajak twisted in his seat, fuming at the mention of Cog. "You mean to tell me there are not only Topsiders in the Machine, but they are with Cog and most certainly *HIM,* and they managed to kill my Feithidi?" Pajak rose from his seat and made his way over to Fausto, lowering himself so they were at eye level.

"Yes. I have seen it myself. These Topsiders are different from what we have learned of them. These ones are strong, smart, and loyal to one another. They think in a way I didn't know was possible. I worry that this may give them an edge that our Kleinmasch don't have."

Pajak rose and walked past Fausto. He traveled slowly down the chamber and moved his gaze from side to side, watching his Breeders. Fausto wasn't certain, whether it was seeing the torture and misery of the Dwellers used as Breeders, or the genius of his ingenuity, but Pajak often paced the chamber, watching the Breeders and thinking.

Pajak stopped as he reached the end of the hall, turning to one particularly sad-looking Breeder. It twitched in discomfort with its head hung low, looking at the floor. Pajak walked over to the creature and drew one of his long fingers across the top of its head. It shuddered and twitched at the contact, causing a wide smile to spread across Pajak's face.

"The presence of these Topsiders intrigues me. I want them, Fausto. You will bring them to me. I have so many things to learn from them. Bring me these creatures . . . alive Fausto, do you understand me?" Pajak pushed the head of the breeder to the side letting it bounce in place before walking back toward Fausto and pressing his hand against his shoulder. Fausto glared into Pajak's eyes, nodding in obedience.

"What sorts of things might you have in mind for the Topsiders?" Fausto had known Pajak for a long time. He knew if Pajak wanted the Topsiders, he had something very specific in mind for their use. Fausto leaned in and allowed a long, thin grin to etch itself across his face.

"My old friend, I have wonders planned for them," Pajak laughed, releasing Fausto and making his way back to his throne. "As you know, I have long had the ability to draft and create many of the Kleinmasch in my image. I toil with their forces and structures and have given life to the lifeless matter I draw from the Machine." Pajak stopped just in front of his throne, turning with one pointed finger raised. "However, I am tired of their existence. I want something more. I want to know the secrets of the Topsiders. I want to create something that *HE* never could. I will learn their secrets, even if it's from the pieces and parts I rip from them with my bare hands. Again, I want them alive, first and foremost . . . if later I must kill, torture, or dismember them . . . so be it."

Pajak spoke like a true creator. Fausto knew Pajak should be the ruler of the Dwellers, not Webley. This drive to do anything necessary to save their people and put them in power was the reason Fausto followed Pajak into the depths of the Machine. There was so much power to be had, what was the purpose of it being all held by one?

"They will be yours soon, Pajak. I will see to this personally." Fausto lowered to one knee and bowed. These Topsiders might just be the thing his master needed to become the true creator, and when that happened, Pajak would keep Fausto by his side. They would be co-creators and would both rule over all of the World Machine.

"Splendid. See that it's done, Fausto. Be sure to take some Kleinmasch with you." Fausto rose from his bow and nodded in agreement.

"Would you like the acquisition quiet?" Fausto asked, bouncing on the balls of his feet and hoping for the right answer.

"I don't care how, I just want it done," Pajak responded in a growl. Fausto smiled. That was the answer he had wanted.

15

Into Aparat

Since they left the platform, time had disappeared, and Arija found herself lost in thought as they flew with Cog. Swooping past structures and mechanical parts, it was nearly impossible for her to appreciate the sights, so she resigned herself to mentally etching everything she'd seen so far into her memory. It had taken her some time to get used to the flight. She and Adal were hanging below Cog from straps protruding from his pack, and the sway of the trip caused her stomach to flip and the coffee she'd had that morning to make a sour reappearance in her throat.

She still clutched Adal's hand. Her stomach had calmed down, and now she was just staring at the blurred metallic town thinking about everything that had happened. She stole a glance at Adal who had been staring at her but shot his eyes away when she looked. Why wouldn't he admit that he had a thing for her? She could see his face flush and feel his heartbeat jump whenever she touched him. What was so wrong with her that he couldn't admit it?

Cog jerked up so quickly that he pulled Arija from her thoughts and she looked up to see what was happening. Adal tightened his stomach in a strange attempt to control the speed at which Cog flew. The sudden rush of air caused Arija's hair to whip around, smacking her in the face from all angles and she let go of Adal's hand to try to wrangle it in.

Arija and Adal could feel their stomachs in their throats as Cog made a final swoop, leveled them out and flew directly at a large wall that seemed to cover the entire Machine, stretching as far as they could see in every direction. Along the infinite walls, giant gears slowly turned and wound. Creatures flew in a "V" formation along the length of the wall. Arija first thought they were birds until they drew closer, and Adal pointed out that their wings looked similar to the ones attached to Cog's pack. Arija looked at Adal, mouthing the word "Dwellers?" and he responded with a shrug.

Banking sharply to the side, Cog drifted into alignment with another platform. Along the sides of the runway were several assorted aircraft, floating in the air with gangways leading from their sides to the platform. Mixed in with the aircraft were several ships sitting on metal railways. There must have been hundreds of Dwellers loading and unloading all assortments of packages, crates, and machinery.

"This place looks like a port or shipyard!" Adal shouted over the blowing wind in his ears. "What is this place?" He looked up at Cog, who either didn't bother to answer or couldn't hear the question.

189

"Be ready. Here we go!" Cog shouted, but, before Adal or Arija could ask what he was talking about, Cog plummeted down toward the docks. Adal and Arija were suspended in the air for a few seconds before their straps pulled taut and they fell, upside down after Cog. Adal screamed at the top of his lungs but Arija's scream got stuck in her throat, and she closed her eyes, frozen by sheer terror. After a few minutes, Arija's stomach lurched into her throat again as she slowed and then with a jerk dropped so that she was right side up again. She cracked open one eye and realized that Cog was slowing as they approached the platform.

With the platform so close they could almost reach out and touch the metallic surface, Arija and Adal slammed their eyes closed again in anticipation of an unknown landing. Cog pulled tightly on their straps to secure them as close as possible. With a final whoosh of air, a gentle thump ended their terrifying descent. Adal slowly opened his eyes and looked around. After seeing they were safely on the ground, a wave of embarrassment washed over his face.

"Hey, don't play it like that! I know you were scared too!" he barked at Arija who was smirking as she fingered through her tangled hair. Cog tugged at the straps, and the two dropped to the ground with an abrupt 'thud.'

"You scream more like a girl than I do," she mumbled. Adal shot a look at her, and she laughed, pushing his shoulder.

"Welcome to the main entrance of Aparat, our capital city!" Cog announced enthusiastically. For a moment, Adal and Arija had forgotten where they were as they bickered and let the relief of finally being on a solid surface wash over them. Snapping out of their own minds, the two looked on in awe at what surrounded them.

All around, Dwellers went about their business. Several unloaded boxes from what Adal could only describe as an old-fashioned steamboat while others barked orders. A group of four women stood in a circle talking and laughing. Their Victorian style ball gowns looked like they were made from the same lightweight leather as Arija's skirt and embroidered with intricate gold and silver designs.

Arija took a few steps toward the group admiring the perfect curls that protruded from their heads. The woman closest to Arija was holding a thin wire parasol made of black lace, and it took a few moments before she realized the women weren't made completely of metal. All four women had beautiful skin in various shades, but the delicate hand that clasped the parasol was made of bronze. The women leaned in close to each other whispering and then leaned back and laughed at whatever gossip was being revealed.

A small pack of boys ran toward the women grabbing onto their dresses and hiding behind them as several older boys came running toward the group wielding various pipes and sticks. Arija opened her mouth to warn the group when the younger boys started to laugh, and the older boys stopped to argue with their mothers. The scene was strikingly similar to any normal boating dock Arija had seen at home if the real world had been stuck in the eighteen hundreds and made of out of metal.

Adal absentmindedly walked into the crowd of Dwellers. He watched the group of women giggle as they glanced at him and he gave the group a small wink.

"Even Dweller woman can't handle how sexy I am." Adal ran his fingers over his eyebrows as he looked back at Cog.

"Those are not Dwellers. Well, they *are* Dwellers, but here they are called Toppers. They are the wealthier group of the Dwellers who can afford to have Adhesion Surgery. They got the name Topper because they want to look like you. Like the Topsiders." Cog watched the confused look on Adal's face.

"The fuck?" Arija chimed in as she eyed Cog suspiciously. "Are you trying to tell me these people want my skin as an aesthetic? That's messed up on so many levels, Cog."

"Indeed, it is, my dear girl. The Toppers are elitist snobs, and Webley and I do not condone anything that happens on the black market. Even though Webley created all the Dwellers, once he gave them the ability to think on their own, he couldn't control them. Years ago, when they saw their first Topsider, many Dwellers became smitten and eventually jealous that you have the ability to go Topside and they do not. Someone, I don't recall who, discovered that they could stretch the pineapple leather over a Dweller's face to mimic human skin. You will usually see Toppers with partial Adhesion because we need the leather for more important things, and the surgery is very costly. But don't worry, they won't hurt you. They simply admire you for what you have and what they don't."

"Other people have been down here before? What happened to them? Are they still here?" Arija couldn't help the string of questions that spewed out of her mouth.

"That's a long story for another time," Cog said as he stared off into the crowd of Dwellers.

Arija nibbled on her bottom lip as she watched Cog, guilt warming her face. Cog had been nothing but nice to them. He'd saved them from the Kleinmasch and opened his home to them. He wasn't there to hurt her. If he'd wanted that, he could have done it while they slept. Besides the leathery skin that stretched the Toppers faces was obviously not human, and it had been dyed in various shades.

Arija turned her attention back to the bustling dock as one woman called a male Dweller over to her. The gold colored Dweller put down the crate he'd been lugging and wiped his greasy hands on his pants. He walked over to the Topper woman, and she leaned in and whispered something in his ear causing a burst of giggles from her Topper friends. The man nodded, taking something from her hand and then went back to work on the airship he had been loading. Arija's brow scrunched together as she watched the strange transaction. There was definitely more to this world than Arija had originally thought. She took a few steps toward the group and tried to get a closer look.

16

A World of Creation and Science

Adal stepped farther onto the dock watching the workers go about their business in awe as if loading and unloading crates was the most interesting thing he'd seen in his life. The steamboat appeared to be sitting on a wide metal beam like the train they had taken when they first arrived. A loud grinding noise was followed by a shout of "LOOK OUT!". Adal had just enough time to move when a Dweller on a basket flew over his head on one of the many wires that stretched the length of the dock. He stumbled backward and hit something hard.

"Oh, my bad . . ." Adal began as he turned, only to be greeted by a large Dweller that looked similar to Webley but with copper skin and without the beard to match. He immediately backed away as the large man peered down at him.

"Careful, Topsider! Trying to work here!" he bellowed, throwing a large crate onto a pallet as it was loaded by a crane onto one of the steamboats. Adal apologized profusely, backing away. Cog's hand appeared on his shoulder and slowly turned him around.

"Careful, Adal. Folks here get testy this time of day. This is when the bulk of the shipments go out to the citizens in the rest of the Machine. Stick close. Webley will be waiting for us at the other end."

"Yeah. Right. I can handle that," he responded, trying to sound reassuring. This place just kept getting weirder and weirder, and every time Adal thought he'd figured it out, something else threw him for a loop. The two turned to look for Arija, only to find her set up on a crate with her notebook in her hand. She fervidly moved her pencil back and forth, desperate to capture every bit of what she'd seen.

Adal smiled. She had a way about her when she drew. She would just throw herself into her sketches and leave the rest of the world behind. Adal watched as she nibbled on her bottom lip like she usually did when she was lost in her drawings. She tapped the charcoal on the tip of her chin leaving a black spot in its wake and then pushed her hair out of her face and dove back into her masterpiece. Adal suddenly wished he could draw so he could capture how beautiful she was at that moment.

195

"Hey, Monet! Let's roll! We're moving out!" he shouted as he shook the lazy look off his face. Arija looked up from her notebook and frowned, then put her nose firmly back into the sketch. After a few more lines, she quickly closed the book and slid it back into her satchel. Arija hopped from her seat and ran over to Adal and Cog.

As she approached, she opened her mouth to speak, but Adal pulled her to him. He couldn't help it, he knew he shouldn't mess with her like this, but he needed to be close to her. Arija was shocked into silence, and she let her rigid muscles go slack as Adal reached his thumb up to her face and wiped the black smudge from her chin. The surrounding bustle died away, and the only thing Adal could hear was his heart furiously pounding in his chest. After a moment he cleared his throat, letting her go and turning back to Cog.

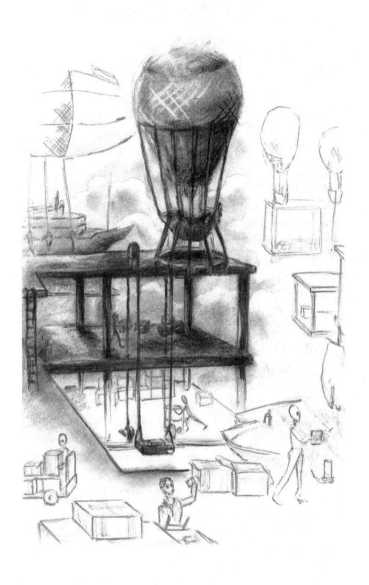

Arija stood still for a moment, reveling in the tingling sensation that lingered where Adal had touched her face, before jumping back into life and trying to act as if nothing had happened. "I can't believe this place! It's like a scene right out of a science fiction book!" the excitement oozed from every word she spoke.

"You aren't kidding. This place is insane!" Adal agreed. The three made their way through the dense crowd. As they neared what looked to be giant doors built into the walls that surrounded Aparat, something took over Adal's thoughts.

"Cog, why aren't these people weirded out by us being here? I mean, they act like we aren't anything special or strange. What's that all about?" Adal accidentally bumped another Dweller. Again, he responded with apologies, but it was near impossible to not run into people in this place. They were everywhere.

Cog paused before he cleared his throat and answered, "This is a world of creation and science. There's little that will surprise the Dwellers. Besides, you aren't the first Topsiders they've seen, and it takes a lot to surprise a Dweller. Just like you humans, the gossip around here travels like an electric current through a bolt." This didn't answer Adal's question, but as long as the Dwellers weren't coming after him with pitchforks, he could handle it.

"'Ere ye are!" bellowed a familiar voice over the commotion. Webley stood several yards ahead of them and was waiving his tree-trunk of an arm excitedly. "What took ye so long! Not like Cog te' lose a race!" Arija and Adal looked to one another and then to Cog.

"Can I have a moment with him?" Cog asked.

"Sure!" Arija pulled Adal's arm so he would follow her a few feet away.

"Take your time," Adal added.

Cog took Webley off to the side to explain what had happened. Arija and Adal were immediately lost to their surroundings once more. Two more Dwellers flew overhead on their carts, causing Arija and Adal to duck though they were actually several feet below them.

"This place is a trip!" Adal proclaimed, turning in a circle.

"Yeah, no kidding. I can't believe what I'm seeing. I don't think I ever want to go home!" Arija laughed, nudging Adal and pointing at a Dweller, almost the size of a small house, marching by. The creature looked like an armored tank turned on its side with arms and legs. Its two large hands were surrounded by over a dozen pipe-like barrels. His chest bore the seal of the World Machine accompanied by a polished badge next to it. The ground shook as he passed them.

"What is that thing?" Arija asked, amazed by its size.

"I think it's like their version of a cop down here. You see the hardware on his hands? What would they need guns like that for?" Adal asked, pointing at the cannon-like appendages.

"I don't know. Well, honestly, I don't want to know. Look at his head!" she said, pointing at the comically small head atop the mechanical man. Adal then motioned to what appeared to be a hatch on its back.

"I think he's wearing that thing." Adal examined what he believed to be a latch that ran the length of its side. "Sweet! Wonder what I need to do to catch a ride in one!"

Arija scoffed and shook her head. "Keep dreaming! I wouldn't let you run around in that thing," she shot back, nudging him with her elbow. The two remained silent until Arija asked what had been bugging her since their attack by the Kleinmasch. "Adal, do you trust Cog?"

"What do you mean?" Adal asked, knitting his brow together and turning to look her in the eye.

"Do you get the feeling he's . . . I don't know . . . maybe hiding something from us?"

Adal arched an eyebrow, but before he could open his mouth to respond, Cog and Webley walked up. Webley's general expression of joy and warmth was replaced with a solemn glare and saddened frown.

"Cog tells me that ye came into some trouble. Sorry 'bout tha'. The World Machine is an amazing place, but some in it would see nothin' but destruction. Those creatures are known in these parts as the Kleinmasch. They are a disturbed breed of Dweller that lives in the depths of the machine. Those particular Kleinmasch are called the Feithidi. Don' ye worry. They don't come up in these parts much."

Webley's bemoan expression widened, and he immediately returned to his warm, chipper self.

Arija shot Adal a look that said she thought there was more to the story.

"'Nough 'bout tha'! Let's get ye two into the city. Should prove to be an amazin' day!" Webley chuckled and threw his arms around Adal and Arija, pulling them close and squeezing them tightly. He smelled of musk and smoke, yet there were sweet tones under it all. Arija was reminded of a tobacco shop that her father took her to as a child, and Adal couldn't help but think of his grandfather.

"Shall we show them anything in particular?" Cog asked.

"Nah! I think they prolly want to see a bit of it all." Webley squeezed Adal and Arija again as if they were his long-lost cousins come to visit. As they approached the giant doorway to the city, several more of the sentries appeared along the gates. They stood motionless, like the statues they resembled, but Adal knew they were alive.

One guard stepped forward from the line and approached the group. His armor was different from the others. Rather than riveted bronze armor, he was made of polished brass, covered with ornate filigree and etched designs. Adal noticed his badge had several more designs adorned within it. He halted his approach before the group, a stern gaze on his face.

"Morning, Webley. Nice to see you today. I see you have brought some Topsiders with you." The guard glared at Adal and Arija for a moment, scrutinizing them. Adal met his gaze and fired a stern expression right back, and Arija clenched her fists in

201

the presence of the stranger's attitude. A Cheshire grin erupted across the man's face, and he roared with laughter. Webley and Cog both followed suit. Arija and Adal looked to one another in confusion and relief, exhaling and relaxing once more.

"Good morning, Captain Silny! How are you today?" Cog asked, extending his hand for a shake.

"All's well 'ere?" Webley asked, slapping the Captain on his shoulder and rocking him sideways. The Captain only laughed harder.

"Ah, there isn't ever anything interesting happening. Things are the same as usual. Kids stealing from carts, bootleggers trying to peddle in the city, my guards want more recreation time. If these are the worst of my problems, I ain't gonna complain. Showing your guests the city today, eh?"

"Indeed, we are! They already had a show today. Kleinmasch herd huntin' in the lower levels gave 'em a what-for! Nothin' my friend 'ere couldn't handle." Webley patted Cog on the back like a proud father.

"Just a few small ones flying around. We came across them chasing some birds. Nothing to worry about." Cog added.

"Ah! Those things need to watch themselves! I'm half-tempted to dispatch a team into some of the smaller nests and start a campaign on them. Keep them in line and remind them their place." Scorned the Captain, his face now genuinely housing a stern glare.

"Well, I think the ones I dealt with won't be a problem any longer." Cog smiled with a hint of sadness in his voice that got Arija's attention. She shot

Adal another glance, but he was happily listening to the conversation, gawking at the large soldier.

"I'm sure. Be that as it may, they have been a nuisance as of late. Some of them have even been trying to raid the ships as they come and go. Hence, why I've had so many of my men out here during the day. Someone needs put those filthy bastards back in their place," the surly captain ranted, shaking his well-armored fist.

"Well, I appreciate the service ye provide the citizens, Captain!" Webley interjected, patting him on the shoulder to calm him down. Captain Silny smiled at Webley and wished them all a fine day. Scooping Adal and Arija once more into his arms, Webley made his way to the base of the giant door.

"Open the gates!" Captain Silny called out from behind them. One of the guards saluted and walked to the center of the wall. From what Arija could see, the guard inserted his giant fist into a hole, turning it clockwise, like it was a key. A low rumble emitted and several of the gargantuan gears on the door's face began to turn slowly. As they cranked in formation, a crease emerged in the door. This grew into a long split as the doors worked their way open.

"Man, you guys don't play around with this stuff, do you?" Adal asked as he peered past the opening and saw that the doors did not open to a city. Rather, the doors opened to yet another large corridor at the opposite end of which were another set of giant doors. "It's like this place just doesn't stop!"

Webley looked down to respond, but something stopped him. A screeching sound came from behind the group.

203

17

THE ADAL I KNOW

Webley and Cog immediately turned in their place, releasing Arija and Adal.

Suddenly, another vicious screech came over the crowd. Shadows flew overhead so quickly that by the time Arija and Adal looked up, whatever made the shadows was gone. Webley and Cog turned, scanning the dock from left to right. All the workers on the dock stood frozen as if they were part of a movie that had been paused.

"What the hell is going on?" Adal asked, a tight sensation returning to his stomach.

"I have no idea. Look at all of them." Arija took a step toward one of the patrons frozen in his place when a bundle of something crashed to the ground ahead of her. Arija fell backward and was caught by Adal who rapidly hoisted her to her feet.

"What the f—" Arija's words were cut off as several more bundles fell to the ground around them. Arija and Adal took several slow steps toward one of the piles, only to have their hearts sink in their chests as if the muscles were cowering. The tattered piles that had fallen from the sky were the shredded remains of arms, legs, a torso, and wings. The shiny surface of the severed parts glinted in the simulated sun, and then chaos broke out.

Screaming and running erupted around them as Dwellers fled from the area of the fallen air guards. These had to have been the same aerial sentries they had seen when they approached strapped to Cog. Adal absentmindedly picked up a badge that looked identical to the badges worn by the city guards.

"These guys are guards!" Adal shouted at Arija as the mob of Dwellers threatened to trample them.

"What did that?" Arija asked, immediately regretting her inquiry. The shambling mass about them erupted in more screams as several Dwellers stood frozen pointing toward the sky at the end of the dock.

"Gearrtha!" One of the Dwellers near them shouted. Two dozen winged creatures swept through the air toward the mob on the dock in a swarm that resembled a military plane formation. They had long, thin wings, two short legs, and sharp angular faces. They appeared to be a strange mixture of a Dweller, and a praying mantis, complete with a mantis' long, bladed appendages.

"They did this!" barked Adal, noting their arms and motioning to the mangled guards.

"Everyone, into the city!" bellowed Webley, waving his arms and pointing to the open gates. Captain Silny and a squadron of his guards appeared at either side of Adal and Arija.

"Get inside! My men will protect you!" Captain Silny commanded.

The mob needed no further instruction. Like a wave of panic and fear, they all turned and ran toward the doorway to the city. Adal and Arija pushed and shoved the metallic bodies of the Dwellers to avoid being trampled as they ran into the corridor. Crashes of thunder erupted as the sentinels aimed their arm-cannons toward the coming assault and fired. The flying attackers expertly maneuvered about the streaks of hot steel that projected from their barrels.

Within a moment, the Gearrtha swooped in and landed upon the dock. Those Dwellers unfortunate enough to still be in the area when they landed were cut down before they even knew what happened. With several perfectly timed slashes and swings, their appendages were severed from their bodies, creating piles of gears and scrap metal all over the dock.

Cog shot a knowing glance to Webley who pursed his lips and gave a curt nod. Cog took out his staff and ran towards the massacre with Webley right behind him. Captain Silny and his men continued firing their weapons and swinging their massive arms at the ones that flew overhead. One by one, dozens of Dwellers fell victim to the savageness of the Gearrtha. Arija stopped and watched as Dwellers all around her dropped to the ground. She ran over to the body of a flying guard and began to sort through the lifeless mass.

"What are you doing?" Adal shouted over the screams when he realized she was no longer following him to safety. He pushed through the crowd of frantic

Dwellers until he was standing only a few feet from where she was squatting over a dead soldier.

"Here!" Arija tossed him the belt that the guard had been wearing. On it was a holster that held a large revolver. He looked at the heavy piece of metal as if the weapon was completely foreign to him. She then tossed him another belt that held rows of ammunition. As he looked at the two; she ran to another corpse and looted the same items for herself, immediately dawning the equipment.

"Oh, you've got to be kidding me! No way in hell!" Adal shouted, holding out the belts as he realized what Arija wanted him to do. Arija clipped her belts into place and adjusted them, giving Adal a look of disgust for the first time in her life.

"No, YOU'RE the one who's got to be kidding. What's happened to you, Adal? You used to be this big, tough man with the ego the size of a small city bus. You were somebody that never ran away from anything. Not a fight, not a chance to stand out, not a single opposition. Since your grandfather died, and we came here, you've been nothing but a little bitch. That isn't the Adal I know. The Adal I know would've already been looking for a way to get in this fight and kick some ass!" Arija waited for a retort, but when none came, she continued. "Your grandfather is gone, but his spirit isn't. It led us to this place. Do you think he would have stood in your place, frozen in fear while innocent people die? I can guarantee you, he would've charged in even before Webley. What are you going to do? Are you going to stay afraid, or are you going to honor your grandfather?"

Arija's swords stabbed at Adal's heart. She was right. He was being a coward, and now people were dying. His grandfather would have been ashamed of him. He wasn't about to let his grandfather's memory be something he couldn't live up to. Adal threw the holster belt around his waist and clipped the buckle. He then slid the bandolier over his shoulder.

"Coward, huh?" Adal said, a grin creeping across his face. The heat from his chest spread to his face and cheeks, and the hairs all over his body stood on end.

"I got your 'coward' right here!" Adal yanked the weighty revolver free, feeling the weight of the pistol in his hands. It was heavier than he thought it should be, but he'd never held a gun before today, so who was he to judge. Adal turned on his heels and looked to the massacre. He cracked his neck to both sides and rolled his shoulders.

"Watch this!" he yelled over his shoulder before springing toward the fight. Arija rolled her eyes, but she was smiling, happy to see her friend back. She sent a silent prayer to her mom to make her strong and then followed him into the battle.

Captain Silny and his men fired at everything that flew and jumped about them. Already, several corpses of the Gearrtha littered the ground around them, but it seemed more had appeared to replace the numbers of the fallen.

The sight of Webley and Cog battling the Gearrtha was something to behold. It was like a scene from Jekyll and Hyde. Their usually kind and pleasant dispositions now contorted into cold killing machines. One of the Gearrtha dodged Cog's strike, ducking under the staff and coming up in time to swipe his

208

claw across Cog's face. The Gearrtha were clearly much better fighters than the clumsy Kleinmasch from earlier that day. Webley even seemed to struggle as he battled four at a time. As one swiped at his face, Webley ducked and grasped two by their heads before they could respond. He crushed their skulls in his palms, dropping them lifeless to the ground in one swift movement.

A shadow moved overhead, and Arija had just enough time to lunge forward and tackle Adal to the floor. A Gearrtha swooped in and swiped its claws at them. Adal rolled forward and aimed his pistol at the creature, firing several shots. The first three went wide, but the fourth shot ripped through the back of the Gearrtha right between its wings. It screeched as it fell from the sky and disappeared over the edge of the dock. Adal's heart pounded in his ears. There was no turning back now. Thinking in the moment, he brought the pistol up to his eyes to examine it. He wanted to know how many rounds it held, so he knew when it was almost empty.

The blued steel revolver had two barrels, one over the other. The rotating cylinder had two sections of chambers, both aligned with their own barrel. He saw that two rounds were missing from the larger, external cylinder and two from the smaller internal cylinder. He gathered it must be alternating shots between the two. Ten rounds for the larger cylinder, six rounds for the internal.

"Sixteen shots! Remember that!" Adal said as he held out his hand and helped Arija up.

"Thanks for the save!" As they approached the battle, the guards fired their cannons in all directions. With every shot, the air shook around them, and plumes of steam erupted into clouds. Captain Silny barked orders around every shot, but Adal and Arija heard none of his words. They made their way toward Webley and Cog, keeping their heads as low as possible to avoid the swooping blades.

Two Gearrtha landed on either shoulder of a guard, and he batted at them with the weaponized arms of his suit. They tore into his armor around his head and yanked him from the suit. One of the creatures held him in the air by his arm, while the second cleaved the appendage from his body. The Dweller guard screamed as he dropped to the floor, a wriggling pile of a man. His mechanical suit crashed limply to the dock; the platform below shaking violently.

The Gearrtha launched into the air and landed next to their fallen prey. Reaching out with his remaining arm, the Dweller tried to crawl away from the insidious Kleinmasch and get to cover. The Gearrtha only watched, relishing in the terror on the Dweller's face as he shouted for help.

"Hey!" shouted Adal and Arija in tandem as they took a step toward the helpless Dweller. The Gearrtha looked up from their victim, surprise covering their pointed faces as the two friends stood shoulder-to-shoulder. One creature cocked its head to the side and let out a predatory cry. Adal and Arija took a fleeting glimpse at the desperate man on the floor and then opened fire on the creatures.

Arija was shocked at how accurate the gun was. Its weight and turnkey mechanics did wonders at taming the recoil. She used to go shooting with her dad, but she'd never shot something like this before. The explosion from the shot and the plume of smoke from the barrels were barely felt in her hand. When Adal had fired at the first Gearrtha, she thought perhaps he had just been making it look easy, now she questioned how he missed the first three shots.

Arija's shots tore through the face of the Gearrtha that screamed its battle cry at them. Adal had only fired one shot, but it punched a hole right through the other monster's neck. Arija could tell he'd never shot a gun before, even though the weapon was crazy accurate, he didn't look confident with it in his hand and his posture was all wrong, mimicking something from a bad action film.

Arija checked that the Dweller was still alive and then she reached down to help him to his feet. She opened her mouth to say something, but then closed it again, unable to think of anything to say that would help. The Dweller looked up at her with fear in his eyes and then ran towards the gate to the city, disappearing into the crowded sea of Dwellers trying to get to safety.

The body of a dead Gearrtha dropped to their feet, causing Arija to jump back. She looked from the

211

corpse to the guard that had just saved their lives and nodded a grateful 'thanks.' He nodded back and went back to shooting at the creatures flying overhead.

"Let's just get to Webley and Cog!" Adal shouted, firing another couple of shots at a Gearrtha attempting to surprise one of the guards.

"All right, just keep moving and try not to get yourself killed!" Arija shouted back as she shot at three passing Gearrtha. The one in the middle screamed as a bullet pierced its stomach and fell from the sky. She aimed her pistol at the other two, but they flew out of her range before she could get a second shot off. Off in the distance, Arija could see Cog still battling with a small group of the attackers, his staff spinning so fast she could only tell it was there by the rhythmic movement of his hands.

As the world exploded around Adal and Arija, they ran as cautiously as possible through the battle, stopping every several feet to fire at a Gearrtha or to avoid colliding with an obstacle. As they got closer to Webley and Cog, Arija got a strange feeling in her stomach. Why was it so easy to pass through the fight? The Gearrtha were everywhere, and yet they seemed to ignore them. Just as this thought occurred to her, Adal turned to look at her, and she froze in terror as a look of pain erupted across his face.

18

The Cliché Evil

Twin

Adal was thrown several yards as the back-half of a Gearrtha's claw collided with his chest. The force was so great that the air left his lungs and he could hear the cracking of his own ribs. The metallic taste of blood coated the inside of his mouth as he slammed into the platform, his body rolling over and over before colliding with a stack of crates that had been left by the Dweller's before the battle began. A too tall stack of crates teetered and then came crashing down on Adal, burying him in a pile of wood.

In the distance, Adal could hear Arija shouting but the pain overtook his thoughts, and his eyesight was fading in and out. Adal's lungs burned, and he struggled to take in oxygen. He pushed up on one crate and daylight spilled in just in time for him to see Arija connect a perfect spin kick and send one of the Gearrthas crashing into a wall. She ducked as another one flew at her and then fired off a barrage of shots. Each shot hit the Gearrtha square in the chest, and it fell to the ground next to her. Arija reared back her booted foot and kicked the dead creature in the head, almost taking it off with her force.

Adal watched as the blurry image of Arija took her aggression out on the Gearrtha that had hit him. He could see his pulse pounding at the edge of his vision until the world faded to black.

Arija looked around, trying to figure out where Adal had landed. Her heart pounded in her ears and rage warmed her face. If she'd gotten him killed, she'd never forgive herself.

"I was starting to wonder if you were ever going to expel your munitions." The voice made Arija jump, and she spun around, gun pointed and at the ready.

In front of her stood a Dweller man, but something about him was different from the others she'd seen so far. He carried himself like he was in charge and the fighting that surrounded them didn't seem to bother him in the slightest.

"What's wrong with you? You need to get out of here! Those things will kill you!" Arija said, keeping her aim on the strange Dweller. He only smiled coldly and shook his head. He looked almost familiar even though Arija hadn't met that many Dwellers. He was clothed head to toe in black leather pressed with straight edges. His hands sat perched on his copper belt, upon which hung two large daggers.

As Arija looked from the weapons back to his face, recognition washed over her. He looked almost exactly like Cog. The only difference between the two was a long, silver scar that ran down the left side of the Dweller's face.

"There isn't much of a reason for me to fear these amazing creatures. You, on the other hand, have no idea how lucky you are." The Dweller said as he let his eyes roam over Arija. Arija took a small step backward, keeping the pistol trained on him even though she knew she was out of bullets. The Dweller clicked his pinkies on the pommel of his daggers.

"Look, I don't know who you are, but you need to get out of here!" Arija adjusted the grip on her pistol. He grinned, looking at the ground by Arija's feet. Arija let her eyes drift down, and when she brought them up again, he was so close that the barrel of her revolver was pressed against his shoulder. A small gasp reflexively escaped her lips.

"Topsiders really are as dim as they seem." With another burst of blinded speed, the Cog look-a-like swung his arm into the air, knocking the empty gun from Arija's hands. Arija brought her leg up and thrust her heel into his stomach forcing him to stumble back a half step. "Mistake!" the Dweller said as he brought his green eyes up to meet hers.

Before Arija could react, he drew his blades and swiped them at the air in front of her. Arija stumbled backward with just enough time to feel a gust of air on her face from the momentum of the blades. A thin strand of her chestnut hair drifted down, a fallen casualty in the fight. Arija planted a firm foot on the platform, looking down at her severed locks.

"You are coming with me, Topsider! Either you surrender now, and I take you to him, or I cut you into pieces and take him what is left." He slid one foot behind the other and poised himself for a lunge. Arija eyed the blades, trying to reason out what to do.

"Screw you! I don't know who *he* is, but there's no way I'm coming with you!" Arija clenched her hands so tightly into fists that several of her knuckles cracked under the pressure. If he was here for her, she wasn't going to make it easy. Even if it killed her.

"Really? Well, that's a shame then, isn't it? I suppose it will have to be in pieces." The sinister looking being snickered, lowering his stance. Arija took a peripheral glimpse around for something she could use as a weapon. The empty gun was only a few feet away. If she could get to it, she could use it as a bludgeon.

"Whose house?" Adal shouted as he lunged forward and surprised Arija's attacker. He threw his legs into the air and connected both soles with the face of Cog's doppelgänger, sending him sprawling sideways and dropping his knives. Adal let out a loud grunt as he slammed back to the platform and rolled away.

Just as Adal had come to moments before, he'd seen a man threatening Arija through a crack in the crates. His ribs burned, but he'd known he couldn't let her get hurt. So, he'd pushed his way through the crates, ignoring the pain in his side, and ran to Arija.

"Oh, hell no . . ." Adal forced out between gasps of pain.

Arija exhaled the breath she'd been holding since the strange Dweller had swiped his knives at her. She ran over to Adal and fell to her knees at his side, trying to help him up. Adal pulled his arms away and shook his head.

"I'm all right, kid! Who's that idiot?" he coughed, trying to regain the wind knocked from his lungs. Arija grabbed at his shoulders and tugged him to his feet.

"Quit being stubborn. We need to get away from here. You're injured!" Arija placed a gentle hand on Adal's ribs causing him to double over. "Why would you just dropkick a guy? What were you thinking? And what the hell was 'whose house'? What does that even mean?"

Adal lazily brushed at his pants. "This my house . . . hey, it seemed like a good idea at the time. You're welcome for the save, by the way!" he responded, slightly annoyed that she was fussing over him.

"Save? You nearly got yourself killed! I had this one!"

"That's not how it loo—"

"The second one isn't so down and out after all. Wonderful. The master will be pleased to have both of you." The dark Dweller sneered, interrupting Adal from only a few feet away. His wicked grin and slanted eyes brought a sinister nuance to his face. He adjusted his jaw where he'd been kicked. His blades

217

were scattered on the platform between them, and Arija glanced down for a split second before refocusing on his face.

"We aren't going anywhere with your creepy smiling ass. Thanks for the offer, but we have better things to do. Like fight these crazy mantis things. So, if you don't mind, step off, or I'll throw you another beating," Adal offered as he took a half step ahead of Arija who yanked at his sleeve.

"What the hell are you doing? If I couldn't take him, you sure as hell can't! Not in your condition anyway." Arija slid her hand down Adal's side to where his empty holster sat on his hip. "Where's your gun?" she mumbled out of the side of her mouth.

"I don't know. It went flying when I did. I'm going to make my move. You make yours!" Adal mumbled back, keeping his eyes trained on his opponent. With his little finger, Adal motioned to the two knives on the platform.

"So, what's the plan, shiny? We gonna do this, or are you going to just stand there and look at me? I mean, I know I'm pretty, but damn," Adal said, the humor gone from his voice. The Dweller's grin faded and his mouth thinned. He closed his robotic hands into fists and lowered his head to his shoulders.

"If you think it's in your best interest, Topsider, please feel free to try your odds. I will greatly enjoy peeling back your skin and seeing what your wet insides look like. When I'm done with you, your mate is next!" he said, flicking his gaze toward Arija.

Arija flinched at the word "mate." She wasn't even Adal's girlfriend, for reasons she didn't exactly understand, and the word brought a sudden embarrassment to her cheeks.

Adal's upper lip twitched as he watched him eye Arija like she was a prize at the fair. His face burned, and his palms got sweaty at the thought of this man with Arija, torturing her or . . . whatever else he had in mind. Adal was ready to put his fist down this asshole's throat.

Without another word, Adal lunged. He swung his right arm at the Cog look-a-like, his fist colliding with his face. A loud, metallic clang was followed by a searing pain rushing through Adal's hand and up into his arm. He could swear that under the ringing of the collision, he heard the small bones in his hand break.

Adal looked from his throbbing hand back to the metal man who stood before him with a bored look on his face. Adal froze as that same, familiar grin returned.

"Thank you for going first. I wouldn't want this to be over too quickly. My turn?"

Before Adal could react, he was grabbed by the collar and hoisted into the air. Adal gripped at the hands around his neck, doing his best to support his own weight. He flailed his legs, trying and failing to kick hard enough to be released.

Using this as a distraction, Arija slid across the floor to the knives. Grabbing the weapons, she pushed herself to her feet. The glint of the blades caught the light and Adal's attacker shot a furious look in her direction. He threw Adal, and the two collided just as she was preparing herself for the attack, causing

219

her to drop the weapons as she slid across the copper platform.

"Clever, Topsider!" he said, walking over to his knives. "I guess taking you alive won't be a possibility. It isn't that I cannot, rather I'm tired of dealing with you and do not wish to face the hassle." The dark Dweller collected his daggers and rolled them around in his hands. He admired the sleek blades of his knives like an artist admiring a finished canvas. Adal tried to stand, but the pain in his ribs was unbearable. He rolled over, looking at Arija's unconscious body. He shook her shoulder, watching her head lull from side to side.

"Shall we get this over with then?" the Dweller walked over to Adal who sat up the best he could, covering Arija with his body.

"Coward! Couldn't handle me when I could fight back, could you?" Adal spat.

"Enough talking. After everything you have tried, I wouldn't want your weak words to ruin this moment for me." He reached down and grabbed Adal by his shirt and pulled him upward. He raised the blade in his other hand high into the air in a grand show of power. Adal tried to fight back, but without a weapon, he couldn't do anything more than stare death in the eye. He refused to die a coward. Adal grunted as he thrust the blade toward Adal's face.

Clang! Adal flinched at the sound.

"That's enough, Fausto. Not going to allow this one, brother!" Cog thrust his staff against Fausto's wrist, halting the attack. Fausto dropped Adal back to the ground and stepped away, turning his attention to Cog.

"Ah! As usual, terrible timing, brother. I was just going to give my new friend . . ." Fausto stopped, his shoulders shaking in a silent laugh. "I mean *our* new friend, a present."

"You need to stand down, Fausto! This isn't going to happen. Not today. Not ever. You can tell Pajak that!" Cog spun his staff around, stepping into a defensive stance. Fausto twirled his knives in his hands and squared off with his brother.

Adal crouched down back to Arija but let his eyes bounce back and forth between the two brothers. *How can robots be brothers?* Adal was pulled from his thoughts as Arija groaned. He brushed the matted locks of hair out of her face revealing a small bump on her head and a droplet of blood trickling down her face. Adal wiped the blood away with his thumb. He sat down beside her, cradling her head in his lap as he stroked her hair. He glanced up, tuning back into the fight.

"Your problem, brother. You never were much for sharing. Nor is YOUR master!" Fausto taunted.

"You're the only one with a master, Fausto. I have a family. One that you walked out on. There's a difference. You never could understand that. Neither could Pajak."

"Enough!" Fausto shouted. "This ends here, Cogsworth!"

Adal brought his attention back down to Arija as the two Dwellers collided with a mechanical clash of sounds. Adal watched Arija's chest rise and fall and her face twitch with each small breath.

"I'm not sure what's worse; getting knocked out like an idiot in the middle of a fight, or waking up to you breathing on me like a creep," Arija groaned. Her eyes remained closed, but she cracked a small smile.

"Damn, kid! Don't do that to me again," Adal spat. "You had me worried for a second. I can't lose you. Now, get it together. I can't keep babysitting you like this. You're jamming up my style." The fight behind him drifted away, and all he could hear was Arija's soft breathing.

She opened her eyes and managed a scowl.

"Correct me if I'm wrong, but weren't you getting choked out? Oh, and wasn't it your butt that knocked me out in the first place? I remember seeing your fat ass flying at me right before it went dark." Arija laughed as she propped herself up on her elbows.

"Yeah, what can I say Arija? Just looking at this ass is enough to make any girl faint."

"I wouldn't brag about that. Not sure it's a good thing, Adal. What happened to that man?" Arija asked, bringing the focus back to the present.

"He almost had us, then Cog came in. Now they're fighting." Adal pointed over his shoulder to where Cog and Fausto were battling it out.

"Wait, what?" Arija forced herself to sit up all the way.

"Relax! Cog has it." Adal turned to motion at the brothers. As if on cue, Cog soared past them and slid to a stop a few feet behind them. Adal and Arija followed Cog with their eyes as he stood and pulled one of Fausto's daggers out of his shoulder. He grimaced as he worked the end of the blade free.

"Oh, brother, you're getting slower in your old age. Is Webley rubbing off on you?" Fausto taunted.

Adal and Arija turned their attention back to Fausto. He looked battle-worn just as Cog did, but he somehow looked like he'd won. He still held the other knife in his hand and idly tossed it up into the air and caught it.

"I see that your master is rubbing off on you. That was a dirty move, indeed. I won't be making that mistake again." Cog threw the knife down to the dock and charged at Fausto.

Fausto let out a battle cry, lunging forward to meet Cog. As they glided over the ground, Adal and Arija realized that the fight was coming directly toward them. They pulled at one another and rose to their feet. With their arms wrapped around each other's shoulders, they moved out of the way. An explosion thundered from where they had just been, and the conjoined pair spun around to see what happened.

"ENOUGH!" Webley's face was red from combat, and he had several small wounds from where the Gearrtha had gotten the best of him. His eyes narrowed with such anger that Adal could have sworn there was actual fire in his eyes. Arija noticed that he still had pieces of Gearrtha stuck between his large fingers and she looked away to avoid thinking too much about it.

"This fight will continue no further!" Webley shouted, looking between Cog and Fausto like a disapproving parent.

"These attempts an' plans of Pajak stop now! I will no longer 'ave him risking not only the Dweller's

223

lives but the Machine itself. You tell him I said to back down. If he 'as an issue with tha', then 'ave him see me!" Webley said, turning his full attention to Fausto.

Fausto remained silent as if he couldn't help but to listen and obey every word that came out of Webley's mouth. Fausto kept his stare fixated on Cog who whistled and then tossed Fausto's knife into the air. As Cog caught the knife by its blade, he threw it at Fausto who caught it inches before the pointed tip penetrated his eye.

"Had enough then, brother?" Fausto teased.

"Enough! The both of ye! I mean it, Fausto, leave!" Webley's voice shook with fury. Fausto calmly slid his blades back into their sheaths. He bowed almost comically low to Webley, then shot a glare at Adal and Arija. He winked at the two of them, turned, and then sprinted to the opposite side of the dock. Once he reached the edge, Fausto spread his arms wide and dove from the platform, disappearing over the edge.

"Well, that was dramatic," Arija said as she watched Fausto plummet over the edge of the platform. "Is he always like this?"

Cog shook his head but said nothing in response.

"Ye all right?" Webley asked, turning to Cog. He nodded silently then motioned to Adal and Arija. "Ye two all right?" Webley asked, stepping over and eyeing them as if searching for injuries.

"Yeah, we're good. This sort of thing happens to us all the time," Adal began, sarcasm brewing with every word.

"We're fine, Webley. Thank you. Just a little sore, really," Arija finished.

"Tha's quite the knock on the head, Arija. Perhaps we should get ye to the doctor in the city." Webley bent over the two friends, looking at the hit she'd taken. Adal did his best to look un-phased by the battle. It was Cog that called his bluff.

"I think they both could use a bit of attention. Adal did well holding his own, but if I know Fausto, those hits were not restrained. Not sure a Topsider can take a full hit from a Dweller." Cog walked over to Webley's side.

"Come. Let's get ye to the doctor." Webley put his arm around Arija. Cog attempted to do the same with Adal but was brushed off. As Adal took his first step, his legs nearly gave out, and a shooting pain erupted from his ribs.

"You know, on second thought," Adal said, putting his arm back around Cog.

"Wait! What about the fight?" Arija broke through, twisting herself in Webley's arm. In the commotion, she'd completely forgotten about the Gearrtha that were terrorizing the docks. Turning to face the scene of the conflict, her mouth fell open when she saw what remained. Several mangled Gearrtha littered the ground about them as the guards marched in formation. The few Dwellers that remained on the docks were helping each other up, and a few Dwellers were pushing the severed parts of both Dweller and Gearrtha alike into neat piles with what looked like large push brooms.

"The fight has been fought an' won, Arija. They weren' much of a match fer the guards. I helped design them suits m'self. Right sturdy," Webley added.

"So, we won?" Adal asked, rubbing his sore ribs with his free hand.

"This wasn't the sort of thing you can win or lose. This was just the tip of the mound. Be warned, this, whatever it was, is not over." Cog's words tore at Adal and Arija's hearts. Seeing things on film or reading them in books had an inert way of removing the severity and emotion of war. Being in this battle, having their own lives threatened and being forced to face mortality, was a humbling experience.

Adal would never admit it aloud, but he had been terrified. He had never met someone, or something, that could take and deal hits like that and keep coming. If Cog hadn't shown up when he did, they wouldn't be there to think about it.

19

I Will Lead Your

Armies Into Victory

Fausto took his time making his way back to The Roost. If any of the other Kleinmasch had failed Pajak like he had, Pajak would have them disassembled and fed to the others.

"Let him try if he fancies a go!" Fausto snapped as he made his way deeper into the Machine. For all of Fausto's strengths, and the soldiers he commanded, Pajak realistically wouldn't have any reservations about having him killed. He damned himself for not planning the attack more thoroughly. In hindsight, he should have kept to his traditionally stealthy ways instead of trying to make a show of it. Get in, get the Topsiders, and get out. But no, he'd brought in the Gearrtha and tried to take on the whole dock. Stupid. He should've at least taken some Umar with him.

The lights dimmed about him as he drew closer to the city. A small group of Baeg scuttled past him, and Fausto kicked at them, sending several flying deeper into The Roost. As he stormed past more Kleinmasch, Fausto shot infuriated glances at them so they wouldn't try to approach or talk to him.

"He hasn't lost much of his step," Fausto said as he thought about the fight with his brother. He lunged from one platform only to free-fall over a hundred feet and land effortlessly on another, his daggers clanking in their sheaths. A small group of Feithidi scattered in surprise as Fausto landed directly behind them.

"I should've had him. He sticks to the same tricks. The same moves. I nearly had him clocked to a pattern. But no, he had to involve that oversized gremlin." Fausto spat at the thought of Webley. He knew Pajak wouldn't be able to see past Webley's involvement. That would be the one point he would latch on to, and he wouldn't even be able to see all the Dwellers that Fausto took out with the Gearrtha.

The Topsiders' reluctance to comply with his orders only further angered Fausto. Topsiders were weak. He knew it. They all knew it. Their soft fleshy exteriors and their slow reaction times made it a wonder they survived at all. So, why were these two particularly difficult to capture. If Cogsworth and Webley had minded their own damn business, Fausto would be enjoying a feast while Pajak tinkered inside them.

Clearing the tunnel, Fausto slapped his hand at one of the long legs of a Cead. The creature let out a surprised bark and looked down at the nuisance below him. Fausto shot a lethal gaze at the sentry, and it immediately snapped back to attention.

On the other side of the tunnel, Fausto stopped to look deeper into The Roost at the hanging nest of the Gearrtha. Of all the creatures created within the Kleinmasch's ranks, these were his favorite. Granted, they were also one of the few Kleinmasch that he'd designed himself. At the time, Pajak had his intensely strong Umar, but Fausto told him they needed shrill soldiers. Assassins that had the skills to dive into battle and create as much havoc as possible. The Gearrtha were born from that.

Since that day, Pajak had allowed Fausto to lead their ranks. Fausto loved nothing more than directing his fierce soldiers into war and watching them destroy everything in their path. He reveled in the praise he received from Pajak when he returned victorious.

This would not be one of those days. A failure that someone would soon answer for. Luckily for him, his creations were too dim to place the blame where it was due. He'd hate to watch his children being slaughtered, but it was either them or him, and Fausto knew how to survive in The Roost.

The grand chamber was surprisingly quiet when he entered. The Breeders seemed eerily still and were not twitching and pumping their hindquarters as they created new waves of Kleinmasch. Fausto froze for a moment and peered around the vast, empty space. Something was wrong.

"Damn." The word was soft, but it still echoed around the walls. Pajak appeared near the crest of the vaulted ceiling and scaled one of the main pillars that ran the length of the room, landing gracefully behind Fausto. Pajak lifted Fausto into the air by scooping two of his long, arachnid legs under his arms, and then threw him across the chamber.

Fausto came to a stop as he slid into one of the pillars. He fumbled with his holsters and tried to draw his daggers, but Pajak was too quick. He jumped on top of Fausto and kicked his weapons away. Pajak's face twisted into a snarl as he lifted Fausto into the air once more. Fausto grasped and clutched at the long spider-like appendages, only to be slammed against the far wall of the chamber. As he fell to the floor, he nudged one of the Breeders on his way down. It squeaked and shivered in fear.

"I told you I wanted the Topsiders! Did I not assign you the task? Did you not promise me I could be tearing out their insides by this evening? Was I *not* fully clear on your duties?" Pajak shouted as he collected Fausto once more and threw him into yet another wall. Fausto's internal mechanics were jarred, and he saw double as he cowered at the foot of Pajak's throne where he'd landed.

"Tell me, have you anything to say for yourself, or shall I just introduce you to your new home with all the other Breeders?" Pajak strolled past Fausto and pulled himself up onto his throne. A part of Fausto wanted Pajak to just end it all. He was a proud warrior, but lying on the cold floor, the pain of the day's battle and the utter disgust of defeat radiating from every nut and bolt in his body, a part of Fausto just wanted it all to end.

It was then that it occurred to him. How had Pajak known of his failure? The only way the master could have known would be if one of his cowardly creations retreated to The Roost and told him. No! He would rise from this day. Things were not over for him by far. Pajak waived his arm, and the large chamber door flew open, and one of his hulking Umar shuffled in.

"Hmm, I think the best punishment for you will be . . ." Pajak glanced over at the wall covered in Breeders where one nest was empty.

"Yes, I think that'll be the best place for you. Perhaps I can find a use in you yet." Pajak motioned for the Umar who slowly made its way down the corridor toward him.

"No!" barked Fausto, pushing himself up from the floor as he covered his head in anticipation of another attack. None came. Instead, Pajak smiled at him and waived his arm for the Umar to stop.

"No?" Pajak reiterated. "Just why, exactly, do you think you have a choice in the matter?" Pajak often enjoyed toying with his prey, but Fausto was not in a toying mood. He was going to speak his mind, and if it came to it, Pajak would have to kill him. There was no way Fausto was going to become a Breeder.

"I did not fail you!" Fausto adjusted his clothing and stood up as straight as he could, ignoring the searing pain that coursed through his body.

"That's not what I was told," Pajak began. Fausto twitched at that statement. One of his men *had* betrayed him. If he survived the night, he would find the traitor in his ranks and rip him apart one bolt at a time.

"As I said, I did not fail you. I had the Topsiders bested and in my grasp. It was not until Webley joined the fray that I had an issue." Fausto knew the very mention of Webley would push Pajak over the edge and sure enough the master twisted in his seat at the mention of the name.

"I had my brother ended too. I had the Topsiders defeated. My men wrought havoc on the dock, claiming the lives of Dwellers and guards alike. Webley was among them. He helped fight back. In the end, we could not return victorious from the battle. If the weak creature that fled and informed you had remained until the end of the fight, surely he would have known this." The more Fausto touched on the subject, the more his own rage grew. He had to catch himself from intentionally bating Pajak into another scuffle.

"Webley doesn't kill machines," Pajak interjected, his voice cold and mechanical. Every letter he spoke twisted with uncertain intent.

"He did today. I watched him crush many of my men himself with my bastard brother at his side. I even watched the Topsiders dispatch of some of my ranks. Had it been only the Topsiders and the guards, we would have been victorious. Even my brother didn't influence the mission other than slowing and irritating me."

"What, and you couldn't tend to Webley yourself? He may have destroyed that which we have created, but certainly he wouldn't hurt one of his own creations," Pajak argued, picking at the arm of his throne as he often did.

"Would *you* have battled him?" Fausto knew the answer before the words even left his mouth.

232

Pajak growled lowly and squeezed the arm of his throne, crushing the metallic parts under the strength of his hand. "I would not challenge me, Fausto. Not today. You're already on the edge with me, and that empty Breeder spot is looking lonely."

"He is protecting them! He defended the Topsiders more intensely than he ever did for us! He killed machines to keep them safe! He has even ordered the recycling of the fallen Gearrtha! What he has done against you today is the reason the mission failed! I was not the reason. This has become a full-fledged war, Pajak, and it is clear what side he has taken. My only question to you is, are you willing to do what is necessary to win?"

Fausto's words echoed through the vast room. Pajak remained silent for a moment, leaning back in his chair as if thinking deeply about his response. Fausto swallowed the nervous lump in his throat. If his plan didn't work, he would be spending the rest of eternity as a Breeder.

"So, you think his actions today were a declaration of war?" Pajak finally asked, his voice finding a strange level of optimism in his question.

"I . . . I suppose so, yes. He doesn't kill his precious Dwellers, but he will eradicate our ranks with no thought," Fausto added, his voice finding a more confident tone.

"He has always admired *his* creations over mine. Webley has never granted respect to our race and, yet, he thinks what he makes is so superior? Then why do our brethren slaughter his creations and consume them? We are the dominant species! This place, this World Machine, is OUR kingdom. And it's time we take it!" Pajak paused a moment as if thinking about what he'd just said before he continued. "Webley thinks his ability to grant 'life' to his creations is something that only he can acquire? I will learn the secrets myself, if I must. I will tear those Topsiders apart. I will learn every part of their 'living' beings. Then, I will use that to grow a new race. Something better than both the Dwellers and Kleinmasch alike. A master creation that will go forth and grow, dominating all in existence, and I will rule everything he has created and mold it to my image!" Pajak rose triumphantly, the thought of war energizing him. Fausto relaxed his tightened gears. His plan had worked.

"War. This will change all that we know. To do this, I will need a General. I will need someone competent to lead my armies and accomplish my tasks. Is this something you think you can manage without failure?" Pajak held up his hand to stifle Fausto's eager response. "Before you speak, you should know that your punishment, should you fail, will be something that has never been witnessed before. I will create something especially for you that will be far worse than anything you can imagine." Pajak lowered his hand, the wicked grin on his face widening, a villainous glare in his eyes.

"Yes! I will lead your armies!" Fausto did not hesitate. He knew there was only one answer. Refusing would have resulted in death, regardless. Besides, he wanted revenge for the day's defeat. He wanted Cog and Webley to both pay for what they had done.

"I am pleased to hear that. I must warn you, this position will not be 'granted' to you. You must earn it. If you are to lead my army, you must prove yourself." Pajak seated himself once more on his throne. His face contorted into the cold look of a businessman and then he raised his arm and waved the signal.

Fausto crouched low to the ground as the floor shook. He shot a stare over his shoulder at the Umar guard walking toward him, small bolts and debris jumping with every step he took. A smile spread across Fausto's face as understanding reached his eyes. Pajak tossed Fausto his blades as he stood upright.

"All right, then. Let's see what you can do," Pajak said as he sunk into his throne, making himself comfortable.

Part II:

The New World

20

You Need To Do What Inside Me?

The doctor's office looked pretty standard, but the parts of the city they'd seen as they limped to the building had been more shocking than what they had already seen of the Machine. The streets were lined with strange vehicles that barely missed buildings and Dwellers alike as they sped around, traversing crowds with surgical precision. Adal thought some cars looked sort of like the old Model Ts he'd seen in magazines, but others were smaller with mechanical wings that ejected from the sides.

On both sides of the street, buildings pierced the artificial sky, and crowds of Dwellers gathered to get a look at the aftermath. Every so often a Dweller would gasp or point as they noticed Adal and Arija being escorted by Webley to the doctor's office. Between the droves of occupants, not a single Dweller looked like another. All humanoid, all in their beautifully articulated Victorian clothing, and all looking at Adal and Arija as though aliens had landed in their midst.

The streets were composed of brick cobblestone, and the sidewalks were a patchwork assortment of bronzed, pink, black, and yellow metals.

Arija had wished, not for the first time that day, that she'd had time to sketch what she had seen. Even now, sitting in the doctor's waiting room, she was too busy dealing with Adal's worried outbursts to pull out her sketchbook.

"I'm just sayin', how in the hell is a Dweller doctor going to know how to treat our 'Topsider' injuries? If he rolls out here with a mechanic's outfit on and some wrenches, I'm out!" Adal protested as he and Arija sat alone in the doctor's office.

"And I'm telling *you* that if you act like a tool in front of the doctor who's only trying to help us, I will break the rest of your ribs," Arija said, trying to keep the stern look on her face. "We have to get checked out, Adal. We got our asses kicked back there. Besides, with everything we've seen, I'd think you could admit anything is possible here."

As soon as they'd reached the doctor's office inside Aparat, Webley had left Adal and Arija with Cog to return to the dock and help clean up the mess left behind from the fight. Once inside the office, Cog had left them alone to find the doctor and see what could be done about their injuries.

Adal's damaged ribs had kept him hunched over for most of the walk to the doctor, but the moments Arija had gasped, he'd pushed his head up and taken in what she'd seen. Now, sitting in the waiting room, his thoughts wandered to his grandfather and the coin. He wondered if maybe his grandfather knew of this place.

Movement in his peripheral brought Adal's attention back to his surroundings. "This place is like a doctor's office mixed with a mechanic's shop mixed with a museum," he said, looking around the room.

Arija couldn't have agreed more. The large room was dwarfed by the sheer number of items within it. Glass cases with jars of parts and things that looked like old-fashioned medical equipment. In a case near the door was what looked like an old brass and wood microscope. The wooden stand held a long brass barrel with a piece of curved glass at the top of it, almost like a child's kaleidoscope. A small rusted piece of metal bolted to the wooden base held a small glass slide with a metallic smear across it. On a counter near the microscope was a strange looking machine with plumes of smoke coming from a thin pipe at the top.

In the center of the room, a reclined chair reminded Arija of a dental chair with a large light attached to the chair and suspended a few feet above it. Beneath it ran several pipes and tubes that connected to various machines looming ominously nearby. Another twitching caught Adal's attention and

241

drew his eyes to a tray of tools a few feet away from the chair.

"What is that?" Arija asked, nudging Adal's shoulder and pointing to the tray. A severed arm of a Dweller twitched reflexively on the tray, its fingers stretching out as if calling for help before curling back into a fist. Several small tools protruded from an open panel on the forearm while a tube ran from where the elbow should be to a small machine with wires that periodically arced with electricity. Following each arc, every few seconds, one digit would twitch.

"I'm sure the doctor has all the appropriate credentials and training . . . to work on Frankenstein's monster," Adal muttered under his breath.

Arija shot him a warning look, and he laughed but immediately doubled over in pain as the laughter pressed on his broken ribs.

"That's what you get!" Arija said, stifling her own laughter. A bang from across the room echoed off the smooth metal walls, and Adal and Arija sat at attention searching the room. An eerily silent moment passed and gave way to relief as Cog appeared from behind one of the large machines.

"Sorry about the wait, you two. It took me a moment to find her. She was tending to a malfunction with one of her instruments."

"Oh *great*," Adal whispered so only Arija could hear. She didn't scold since she couldn't help but think the same thing. Hopefully, that wasn't a machine that the doctor planned on using to help them. Then again, they both wondered if any of the machines in the room could be used to help them.

"I know that this may all seem a bit strange to you, but please give her an opportunity," Cog began, making his way over to Adal. Before either of them could formulate a question of their own, another sound echoed through the room, and a Dweller woman appeared from behind the same instrument Cog had emerged from. A warm smile creased her bronze face as she walked over to them. The doctor.

Adal couldn't help but notice the doctor wore a waxed canvas mechanics apron, and his heart sped as he wondered what she was going to do to him. Adal and Arija shot one another a weary look and placed their fists on the arms of their chairs directly next to each other. They made three bumps with their fists; Arija's 'scissors' beat Adal's 'paper.'

"Shit!" he shot under his breath. Looks like he would be the guinea pig after all.

Her pants were tucked into large, leather boots, and under her apron, she wore an oil-stained white shirt with rolled-up sleeves that fluffed out from the sides. Adal noticed the shirt was clearly much too big for her small frame. Her hair was a mass of titanium formed into a tight bun with several twisted shavings creating a couple of stray curls that framed her face. Her cheeks were round with two small divots in the center that looked like dimples. A set of wire-rimmed glasses hung around her neck along with a unique leather choker that seemed to be crafted from old machine clockwork pieces bound by a bright-pink copper wire.

When she looked up, Adal noticed that her eyes were an unnaturally beautiful shade of blue. They shone like Aquamarine in her softened expression. He couldn't help but think if a robot could be beautiful, she would be.

243

Just as she stopped in front of them, Cog straightened his stance, his chest sticking out like a proud bird.

Aww. That's cute, Arija thought as she watched Cog trying to get the doctor's attention.

"Avani, these are the two Topsiders I was just telling you about," Cog sputtered, trying to keep his chest out while he spoke.

Adal picked up on the situation and snorted a laugh before wincing in pain from his ribs. "Smooth, boss."

"Why thank you, Cog. I would have never guessed," Avani teased, smiling and giving him a small wink. Avani was sweet and her voice soft. As she joked, Cog smiled an awkward half grin and laughed lightly, putting his hand on Adal's shoulder and trying to look casual.

"Hey. Ey EYYY!" Adal bellowed, his face scrunched in pain.

Cog's confident face turned down as he rubbed Adal's shoulder and said, "Oh, Adal, I am so sorry!" He pulled back, obviously not intending to cause pain, Cog only needed to find something to do with his hands other than nervously fumbling with them.

Avani bent over Adal, placing her hands on his shoulders softly and examined him.

"It looks as though you have taken some nasty hits. Let's see if we can get those taken care of, no? Please follow me to the examination chair." Avani motioned for Cog to help her move Adal, and the two of them slowly brought him to his feet. The adrenaline from the fight had thoroughly worn off, and Adal could feel every aching muscle and twisted bone in his body. As he rose, he shot a nervous look at Arija. She smiled and shook her head, making a scissor motion with her fingers. Adal grunted as Avani and Cog guided him across the room to the chair.

"Just relax. I promise I will take good care of you. Adal, is it?"

He nodded.

"Adal, my name is Avani. It is very nice to meet you." Avani adjusted the light above Adal's head so it didn't shine directly into his eyes. She fumbled with a tray of instruments out of sight, and Adal tried to twist so he could see what she was doing before the pain forced him to stop.

"So, uh, you've treated Topsiders before?" Adal asked, failing to hide the tremble in his voice. He jumped when Avani suddenly reappeared and stood over him, surveying his chest.

"Oh, absolutely!"

"Really?" Adal sighed a breath of relief.

"Not in the slightest," Avani giggled, letting her amusement dance at the edges of her mouth. The relief Adal had released was immediately sucked back in.

"Relax, Adal! I have studied Topsiders for a very long time," Avani continued through her amusement. "I am well aware of your 'unique' structures. Biological organisms are so sensitive. I promise I know precisely what I am doing." Avani reached over to a tray of instruments and produced a small hammer and hand saw. "Now, how do I remove your arms and legs again?"

Before he realized what he was doing, Adal panicked. Immediately two cold hands were holding

246

him down in the chair. For a quiet, soft-spoken Dweller, Avani was strong enough to keep him in the chair despite how hard he fought.

"Adal! Adal! Calm down, I am only kidding. Look, no tools. I am only examining you." Avani released him and waved her empty hands in the air.

Adal looked from her hands to the tray beside the chair then to Arija and Cog on the other side of the room. Cog was snickering while Arija doubled over, gasping for air as she tried to contain her laughter. Adal relaxed back into the chair.

"I'm glad you two are having a good time with this," he said before bringing his eyes back to the doctor. "So, you have jokes, huh?" he asked, his mouth slightly gaped and his tongue pressed to the inside of his cheek.

"One or two. I will say I generally don't get as much response from my patients as this. I think we can be friends." Avani held out her hand. Adal looked at her hand for a moment then smiled, shaking it.

"Yeah, you're all right, I guess. Seriously though, don't stick me with anything or break out those tools without warning me." Adal adjusted himself in the chair. Avani smiled, stepping away again for a moment and returned with a large black screen.

"Well, Adal, it looks like your endoskeletal structure may have taken some integrity damage. I will have to get an examination of your internal mechanics to better assess the situation." Avani wheeled the strange machine to the side of the chair and unlocked a retractable brass arm.

Adal's eyes widened as he thought about all the horribly painful things this weird contraption

247

could do to him. "Wait, you need to do what inside me?" he looked from the screen to the tools that sat just out of reach. Avani followed his gaze to the tools, then looked back to him and laughed.

"Relax, Adal. I am going to x-ray your chest and see if you have any broken parts unless you want me to open you up like I would do to a Dweller? Honestly, I *am* a doctor. Trust me when I say I mean you no harm."

Adal looked back to Arija, who was sitting on the edge of her seat as if watching her favorite show.

"Hey girl, you enjoying the show? This isn't an episode of Dr. Who, you know," he barked at her causing her to grace him with one of her smiles.

"Hey, she had to start somewhere. I'm just happy she got her fun out on you first!" Arija replied.

"Oh, do not worry, Arija. I have plenty of fun for you as well." Avani looked at Adal and winked. Arija's face went pale, and she slid back into her chair, suddenly not feeling like gawking. "Now, please remain still. I am going to turn this on and examine what is damaged. If you move, it will make it difficult for me to identify smaller injuries."

Adal nodded and tried to relax. Avani pulled the arms and extended the apparatus over Adal. The side that faced him was not the black surface he had seen as the machine was wheeled over. Instead, he looked at a dim reflection of himself in the silver metal at the back of the instrument. Avani aligned the device, placed a protective mat over his chest, and flipped a large switch on the side of the x-ray machine.

An immediate image appeared on the screen. Arija could see it from across the room and couldn't help but stand and walk over with Cog in tow. Avani inspected the image in an intense silence. As Arija approached, she could see the glowing blue image of Adal's skeletal structure. His bones moved slightly as he breathed, but aside from that, she could very well have been looking at a photograph of a skeleton.

"Ah, there they are!" Avani declared, pointing to the three lowest ribs on Adal's right side. Sure enough, as Arija and Cog leaned in to examine her findings, it was apparent that two of the ribs were completely broken, and his lowest rib was fractured.

Arija sucked in a breath, squinting as she looked at the screen. "Man, Adal, that looks like it hurts!" scanning her eyes over the rest of the image, she looked for any other breaks. Nothing. Avani must have come to the same conclusion because she stepped away from the screen nodding.

"I am so sorry that you were hurt so badly," Cog began, shaking his head. "I should have been there with you sooner. This is all my fault."

"Hey man, you had business to handle. This isn't on you. We chose to fight," Adal responded, trying to comfort the man. Adal wasn't in practice of allowing others to dictate his actions. He made his own choices and wasn't about to let Cog blame himself for his call.

"Adal is right, Cog, this wasn't your fault. It was our choice. These are our wounds." Arija placed her hand on Cog's shoulder.

"Thank you, both. I swear, this won't happen again with me around."

Avani moved to Adal's side holding a silver medical tray with a large syringe, a vial of some metallic liquid—maybe mercury, and an odd device that reminded Arija of a gun.

"What's all that for?" Adal asked, still not convinced Avani wasn't going to try to experiment on him.

Avani placed the tray on a stand and sat next to Adal. "You have two solid breaks in ribs eight and nine, and rib ten is fractured. I must mend them, or your internal injuries will worsen, and your pain will only increase. This is the only way I can fix that for you. Well, other than cutting you open, that is. I would prefer not to as I have no way of replacing your blood."

Adal rolled in his chair so he could glare at Arija. She gritted her teeth and shrugged at him, forming another 'scissor' with her fingers. Adal extended his middle finger causing Arija to slap his hand away.

"Calm down, Adal. If this is what we have to do to get you fixed, then this is what we have to do."

Adal relaxed into the chair, bringing his eyes back to Avani. "All right, what's the procedure?"

"It is simple, really, I promise. I inject you with this," Avani held up the vial of liquid metal, "then I use this device here," she raised the strange looking guns and showed Adal and Arija, "to guide the liquid to the location of the broken ribs. I will be watching the whole procedure on my screen here as the metal shows on this x-ray. Once it is in place, I pull the trigger and release a concentrated wave of energy that reacts only with this special mixture of mine. It will instantly harden and bridge the broken and fractured gaps." Avani's piercing eyes gleamed with excitement and pride as she walked the two Topsiders through the procedure.

Adal couldn't help the sinking feeling in the pit of his stomach. This was too weird. He shot one more nervous look at Arija who only shrugged in response. She was right, it's not like he had any other choice. It all seemed strange, but the basic theory was sound. Avani produced a large needle and inserted the tip into the vial of metallic liquid. As soon as Adal's eyes landed on the gargantuan needle, his head started to spin, and he gripped the arms of the chair as hard as he could to stop himself from passing out.

"Wait a minute! Did you get the biggest needle you had? You could just stab me with a freakin' pole, would be the same," Adal stuttered nervously.

Arija couldn't contain her laughter. "The big, bad Adalwolf Stein is scared of needles? You learn something new every day."

"I'm NOT scared of needles. But that thing? She might as well be holding an icepick!"

Avani looked at Arija and Cog, smiling and shaking her head.

"Adal, I have to do this. It's the only way I can set your breaks without physically opening you up. I promise this syringe is micro-sharpened and has been designed so you won't even feel it. This entire process won't take but a moment and you will feel worlds better." Avani's smile widened, and Adal thought she looked sincere. His face warmed, and he dropped his eyes to his lap. She was treating him like a toddler. At this rate, he wouldn't be surprised if she gave him a lollypop for being a "brave boy."

251

"Really? That sharp?" Arija asked, impressed with Avani's technology. Avani shot Arija a brief look as she widened her eyes and shrugged. That was the most obvious 'I dunno, I guess so' expression that Arija could imagine and suddenly, she was just as nervous as Adal. Though Avani seemed rather intelligent, she had a wit about her and a cavalier 'let's wing this' attitude that Arija would have admired if the woman hadn't been working on her best friend. Arija squeezed Adal's hand as Avani bent down and picked up a large, brass cone from the floor that was attached to a long, thick tube.

"I know what will help." The doctor brought the brass cone up to her lips and yelled, "Kip!" into it.

21

THE NAME'S KIP

A loud metallic squeaking filled the room, like the world's worst shopping cart.

In the corner of the room, a metallic ladder led up to a hatch like you would see in a submarine. The giant wheel in the center of the hatch spun in place and sounded like it hadn't been opened in sentries. Arija pressed the palms of her hands to her ears to dampen the screech. A sound like a vacuum seal being released echoed, and the hatch opened. A small Dweller boy dropped out of the hatch and slid down the ladder without stepping on any of the rungs. He landed with a loud 'clunk' on the floor at the bottom.

"The mobile clinic is almost up and running, mum. I just had to adjust the throttle and . . . WOW! TOPSIDERS!" Kip stopped mid-step as he spun around and noticed Adal sitting on the doctor's chair. He paused a moment and then ran over to Arija. He picked up her hand and ran his cold, small fingers across her skin.

Age wasn't really something that Webley and Cog had explained to them before, but if Arija had to take a guess, she would have said that Kip was about twelve or thirteen in human years. He had small rust-colored freckles on his smooth brass face and wore oversized grey pants held up by suspenders. Under the suspenders was an oversized white shirt with the sleeves rolled up just like Avani's. Kip dropped Arija's hand, removed his newsboy cap and lowered it to the ground as he bowed. "The name's Kip, miss," Kip said as he tossed his cap back onto his head and walked over to Adal. He leaned over the edge of the examination chair and slowly poked Adal in the arm.

"Hey kid, that's still a bit sore, bro!" Adal responded, wincing as Kip's finger jabbed at him.

"Wow, really? Neat!"

"Kip, focus. Our guests could use a boost after their day. Would you mind terribly retrieving some coffee that we got from Webley? I think the warm drink will do you both some good and relax your muscles. Webley roasts the best beans!" Avani nodded toward Kip and then toward the door she had entered earlier.

"All right, mum. I can do that!" Kip turned on his heels and sprinted to the back of the room, disappearing behind the clutter of machines.

"Is Kip your son?" Arija asked.

"Yes. Kip was orphaned as a baby, and I decided the world was too cold for such an innocent thing to be alone like that. So, I took him in and have been teaching Kip all I know ever since. He is a great kid." Avani offered a smile as if she were remembering a lifetime of wonderful memories. Adal had a flash of his father and wished he was as soft and

254

chill as Avani. The only memories Adal had of his father were of him pushing him and being hard on him for no reason. Adal was a smart guy, but nothing was ever good enough for his dad.

"Mobile clinic?" Cog asked as he turned his attention to Avani, a skeptical look on his normally smooth face.

"Yes, my mobile clinic. Why shouldn't those that live out in the Machine get the same medical treatment as those that live in the city? That flying cart will allow me to do so. Kip has really come along, and it is impressive what he has done with it. You should see it sometime. Maybe I can take you for a ride." Avani pressed on Adal's chest, aligning the broken bones with her fingers.

"I, uh, would like that . . . I think . . ." Cog sputtered.

Arija looked at him, a small smile on her lips. If Cog could blush, he would almost certainly be doing so. It was sort of cute the way Cog fell apart when Avani was around.

Avani pressed on Adal's ribs again eliciting a grunt of pain. She aimed the large needle directly at his chest.

"Hey, shouldn't that go into my arm or something?" Adal stuttered, stalling.

"Not at all. I don't want this in your bloodstream. Too difficult to guide the metal where I need it. I'm going to inject it directly into your chest cavity. Like this."

Before Adal could reply, Avani stabbed the needle into his chest and pressed down on the plunger. Every drop of the liquid metal flowed from

255

the reservoir, disappearing into Adal. He gritted his teeth in discomfort, but Adal soldiered through the injection better than Arija thought he would.

Cog nudged Arija, pointing at the screen. As soon as the metallic fluid entered Adal's chest, it appeared as a blue-white substance on the x-ray. It beaded and spread inside his chest. Arija felt her heart begin to race as she watched the metal seep into every crevice and around his lungs.

"Dr. Avani . . . The liquid is going all over. Is that normal?" she asked, concerned. Adal looked at Arija, and she squeezed his hand. At the moment, she knew she was far more terrified than Adal could have been, and she was happy he couldn't see the face she was making.

"Relax, my dear. You will see," she insisted, finishing the injection and retrieving the gun from the tray along with three small disks.

Kip returned with a tray of four cups and a metal pot of coffee. He nearly spilled the entire tray as he hurriedly put it down on a small table next to the waiting chairs and ran back over to watch the screen like a kid missing his favorite TV show.

"Wow! That's what your insides look like? Where are all the gears?" he asked, squeezing between Cog and Arija.

Avani giggled but didn't answer him. She turned the screen to improve her view and placed the three small disks on Adal's chest, one over each break. The spreading of the metal over Adal's insides ceased, and as if being called to attention the liquid slowly began to retract.

Each bead of metal moved toward the areas where Avani had placed the disks. Like a magnet pulling on the metal, the liquid pooled over Adal's broken ribs. Avani then produced her gun and lined the tip of the barrel with the first magnet. Once she had everything in place, she pulled the trigger, and a dim flash of light emitted from the barrel of the gun. The liquid instantly solidified around the bone. She moved the gun from one disk to the next. In under a minute, Adal's ribs had a thin coat of metal over them, the broken and fractured areas nowhere to be seen.

"Wow! That was cool!" Kip announced stepping around the side of the screen to Adal. "Can we break something else and do it again?"

"Hell no!" Adal barked, sitting up in his seat.

"Really? Aww man, no fun! How do you feel?" Kip asked, poking at Adal's ribs with one small, curious finger.

"Actually . . . better." Adal rubbed his hand over his chest and smiled.

Arija was in shock. She couldn't believe it worked.

"Fantastic! I am glad to hear that. You will still be sore for a little while. There isn't much I can do to reduce the bruising, but the bones won't be breaking again any time soon! Now, as for the rest of you . . ."

Much to Kip's pleasure, Avani spent the next hour performing the same procedure for several other areas, mostly in Adal's hands from the haymaker slug he'd thrown at Fausto.

After a while, the pain of the procedure and the general discomfort subsided, and Adal and Arija found themselves talking and laughing with Kip. Adal sipped his coffee, listening to the barrage of questions that came from the curious boy.

"What's the Topside like? Do you guys have a Webley too? What sort of machines are there? Can you show me?" Kip fired out questions quicker than Adal and Arija could answer them.

"All right, Kip. I think it's time you went back to working on the mobile clinic, don't you?" Avani stood from her seat and gave Adal one final check.

"Awe, can't I stay?" Kip pleaded as he slouched his shoulders.

"Kip, I need you working on the clinic. The Topsiders will be in the Machine for a while. You will have other opportunities to hang out with them. Now go. We need to have that thing functioning as soon as possible." Avani waived her hand at Kip, who sighed and slowly trudged back to the stairs.

"Hey, when you guys are all done, you should come up and see it. It's really neat!"

"Kip, I'm sure they would enjoy seeing it later. For now, I must finish," Avani said as she crossed her arms in a motherly manner. Kip sighed and disappeared through the hatch, leaving it open.

"See? That wasn't so bad now, was it?" Arija said as she reached a hand out to Adal, helping him sit up in the chair.

"You got jokes too? Well, keep it up, because it's your turn in the chair now!" Adal laughed as he hopped from the seat and broadly gestured to the chair like he was presenting a prize.

"I, uh, think I'm all set. Just a few bumps. Nothing that really needs any medical help." Arija put both hands in the air as she slowly backed away from the chair.

"Oh no, 'man up,' remember? Or are you going to admit that I can handle more than you?"

258

Adal knew the buttons to push just as she did. She glared at him and turned up her nose, hopping into the seat.

"Ah, Miss Arija. Let's have a look at you." Avani began her assessment of Arija's injuries. Fortunately for Arija, there weren't any broken bones, but Avani did note the nasty hit she'd taken on her head needed mending.

"Well, we can stitch that right up!" Avani immediately produced another large needle and a spool of thick thread from her apron. "This will only take a moment."

"Uh, sorry, but do you have something that isn't so, well, large? I've had stitches before, and that thread looks more like a rope!"

Avani paused for a moment and examine her tools. "Well, I suppose I could do something else. I had read of your stitching measures, but I wasn't aware of a size standard. My apologies for that. Still should be an easy fix." Avani shuffled over to one of the glass cabinets and produces a small jar with a sludgy brown liquid inside.

"This is an adhesive. I use it to bind the leather aesthetics to the Toppers that come in. Should do just as well here. It's made organically from sap. Shouldn't cause you any issues." Avani turned on the light above Arija's head to look at the wound. Adal stepped behind the chair to get his own look, happy that finally, it wasn't him being poked and prodded.

"No worries, Arija. Shouldn't be too bad. Man, that's a bad gash. Looks like that would easily need a few stitches. Nothing wrong with being held together with glue. Might make styling your hair easier to be sticky anyway," Adal teased.

"Hey, you're the vain one here!" Arija barked. Avani pressed on Arija's side and slowly rolled her to face away so she may better access the slice on her scalp.

"You know, it may be better if we just shave off all of this hair. Easier to get to the wound," Avani parted Arija's hair, but the smile on her lips betrayed her. She pressed hard on the wound, closing the gash and holding the skin together. Arija didn't reply, she just scoffed with a 'you just try it' expression.

With the flesh clenched into place, Avani applied a thin layer of the brown paste to the wound. Arija winced as the cold sensation raced down her neck and the gash in her head started to throb. With teeth clenched so tightly she was sure she would chip her tooth, Arija glared at Adal, squeezing his hand but refusing to show more pain than he had. Avani grabbed the same gun she'd used on Adal, and lit up Arija's scalp, instantly hardening the glue.

"All done!" Avani announced, releasing Arija's hair. "Now, same thing goes for you as well. This will be sore for a little while. Just take it easy and try not to re-injure yourself. I am not entirely sure what other broken things on you two I can successfully fix without removing them and replacing them with parts I have lying around my shop."

Adal and Arija looked at one another, mirror expressions of horror covering their faces.

"So, what are the plans for the rest of the day? Will you be tending to the docks?" The mood drastically changed when Avani mentioned the battle. With everything that had happened and all the anxiety about being experimented on, Adal and Arija had momentarily forgotten about what put them there in the first place. Cog frowned and shook his head.

"Webley went back to help clean that up and work with the rescuers in bringing in the injured. He insisted I get these two to you and see that they are taken care of, then he wanted me to show them around the city. Honestly, I would much rather be there helping. No offense." Cog turned and nodded towards Adal and Arija.

"Let's all go back there and help! We don't mind, really. It's the right thing to do," Arija interjected.

"Seriously, we should be there helping anyway," Adal added.

"No, I must honor what Webley wanted. He doesn't want you wrapped up in that sort of mess. What caused all those deaths is the one sickness we have not been able to purge from the Machine. Believe me, Webley would be ashamed if you went back to help," Cog replied.

"Well, why don't I help? You can still take them around the city, and I will make sure that Webley gets on all right." Avani offered.

"No, I couldn't let you do that, really." Cog apologized, placing one timid hand on her shoulder and then quickly removing it.

"Why don't you both go?" Adal added.

"Yes! We'll be fine. Honestly, what else can happen? You two go on," Arija hopped off the chair and grabbed Adal's hand.

"Well, how about this then: Cog, you and I will go back to the docks and give any help we can.

261

Adal and Arija, perhaps I can ask Kip . . ." Avani hadn't the chance to finish her thought when Kip leaped from the open doorway and slid down the latter.

"I can show them around the city!" Kip shouted enthusiastically, not caring if they knew he'd been eavesdropping.

"Look, I appreciate the gesture, but after a day like this, really, perhaps this isn't the best idea. I . . . uhh . . . I think." Cog broke away, glancing at Avani for reassurance.

Adal and Arija both locked on to him with the same expressions. Their eyes bugged wide, and their heads cocked to one side. Cog studied them in confusion for a moment before Arija motioned toward Avani with her eyes. She was busy cleaning up and putting her tools away.

"No, really. We'll be fine," Arija insisted, punctuating each word as she tried to get a silent message to Cog. This was a lot easier when she was communicating with Adal.

"Yeah, really. Kip has us covered," Adal added, pointing toward Avani and then back to Cog as if saying "GO WITH HER." Cog looked blankly at them, not understanding their cryptic messages. Avani stopped picking up and turned to address Cog.

"You see, Cog. They will be just fine. Besides, we can be more effective if it's just us. I mean no offense to the two of you, but this sort of thing is best left to us. We have our own processes and ways of dealing with situations like this. We are very lucky that, due to the response of the Watch, most of the damage was only to transport crafts and other structures. The loss of life was minimal."

"So, can we be off then?" Kip took a few steps toward the door, looking between Avani and the Topsiders.

"Yes, go on ahead. Just be careful and keep an eye on them, Kip. Don't go on one of your little adventures. This has been a trying day for all of us, I am sure of it. Cog, if you would help me put these things away, we can be off too."

22

The Way the World Works

They weren't more than five minutes from the shop when Adal began to question his decision to be led around the city by Kip. As they attempted to take in everything about them, the two new-to-towners were subjected to a hyper-active Dweller child making their ability to sightsee nearly impossible.

"This is the place. Isn't it neat? Bet you haven't seen a place like Aparat before, have you?" Kip walked several feet ahead but turned so he was walking backward, keeping his attention on Adal and Arija. Every so often, Kip would unknowingly bump into someone trying to get around him, and a barrage of curses would be heard as the young child tried to apologize to the busy Dwellers.

Adal and Arija had never had so many people

pause from their daily lives and examine them before. Several Dwellers even stopped mid-step and gaped at them. Arija was quickly finding out that she really hated being the center of attention, but Adal couldn't have been enjoying himself more. Kip picked up on Arija's discomfort and drew the attention back to him.

"Hey, if your eyes are broken, I can fix those for you!" he shouted at a Dweller couple that were so busy staring they wouldn't move out of the way to let the group pass. Adal cracked a smile as Kip shooed the couple away and then turned a smiling face back to him. Kip was confident with an attitude that reminded Adal of someone he knew.

Arija, being so uncomfortable with all the gawking, focused her attention on examining every part of Aparat. She was itching to stop dead in her tracks and sit on the ground, drawing the city as it presented itself to her.

"So, did Webley build all this?" Adal asked, bringing Arija's attention back to the group. "I mean, how long could this have taken?"

"I have no idea, but there's no way he did all this without help," she added.

"We all build this place!" Kip interjected, tripping over a stack of papers as they passed what looked like a newsstand. The older Dweller that occupied the stand shouted at them as they passed but the group didn't heed him any mind.

"Damnit, Kip! You wreck my papers, and I am sending Avani a bill!" the owner shouted, not even paying attention to Adal and Arija.

"Yeah yeah, put it on my tab, Mr. Nuts!" Kip waved the vendor off.

"That's Mr. Naught, you little shit!"

Adal shot the newsstand owner a look, and the old Dweller fell silent and sat back down in his seat.

"Hey, Kip, we appreciate the tour, but could you please try to not draw so much attention to us?" Arija asked as softly as she could.

"You two stick out like a broken gear," Kip said between bouts of laughter. "Believe me, you aren't sticking out because of me!"

Adal couldn't help himself but snort. "Shit, you said it, man!"

Kip let out a proud grin, and Adal clapped his hand on the top of Kip's head, smashing his newsboy cap into his hair and ruffling the short strands.

"Great, I already have to deal with one of you, don't you go corrupting Kip!" Arija sighed, hopping over a large puddle that Adal failed to notice. Adal pulled his sopping wet foot out of the puddle, cursing as he shook the water from it.

"Ha! Sorry about that! Those puddles can be tricky. I would have driven you around the city, but mum took my driving privileges." Kip shrugged like it was the most normal thing for a child to say.

"Wait a minute, Kip. Are you telling me you can drive? Aren't you a little young?" Adal broke in, remembering the huge fight he'd had with his father about getting his permit last year.

"Oh yeah, I can drive anything. In fact, that's how mum found me. She was out in the Machine one day, and I tried to steal her car. In my defense, she left the keys in it." Kip stepped backward into a large cart, spilling a small bag of oranges to the ground.

"Hey, kid! Watch where you're going! You're going to pay for those if they're bruised!" the owner of the cart shouted without dropping the cigarette from his mouth.

"All right, Kip. You need to slow down and relax. This place is amazing, but maybe it would be better if we got to see it without angering everyone in the city?" Arija suggested.

"Ha! Don't worry about these guys. Most of the people on this street are either Toppers or Bours. They all have their head up their own cans." Kip justified.

"Bours?" Adal cocked his head to the side and scrunched his eyebrows together.

"Yeah, you guys have a lot of different names for Dwellers. What do they all mean?" Arija added.

Kip stopped in his tracks and leaned against the side of a building. Wire silhouettes displayed ornate clothing in the shop window next to him. A deep burgundy gown with black and gold lace and a thick black corset top hung in the window, and Arija wondered how much a dress like that would cost and what they used as currency down here.

"Ok, so here's the story: You already know we are called Dwellers. Well, there are different kinds of Dwellers depending on where you live. There are three types . . . okay, there are technically four, but no one even recognizes the fourth one." Kip shifted so that his foot was planted against the side of the dress shop and his arms were crossed over his chest. "There's the Toppers. The wealthy assholes that like to go around pretending they're better than everyone else because they think they look like Topsiders. There's the Bours. Those guys are below the Toppers. They are all the workers and 'normal' Dwellers you

267

see everywhere. Truth be told, without them, I'm not entirely sure this place would keep going. Below the Bours are the Desps. They live in the crevices of the city or in small settlements in the Machine. Everyone pretty much looks down on the Desps. The Toppers see them as a bunch of criminals, useless machines, and a general plight on their perfect city, but I grew up as a Desp before Avani took me in. They aren't all bad, they just . . . it's a tough life out there for the Desps."

"So, this is like your class system then?" Arija asked.

"Yeah, I suppose you can call it that. Though some of them have no class at all," Kip joked, snorting.

"What about the fourth group?" Adal moved to lean against the building next to Kip. "You said that technically there was a fourth group. Who are they and where do they fall?"

"Oh, right. The fourth group is called the Radix. These people were the first. The founding Dwellers made by Webley himself. There are only a handful of them, but because they were all handmade by Webley. They are held in higher respect, have special abilities gifted to each one, and they all serve a much higher calling than the rest of the Dwellers. You ask me, the Radix are the top of the top. The Toppers are no better than the Desps that they hate if you ask me. The only difference is their money. Without that, the Toppers would be the scum they accuse the Desps of being."

"Oh, wow. So, there's a whole class of Dwellers made specifically by Webley? Do you know any of them?" Adal asked.

"Ha, sure do! Let's see, there's Cog, Captain Silny, my mum, of course, and a few more you haven't met yet."

"Wait a minute. If Webley made this place and only made a handful of Dwellers, how do you guys make more?" Adal couldn't help but ask. In part, he imagined a sort of large factory with giant machines pumping out Dwellers and one guy at the end just putting batteries in them.

"Well, uh, that's kind of a personal question, don't you think?" Kip started.

"Oh," Adal responded, as he realized exactly what he just asked their young tour guide. Kip paused a moment as if trying to figure out the right way to explain the reproduction of his species.

"We make more by assembly," Kip finally said.

Arija punched Adal in the arm. Even though she'd been wondering the same thing, she would have never considered asking something so embarrassing to someone so young.

"Assembly?" Adal continued, ignoring the pain in his arm. Yeah, it was a strange thing to ask a kid, but the word "Assembly" made it seem like maybe it wasn't as intimate as it was for humans. Adal was wrong.

"Yes. OK, so here's how THAT happens: each Dweller male is made with a singular key. That key is housed in the index finger of his right hand. Each Dweller female has a keyhole just over where her heart is. When two Dwellers decide they want to, uhh, have a baby, the male inserts his key into the female's heart. The key detaches from the male and

269

disassembles in her heart, becoming the basis of what will grow and develop into a baby Dweller. Any other questions?" Kip was staring at the ground kicking a small rock.

Adal opened his mouth, but Arija jabbed him in the side, forgetting about his bruised ribs. She needed him to stop asking the kid so many awkward questions.

Adal gasped at the hit and rubbed his sore ribs, shooting her an evil look. "All right, never mind then. Kip, let's get going."

"Yeah! Sure thing! Hey, do you guys want to see something REALLY cool?" Kip asked, looking up and down the street.

"Yeah, why not," Arija agreed.

"Lead on, kid," Adal motioned up the street.

Kip was more than grateful for the change in subject. He pushed off the wall and jogged several feet ahead, stopping at the mouth of an alleyway. He looked down the passage, then back to Adal and Arija. A grin stretched so widely across his small face that Arija could almost hear his metallic cheeks creaking.

"It's this way. Just follow my lead and play it cool. They know me but don't really like outsiders. Don't worry, I'll vouch for you, so it'll be fine." Kip turned and made his way down the alley.

"Adal, I swear to God . . ." Arija began, shaking her head.

"Relax. I got this. I'll keep Kip on track," Adal assured, chasing after the small Dweller. Arija sighed and followed. As soon as they made the turn down the alley, Adal paused to give himself a moment to take it all in. Dim, yellow lights ran the length of the brick walls of the surrounding shops. A large assortment of indescribable machinery and trash cluttered the path, making the alley nearly unpassable. What could be found down an abandoned alley that could be *cool?*

Kip was already halfway down the street, climbing over what looked like a pile of junk. Adal could feel Arija's glare boring into the back of his head. "I know, I know. Let's just keep lookout," he replied without turning to acknowledge her.

23

HAZARD DICE

Arija glared at the back of Adal's head as he walked. She squinted, trying with everything she had to set his head on fire with her thoughts. They had just barely survived the fight with Fausto, and here they were off on another adventure to God knows where as though none of it had happened. There was a sinking feeling in her gut like she'd swallowed a boulder. This wasn't going to end well.

Adal stopped, and Arija peered around him to see what was going on. They had caught up to Kip, but a large mound of discarded trash and metal parts two-stories high blocked their way. The feeling in Arija's stomach deepened. They were trapped. She sucked in a shallow breath, opening her mouth to suggest they go back the way they came, but before she could say anything, Kip motioned to the brick wall of the building next to them. A crudely drawn pair of dice was etched into one of the bricks.

"That's how you know where they are." Kip's small voice bounced off the walls and the pile of trash making it sound louder than it actually was. Without going into any further detail, Kip walked to the scrap pile and lifted a tarp that hung to one side. Beneath it was an opening that led into the pile. He turned and waved for Arija and Adal to follow. Arija gave a cautious glance to the empty alley behind her and then followed Kip and Adal into the opening.

Past the blockade, Dwellers walked in masses about the narrow alley. It was like stepping into a new world. Lights were strewn about haphazardly, tables were packed with Dwellers talking and eating, there were vendors peddling goods, and what sounded like a loud mixture of rock and opera music was playing.

"What?" Adal turned to look back at the blockade. "How? Why . . . uhh, why didn't we hear any of this on the other side of the tarp? We were just ten feet away and nothing."

Kip gave a silent laugh. "Disruptors," he said as if it were the simplest thing in the world. "How else could we do that? It keeps the local crowd and curious walkers away. Best part, most flat-foots won't even come down the alley. This place is a secret. It's where I go to have fun when I'm not working on mum's machines." Kip dogged the other Dwellers in the

273

crowd effortlessly, but Arija was not as lucky. As she walked, slack-jawed and curious, she bumped into virtually everyone and everything that crossed her path.

"I'm not sure we should be here." Arija eyed a group of Dweller men who looked like they could be serial killers, beating the crap out of another Dweller with bent up pieces of metal. Everywhere she looked, men seemed to be gambling, drinking from large copper mugs, and any time a Dweller thought someone else was looking at them funny, another fight would break out.

"Yeah, I'm not sure about this one either. I feel like the kid just took us to a members only biker club," Adal added as he stepped around a Dweller passed out in the middle of the walkway.

"Are you guys coming or what? The fun stuff is up here," Kip said as he disappeared from sight around a corner. Adal looked at Arija for confirmation. She had suddenly become hyperaware and was eyeing everything with a skeptical stare. She glanced at Adal and then tapped the side of her face by her eye. Adal gave her a curt nod, understanding that she wanted him to stay alert. As they rounded the corner, Adal was stopped by a small metallic hand to his stomach.

"Mother—" Adal gasped, bending at the waist.

Arija couldn't help it, and she let out a small laugh as she patted him on the back. "Whaddya learn?" she teased, grabbing Adal by the shoulder and pulling him upright.

"Sorry, I didn't want you to interrupt the game! They don't appreciate it much if you throw off their rolls. Back Slangers are very particular about how they roll the dice." Kip pointed to a group of Dwellers all kneeling in a circle. In the center of the circle were several small piles of gold coins. Each of the coins had the anvil and hammer seal engraved into its face.

One Dweller was viciously jiggling his hand and kissing the tops of his knuckles. "My main will be eight. Come on baby. My main will be eight." He threw the dice across the circle, and everyone leaned in to see what he rolled. Adal tilted his head and tried to see what they landed on, but he could tell by the Dweller's reaction that it wasn't what he wanted. "DAMN!" the Dweller punched his fist into the concrete, a small crack appeared where he hit.

"That's number three, you lose!" barked another Dweller as he snatched up the dice. The sore loser rose from his spot and shouted further obscenities before stomping away.

"What are they playing?" Adal asked as he watched the losing Dweller disappear down the alley.

"Hazard Dice. It's a fun game once you get the hang of it. I never lose," Kip proudly puffed out his chest. Not being able to help themselves, Adal and Arija inched closer to the circle of gamblers as the crowd began to energize and a new player picked up the dice. Several other spectators did the same and crowded around Adal and Arija, pushing them closer to the circle.

"So, how do you play?" Adal turned back to ask Kip, but the kid was gone. "Kip?"

"Where'd he go?" Arija asked, concern pouring from her voice. She swiveled her head from side to side looking for their tour guide, but the crowd of Dwellers had almost doubled now that a new player was in the circle. This wasn't the sort of place she wanted to be lost in. A burst of cheers made Arija flinch, and she momentarily turned her attention back to the game.

Several of the gamblers were scooping up their chips and stepping back as a Dweller entered the ring holding Kip by the scruff of his collar. He was smaller than most of the other Dwellers they'd seen with slender features that reminded Adal of a teenaged boy. Once everyone's attention was on the newcomer, he threw Kip to the ground in the center of the circle.

"Look what I found, fellas! The little rodent has come back to play! Didn't I warn you what would happen if you didn't stay away from here, little rodent?" The teenaged Dweller snarled as he spoke like he'd smelled something disgusting. Kip tried to stand, but the Dweller only kicked him back to the ground again with the tip of his black leather boot.

"Let it go, Lupo! I won those games fair and square!" Kip shouted, adjusting his cap as he was finally able to stand.

"Fair my ass! You cheated! You know it, I know it, everyone knows it. You always cheat! I told you if you ever drug yourself back to my alley I would break you down piece by piece until you're nothing but a pile of scrap! Guess that's what you want since you're back here like the dumbass you are." Lupo reached for Kip, only to be kicked in the shin. He howled in pain and rubbed his leg.

"You little shit! I'm gonna break you down into so many pieces, even your whore of a mother won't be able to put you back together!" Lupo grabbed Kip by his collar, yanking him into the air.

"Put the kid down!" Adal pushed through the crowd followed by Arija and stepped into the circle. The previously cheering crowd suddenly fell silent as the Topsiders faced off with the bully.

"Topsiders! What the hell are they doing here?"

"They are my friends!" Kip choked out, trying and failing to swing his legs and kick at Lupo.

"Hey! I said drop the kid, or I'll drop you. Not going to repeat that, asshole!" Adal took several steps into the center of the circle, his fists clenched, and his jaw extended out as he scowled.

Arija was right behind him, surveying the crowd and assessing who and what could be a possible threat. Adal usually had tunnel vision when he got into confrontations, so it was up to Arija to keep an eye on their surroundings. She had to make sure he didn't get them into more trouble than he could handle.

As they neared Lupo and Kip, a fat gold-colored Dweller stepped out from the crowd and stood next to Lupo. He wore green leather overalls ripped up one leg and covered in mysterious black stains. His tungsten hair stuck out of the top of his head like a patch of neatly cut metallic grass and covering one hand was a small patch of stretched leather skin the color of the setting sun.

A sound caught Arija's attention, and as she glanced over her shoulder, she saw two more Dwellers step into the circle. Adal continued toward Lupo and his friend, completely oblivious to the other two Dwellers that had entered the ring behind him.

Arija focused her attention on the newcomers, blocking the distance between them and Adal. One was taller with short cobalt hair and a white leather vest left open revealing his smooth cobalt chest. His long wiry legs were covered in thick black leather and stuck out of a torso that seemed too short for his size. The other Dweller was more Arija's size with thick, black-rimmed glasses on a round bronze face. He grabbed the edges of his brown leather pants and hiked them up, adjusting his belt and tucking in his shirt. One of his arms was completely covered in stretched leather and crudely pinned to itself. The golden brown fake skin was too tight in some areas and too loose in others like a back-alley facelift, and Arija cringed at the sight.

"Oh! A Topsider with a sense of humor! Why don't you mind your business? This is between me and this worthless little shit!" Lupo shook Kip, the kid swinging like a rag doll under the bully's grip.

"Last time. Put the kid down," Adal commanded.

The tall Dweller and the one with glasses took a simultaneous step toward Arija, looking past her to their leader like she wasn't there.

"Not the best decision, boys. If I were you, I wouldn't pick this fight . . . but if you insist, you'll have to go through me first." Arija clenched her teeth as she grinned, positioning her weight on to the balls of her feet.

"Remember, you can't punch them," Adal whispered to Arija without turning his head to look at her.

"Elias. Coffee shop," she replied, bringing a smile to Adal's face. He knew exactly what she meant, he would handle Lupo, and she would take out his friends. Lupo took another look at Adal and Arija, growled through his teeth, and then threw Kip to the ground.

"Split, kid. Get out of here." Adal waved his hand at Kip who stood and backed away to the edge of the crowd.

"No, stay. When we're done with your friends, we'll get to you, I promise." Lupo looked over his shoulder at the young Dweller and winked. Kip spat at the ground in attempted bravado.

"Beat it, Kip!" Adal bellowed. Kip jumped in place, and then slowly slunk away into the crowd, vanishing from sight. Once he was sure Kip was gone, Adal turned his attention back to Lupo.

"So, Topsiders here to save the day, eh? Isn't that cute." Lupo slowly walked in a circle around Adal, his face scrunched up like the cocky teenager he was. His smile was two gnarled rows of crooked teeth, several covered in rust.

"What do you say we make an example of these Topsiders and find a better use for them?" Lupo posed to his crew who all grunted their approval.

Arija felt her muscles tighten as the two Dwellers in front of her began to bob in place, preparing to attack. They shifted their weight onto the tips of their toes and hunched down, leaning slightly in her direction. Arija tried to hide the smile that lingered at the edges of her mouth. Telegraphing. She knew exactly what their next move would be, and she was prepared.

"Look, man, this doesn't have to go this way," Adal was saying, trying to end the fight before it began.

"Oh, excuse me! I thought we were having a nice conversation here. Do all Topsiders have such an attitude? Maybe spending some time with the Toppers will change your perspective. Or, rather, as a Topper," Lupo laughed, a wicked, throaty sound that made Adal want to cough.

The group around them waited in silence to see what would happen next. Not a single Dweller moved as the scene unfolded. Arija kept glancing at the crowd, scanning for any other possible threats, but she didn't want to pull her eyes away from Legs and Glasses.

"Want to run us by that one more time?" Arija joined the conversation, bouncing her eyes between the two Dwellers in front of her and the crowd.

"Oh, the female speaks! Let's hope she's more entertaining than her male counterpart. One thing that makes me so good at what I do is that when I see an opportunity, I never pass it up. Some may see you two as pests. Two ignorant Topsiders walking around the Machine and sticking their noses into everyone's business. Me? I see a business opportunity." Lupo took a step sideways towards Arija.

"Don't touch her, or it will be the last thing you do!" Adal growled.

"Oh, are you going to protect your mate? How quaint," Lupo said, but he retreated the step anyway.

"It's not me you should worry about," Adal added. "I wouldn't piss her off if you value your extremities."

Lupo looked from Adal to Arija and then back to Adal again, trying to figure out what exactly he was trying to do.

"As I said . . ." Lupo continued, "I don't miss out on an opportunity. Looking at you two, I see a fortune I need to cash in on. Can you fellas imagine the bit some Toppers would pay to replace their fake leather skin with a full, real Topsider skin suit?"

The hair on the back of Adal's neck stood at attention, and his muscles went rigid as he fought the urge to drive his fist into Lupo's face. Arija broke her gaze briefly from the two Dwellers and looked over her shoulder to Adal, her eyebrows knit together and a sour taste in her mouth. This definitely wasn't going to end well.

Lupo walked over to Adal who stood like a statue, his fists so tightly clenched that his knuckles popped. The Dweller leaned in until their chests were touching and ran his long finger across Adal's cheek. "Think of the bits I'll get with real Topsider skin."

"Look asshat, you need to stop this. I'm not warning you, I'm telling you. You don't want to go down this road." Adal knocked Lupo's hand away and tilted his head, pointing his chin at him. He raised his hands, pushing at the air between the two and signaling for the Dweller to back up.

Lupo took this gesture as fear, but Adal knew you never get into a fight with your hands down.

"Oh, what a rich ideal. The fact is, there's nothing you can do to stop me. If I say you're just parts, then you're just parts. That's how it works out here." Lupo extended a thin finger and jabbed it into Adal's right shoulder.

Adal took a deep breath and stepped back. He was going to enjoy kicking this guy's ass.

"What's the matter, Topsider? The reality of your situation sinking in. Feeling beaten already?" Lupo joked, laughing and nodding to his lackeys.

Adal slowly shook his head. "No, it's not that. I just really don't want to get stuck with that damn needle again." Adal looked over to Arija, who rolled her eyes.

"You . . . what?" Lupo looked between Adal and Arija, confusion covering his metallic features. Before he could react, Adal reared back and thrust his right leg into Lupo's chest. A metal crunch rang out as Lupo's face fell blank from surprise and he stumbled backward into his friend who still stood behind him.

Taking the opportunity, Legs and Glasses lunged at Arija. She expected it and charged lower toward their legs. Using their body weight against them, Arija flipped them over her shoulders, and they landed with a hard metallic 'thunk' on the ground behind her. She pivoted on her toes and dove at Legs.

The Dweller next to Lupo charged at Adal, and he flinched, throwing a powerful right hook out of reflex. A sharp metallic 'ping' echoed off the walls of the alley as Adal's fist made contact with the Dweller's face, creating a small dent in the teen's cheek. Adal looked at his balled-up fist with wide eyes.

"Now that's what I'm talkin' about!" he shouted as he stepped toward the staggered attacker, hands at the ready. The metallic mixture Avani had injected into his hands to fix his broken bones had made them immensely powerful and resilient. He was finally on an even playing field with the Dwellers. This was going to be fun. The Dweller stumbled back, running his shaking fingers across the dent in his cheek.

24

OFF WITH THEIR SKIN

Arija gained purchase over Legs and interlocked her legs with his, twisting them about. She applied leverage to the top of his foot and wrenched it backward. The Dweller shouted in pain as small creaks, cracks, and pops came from his ankle and leg.

"Looks like you won't have a leg to stand on," Arija grunted to herself. She snickered at her own pun as another 'pop' echoed from the Dweller's leg.

"Really?" Adal scoffed, ducking a follow-up volley of enraged swings from Lupo and his follower.

"Mind your own business!" Arija shot back as Glasses got to his feet. He stalked over to her and kicked her in the side of the face. Arija's world spun and as she let go of the other Dweller she felt herself being dragged across the ground. She reached up and grabbed both of his arms and used her weight to pull him down to her level. Arija locked his wrists and flipped her feet into the air, pressing them against the Dweller's throat. Glasses gasped and grabbed for her feet as he was forced forward.

"I'll kill you both and then skin you alive!" shrieked Lupo as he desperately swung at Adal who ducked under the flurry of strikes and brought his right fist up under Lupo's chin, sending him sprawling backward. In the shuffle, the second Dweller rushed in, forcing Adal to punch at him with his left hand. A dull thud followed by a burning pain shook Adal. That hand was still all skin and bone.

"Daaaaaaaaamnit!" Adal shouted, recovering and swinging his right hand at his attacker, but he was distracted by the pain, and the swing went wide. The Dweller collided with Adal's waist, thrusting him back as the two fell to the ground in a twisted pile of man and machine.

Adal's skull collided with the hard ground, the ringing in his head unbearable. In a fit of desperation, he blindly swung his right arm upward, and it connected with his attacker's left eye.

Arija lay on the concrete with her feet stretched over her head, still pressed against Glasses' throat. She wanted to go to Adal, but she couldn't let go of Glasses, or he would crush her face with the weight of his body. Legs had crawled away to the edge of the crowd, nursing his broken appendages, but Glasses just wouldn't quit.

As Arija shifted her weight to position the Dweller's arm behind his back, he was able to free himself and grab her by the throat. "I . . . don't . . . think . . . so," she gasped, pressing her foot into his chest and thrusting outward. The Dweller's grip weakened just enough for her to grab all the fingers on his left hand and yank them backward. The sounds of them breaking reminded her of snapping twigs, and Arija cringed. He shouted and released Arija, reflexively bringing his other hand to his broken fingers. She took this moment to plant the heel of her boot into his jaw, causing him to jerk away and roll to the edge of the crowd of onlookers.

The metallic taste of blood filled Adal's mouth as the Dweller punched him in the jaw. He spat crimson liquid into the Dweller's eyes and followed with another powerful swing of his right hand. The

Dweller slumped to the side, a wheezing sack of metal, and Adal rolled out from under him then pulled himself to his feet. Just as he was about to kick the Dweller in the ribs, a loud 'pop' made him jump, and several of the onlookers scattered.

At the edge of the circle, Lupo stood like a statue, with a pistol pointed in the air. The corner of his right eye twitched as he lowered the gun and leveled it at Arija. Adal prepared himself to charge, only to have Lupo turn the gun on him. He waved the gun erratically back and forth between the two like a psychotic game of eenie, meenie, miney, mo.

"That's enough!" Lupo shouted. Brown liquid sprayed from his mouth with each word. Arija slowly rose to her feet, both hands in the air, and her eyes trained on the gun. Lupo was too far away for her to risk rushing him, and as she tilted her head toward Adal, he seemed to know what she was thinking, and he slowly shook his head "no."

"You . . . you . . . assholes! Enough fighting! Enough snarky remarks! I may have been overzealous with the idea of skinning the two of you and selling your skin. To be honest, it would have taken some time to find a buyer with enough money to afford the goods. But now I think I'll do it for fun." Lupo turned his attention to his broken and cowering friends. "You three, get off your asses!"

His men grunted as they collected themselves and helped one another up. Lupo snarled impatiently as he waited for them to get to his side.

"Oh, this is ridiculous. The three of you are useless! What's wrong, too much time spent robbing old ones and not enough time actually being Back

Slangers? Fine!" Lupo took a half step into the circle and opened his mouth to address the crowd.

Before he could utter a word, Arija spoke. "What's the matter? Need to hide behind your little gun and your friends? Maybe if you just put the gun down and politely apologize, my friend and I won't have to hurt you again."

Adal furiously shook his head at her as Lupo turned his attention back to her and aimed the gun at her head. "Is that so?"

"Hey man, bring that over here! You going to let her mouth get to you? I'm the one that beat your ass!" Adal stepped toward Lupo, hands out in an attempt to shield Arija.

"Fine! The two of you want to play this game? I can abide. The lot of you!" Lupo looked past Adal to the crowd. "The first one to bring me their skin will get thirty percent of what it takes in!"

Adal glanced back at the group of men that stood directly behind him. Several of them were whispering to one another and nodding as they looked at Adal and Arija, like a hunter on the prowl.

"Hey, girl! You good?" Adal said over his shoulder, splitting his attention between Lupo and the buzzing group of onlookers.

"Oh, sure thing. No worries here!" Confident sarcasm dripped from each word Arija spoke.

"Not so smug now, are you?" Lupo laughed as the worry spread across Adal and Arija's faces. A Dweller man standing next to Adal produced a small pocket knife and wiped the blade on the side of his dirty, brown pants. The tension in the circle thickened like the air was made of maple syrup. As Adal looked

287

around at all the sad, angry, reluctant eyes, he said a silent prayer they'd find a way out of this.

A distant sound tickled at Adal's ear and as he brought his attention to it, the sound morphed into the crunching of metal. Adal and Arija looked at each other, their faces screwed up in confusion as the sound grew progressively louder. Suddenly, an explosion burst from the mob sending the Dwellers nearest to Adal flying through the air and their various parts raining down on them.

Arija leaped from the path of the explosion and rolled over to where Adal stood, stunned. A car plowed at full speed through the huddled mass, casting aside all the would-be attackers. Everything happened so fast that Adal didn't have time to process how a car could have gotten into the alley in the first place.

Lupo raised his gun to fire as the car fishtailed toward him, but before he could shoot, the trunk of the large car smacked into him, sending him sailing through the air and his gun landing with a loud bang on the roof of the car.

"Sorry to interrupt the party, but are you two ready to go yet?" Kip panted through the broken glass of the shattered driver-side window. Adal and Arija stood petrified for a moment, minds buzzing as they tried to piece together what had just happened. A few the Dwellers near them started to pick themselves up and were no doubt thinking the same thing.

"What the hell is this?" a petite Dweller woman shouted.

"Hey, that's OUR payday!" The Dweller with the pocket knife said as he brushed the dirt from his pants and went to stand next to the woman.

"Get in the car!" Adal and Arija shouted at one another in tandem. Without thought, they both grabbed the handle of the door to find it had been jammed closed in the impact. After a few good pulls, Adal gave up and grabbed the handle for the back door. Luckily it was still in working order, and the two pushed themselves into the car, slamming the door behind them just as a short navy-blue Dweller smashed his fist into the window.

Arija fumbled with the door, holding the handle while the Dweller tried to pull the door open. "Where the hell is the lock!" she screeched as the door came open a few inches and she pulled harder on the handle, slamming it shut again. Adal leaned over Arija and ran his hand along the top of the car until he found a switch. He pressed the switch, and the door made a faint clicking sound. Arija kept her shaking hands on the door handle even as the Dweller gave up and started to kick the rear tire of the vehicle.

"Drive! Drive! Drive!" Adal shouted as a rock came bursting through the window and nearly hit Arija in the face. A surprised yelp escaped her lips, and she grabbed the rock and threw it back through the shattered window.

"Hold onto your nuts and bolts!" Kip slammed on the accelerator, peeling the tires and kicking up enough street dust to give them a cloud to escape in. The vehicle jerked forward and threw Adal and Arija against the soft, leather seat. The gun that had landed on the roof of the car slid through an open sunroof and hit Adal in the stomach before settling in his lap. He gasped as Kip drove rampant through the narrow alleyway, striking virtually everything ahead of them like a kid playing a video game.

"Kip, careful! You're going to kill someone!" Arija shouted. She skooched up to the edge of her seat to watch as Kip rounded another corner. The car tilted, lifting slightly onto two wheels and Arija slid into Adal, bracing herself on his door so she wouldn't fall into his lap.

"Now really isn't the time for that, Arija."

Arija jabbed her elbow into Adal's groin as she pushed herself up resulting in a loud groan from Adal. Several loud bangs erupted behind them, and the rear window exploded, sending shards of glass raining over them.

"Kip!" Arija shouted as she covered her head with her hands. "Are they shooting at us?"

"Well, they aren't throwing us a party!" Kip replied, pressing harder on the accelerator. Several more shots pierced through the air and Adal leaned down, fumbling with the pistol that had fallen to his feet.

"I'm over this!" he yelled, leaning halfway out of the window and taking aim at the pursuing crowd of Dwellers. Several Dwellers were wearing fliegensacks and waving sticks, pipes and some even had small guns as they struggled to catch up to the car. One thin, wiry Dweller that looked like he couldn't be a day over fifteen had a pile of rocks and was struggling to keep himself flying straight while aiming at the car. He zig-zagged down the alley, and as they took a turn, he lost control and spun into a cluster of trashcans. Adal leaned over the back seat and took aim through the broken back window. The car bounced and shook as it barreled over the cobbled stones, but Adal squinted his eyes and fired at the closest Dweller he could see with a gun.

"What are you doing?" Arija demanded as he fired a second round.

Adal was certain he hadn't hit anyone, but the shooting alone was enough to cause some of them to scatter. Ahead of them, a large container stuck out from the side of the building near the exit to the secret alley.

Arija wasn't sure what the container was, but she saw a chance. She snatched the gun from Adal. "Give me that!"

As the car drove under the container, Arija leaned out of the window and fired four shots at the base of the giant drum where a large pipe fed into it. The pressure from the container's contents forced the pipe aside, and a violent flow of rust-colored liquid spewed out, covering the street. The car had just enough time to get out of the way of the flow as it hit the ground, but several of the closest Dwellers were enveloped by the thick liquid.

"Ah man! What is that stuff?" Adal asked, clenching his face in disgust and the possibilities.

"Did the job, didn't it?" Arija blew the thin line of smoke from the barrel of the gun.

"I mean, I could've done that," Adal mumbled sheepishly.

"It was just cider. These guys store it in those towers like that so they don't have to worry about tons of barrels sitting around. Limited space in these alleys you know." Kip yanked the wheel and sent Arija and Adal colliding into one another again as he finally brought them to the main road and forced his way into traffic. A barrage of horns and shouting was met with a sigh of relief from the two terrified passengers.

"You guys all right? That was amazing!" Kip let out a manic laugh. "Life was never this exciting before you two showed up. Now that I got us some wheels, let's start the official Kip tour!"

Adal stared, his mouth slightly ajar. He turned his head to find Arija staring right back at him, shaking her head. Somehow, he doubted Kip had any difficulty getting himself into trouble.

25

THE CREATOR

To both Arija and Adal's relief, the next several hours of the tour went on without much of a fuss. Agreeing to his begging passengers, Kip reluctantly kept the rest of the tour tame by showing them what he called "Topper fluff."

Amazing structures and machines were intricately woven into the fabric of the seemingly infinite city, and at some point, Arija had climbed into the front seat with Kip and drew as she stared out the window. She had begun to warm up to the kid. Sure, he'd gotten them into that whole mess, but he'd also saved their asses. Glancing over at Kip, who was droning on about the place he'd stolen his first something or other, Arija tuned him out and continued her sketch with the cap that always sat perfectly on Kip's head.

Adal lazily watched Arija draw wondering how in the hell she had managed to hold on to that book this entire time. He leaned against the window and watched as building upon building passed as Kip explained how the city was designed into levels.

"If you really wanna see something cool, we gotta go up!" Kip twisted in his seat to look at Adal and narrowly missed an oncoming car who blared its horn at them. "One day, when I can get us a Fliegenmobi . . . oh uh, that's a car with wings. Once I can nab us one of those, we can really have some fun!" Kip said as he practically bounced in his seat with excitement. After everything they'd been through that day, even Adal wasn't sure if that was a good idea or not.

As they turned onto a side road, a Topper woman pushed open the door to a large brick building. Her light blue ruffled dress was hanging off one shoulder, and she looked side to side before she stepped out of the building, pulling a Dweller man behind her. As Kip got closer, Adal recognized the Dweller as one of the dock workers. The Dweller leaned in, planting a lingering kiss on her cheek, causing her to giggle and push him away. She stepped back into the doorway and waved him goodbye as she nervously glanced around the street again and then quietly shut the door behind her.

"What was that about?" Adal asked, pointing to the Dweller who was adjusting his suspenders on the side of the street.

"Oh, that? Just a little bit of Topper fun. They like to slum it with the dock workers every now and again when their husbands are out in the Machine. Everyone knows about it, but it's something no one talks about." This time Kip kept his eyes on the road as he spoke. Adal didn't reply, he just looked out the window, watching the dock worker make his way down the road.

Eventually, they came clanking and grinding to a halt just around the corner from Avani's shop. Kip didn't dare venture much closer than that, for fear that his mother would see he'd stolen another car. Adal couldn't help but admire the kid. He had a cavalier "don't care what happens as long as it's fun" attitude that made for an interesting day, to say the least.

"All right, you two. We're back. You can go about your boring evening with Cog and Webley. I'll leave you here to make your way back in. I have to get rid of this thing before mum sees me. Just tell her I went up and started working on the mobile clinic again."

Adal leaned forward and patted Kip on the shoulder. "Thanks, little man. This was a cool day after all. Take it easy." With a final tap of appreciation, Adal slid over the seat and stepped out of the car.

Arija forced her lips into a thin smile. "Yes, thank you for the tour and for not entirely getting us killed. Do me a favor, don't get into any more trouble tonight?" Arija winked as Kip wildly nodded his head, a toothy grin stretched across his freckle-spattered face.

"No promises, miss. Can only do what I do."

Arija collected her bag and stepped out to the curb with Adal. With a final wave at his former passengers, the tires peeled once more, and steam poured from beneath the car before Kip rocketed off down the street and disappeared around the corner.

"That kid is going to get us killed," Arija said, shaking her head.

"Yeah, but what a way to go out!" Adal laughed, putting his arm around her.

"Hey, you all right? Hasn't really been the most chill day we've had together." Adal straightened up, his smile turning down.

"I'm fine. Definitely not a normal day, but we survived it, so that's something." Arija smiled at him and nudged him in the ribs, pushing him away playfully. "No thanks to you, that is!"

"What the hell did I do?"

"Really? We going to start on this one?" Arija raised an eyebrow and tilted her head.

"You mean when I kept those guys off you in the alley or shooting at them to slow them down? You wouldn't be here if it weren't for all of this." Adal grinned and stretched his arms out, flexing to show off his muscles.

"Oh, my hero . . . NOT! You mean when I took down two Dwellers using only my momentum and locks because I don't have some super fist? Nice going, by the way, *Hulk smash*. Oh, how about when I fired the shots that actually stopped the mob from chasing us? Jeez, what would have happened if I didn't have my big, strong Adal with me?" Arija rolled her eyes, doing her best to look fragile and delicate, all while laughing at Adal.

Adal thought in silence for a moment and then grinned back. "See! You did notice!"

Arija scoffed and walked past him toward Avani's office.

"Ah, don't be like that!" Adal shouted, jogging after her. He picked her up and spun her around, placing her gently down on the ground in front of him. Arija had to fight the desire to laugh and instead buried her elbow once more into his ribs.

"You can fight it, but I know you like it," Adal said between coughs. Since they'd both come to the Machine only a day ago, the two hadn't had the chance to just hang out and get a feel for what was going on. Webley and Cog's plans for them kept them occupied. Neither of the two would admit it, but they were enjoying this moment together. It reminded them that no matter what happened in the Machine, they still had each other's backs.

Adal wrapped his arm around Arija's shoulders, and she playfully hip-checked him as they walked into Avani's office.

A familiar laugh rumbled through the room, and they immediately knew Webley was back from cleaning up the docks. As Adal and Arija entered the main room from the foyer, they saw Webley, Cog, and Avani standing in the center and Webley was doubled over in a fit of laughter.

"'Ello there!" Webley boomed, raising his hands high and scooping both Adal and Arija up into a bear hug. "Welcome back from yer tour. 'Ope ye enjoyed what ye saw of the city." Webley squeezed once more and put them down.

Adal and Arija gave a nervous laugh as they looked at one another, silently deciding to keep the day's events to themselves.

"It was great," Arija began, re-parting and smoothing out the hair that Webley had ruffled when he picked them up.

"Yeah! This place is ridiculous! I really can't believe this whole place is down here." Adal added, nervously tugging his shirt straight.

"Well, today was not the most pleasant of starts on your adventures in the Machine. Hopefully, there won't be any future issues," Cog interjected, joining Webley like a concerned parent.

"I think you just need to watch over these two a little better." Everyone turned to Avani as she spoke. "This place can be amazing, but there are still, and always will be, dangers. It's the nature of the Machine. I see it all the time. Just promise you will watch over these two."

"Avani, I can promise ye tha' there won' be any more funny business with my guests. Today was 'orrible, but I think I've taken care of tha'."

Arija watched Webley as he spoke. She wondered what he meant by he'd taken care of it. She looked at Adal who was curiously inspecting his right knuckles. How was Adal ever going to explain the metal in his hand if he ever had to get medical attention back home?

"Thank you, Webley. On that note, where is Kip? How was he as a tour guide?" Avani inquired.

"Oh, uh, great! He really showed us . . . uh . . . all the different parts of the city." Arija tried her best to sound collected and believable. She shot a look at Adal whose eyes widened as the attention focused on him.

"Yeah! He was a perfect guide, very . . . entertaining," Adal coughed as the last word caught in his throat. Avani's smile thinned slightly, and she took a few steps toward them. Her raised brow reminded Arija of her father when he caught her in a lie. Damn.

"Really? That's nice." Avani took a few more steps toward Adal, her hands planted firmly on her hips. "Tell me, where is Kip now?" She narrowed her eyes and looked back and forth between Arija and Adal, gauging their expressions.

"Oh, uh, he said he had to work on the mobile clinic. Good guy, Kip. All he talked about the whole tour was getting back here and finishing up the clinic for you," Adal lied, his voice shaky.

Avani's eyes sharpened. "OH! He stole another car, didn't he? I am going to hide all his tools when I get ahold of him!" Avani barked as she turned on her heels and marched off into the shop.

"Way to lay that one on thick, Adal!" Arija slapped him on the back.

"My bad!"

Webley started to roll with laughter and Cog looked off to where Avani had disappeared, his mouth hanging slightly open as she disappeared around the corner. Arija smiled as she watched Cog. He was a little strange and gave her weird vibes when they first met, but now she could see he was just terribly awkward.

"Oh! Tha' Kip sure is keepin' her busy! Wha' do ye two say? Want te get back to the house? Been a bit of a long day, no?" Webley walked past them and made his way over to the door, opening it and waving his arm outside.

"I'm down for that. One thing, though; can we NOT fly back?" Adal asked, shaking his head at the thought of having to fly anywhere any time soon.

"Yeah, I'm with him on this one," Arija added.

"I think a ride in the rail car might be in order. Webley, what are your thoughts?" Cog pulled his attention away from Avani and back to the group.

"Well, I don' see why not!"

The ride back went without incident or excitement at all, really. Webley remained silent for the most part, conducting and operating the rail car as they sped through the Machine towards his home.

Arija and Adal sat in silence, peering through the glass at what sights they could behold before they became an indistinguishable blur. Cog was working in a box attached to the wall next to the control panel adjusting various things that neither Adal nor Arija could see.

"Webley, did you adjust these capacitors?" Cog peeked his head out of the box, his face streaked with oil. Webley only shrugged his shoulders and grunted. Cog dove back into his work.

Arija leaned her head on Adal's shoulder as she watched the mechanical world fly by. A few minutes later Cog stuck his head back out of his box. "When did we upgrade these components? They aren't functioning well with the connectors at all. That is why this thing is sluggish." Again, Webley only shrugged his shoulders, and after a few seconds of silence, Cog huffed and dipped back into his box.

Finally, there was a high-pitched screech followed by a plume of steam as the railcar came to a stop in front of Webley's house. Exhaustion had taken over Arija's body, and she lazily slid herself from the seat, climbed out of the railcar and into Webley's house as if she had done it a thousand times.

Webley, Adal, and Arija sat in silence at the table as Cog served a steaming bowl of some sort of soup. Adal hadn't spoken one word since they'd gotten on the railcar and the aches and pains that covered his body had made themselves known as his whole body throbbed. Adal looked across the table to Arija who was propped up on her elbow, spooning chunks of broccoli into her mouth. Even Webley was abnormally quiet, the only sounds in the house those of Webley slurping his dinner.

"Well, I think some coffee is in order." Cog's voice shattered the silence. "Everyone into the study and I'll bring some in."

The fire crackled as they all sat in comfort on the oversized leather seating. Arija had begun to thumb through a large book of paintings sitting on the small coffee table in front of the couch. Adal was staring off into the rolling fire, casually sipping his coffee and both Webley and Cog alike just sipped their cups and stared awkwardly off into the distance.

"So, what's the deal with this place?" Adal finally asked, finishing his cup and sitting back in his seat. "Like, you built this place, but where did you come from? What started all of this?" Once Adal's first question came, the rest followed like a bunch of sheep jumping off a cliff.

Arija put her book down and leaned back on the couch.

"Well, time works differently down 'ere, Adal. Things happen . . . slower. Yer parents probably 'avent even noticed ya missin' yet. As fer how I made my machine, those 'er long tales te' be told, Adal. The day 'as been long a'ready. Ye sure ye want te' hear it all?" Webley asked, putting his bowl of coffee down and leaning forward.

Adal nodded.

"All right then. Fact is, I made this place. Long ago. Now you see all tha' is around. Simple enough. Well . . . uhh . . . I'm rubbish with stories. I tend te' forget parts and glass over others. I think it's best if Cog takes this one." Webley took another sip of his coffee and leaned back in his chair.

"Ok. You want to know it all? After all you have seen, I think that . . . we think it is only fair." Cog took a deep breath and looked back to Webley, who nodded a single, slow nod to his friend.

"All right, it all began in a time before time was even a notion. I told you once before that Webley was a Creator, and I assume you took that as he fancied building things. This is true, but not the entire truth. Webley is a Creator, an old race of creatures that spends their days building life from nothingness. There are entire worlds out there that the Creators call home." Cog paused, watching Adal's and Arija's reaction.

"You mean like aliens?" Adal asked after a moment.

Cog didn't reply, he just scratched the back of his head and continued with his story. "So once, from a timeless time, a Creator came to a dead rock in a galaxy lost to the rest of creation. The Creator's

303

journeys took him to many places, but something about this system sparked his interest. So many lifeless, dead structures sat like blank canvases in a dance with a star. This Creator decided to take a brief stay on one of these structures and do what he was born to do—create."

"Wait, lifeless structures dancing around a star?" Arija began before Cog interrupted her.

"Yes, my dear. He came to this planet. The Creator burrowed deep in the core of Earth in search of a quiet place to do his work. In the beginning, he had only his ship as a home and very little to work with, venturing forth to collect the planet's natural metals so he may create. After a time, the creations began to take a form and function. Within several eons, large machines occupied the center of this planet. Massive furnaces sprung up and began to heat the lifeless structure. Gears of immense size rotated the dead structure around its star. Eventually, a grand machine, the likes of which no Creator had ever accomplished on their own, came to life from the dark."

Adal looked at Arija, wide-eyed, but she was fixated on Cog, trying to make sense of what he was saying.

"Alas, even with such creations and accomplishments, one will grow lonesome without the accompaniment of others to share in life's experiences. So, one fateful day, the Creator decided to make another creation. He gathered his best materials and crafted a living, aware creature to spend his time with. He made himself a son. A son to, not only provide him with family and company, but a son to help him build. Although the Creator was able to

304

bestow life into his creations and give them a soul, the Dwellers he created were only able to create a shell of a being that could follow orders but weren't sentient. Only the Creator could give true life to his creations."

Webley shifted uncomfortably. He stood like he was going to leave and then sat back down, shifting his weight from one side to the other before slouching back into the chair. Cog waited until Webley settled in his chair, giving him a look before continuing.

"The two were a family, and they worked together crafting machines and drafting new ideas for further creations. Eventually, the Creator and his son decided that it was time to grow their world. So, they set out creating several more sentient beings. These would be the first of the Dwellers. Though similar to their future lines, these were very special Dwellers embossed with special skills to help grow the world they were creating. First came twin brothers, to help with general creating and maintenance of the machines. Next came a woman to help in caring for the sick and injured. The third was a mighty warrior created to protect those that dwelled within the Machine. Next came two pairs of men and women that would help bring forward the future generations of Dwellers. Finally, they created a child to always remind the group that they stood as a team and they lived in harmony for many years."

Arija looked at Adal. When his eyes met hers, she mouthed "Radix," and Adal nodded back as he remembered what Kip had told them earlier that day.

"Then it all changed. Unbeknownst to the Creator or the Dwellers, life had taken form on the top side of the planet. The large furnaces the Creator

305

had crafted were heating the planet so that it was livable to other beings and the gears the Creator kept turning to keep the Machine functioning were slowly rotating the planet and causing weather to form and life to grow. One day a human male found his way into the Machine through a tunnel the Creator had made when his ship first burrowed into the planet. The Dwellers were all very excited and intrigued to see this new type of creature, so the Creator set out to investigate the Topside. The other Dwellers begged the Creator to let them come with him, but not knowing the dangers they might face, the Creator insisted that he go alone. Several days later, the Creator returned to the Machine and sealed the hole to the Topside. He refused to talk about what had happened while he was away, but he brought bags of seeds and plants which we have used to create the gardens you see today." Cog paused and took a sip of his coffee.

"Several years later, the Creator installed the elevator you took to get down here so he could make short trips to the Topside and gather knowledge and supplies, but he never spoke of his journeys, and he never let another Dweller accompany him. After a while, the Creator's son grew jealous of his father's ability to create life. So, one day, he went to his father and asked what the secret to giving life was. His father refused to tell him. The secret to life was something only a Creator can have knowledge of. This enraged his son. And this was the beginning of the Great Divide. Eventually, the eldest son decided that if his father would not share his knowledge with them, then he was just a slave to his father, so he began to spread lies into the ears of the Dwellers to turn them against the Creator. Some heard his wickedness while others sided with the Creator and denied the son his audience."

Arija thought back to the fight they'd had with the Dweller at the docks, and everything started to make sense. He'd wanted to take her to him. Whoever he was, he must be a follower of the Creator's son.

Cog continued. "Fights broke out between the two groups. In one of those fights, the child that was meant to keep them united was killed. Each of the remaining Dwellers took a side during the Great Divide. The twins chose opposite sides, the warriors and caregiver sided with the Creator, and the birthers also split evenly between sides.

"The Creator didn't have the heart to choose between his creations, and so he refused to go to battle. This left the long war to be fought amongst the Dwellers alone. Once it was all said and done, all four of the birthers were dead. The remaining twin and the son were defeated in battle and cast out into the depths of the Machine where they remain to this day. It was left to the remaining three and the Creator to start again and rebuild. Though this war was fought and lost long ago, the fire that birthed it still smolders and occasionally flares up. This was what you had the unfortunate luck of witnessing today."

Arija and Adal sat in silence. At some point during the tale, Adal's mouth had fallen open, and there it remained. He tried to think of questions to ask, but his mind was a muddled mess. "Wait, so you . . . and we are . . . but then . . ." Adal spat out incoherently. To him, it sounded like a fairytale version of the Bible. Adal couldn't believe any of this was real, but as he thought about everything he'd seen, he realized that anything was possible.

Arija's eyes could not have been any wider. Her mouth had run dry as she became lost in the story, and her head was spinning from the information overload. "What was his name? The one that betrayed everyone?" she asked quietly, leaning further forward and realizing she had been on the literal edge of her seat for the entire story.

"The son? His name was Pajak. The twin that followed his new master into madness was Fausto," Cog said, falling silent and staring at his two overwhelmed and befuddled guests. Arija thought about the Dweller on the dock and how eerily similar he looked to Cog.

Webley sat in silence, lost in the warm dance of the fire, a soft look of shame and sadness resting on his face.

"Hey man, are you all right?" Adal broke in, addressing Webley.

Webley let Adal's words hang in the air for a moment before he gave a slight sniffle and brought his attention back from the fire to the room. "I'm all right, Adal. Thank ye' for the ask. I think it's time fer' bed. We all need our rest fer' tomorrow. Gonna be another grand day."

With those words, Webley rose from his seat and bowed to Adal and Arija without making eye contact before abruptly walking toward the kitchen and disappearing through the door.

"Perhaps he is right. Maybe we should be off to bed then." Cog stood from his seat and walked over to the staircase that led to the upper level. Arija and Adal slowly rose from the couch. Everything felt so strange now with this new knowledge. Maybe a good night's sleep would help.

Halfway up the spiral stairs, Arija paused and turned to face Cog who still stood at the base of the steps. "So, today, all those things that attacked us. Webley made?"

"No, my dear. Those were bastard creations made by Pajak. Their only purpose is to follow orders. They don't have a soul. That is why the guards had no pause in dispatching of them. They are not true creations."

"What about the Dwellers that fought with us today on the dock? The ones that died. What did you guys do with them?" Adal asked.

"That is likely the only good news of the day. So few Dwellers truly fell today that Webley was able to act in time to save them. Had the destruction been greater, he may not have been able to do so. With that, some Dwellers are missing, and I do fear their fate, but there is nothing that can be done for them now. Please, get some rest. It has been a long day for us all."

With Cog's final request, Arija and Adal bid him goodnight and made their way to their rooms. That night, they slept hard, but their dreams were plagued with sporadic nightmares of a dark kingdom with demonic machines. Little did they know their nightmares were more of a reality than they ever could have imagined.

Part III

The War

26

SHOULD WE BE GETTING OUR ASSES OUT OF HERE?

The next morning, Adal found himself blankly staring at his reflection in the mirror. The dark circles under his eyes and scruffy stubble on his face reflected how poorly he'd slept. Images of Creators from other planets and Dwellers chasing after him with razor blades had haunted his dreams and caused him to toss and turn all night, repeatedly waking up drenched in sweat.

Adal reached for the brush, unable to pull his eyes away from the distorted image of himself in the mirror and dragged it over his head lazily. The weight of everything he'd learned and seen had finally settled in, and he felt like he couldn't breathe. How could he focus on how he looked when there were giants on other planets bringing inanimate objects to life that wanted to kill him and wear his flesh like some creepy sci-fi version of *Silence of The Lambs*? Life would never be the same knowing what he knew. He gave up on his appearance and shuffled out into the hall.

Arija sat on the edge of her bed, notebook in hand, staring at a mostly blank page. She'd been unable to sleep more than an hour at a time without waking up in a panic. At some point, she'd decided to put her thoughts on paper. Arija dragged her pencil around the question mark she'd made in the corner for the thousandth time. She was too tired to be creative, and there were too many questions clouding her mind.

She glared up at the clock and watched the seconds count down until her alarm broke the silence. Then she slid the sketchpad back into her bag and pulled her legs up onto the bed and sat cross-legged as the alarm sounded for a few minutes. Finally, she pulled herself off the bed to shut it off.

Arija ran her fingers through her tangled mess of hair and dressed in the same outfit she'd worn the day before. She longed for the days when her only worry was whether she was going to win her track meet. It was time for them to go home, and she would say as much to Adal when she saw him. Things needed to get back to some form of normalcy, or she may never have a good night's sleep again. With this thought, Arija grabbed her bag and slipped out of the room.

Out in the hall, Adal was waiting for her, slouched against the railing like he was using it to hold himself up. His usual grin was replaced with a solemn stare, and Arija knew he'd gotten as good of a night's sleep as she had. He glanced up at her, and she nodded, unable to force her mouth into a smile.

"Sup?" Adal managed.

"Yeah," Arija replied as Adal pushed off the railing and they made their way down the stairs. An awkward silence hung thick in the air as Adal and Arija stepped into the study. The house was strangely quiet. No Cog greeting them with his annoyingly cheerful grin and coffee, no Webley stomping around preparing for whatever they were going to be doing today.

In the study, the fire had long gone out, yet the smell of smoke still filled the room. Arija looked around, hair suddenly on end until she spotted a platter of fruit on the coffee table and a note sitting at the corner of the table. She walked over to the kitchen and cracked the door to look inside. She turned to Adal and shook her head. Adal walked to the table and picked up the note.

Adal and Arija,

We had to tend to an issue this morning. Please, enjoy the breakfast we left for you, and we shall be back shortly.

-Cog

"Looks like we're flying solo today." Adal tossed the paper back to the table and turned to Arija.

"Looks that way. Great. It isn't bad enough they dropped that bomb on us last night. Now we're stuck sitting here waiting. We really need to get back home, Adal. Things have just gotten so . . . complicated, and I just want to be back in my own bed." Arija walked over to the table and picked up the note once more, only to roll her eyes and crumple it up.

"Hey, what's the matter with you? Normally you don't throw attitude around unless it's warranted. Did I miss something?"

Arija sighed and plopped down on the couch. She un-crumpled and re-crumpled the piece of paper a few times before she started to speak. "It's just, well, all my life, I was raised in my family's faith. Being told of a higher power, creation, God's gifts, and so on. Now, I'm sitting in this world under ours, hearing the news that Webley created this place. That there are other Creators out there doing the same thing, what does that mean about God? Am I wrong? Are we wrong? This is just too insane." Arija huffed as she spoke, exasperated and frustrated.

Adal sat down on the couch next to her and put his arm around her, squeezing her into a side hug.

316

"Hey, kid, I get it. I've never really been religious, but I know this is about what you believe. This has to hit heavy. Here's how I look at it. Webley created this place, and all the things in it all came from him. Everything is mechanical and weird to us, right? We've only seen versions of people, but these Dwellers aren't like us. If a Creator like Webley had made us, then this place wouldn't be a thing, and if it were, it would be just like back home. Webley may have made this place, but we come from something else. That's what I believe. Basically . . . I guess what I'm trying to say is that there's room for God *and* the Creators to exist. Don't let that faith leave you. If this world is possible, so is ours. So are others. Besides, right now, we have other things to worry about."

"Like what?" Arija asked, her brows furrowed as she raised her head to look up at him.

"Like where in the hell we are going to get some coffee in this place!" Adal laughed. Arija let the rise and fall of his chest rock her to a slightly happier place. She smiled back at him and threw one of her own arms around him, squeezing tightly.

"You know, sometimes you aren't as dumb as you look," Arija teased. She caught Adal staring at her mouth, and when he glanced up to meet her stare, she found herself unable to look away. The world around them muted to nothing. Adal lowered his head as Arija tilted hers up. She leaned closer to him, so close she could feel the warmth of his breath tickle her lips. Her heart was pounding, fighting its way out of her throat. Finally, Arija closed her eyes, needing to enjoy every second of what was about to happen.

317

"I don' care what yer think! Tha' is the plan. You take 'em out o' here, and I'll handle this!"

The door smacked the wall as Webley burst into the room, ruining the moment. Arija and Adal pushed away from each other like two teens that got caught kissing by their parents. Adal cleared his throat and leaned back on the couch as if nothing had happened while Arija jumped up and took a few steps away from the couch. She stole a glance at Adal and silently wished that Webley and Cog had come home just a few minutes later.

Webley looked as though he had just been through hell. His clothing was tattered and torn, and there were several deep scrapes across his face. Cog came in behind him with several small dents in his legs and arms. Neither Webley nor Cog was paying any attention to them, and the embarrassment quickly left Arija and was replaced by fear.

"Webley, this isn't the time. Let me help you. They will be safe here! We must do this together. Now is not the time for you to take this up," Cog huffed, chasing after Webley and slamming his hand on the bookshelf as he leaned his weight against it.

"Cog, move yer' hand! You saw it too! We both barely got out o' there. Ye need te' get them outta here!" Webley pushed Cog's hand away and pulled on one of the larger books on the shelf. From behind the wall, there came a clank, followed by a metallic rumbling as the shelf slid up the wall toward the ceiling, revealing an assortment of strange looking weapons.

Adal stood from the couch, doing a double take at the small arsenal as his mouth dropped open in awe. Adal let out a loud whistle, and the room fell silent. All three turned to him. "What in the hell is going on right now? Should we be getting our asses out of here or what?" Adal asked, still staring at the weapons.

"There isn't time, Adal. We need you two to stay put. There is a little problem, and we have to leave you to take care of it," Cog justified.

Arija scoffed. "Really? You need an armory to fix a *little* problem? Cog, I like you and all, but you might want to come up with a better lie than that!"

"Get them outta 'ere, Cog!"

"Really, there isn't time." Cog turned back to Webley.

"Hey, first off, we aren't going anywhere. Secondly, you need to tell us what happened. We can help," Adal added as he walked over to the wall of weapons.

"The Gearrtha tha' attacked ye' yesterday. They are back, an' they are runnin' amuck in my machine. This mornin' they attacked one of the furnaces. If we hadn't gotten there in time, they would have cast us into cold an' darkness!" Webley's voice shook with anger and a hint of worry.

Adal looked at Arija. Her face contorted with concern and fear. If Webley was scared, then things had to be a lot worse than Adal thought.

"All right. Well, you beat them yesterday. Can you fix the furnace?" Adal asked. Webley could fix anything. Adal didn't see what the big deal was.

"We only managed to stop their attack, but they aren't finished. As we left the area, they followed us. If we are correct, they will be here any minute, bringing the fight to the house," Cog explained as he stuffed ammunition into a bag.

Adal felt his stomach lurch. He flashed back to an image from the battle the previous day.

"So, they attacked a furnace?" Arija asked, finally breaking her cautioned silence. "Cog, you told us last night that this machine is what powers the world, basically. The mechanics here directly affect the surface. So, what happens if you can't fix the furnace?" Arija asked. Cog and Webley fell silent, their eyes focusing on anything other than the two humans in front of them.

"Once, long ago, during the first war, one of the furnaces was destroyed, and Webley couldn't fix it right away. Half of your world froze," Cog replied bluntly. Time was running out, and he didn't have the desire to ease the two Topsiders into the situation gradually.

"Wait, what?" Adal asked.

"Yes. Do not worry, though, we have a plan to stop them. What we need to worry about at the moment is getting you two to safety."

Cog turned to Webley, but Adal interrupted before he could speak again.

"Wait a minute. You mean to say the last time you all had to handle your business, you caused an ice age? I mean damn! I sure as shit am not about to leave you guys here to fight this fight without me! I like to keep my world, you know, livable." Adal's face grew hot at Cog's matter-of-fact way of talking about the situation. What about his mom and dad? What about Arija's family? He couldn't sit around and just let another ice age kill everyone on Earth.

"Adal, I appreciate yer' stance. But the fact is, this isn't yer' fight. I can't ask ye' te' join in." Webley walked over to Adal and placed his large hand on Adal's shoulder. "We need te' get ye' out of here."

The distinct sound of a shotgun racking made both Adal and Webley jump, turning back to face the shelves. Arija stood next to it, holding an arm's length shotgun with an ax-blade stretching from the barrel. It was like a Viking discovered firearms.

Arija ran her eyes over the weapon in her hands, a small smile playing on her lips. "Look, I'm over all of this. Just . . . I'm done! We're in a world that's in the middle of ours, science doesn't matter anymore. Logic doesn't matter anymore. I have no idea where we came from or what to even believe and these . . . these . . . assholes are constantly trying to pick a fight with us. One thing my father always taught me was to be smart enough to know my boundaries and how to overcome obstacles. My mother taught me that when things in life hit you, hit them back even harder. Now, I'm done fighting over this. All I want to know now is; how hard does this thing hit?"

Adal was breathless. Webley and Cog turned and looked at him, only to have him shrug back at them. Arija had always been the "kick-ass and take names" type, but he had never seen her like this before. If he was honest with himself, it was pretty hot. He shook his head to clear his thoughts.

"Damn kid, save some for the rest of us! Look, guys, Arija's right. This fight is about all of us now. You need as many people as you can get to fight, and we aren't exactly helpless kids. So, are we going to do this thing or what?" Adal wanted nothing more than to run over to the wall of weapons and start picking up the baddest ones, but he waited to gage Cog's and Webley's responses first. The two hosts looked at one another, having a silent conversation before turning back to Adal and nodding.

"All right, then. The fight is upon us all. Know this, we will do what we can to help you, but likely the two of you will be on your own," Cog warned.

"Aye, this won' be the place fer' rescuin'. This will be nothin' but fightin'," Webley added.

Adal and Arija nodded in unison.

27

SUIT UP

Adal could feel his heart pulsing in his clenched fists. He was rigid with a strange combination of excitement and fear. A singular thought raged through his mind so loudly that he was impressed he could even still hear Webley and Cog speak. *Bro, what the hell are you doing right now?!*

Arija, on the other hand, had gone cold to the moment. She felt like she had done nothing but fight since they came to this amazing place. Her family had come from a place of constant war, and somewhere deep within her, an ancestral rage burned for being thrown into combat. She tightened her grip on the surprisingly light weapon. The bronzed stock and forward grip were warm to her touch. Her eyes danced over the ax blade that suspended underneath the barrel. Clearly, that would be "Plan B."

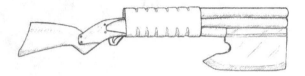

"All right then, Arija, if this is going to happen, I think I may have some tools you will like." Cog broke the silence, walking over to her.

"Adal, I think ye' may like what I got fer' ye'," Webley added, slapping his massive hand on Adal's shoulder like a proud father.

Webley and Cog then set about the next several minutes providing the young Topsiders with enough armaments to take on their own army.

Webley drew a large case from one of the shelves and brought it to the table, slamming it down. Adal hardly had a moment to appreciate the delicately hammered and riveted texture of its surface before Webley threw the lid open and began to shuffle through its contents and withdraw items, clumsily slapping them down on the table. Once he had taken out all that he had been looking for, Webley closed the lid with a heavy thud.

"Firstly, put this on. Ye' will need it." Webley thrust a thick belt with a holster attached to it to Adal who clipped it around his waist. "This 'ere will be yer' best friend in a pinch. A revolver of m' own design. This is how ye' open it te' reload." Webley pressed a button, and the cylinder jutted out from the side. "It's balanced an' calibrated to where ye' won't even feel the recoil. Ten shots in there!" Webley thrust the gun into Adal's hand and grabbed another weapon. "Now, these are a set of forged Damascus tungsten knuckles. Also, m' own design. I saw that ye' are a fan of pugilism so these may find ye' well. Will near crush anythin' ye swing at! Ye'll find plenty of munitions in tha' bandolier belt ye' got on. Oh, an' the last bit fer ye' . . ."

Webley picked up the last weapon on the table and tossed it to Adal—a shotgun of sorts. Similar to the one Arija had chosen. Only this one had two large drums on it, and the racking mechanism was a lever that a hand slid into on the grip. Adal took a moment to take it all in.

"Tha' there is a personal favorite o' mine. Rotatin' drums hold fifty rounds o' ammunition. Ye' eject them from here and slap a new one in just like tha'. Rock that lever to load the next round. Simple. Oh, and take these replacement drums." Webley handed Adal two more drums attached to a leather sling. As Adal threw the leather sling over his shoulder, the weight of the situation finally hit him. He was about to head into a war that only forty-eight hours ago, he didn't even know existed.

As Cog finished pointing out the particulars of her shotgun, Arija had a flash of her mother. The warrior that taught her to always be strong and fight the good fight. The woman who was strong enough to leave her home country to give a better life to her daughter. Arija had to preserve that life with everything she had. Her father's typical lecture about always considering all the possible outcomes of her actions crept into her mind. Since her mother had passed, she had developed quite the temper with the world and was quick to fight, but now she was wondering what she had just gotten the two of them into.

Cog cleared his throat as he finished removing his own set of weapons from the shelves and placed them on the opposite end of the table before her.

"Two blades. I figure you are a little too smart to get caught in close quarters, but these will get you out if something should happen. Laminated and folded titanium, lighter than the air around them, but will cut through anything." Cog reached out and took the shotgun from Arija's hand. "While I agree that this weapon is formidable, it is a bit clunky. For you, I think this is better suited." Cog pulled another rifle off the wall of weapons and held it out to Arija. This rifle was much smaller, having been filed in half.

With a flick of Cog's wrist, the bottom section sprang upward, and the weapon extended revealing a long, polished barrel. "This is fed in a similar fashion to Adal's weapon. There is this drum underneath that holds twenty-five rounds. When all shots have been fired, simply press this button here, and insert the next cylinder. Simple. This scope is designed to zoom in and out by drawing this small bar up and down. Lastly, with this, there are sights on the side. If an enemy gets too close for the scope, you can use these sights, and when you need to move, this folds the entire weapon in half so that it may be more easily attached to your back for travel."

Arija stood in silence as Cog pointed out all the weapon's features. She pressed the butt of the rifle to her shoulder and squeezed the foregrip in her left hand. Everything was moving so fast. Only a few days ago she was worried about her next algebra test, and now she was preparing for battle. How had things gotten this far gone? She flicked her gaze toward Adal, her eyes squinting as she watched him studying his weapons. He widened his eyes when he caught her staring and nodded his head back. Whether they wanted it or not, Adal and Arija were going to war.

"Wait a minute! What is all of this stuff exactly?" Adal finally asked, motioning to his and Arija's equipment. "I thought you guys didn't believe in fighting or killing one another. You spent all night blabbing about how you couldn't kill your own creations and yet here we are, standing in an armory disguised as a library. What's that about?"

"These are relics from th' past," Webley explained from his post in front of the fireplace. He'd taken down a large gun and hammer/wrench that clung to the wall. "They 'aven' been used since then, but I can assure ye, they will get the job done. An' ye are right, we don' kill one another in my Machine! A Dweller is a sacred and loved creature, an' they should all strive to love one another. These things . . . these Kleinmasch, as he calls 'em, they aren' Dwellers. They are somethin' else, an' they have te' be stopped or all Dwellers are in danger."

Arija looked down at the weapon in her hands. If what Webley said was true, then these things were

327

over two million Earth years old. Were these weapons safe to shoot? Time alone should have seen these deteriorate even if properly cared for. Then again, Webley said time moved slower here, so maybe they would be fine.

Adal was insecure for the first time he could remember. Yeah, sure, sometimes he spoke a big game, and usually, he didn't have an issue backing it up. But this was different. This time, he wondered how he was going to do this. This wasn't some bully talking shit, this was life or death, and if something went wrong, he could lose his best friend.

"I know this is a lot, but we haven't the time," Cog started, seeing the look on Adal's face. "You should also take these, just in case." He tossed a backpack to Adal and one to Arija. "I repaired your fliegensacks. If things get too heavy to handle, you need to get out of here. Understand? Go back to the elevator and wait for us."

"On tha' note, ye should give Avani a call. She should be 'ere fer' what comes after," Webley added. He'd broken open the barrel and stock of his rifle and inserted two rounds.

Adal was shocked at their size. Each bullet was the length of Adal's hand, but they looked normal compared to Webley's as he slid them into the barrel.

Cog made his way into the kitchen and out of sight, leaving Adal and Arija alone with Webley.

"I have te' say, I'm sorry fer' all this. I'm sure ye didn't find this place an' think ye would be fightin' a war. Somethin' is wrong in my Machine, and I plan on gettin' te' the bottom of it." Webley turned from them and slung the large tool over his shoulder and clutched his heavy gun.

Adal's thoughts fell to his grandfather. Grandpa Lawrence hadn't been older than eighteen when he'd taken up the calling to fight evil. Was it really so crazy to think he couldn't do the same? Weren't these people in need of help just like the people that Grandpa Lawrence fought for? Adal remembered how his grandfather would tell the story of the first time he'd been thrown into battle. How scared he was, but how, with the support of his fellow soldiers, he knew he could do some good. In a way, Adal felt closer to his grandfather at that moment than he ever had while he was alive.

Arija's thoughts drifted to her family again. The struggles and tales of horror her mother had faced in her homeland. Israel had been at war for thousands of years. To some, war was all they knew. Aliza Rapp often told a young Arija that had she not met her father and had the strength to seek a better life, she would have been consumed by death. At a young age, Aliza had been trained to kill. War had a way of killing youth and replacing it with a cold killer.

Arija loved her father very much, but he was a peaceful man. Her mother often said he was the cool air that helped tame her fire and encouraged her to strive to be more like her father, but today, Arija would embody her mother. Arija sucked in a breath of the musky air from the study and whispered a silent prayer to her mother for strength as the door to the kitchen flew open.

"She's on her way with the mobile medical vehicle just in case. I also urged Captain Silny to put all his men on the city gates" Cog announced, joining the group once more.

"Good, now tha' tha's settled, it's time te' get ready. I can smell 'em gettin' close." Webley's voice had drawn cold as he spoke.

"You ready for this?" Adal whispered to Arija.

"I am if you are," Arija replied, doing her best to sound confident, though her heart beat so fast she was certain he could hear it.

"We got this. Stick close, and watch one another's asses, and we should be all right," Adal added. "And lucky for you, I have a great ass."

"What ass?" Arija scoffed, rolling her eyes with a forced smile. Her pulse slowed slightly, and she knew he would have her back. If something was going to take one of them out, it would have to take them both.

Adal focused on the faint lavender smell of Arija's hair. Somehow it also smelled of the coffee they never did get that morning. He smiled. She was his best friend, and he knew she would always watch his back. He watched her fiddle with her pack, a small frustrated wrinkle forming on her forehead when she couldn't figure out how to latch one of the buckles. If they got out of this alive, he was going to tell her how he felt.

"All right then. Let's get this done," Webley commanded taking a deep breath. As they walked away from the rack, Arija stopped and grabbed a small silver pistol off the shelf and slid it into her belt line at the small of her back. She fisted a stack of magazines into her pocket, but as she turned to catch up with the rest of the team, she found them all staring at her.

"You know, perhaps we can be a little more tactful," Cog said as the rest of the room fell silent, waiting for his plan.

28

A Rootin' Tootin' Good Time

Cog, Webley, and Adal were lined up outside in Webley's backyard. Arija followed them with the crosshair on her rifle from the second-floor window. She couldn't hear them talking, but Adal was doing something stupid.

Typical.

Adal could rarely take anything seriously.

Arija pulled her face away from the rifle and rubbed her eyes. Adal was a dork, and he'd probably get them both killed, but she couldn't help thinking about their almost kiss that morning. Arija shook the thought from her head and focused back on the three men standing in the backyard. She would have to worry about her non-relationship with Adal another time when they weren't in danger of death.

When Arija brought her crosshairs back to the group, they were all standing in a line in the middle of the yard, hands poised on their weapons, awaiting battle. All they needed was a cheesy whistling sound and a tumbleweed to make this the weirdest western she'd ever seen. She allowed her sights to slide up to the world beyond the yard. Nothing seemed out of place. Just a few Dwellers milling about and a flock of birds sitting on one of the beams.

Adal clutched his shotgun. His palms were sweaty, and his heart was pounding with the anticipation of battle. He mentally ran over the position of where each weapon was on his body. For some reason, each fight he'd gotten into in this place had resulted in him getting thrown or slammed into something, and the wind being knocked out of him. If this got hairy, he wanted to remember where each weapon was in case he had to go for one under duress.

Adal looked over at the two men standing with him. Webley stood in humbled silence, his breath rumbling from his chest like distant thunder. Cog twirled two revolvers, his weapons of choice for the

333

day, over his fingers. He wouldn't dare pull his eyes away from the gate that led into the Machine, but Adal knew somewhere behind him Arija was watching his back. His eyes danced over the distance and surrounding structures, not really sure what he was looking for. He figured he'd know when he saw it.

"All right, Cog. This is yer part." Webley's voice broke through the sound of Adal's beating heart.

Cog nodded, turning to Adal. "Remember, if it gets bad, you two get out of here. Take care of yourselves." Cog turned his attention to Arija and gave her a thumbs up. He couldn't see her in the dark frame of her perch, but that was the point. Cog knew she was watching them. He took several steps forward, and with a jolt, his wings expanded outward from his pack. Before Adal had time to register what was happening, Cog took off into the air, disappearing from sight.

"Ye prepared fer your part?" Webley asked Adal, not bothering to turn and face him.

"About as much as I can be. You ready for yours?"

Webley responded with a low grunt as he stared off into the distant Machine. Adal let his eyes run over Webley's focused face and wondered if it was possible for a Creator to die. This must be what his grandfather had described to him as the "thousand-yard stare." *When a soldier is lookin' death in the face, you can see the fear in their eyes 'cause they know it's coming. That, son, is called the thousand-yard stare.* Adal turned his head toward the window he knew Arija was perched in. He needed to know she was there. That she had his back in case something happened. A slender hand crept from the darkness and formed a thumbs up.

Adal turned to Webley to ask another question, but Webley threw a finger in the air between them, silencing his question before it could be asked.

The sound started off small—a static white noise hanging in the background of his thoughts. Adal could barely make out what it was, but after a while, the sound grew. Adal leaned toward the gate, straining to hear, when something jetted ahead of them, scaring the crap out of Adal. He clumsily swung his rifle around and fumbled with the trigger before realizing it was only Cog.

"Here they come!" Cog shouted as he turned away and flew off behind the house, continuing his patrol. Adal jerked his gaze from side to side, but he couldn't see anything.

"He wasn't kidding. Here they come, and they look pissed!" Arija's voice drifted down from the window above. Adal brought the rifle up to his line of sight and scanned the horizon. His heart hammered in his chest. The edges of his vision darkened. He slowly moved his finger to hover over the trigger. His body shook, and he tried to calm and control his nerves.

Like a piling horde, hundreds of Gearrtha and Feithidi flew toward them, wings out. Adal felt his stomach lurch as he tried to comprehend the magnitude of the inevitable attack, but it was difficult as they moved like any swarm of insects might. It was almost comical how outnumbered they were, and Adal found it impossible to focus on any one of the creatures.

"Remember, if they overcome ye, get back in the 'ouse!" Webley commanded, cracking his neck. The horde was nearing closer and closer, and all Adal could do was wait.

Arija could see Adal shaking from where she sat. A sudden guilt consumed her, and she wanted nothing more than to be down there with him, but she could offer the most help from her post. She trained her sights on the incoming horde of Kleinmasch, her finger poised over the trigger as she waited for the right moment.

"'ere they come!" Webley shouted, raising his large gun into the air. At that moment, it was like a switch flipped in Arija's head. Her unruly heartbeat settled and all sounds around her muted. All that existed was the Gearrtha in her crosshairs. She took a deep breath and held it, counting to three before exhaling and squeezing the trigger.

As the swarm neared the house, Adal felt his nerves calm. His shaking fingers steadied, and his heartbeat slowed to a rhythmic beat. A thunderous eruption followed by a plume of smoke emanated from beside him as Webley fired his first shot obliterating nearly a dozen Kleinmasch and sending small fragments of debris into the air around them. The strong odor of burnt iron filled Adal's nose, and he flicked his eyes toward the giant next to him as time seemed to slow to a crawl.

"Damn! What did you put in those things?" Adal shouted over the sound of crunching metal.

"Huzzah! Ye think tha' was somthin', ye should give yers' a go!" Webley bellowed.

Adal opened his mouth to reply as a set of rapid-fire shots came from overhead.

Cog hovered above them laying waste to any creatures unfortunate enough to be caught in his sights. Once the focus was on him, Cog elegantly spun in the air and led droves of the creatures away from Adal and Webley. As Cog disappeared around the side of the house, one by one, Kleinmasch fell from the sky.

Webley grabbed the large wrench slung over his shoulder, clutching it in his hands. The gentle giant's face contorted into something hideous as he screamed and charged forth, leaping fifty feet into the air and colliding with several of the creatures, instantly crushing and dismantling them. Webley grabbed a metal beam with one meaty hand and swung the wrench with the other, demolishing several more Kleinmasch.

Adal raised his shotgun, focused on a group of Kleinmasch on the platform just outside the gate. "You're mine!" he shouted, charging forward at the creatures. They screeched at him and raised their bladed appendages as he neared. Adal stopped only feet from the group and aimed. He slid his finger to the trigger and squinted one eye as he focused on the Gearrtha in the middle. Three loud bursts erupted from behind him, and the creatures' faces exploded in a burst of metal. Adal paused in shock, at first wondering how he was able to shoot them without pulling the trigger.

"What the hell? Those were mine!" Adal shouted, turning to face Arija when he realized what happened.

"Didn't see your name on 'em. Not only do I have the first kill, but I'm winning too," Arija teased, shooting at a fat Feithidi that swooped over Adal's head and dropping it from the sky. Adal's competitive side roared to life. He raised his weapon and began to fire at everything that moved.

29

BILLY BADASS

Arija laughed to herself. Adal was so easy to play. She'd seen how scared he had been and knew the second she turned it into a competition, he'd get his head out of his ass. The swarm of Kleinmasch hadn't fully engulfed the house yet, but there were far too many of them for Arija's comfort.

Dozens of Kleinmasch flew about in a frenzy, many of them too fast or too close for her to get a good shot at. Arija squeezed the trigger as a Feithidi came flying at her, and before she could register whether she'd hit it, it was plummeting to the ground, lifeless. She exhaled the breath she'd been holding and loaded another round.

Arija was a terrifyingly good shot, but she didn't really have the time to think about what that meant or if it was hereditary. It also helped that the weapons Webley had given them were eerily accurate.

She hardly had to do anything other than point and shoot. Honestly, if Adal could do it, anyone could do it. That boy's hand-eye coordination wasn't anything to talk about. With her mind wandering back to Adal, she allowed her sights to settle back on him.

He was rolling to the side and shooting down two Feithidi. Arija was convinced he was doing his best to look like he was in a movie. A Gearrtha swooped in at him and its bladed arm nearly cleaved his leg. Arija followed the Gearrtha until she was certain she'd land a kill shot, and then she squeezed the trigger. The Gearrtha slumped to the ground next to Adal, and he hopped to his feet, brushing himself off.

"I'm good!" Adal shouted, picking up his gun and racking it. Arija watched as small spider-like creatures swarmed in on the dead Gearrtha. Their small legs gliding over the monster so fast she could hardly see them moving. After a few moments, the Gearrtha's arms started to twitch, and Arija realized it was coming back to life. She hovered her cross-hairs over the pile of Gearrtha and Baeg and pulled the trigger.

"Careful! This isn't a game, Adal!" Cog's voice shouted from overhead. He had just dispatched of his pursuing party and was swooping back to keep the horde focused on him. Adal looked up and raised his shotgun, firing a round. Cog flinched as the projectile flew over his shoulder and the shot landed square between the eyes of a Feithidi behind him. It was too late for Cog to move and the massive body of a dead Feithidi collided with him in the air, sending Cog down onto the platform.

A wrenching crash was followed by the momentum of the hit rolling both Cog and the lifeless Feithidi across the deck and sliding off the edge. Adal shouted as he charged to save Cog. The two slid from sight as Adal dove to the ledge, his hand outstretched.

"NO!" Arija shouted and involuntarily jerked forward as she watched Cog slip off the platform just as a Gearrtha shot up from below toward Adal, its appendages swiping at him as it flew upward.

Adal peered over the edge of the platform to see Cog hanging on to a small piece of metal jutting out of the side. "Hold on Cog. I gotcha." Adal grunted as he reached one arm down toward Cog, holding on to the edge of the platform with the other.

Cog's wings were completely mangled, and his fingers shook as he struggled to hold on to the jagged piece of metal. "I don't think I can hold on anymore, Adal." Cog's words came out in a rasp and Adal could barely hear him. "Tell Avani that it's always been her."

"Come on don't say that man, I got—" Adal was caught off guard as the Gearrtha's bladed arm struck the platform next to his head. Adal rolled to the side to avoid a follow-up attack, but when he looked back toward Cog, he was gone. "NO! COG! COG!" Adal yelled as he pushed himself away from the Gearrtha while simultaneously searching the void for his friend.

Arija pulled the trigger only to hear a small click. She pulled it again and again, desperate to save Adal from being shredded to pieces, but it was useless. She was out of ammunition. The Gearrtha landed next to Adal and shrieked as it raised its lethally sharp arms.

Arija reached into the back of her belt and took out the small pistol she'd grabbed from the shelf. She didn't aim or try to steady her shaking hand. Terrified she would lose her best friend, she pointed the pistol in the Gearrtha's general direction and began jerking the trigger.

Shots rang out at the Gearrtha standing above Adal. Sparks flew past Adal's head as one of Arija's shots hit the creature in the shoulder, taking its attention away from its prey. The Gearrtha reared its head, steadying his gaze on the window in which Arija was perched. It extended its wings and lunged through the air toward its new target.

Adal spun around at the piercing shriek that came from Arija's window. Even from this distance, Adal could see the Gearrtha at the ledge of the window, tearing at it. He had no idea what he was going to do, but he knew he had to do something. Arija was in danger.

The Gearrtha slammed into the window, too big to fit through the small hole. It flew back a few feet, shaking off the impact and then slammed into the window again. This time, Adal could see the window frame start to bend inward, and he jumped to his feet.

He looked around for something to help her and found that Webley had the majority of the attacks focused on him in the air. Adal removed his pistol from the holster and took aim at the creature and lined up the shot. But he couldn't bring himself to fire.

"What if I miss or it goes through him! What if I hit her!" Adal barked at himself. With only an instant to consider his options, Adal holstered his weapon and charged at the house. He didn't know what he was going to do, but it was his only option. Adal saw a small table adorned with several pots against the side of the house. He gathered as much speed as he could, leaped into the air, and sprung from the small table with just enough force to grasp the edge of the roof.

Adal clung to the structure for life. There wasn't enough time to do that again. Tightening his chest and arms, he managed to pull himself up and roll onto the roof. As he turned over on the ledge, his pistol slipped from its holster and fell to the ground.

"Damnit!" Adal shot his gaze from side to side looking for something to use as a weapon, then he remembered the tungsten knuckles Webley had given him. Adal went into his pockets and slipped the metal objects over his fingers.

The Gearrtha let out another wail and ripped away a sizable portion of the window frame, giving it enough berth to enter the house. There was another terrified shriek from inside the room, and Adal ran toward the window.

The creature was crouched down and had one bladed arm in the hole of the window, swiping blindly at Arija. Adal grabbed the Gearrtha by its back. He slid his arm under its wing and placed the palm of his hand on the back of its head, bringing it into a half nelson. The Gearrtha reared backward and out of the opening of the window. Its right arm swiped upward at Adal, but he was expecting it.

"Whose house is this?" he shouted, enjoying the re-use of his catchphrase. Adal brought his free arm up, repeatedly punching the Gearrtha in the head with his tungsten knuckled fist.

The groaning sound of metal giving way filled the air as the Gearrtha let go of the window and stumbled backward, focusing its attention on Adal. Adal used his momentum and spun the creature around so that he was facing the edge of the roof. He brought his fist down again into the Gearrtha's head, his heart skipping a beat when a fist-sized dent appeared in the creature's head. Adal released the beast from his grasp and stepped away as it stumbled about like a zombie running on fumes.

The Gearrtha couldn't see with its head dented in so far that its eyes were no longer visible. Adal figured it was probably dying, but it turned and dealt a few clumsy swipes in Adal's general direction. Not wanting to take any chances, Adal rushed in and struck the creature just under its gaping mouth, crushing the remainder of its insect-like face inward. It gurgled a muted response before it collapsed backward, falling from the roof.

344

"Arija, you all—" Adal turned to the mangled window to check on Arija, but as soon as he set foot in its tattered former frame, a sharp pain erupted along his side. Suddenly he was smashing onto the adjoining wall of the home's exterior and rolling onto the roof again. Another Gearrtha had blindsided him by the window, mouth outstretched in a screech.

Adal looked down at his hands to find that his knuckles were missing. They had slid from his fingers and joined his revolver on the ground below. As the Gearrtha stomped its way across the roof toward him, he used what energy he had left to push himself up. He curled his fingers into fists, waiting for the creature to make its way to him. While his left hand may have been useless against these things, he still had one bionic hand, and he intended on beating this thing to death with it. The Gearrtha poised itself before Adal, a look of animalistic intent on its mechanical face. It glanced to its fallen comrade, then back to Adal.

"Let's go! I don't have all day," Adal huffed. The Gearrtha screeched a high-pitched noise that Adal thought would shatter glass and then its expression went limp. The light in its eyes faded to blackness, and before Adal could assess what was happening, its head fell from its shoulders and rolled off the roof. The headless body of the Gearrtha teetered and then plummeted to the ground clearing Adal's view of Arija, standing with a blade in each hand and a smug grin on her face.

"Yeah . . . I was just about to do that," Adal stammered, with a nervous smile.

"Oh, I'm sure you were. It's not like you've ever needed me to bail you out or anything. Regardless, you're welcome," Arija winked.

"Uh, Arija—" Adal pointed behind her, his eyes wide. She spun around, blades up and ready for the next fight. Webley had disappeared from the air, and more than a dozen Gearrtha now hovered over the backyard. All eyes hungry for revenge and staring at them.

"So, what's the next move?" Adal asked through the side of his mouth.

"What happened to Billy Badass?" Arija looked from side to side for an escape plan. Jumping into the window wouldn't help. The window was now completely dented in with bits hanging off, and there was no way it could withstand that many Gearrtha.

"I mean . . ." Adal started, but before he could finish two blinding white beams of light filled the air around them. Adal slammed his eyes shut, bringing the palm of his hand to his face.

"What the—" Arija began but was cut off by a deafening air horn. Adal slapped his hands to his ears and crouched down, trying to shield himself from the incessant wail.

Arija jumped back just as a large flying vehicle crashed through the swarm of Gearrtha, sending parts flying in all direction. What Arija could only imagine was a Fliegenmobi flew past the house. There was a giant, red cross painted on the side. The mobile clinic.

The machine landed as another dozen Kleinmasch charged in. Arija pulled Adal to his feet just as a large door opened, splitting the cross down the middle. Kip poked his head out from inside the craft.

"Here comes the boom!" Kip shouted, tossing two balls into the air toward the mob of Kleinmasch. Adal pushed Arija up against the side of the house, covering her with his body. When the smoke cleared, there was nothing left of the swarm of Kleinmasch. Adal ran his thumb across Arija's cheek, wiping away a black smudge of soot from the explosion.

"What the hell are they putting in those things?" Arija coughed out as she pushed away from the building.

"I don't know, but remind me to duck next time." Adal stepped to the edge of the roof, surveying the damage. Kip hopped out of the mobile clinic, slid off the roof, and ran to the center of the yard as the craft rose into the air and tore off, plowing into everything that moved.

"Careful with that, Mum! The cyclic rate of the engine is still a little off!" Kip shouted, throwing another grenade into the air from a pouch he had around his shoulder. Several more Kleinmasch were obliterated by its explosion. Kip pointed to one of the Feithidi at the edge of the group. The Feithidi narrowed in on the small prey on the platform and charged at him. At the last moment, Kip let the grenade fly and took cover. It landed directly into his attacker's mouth. The ensuing explosion sent shrapnel everywhere, successfully shredding two Gearrtha flying nearby.

"What is it with that kid?" Adal asked, a hearty, singular laugh leaving his lungs.

"Like you're any better," Arija shot back. "I don't know what gets into either of you to make you do the insane things you do!"

A large shadow appeared from overhead, and Webley emerged into the fray, a Feithidi in his arms. He spun it around like a melee weapon, striking other Kleinmasch as they neared. The swarm seemed to never end. The mobile clinic spun overhead as it collided with several more flying creatures, but Adal could see that several Gearrtha had attached themselves to the side of the craft and were trying to get in.

"Arija, it's time for the surprise! Do it!" Webley's voice thundered over the chaos. Arija grabbed Adal by his shirt and yanked him back into the window.

"What's going on now?" Adal asked, confused. He watched as Arija lifted a giant gun from the floor and set it in the window. She then slid over a large case and opened the top of it, removing a chain that connected a slew of rounds and slapped it into the weapon.

"Whoa! What is that?" Adal asked, running his fingers over the gun.

"A surprise," she answered with a devilish grin.

"Hey, let me shoot that thing!"

Arija laughed, tossing him the small pistol. "Here, use this. If you can handle it, that is." She squatted behind the large machine-gun and took aim out the window.

"Ah, what the f—" Adal began to protest, only to have the rest of his sentence drowned out by the deafening fire of the giant gun. The air in the small room fluctuated with every shot and flash of light. Casings jetted across the room as Arija delicately swayed the barrel back and forth, slicing through the Kleinmasch in droves. As Avani flew past in the medical craft, Arija did her best to align her shots to clear the clinging Gearrtha from its sides.

Adal stood in dumbfounded silence, looking from the small pistol in his hand to Arija's canon. He peeked out the window to see that everyone, including the Kleinmasch, had stopped fighting and were gawking in Arija's direction.

Kip stared up at the window, his mouth curled into a smile as a Feithidi snuck up behind him.

"Kip! Trouble!" Arija shouted over her shoulder to Adal as she concentrated on moving from one Kleinmasch to another.

Adal swept up next to her to peer out the window. "Kip! Run, bro!" Adal shouted, leaping from the open window and sliding down the roof. Kip turned just in time to see the creature coming for him. He spun around and ran toward the house. As Adal jumped to the ground, he fired several shots from the pistol and charged toward Kip.

The Feithidi stretched out one of its long legs in an attempt to grab Kip. Adal reached Kip at the exact same time, grasping him around the waist. He threw all his weight into him, lifting Kip from the ground and the two rolled forward from the path of the charging Feithidi.

"Clear!" Adal shouted in the general direction of the window. Before the Feithidi could take more than a few steps, it shook as Arija pumped several rounds into its body. It dropped to the ground, riddled with bullet holes.

As the parts and sparks flew past them, Adal rolled to cover Kip from the debris. Kip's shirt was mostly torn away, and underneath the fabric was a strange device. It looked very similar to the corset that Arija was wearing and peering out from the top was what appeared to be cleavage. As Adal's mind pieced things together, he pushed himself off Kip, his mouth hanging open.

"Kip . . . you're a girl?"

Kip's face went blank, and his lips thinned as a scowl developed. "I'm not a . . . you're a . . . shut up!" Kip slugged Adal in the arm and pushed to his feet. He pulled as much of his shirt closed as he could and ran into the house.

"What the hell was that?" Adal said, to no one in particular as he watched Kip disappear into the house. After a moment, Adal looked around. For the first time since the fight had started, the air around the house was cleared of Kleinmasch. The ground around him was littered with parts of fallen machines, and everything had fallen silent.

"Adal! Are you all right?" Arija shouted from the window. "Where's Kip?"

"I'm good. Kip ran inside. You good? What can you see?" Adal brushed the debris from his pants as he spoke.

"I'm just peachy. I think they're all gone. The last of the swarm followed Avani and Webley over the edge of the platform."

The air between them hung heavy. Catching a glimpse of metal, Adal walked over to the edge of the yard to collect his knuckles and revolver. He then wandered around the backyard kicking every large piece of the Kleinmasch to make sure they were all dead.

Arija scanned the edge of the platform, looking for any sign of more Kleinmasch. Nothing.

The medical vehicle piloted by Avani flew into sight and toward the house.

"Incoming!" Arija shouted, her heart rate increasing. On top of the craft, Webley held on to its roof, crouched down with a solemn smile creasing the edges of his mouth. Adal put his revolver back into his holster and adjusted his clothing.

Arija watched as the burst of air from the mobile clinic rattled and shifted the smaller pieces of the fallen Kleinmasch. She rubbed her shoulder where the recoil from the automatic firing had repeatedly jammed into her. She couldn't wait to get down to Adal and the rest of the group. She climbed back out onto the roof, took a deep breath of fresh air, and then slid down the side of the roof, landing on the ground below in a crouch.

"I can't see any more of them, I think we're good," she announced, walking over to Adal and giving him a hug. A loud commotion came from the craft as it landed, and Webley hopped from the roof, slamming to the ground.

"Ye' two all right?" he asked, walking over to them. The hatch from the ship opened, and Avani came charging out, running at the two weary Topsiders.

"We're fine. Give us something harder next time," Adal joked, trying to sound calm.

"Yeah, no problem at all. Used to do that all the time back home," Arija added, but her hands were still a little shaky.

"Where is Kip? Is he all right?" Avani asked, a slight tinge of panic in her voice as she approached. She looked slightly frazzled herself but sounded more concerned for Kip than about what she had just gone through.

"Kip is all set. He just ran inside after we took care of the last guy. No injuries, I think he's just upset." Adal glanced toward the house, his eyebrows knitted together.

"Kip was upset? That isn't like him at all. What happened? Are you sure he's all right?"

"I promise, Kip is all good. Look, when we were fighting, that big one came in. We ended up rolling, and it reached for him . . ." Adal gave up being coy. "Look, his shirt ripped open. I know Kip is a girl. She got upset and ran inside."

Arija analyzed Adal's face for signs of the joke she assumed he was telling. She turned to look at Avani who had brought her hand to her cheek and was smiling as if she knew the inside joke.

"Kip is a boy," Avani stated plainly.

"I saw what was underneath. Well, I mean, the corset and the uhh . . . uhh . . . cleavage. Kip is a girl. How could you not know that?" Adal's face warmed from embarrassment. How could they have missed that? Avani was basically Kip's mother, and Webley is supposed to know every part of the machine.

Arija didn't know how to react. So, she didn't. She stood, confusion playing on her face and embarrassment flushing her cheeks.

"Here in the World Machine, there are many different creatures from many aspects of creation. You can make yourself anything you could ever want to be. It does not mean that there is something wrong with you. On the contrary, it means you are an individual and your own being. Kip decided that though he was made in the form of a girl, he was, for all intents and purposes, a boy. So, he is a boy. It is not on the rest of us to define others, only to accept them for what they are. Kip is a wonderful Dweller, smart and cunning. Don't diminish who he is by being blind to that," Avani offered softly.

Avani's words weighed heavy on Adal's mind. He felt like a complete idiot. He didn't care if Kip was

353

a boy or a girl or whatever. Kip was a good kid and had saved his ass many times. That's all that mattered. "I think maybe I should go inside and apologize or something."

A wide smile creased Avani's face, but her eyes remained narrow and analytical. "Maybe that would be best. After all, he did bail you out yesterday, no? Don't worry, he told me all about it. Never been good at keeping secrets, that one."

"I think I'll stay out here and help with this mess," Arija interjected, trying her best to break the awkwardness of the situation.

"I will be off t' look fer Cog. Not like him te' be knocked from a fight an' stay out," Webley added, concern in his voice.

"Wait, where is Cog? He was taken down? Down were?" Avani's voice suddenly filled with panic.

"He got knocked out of the sky and slid off the platform. I tried to reach him, but . . ." Adal let his words trail away. Avani's face contorted into one of horror as she looked from Adal to Webley and back again.

"Relax. I will find him. I sense tha' he's still 'ere," Webley replied, his voice calm and even. With that, he turned to face the end of his backyard and leaped into the air before disappearing over the edge. Even with Webley's reassurance, Avani's features were still creased in concern.

"I'm sure he'll be fine. You're here to help when they come back. If Webley isn't worried, it will all be fine," Arija reassured her. "Come on, let's clean this up. Adal, you go inside and check on Kip. This time, try not to be a jackass to the kid." Arija took charge of the moment. She'd seen enough pain for a lifetime, and this group didn't deserve to have their hopes dashed now. As she saw it, it was probably best to stay task-focused and give Webley time to find Cog, instead of sitting around and worrying about him. Avani nodded in agreement, and Adal snapped a quick and sarcastic salute before making his way into the house to look for Kip.

30

You Like My Knockers?

Adal used the time it took him to walk into the house to think about what he was going to say to Kip. Kip was a cool kid, and Avani was right—he had saved their asses twice in two days. The last thing he wanted was to ostracize him or make him feel little. Adal thought back to his home, not for the first time since they'd entered the Machine and the issues he'd had with Elias. That guy was an asshole, and Adal didn't want to resemble him in the slightest.

As he entered the house, Kip was sitting in the den next to the shelf of weapons they'd left open. He'd brought several of the more impressive pieces of hardware they had left on the shelves down to the table and was mulling over them. When Adal entered the room and walked over to the seat across from him, Kip wouldn't even look up at him.

"Hey, bro. How you feeling?" Adal asked nervously. He didn't want to make it any worse, but he hadn't the slightest clue what he should say. Kip didn't respond immediately. He picked up one of the ax-guns and looked at the blade of it, running one small finger down the steel.

"I'm fine," Kip said bluntly. "I didn't need your help, you know. I was there to save you guys." Kip dropped the gun on the table and leaned back in the chair. He crossed his arms over his chest and trained his eyes on the fireplace. Adal sighed and shook his head, sitting in the seat across from him.

"I know that, bro. Seriously. I owe you thanks like ten times over. You saved our asses more than once, and I appreciate that." Adal noticed a pitcher of water sitting on the table. It hadn't been there that morning. Kip must have gotten it when he came inside. He had a strange thought as he reflexively picked it up and took a swig straight from the pitcher: Do Dwellers drink water? The thought tore at his brain for a couple of minutes while the two sat in silence.

"Yeah, well, you're welcome I guess. I mean, you two would have gotten yourselves killed by now if it wasn't for me. Just saying." Kip played with the tip of his knee, running his fingers over it again and again. Adal smiled and shook his head.

"Hey man, I know it. You're a pretty cool dude. You got the brains and kick-ass toys to boot. The way you came in today, that was dope." Adal took a long swig of the water, not realizing until that moment how thirsty he was.

"Oh, so you liked my knockers?" Kip asked, finally bringing his eyes to Adal's. Adal spit the contents of his mouth into the air, spraying water all over the table and Kip.

"What?!" Adal coughed as his lungs tried to force the water out of his windpipe.

Kip ran his palm across the side of his face, wiping away the droplets that had landed there. "My knockers. The bombs I made. They're pretty cool, huh? The mixture inside is my own design." Kip's voice softened, and his pitch relaxed. He had lost the somber tone from when Adal first entered the room.

After a moment of coughing and realizing the lack of slang terms in the Machine, Adal was able to compose himself. "Oh! Yeah man, those were sweet! What did you put in those things?"

"Well, it is simple really. I take a bit of—" Kip was cut off as the door burst open and Arija stepped into the room.

"Webley found Cog. He was unconscious several levels below. He just came back with him. Come outside!" Arija commanded, a strange mixture of both relief and concern running rampant across her face.

As Adal pushed through the door, followed by Kip and Arija, they were greeted by Avani and Webley standing over a motionless Cog. Webley seemed to look fine at first, but once they got closer, Adal noticed the giant was nervously rubbing his hands together as he examined Cog.

Avani had a small pack of tools next to her on the ground, and she was tapping Cog in the chest and running a small box across his eyes.

"He's alive. He took quite a hit. It looks like something landed on him." As Avani spoke, Adal felt his stomach jump into his throat. He had shot down that Feithidi that collided with his friend in the air. This was all his fault. He looked at Arija, but she was entirely focused on Cog. He then looked to Webley, and a strange frustration came over him. If Webley was so powerful, why couldn't he just fix this?

Arija was staring at Cog, but she was thinking about Adal. She knew he had to be kicking himself, even though this wasn't his fault. She could practically feel his anxiety as she watched him shift his weight from one foot to the other in her peripheral. This wasn't his fault. He may have actually saved Cog by killing that thing first, but she knew he would blame himself no matter what her justification. So, she decided it best just to let it go for the moment. This wasn't the place. Instead, she watched Kip help Avani.

"He's a tough one. Should pull out o' it soon 'nough! Always been a fighter, this one." Webley sounded more like he was trying to convince himself than anyone else in the group.

Avani continued to check Cog over and monitor his responses. After withdrawing a string implement that she had inserted into his ear and watching something on a small screen, she put her tools down and leaned over Cog.

"All right. That is enough of that. You are in there! I know it. Time to wake up," Avani demanded sweetly. She leaned further over Cog and pressed a lingering kiss on his forehead.

"If . . . if I pretend to be out a little longer, could I venture another kiss?" A soft-spoken voice broke the silence.

"Ha! Tha's my boy! Cheers!" Webley thundered, his shoulders sinking into his frame as he relaxed. A smile erupted over Adal and Arija's faces as he spoke. After all that had gone down, it felt nice to have something good happen.

"Well, I'm not sure if that is a medically sound theory, Cog. Perhaps we can reassess your theory at a later date." Avani smiled at him, tapping him on the cheek playfully. Cog lay on the ground for a moment, just looking up at his love and her back at him.

The moment was interrupted by a slight rumble at their feet. Arija couldn't help but think something very bad was about to happen. Arija glanced at Adal, the corners of her lips turned down, but before she could say anything, Webley came crashing into them, sending them both sliding across the ground. Avani's ship came barreling through the air towards them, and when Arija could clear the spots from her eyes and look around, Avani was gone.

"What the f—!" Adal shouted as he rolled across the yard.

"Son of a bitch!" Arija yelled as she slid into Adal. They came to a stop and allowed the dazed world about them to come back to normal.

A large creature came into focus. Somehow it had managed to sneak up on them, which sounded ridiculous considering its size.

It resembled a giant mechanical tarantula had to be at least four stories tall and several times that in width if you counted its legs. Its behemoth body shook everything under them as it moved, casting various objects aside as it crunched through the bent and broken Kleinmasch.

The Umar.

Before Arija had time to process what was happening, Webley was on his feet and at the monstrosity. Arija waited a moment until her world stopped spinning, looking around to examine the situation. Avani was sprawled out halfway across the yard. Her mobile clinic was dented in on one side and teetering on the edge of the platform. Arija watched, dazed, as the mobile clinic groaned and then tipped over the edge of the platform falling into the Machine. Webley's shouts pulled her from her daze. She shifted her weight so she could see him banging his fists on the creature's exoskeleton.

"What the hell is that thing?" Adal shouted, scooting himself closer to Arija.

"I don't know, but we have to help," Arija's voice quivered as she stared back at Avani. "You get Cog, I'll get Avani. We need to bring them away from the fight before they're trampled." Without waiting for a response, Arija pushed herself up and ran toward Avani.

Adal scrambled to his feet and ran for Cog, who was writhing on the ground, trying to pull himself up. He could see Webley and the Umar fighting in the distance. The remnants of a Feithidi was thrown through the air as the Umar reared back and swung one of its legs at Webley, sending him backward. Adal dove forward into a roll, coming to a stop next to Cog.

Arija slid to Avani's side hands up as if she were afraid to touch her for fear she'd break into a million little pieces. Avani's clothes were ripped, and portions of her arm had been peeled back, revealing hundreds of small cogs and gears surrounding a long, thin metal pipe that almost looked like a bone. The delicate clockwork mechanisms weren't moving. Arija had a sudden sinking sickly feeling in her stomach. Small parts from the corpse of a fallen Kleinmasch rained down upon her, but Arija didn't look up. She couldn't wait while Avani potentially died in her arms, so she slid her arms under Avani's and began to drag her across the platform.

362

"Let me in the fight!" Cog yelled at Adal as he dragged him across the yard and toward the house. Adal did his best to ignore him, but the more Cog protested, the more he squirmed, and the more difficult it would be to pull him to safety. The wail of crushing metal came from behind Adal, and he glanced back in time to see Webley drop onto the back of the Umar's head and pound his fist into it. The creature reared back and tossed Webley from his perch. Adal turned again, using the strength of his legs to pull Cog to the side of the house just as the Umar plunged its feet into the ground where Cog had been laying. Arija was leaning against the side of the house staring at Avani with a blank look on her face.

"How is she?" Adal asked as he slid Cog up next to Arija. Arija didn't respond, she only looked up at him with tears in her eyes, and her forehead furrowed in anger. After an intense moment, she just shook her head, bringing her eyes back down to Avani who lay motionless on the ground.

"What happened to her?" Cog's voice hitched, and he crawled toward Avani.

"That thing threw her mobile clinic, and I think it crushed her" Adal answered quietly, not sure how to say it. Cog leaned over Avani's body, lightly brushing his hand across her face like he was trying to wake her from a deep sleep.

"NO!" Cog yelled. "No, no, no, nonononononono" Cog cradled Avani's head in his hands. He pulled his body as close to her as he could get and laid down next to her. "Shhhhh. It's ok. You're ok." Cog was whispering as he kissed her forehead like she had just done to him only moments before.

Arija tugged at Adal's shoulder. "We have to do something! That thing is still out there! We need to find a way to help Webley." Arija pulled back from the group, skooched her body down the side of the house, and carefully peered around the corner. "Why can't he take that thing down?" she mumbled under her breath as she felt Adal press himself up behind her.

"What's the plan? That thing looks like it isn't playing games." Adal watched as Webley slammed his fist into one of the Umar's legs only to be kicked away by another one of its legs.

"Well, neither are we." Arija turned back to face Adal. She nodded her head toward his pistol.

"Let's get this party started then." Adal pulled the pistol from his holster and cocked the hammer back.

Arija pulled out the small pistol she had tucked away in the belt of her skirt. "Me first!" She barked, rolling around the corner and leveling the sights of the pistol with the head of the Umar. Webley was underneath one of its tree-sized legs trying to rip its leg from the socket. Arija took a deep breath and squeezed the trigger. Sparks shot from the Umar's face as the bullet plunged into its head.

The creature reacted like someone swatting away a mosquito. It swatted one leg toward its face and then continued to kick at Webley, sending him hurling through the air toward them. Adal tackled Arija to the ground as Webley smashed into the side of his house, denting the siding.

Adal raised the gun and began firing round after round at the Umar. "Come and get some!" he yelled. The Umar turned its attention to him, stomping toward him and giving Webley time to collect himself. The two Topsiders alternated firing and maneuvering to avoid the crushing legs of the Umar. It was like a strange interpretive dance.

"Webley, what the hell?" Adal shouted, trying his best to reload his revolver while Arija distracted the Umar.

"Can't break through its armor. This ain't one o' my makings, Adal!" Webley grunted as he attempted to rip into the creature's side, succeeding only in getting swatted away once more.

Adal slapped his revolver closed and raised it for another shot.

"Need. Another. Plan!" Arija panted as she emptied the last of her ammunition.

"Yeah, no shit!" Adal replied, realizing he too had run out of rounds. "Webley!" Adal shouted after a minute of realizing they only had one option. The giant didn't respond, but he glanced down at them as he punched the Umar in the side. "We'll keep him distracted!"

Webley went back to trying to rip the rivets out of the Umar's side as Adal reared back and kicked the side of the Umar's leg. The giant spider raised his leg to stomp Adal, but he grabbed the Umar's leg and swung himself around out of reach. Arija jumped onto one of the Umar's other legs and held on for dear life as it tried to shake her off. Adal picked up a severed arm of one of the dead Kleinmasch and smashed it into the beast. The Umar shifted its weight back and forth a few times like it was trying to decide who to focus on before it gave up and brought its attention back to Webley.

All at once, a deafening sound pierced through the battle and the Umar started to violently shake as hundreds of bullets tore into its side. "This is for my mum!" Kip shouted from the second-floor window. Adal and Arija both looked up to see Kip standing in the window of Arija's perch with the giant machine-gun.

"Damn, that kid doesn't play!" Adal dropped the useless arm he'd been holding, suddenly embarrassed by it.

"Uh, Adal . . ." Arija motioned back to the Umar, who had turned his attention to Kip. "This kid is going to get me killed!" Arija protested, sprinting toward one of the spider's legs as it slammed to the ground.

Before Adal could ask what she was doing, Arija jumped onto the leg, digging her fingers into the small holes that held the rivets. Once she gained her balance, she reached up for the next hole, shoving her foot into one below her like she was climbing a rock wall.

The Umar didn't seem to notice her until Arija took one of the blades Cog had given her and stabbed at the litany of pipes and tubes that ran the length of the Umar's legs. A burst of rusty brown liquid sprayed into the air covering Arija. With the back of her hand, she wiped the liquid away from her eyes and stabbed at the spider's legs again. The Umar let out an electronic shriek and shook Arija from its leg, sending her somersaulting through the air.

Adal shouted a guttural charge as he ran toward the Umar. Just then, he remembered that he was wearing a fliegensack. He bent down and released the compressed wings with a sharp echo before launching himself into the air toward Arija. He collided with her just a few yards from the platform, wrapping his arms around her and speeding toward the roof of the house.

"You're welcome," Adal whispered as they circled in the air before landing next to the house.

"Yeah, that's one to my . . . how many times have I saved you?" Arija smiled up at him then turned to run back toward the Umar. Adal paused for a moment and retracted his wings before following her.

Webley had managed to rip several small panels of the Umar's armor away and expose the delicate mechanical workings beneath, but it proved nearly impossible for him to get to the vitals. Kip continued his assault, unfazed by the looming doom. It was like that kid thought everything was a game.

"All right, what's the next idea?" Adal asked as he caught up with Arija.

"Repeat step 'A'!" Arija bellowed, charging back into the fight. Just then, the Umar reared one of its front legs and lunged at the house, desperate to get to Kip.

"Kip! Get—" Adal started, but before he could finish his warning, the Umar brought its leg down on the window of the house, nearly crushing the entire side of Webley's home. The explosion of debris cast Arija backward, forcing Adal to run in and catch his falling friend once more. The two met in mid-maneuver and fell to the ground.

"Kip!" Adal and Arija screamed in unison.

Webley bellowed with rage and tore at the Umar's back. "Ye' blasted machine!" The Umar turned its attention back to Webley, removing its leg from the side of the house and turning about in circles to dislodge him. The two titans churned over and over as they took their shots at one another. The Umar turned at just the right time, and Webley slid from its back, rolling over and over before coming to a stop at Arija and Adal's feet. The two Topsiders looked down at the master of the Machine, frozen in fear. If Webley couldn't beat the Umar, no one could.

"Any ideas now?" Adal asked, looking from Webley to the crushed home, to the Umar. Webley was knocked out at best, Cog could hardly move, Avani was probably dead, and Kip was nowhere to be seen. Adal looked up at the Umar to see its coal black eyes glaring at him.

"We go for the sides. It has to have a weak spot. If we get in there, we have him." Arija replied, taking out the other knife and clutching both blades in her hands.

"All right . . . any ideas how we are going to get in there?" Adal asked, taking out his knuckles and looking at the massive legs that had taken Webley down.

"Haven't gotten that far yet," Arija replied. The Umar shuddered and took a step toward them.

"You ready?" Adal asked.

"Not even close! You?" Arija replied.

"Always." Adal tried not to sound as terrified as he truly was. A shrill shriek startled Adal, and he turned to see Cog running at them, his face twisted into a mask of furry.

"What's that?" Arija asked, pointing to a satchel that Cog clutched in his hand.

"Oh no . . . Those are Kip's Knockers!" Adal yelled.

"His WHAT?"

"Just run!" Adal pulled her by the shoulder, making a full sprint toward the edge of the platform. As they neared the open void, Cog met the Umar in the center of the yard and leaped into the air toward the Umar's open mouth.

"Jump!" Adal shouted, taking Arija by the hand.

"Are you insane?" Horror was plastered on Arija's face.

"Now!" Adal commanded.

Arija squeezed her eyes shut as she jumped from the platform. Her heart was in her throat, and she could hear its furious pounding in her ears.

"I hope you're hungry," Cog's muffled words penetrated the air as it rushed around them.

As Arija and Adal cleared the edge of the platform, the sound and air around them was sucked away. A ringing erupted in Arija's ears as a massive explosion tore through the air. Falling below the platform, Adal stole a glance at the underside of Webley's home. A column of crimson and orange flames spewed from all four sides of the structure.

Adal deployed his wings, but he never let go of Arija's hand. A few seconds later, Arija released her wings as well and floated up so she was even with Adal. They drifted to a slow stop, hovering in silence, watching the sky above them burn and crackle. The smell of smoke and explosives putrefied the air around them.

Arija wiped a tear from her cheek. "What do we do now?" Her voice was cold as she spoke. They were all gone. She could hardly believe it. In the few days since they'd been in the Machine, she'd grown closer to them than she had to most people Topside. And now they were just . . . gone. A horrifying thought crept into her mind and the gravity of what this meant hit her. If Webley were dead, Pajak would be free to run the Machine, and with the furnace destroyed, the entire world would die.

"I don't . . . they are . . . I don't know." Adal's words pulled Arija from her thoughts. A small click, like someone cocking a gun, came from below them. Looking down, deep in the shadows below them, something was moving. Adal and Arija looked at one another and then turned themselves to fly closer to the sound.

Nearing the shadows, they came to an abrupt stop, floating behind a pillar. With precision maneuvering, they landed on a cross-section of beams just wide enough for their feet. Arija crouched down so she could hear what was happening.

"Search all of it. I don't care if you have to bring back everything. The master wanted both of them, and he won't be happy about this. Bring me whatever parts of the Topsiders and Webley that you can find."

Turning around the edge of the structure, but doing their best to keep in the shadows, Adal and Arija were met with the cold silhouette of Fausto standing on a small platform and speaking to a group of Gearrtha. Adal felt the sudden urge to punch the Cog look-a-like in his stupid smug face. Feeling his anger, Arija pulled back on her friend's shoulder, yanking him away. Adal turned to her, and she just shook her head. Doing something stupid now would only get them killed. Fausto had proven strong enough, but with a group of Gearrtha, they didn't stand a chance.

"Then, once you have collected ALL the parts, make sure you bring back what is left of the master's special gift. I am certainly not going to do that myself. Do you think you idiots can handle that?" Fausto spoke the last sentence slowly like he was speaking to a group of toddlers.

"Good, then I will make my way back. Be sure to send word if you find anything else of interest." With that, Fausto jumped off the beam he had been standing on and disappeared into the Machine.

The Gearrtha shot up into the air toward Webley's home, flying past Arija with enough force to push her hair into her face. Adal turned and looked at Arija and tilted his head.

"Let's follow him," Arija whispered and jumped off the beam to follow Fausto into the Machine. The dim lights of the machine danced and moved about them as they darted from one place of concealment to the next, making sure to never lose sight of Fausto. This had been a coordinated attack, and Adal and Arija were hell-bent on getting to the source of it. As they hopped from one beam to another, they lost track of how far they were traveling, moving further and further away from Webley's home.

371

After what seemed like hours of watching Fausto walk and leap from surface to surface, platform to platform, he came to a stop on a large dock near a giant, spinning gear. As he landed softly on the metal surface, Fausto took a moment to stretch his arms and look about the cold machine. He walked to a gap in the turning wheel and disappeared from sight.

"Do we follow him in?" Arija whispered.

"We can't lose him now. Just be ready," Adal replied. After checking the area for threats, they slid out from behind their concealment and swooped down to the platform. With their wings in their packs, they began to silently make their way across the platform.

"You know what to do when we get in there, right?" Adal looked at Arija, his lips thin and eyes narrow. She nodded and took out her blades. They stepped through the gear only to find it led nowhere. A chill ran through Adal's body as he realized it was a trap.

"Whose house is this?" A voice echoed off the steel walls of the empty room. Before Adal could turn, a sharp pain reverberated through his head and then his world turned. He had a second to see Arija lying next to him, her eyes wide with terror before there was a burst of pain behind his eyes and everything went black.

31

A Shitty Sci-Fi Movie From The Eighties

Adal woke to a throbbing pain in the back of his head. From where he lay on the floor all he could see was a strangely beautiful ceiling. Web-like etchings covered the entire ceiling, and there were small gems scattered in various parts of the webbed design.

"Adal . . . you with me?" Arija whispered, her voice stressed with confusion and pain.

"I think so. I don't think I'm dead yet." He couldn't help how his voice hitched at the word 'yet.' He slowly stretched his hand outward, feeling for Arija's. When his fingers brushed hers, he let out the breath he didn't know he'd been holding. She wrapped her fingers around his and squeezed, reassuring him, or herself.

"Not dead yet? That's awfully optimistic of you, wouldn't you say?" A voice echoed through the room. Adal jumped, and he pushed himself up to a sitting position. The room spun around him, but he slid himself over to Arija, his eyes roaming the space for the source of the voice.

Arija looked around the room as she pressed her back against Adal's. Large pillars ran the length of what she could only describe as a palace hall. At one end, a set of gigantic doors stood closed, a spider web etched into their surface. On one side of the hall, a row of what looked like Dwellers attached to strange devices ran the length of the wall. Their dead expressions brought a chill to Arija. Along the opposite side, a large, dead creature like the one that had attacked them at Webley's house lay lifeless.

At the end of the hall, a man sat on a macabre throne, a smug look on his face. He didn't seem to care that the two Topsiders were in his midst as he toyed with what seemed to be a living Dweller's face protruding from his armrest. Standing next to the throne was Fausto, leaning against one of the pillars, a sinister grin on his face. Arija pushed to her feet, steadying herself before reaching a hand down to help Adal.

374

"Who the hell are you?" Adal took a half step forward. Fausto glanced over at Pajak who started to laugh. After a second, Fausto also started to laugh but immediately stopped when Pajak shot him a dirty look.

"Where are we?" Arija asked, changing the question to avoid Adal saying something that would get them killed more quickly. Adal's ego usually won out over rational thought.

"Well, for two Topsiders lost in a strange world, the two of you certainly demand quite a lot. Fausto, are these the two that bested you on the doorway of the city? I cannot imagine how. They appear just as foolish as they are scared." At Pajak's condescending words, Fausto stirred, his face twisting at the implications.

"Either way, I suppose I could enlighten you. I am having too much fun to end this too quickly. You stand in the great hall of my kingdom. I am Pajak, and you are now within my Roost, the capital city of my children, the Kleinmasch. Welcome, Adal and Arija, to your end." Pajak pointed a finger at Adal. "Which one are you? Arija is it?"

Adal clenched his fists and tightened his jaw. "Now that we have that out of the way, exactly what is it you want? I have better places to be than in some Dracula-wannabe robot's house with his minion that has to sneak up on people to win a fight. What's the matter, Fausto? Couldn't get the job done, so you ran to daddy for help?"

"You will speak when instructed, Topsider!" Fausto yelled, stomping one foot on the ground like a spoiled child having a tantrum. "I suggest you close

375

that mouth of yours, or I will have to remove your lower jaw."

"Look at you go! You do have quite the burning fire in you, don't you? I can't wait to rip it out and see what makes it burn." Pajak turned his attention to Adal as he rose from his seat. Four long, thin, spider legs lifted Pajak into the air and set him down gently at the foot of the steps that led to his throne.

"What is it with you people and spiders? I feel like all we need is a large can of raid in here," Adal muttered.

Arija couldn't help the laugh that escaped her lips. The scene felt like a shitty sci-fi movie from the eighties. She moved closer to Adal and grabbed his hand. If something was going to happen, they had to act together, and that was her way of reminding him of it.

Fausto stepped away from the throne and followed his master as he slowly made his way down the walkway ahead of them, towards Adal and Arija.

"The two of you speak with such conviction. Topsiders are an amazing race, are they not, Fausto? I cannot wait to see what makes them run." Pajak's eyes narrowed, and he twisted his head from side to side as he examined his new prey.

Arija shot a nervous look at Adal and squeezed his hand. "You two need to step back!" Even with her knife, she didn't think she could take on Fausto and Pajak. "Fausto, didn't you have enough problems taking me on yesterday? Are you sure you want to take on the both of us?"

Fausto's lips thinned, and he crossed his arms over his chest. "You had the good fortune of catching me on an off day. I can promise you, today will not be the same. Especially without your little toys." Fausto removed two daggers from his belt line and a set of knuckles from behind his back and cast them to the floor. The crash of metal on metal was jarring, and Arija's heart leaped into her throat as she slid her free hand to the small of her back. Arija shot a panicked look at Adal only to find that his face mirrored hers.

"Oh, now, there is no need for that. Really, it isn't like this situation will devolve to fighting anyway. After all, why would it? It isn't as though you have the slightest chance of surviving. I will take you, rip you into pieces, and discover the secrets of your life. Then, no matter what secrets he may keep, I will have my own ways of creating sentient life. I won't need his—" Pajak's monologue was cut off as Adal finally put two and two together, and found them to, in fact, equal four.

"Wait a minute! You're the ones from the war? It was you that turned everyone against themselves? You?" Adal's heart raced as he recalled the story Cog had told them about the spoiled child that destroyed their society. It was this guy? This Dr. Octopus looking mother fucker was the reason the world might end? "For what? The chance to play God and make these . . . what do you call your science experiments again?"

Pajak brought two of his spider-like legs to his knees and doubled over in laughter. "My Kleinmasch are living, that is for certain. What they have in function, they lack in the spark of life. They are not cognitive creatures. They are driven by the basic instincts of feeding, completing assigned tasks, and growing like the horde that they are. To give them life and awareness would truly make them a superior race of creature. Far above that of Webley's Dwellers. Nevertheless, that time has passed. I no longer wish to create a better machine. Wish to create a better Topsider. Ones that are not as weak as you, but have your powerful resolve. Soon I shall have those secrets."

"Sounds like someone wasn't held enough as a child. I can tell you one thing asshat, you touch either one of us, and you will eat that hand!" Adal barked, taking a step toward Pajak and pushing Arija behind him.

"Still think you can survive Topsider? I'm the most powerful creation in the Machine. Even Webley could not stop me." Pajak snaked two of his legs around, yanking on Adal's vest playfully.

Adal slapped his mechanical hand away, and Pajak made a show of shaking it like he was hurt.

"He couldn't stop you because he still loved you even though you betrayed him! But I can promise you, I won't have the same problem." Arija's voice was hoarse, and she prayed they couldn't hear the small quiver.

"Child, it is over. Even your Webley was no match for my Umar! He may be the master of all his creations, but when he faces my might and intellect, he is subject only to his brute strength. I built something stronger than he. And now I will take you out too." Pajak took several steps forward, closing the gap between them.

"You know, maybe I should just dissect one of you and keep the other as a pet. Wouldn't that be splendid? How about it, Arija? Would you like to be a pet?" Pajak reached out and ran his thin fingers across the cuff of Arija's corset.

With unyielding reflex, Adal threw his right hand out and caught Pajak's outstretched appendage. "I warned you . . ." Adal brought his foot upward and kicked Pajak in the groin. A dull, metallic clank was followed by Adal shouting in pain.

Pajak and Fausto roared with laughter. "Was that your master plan of attack?" Fausto gasped in between bouts of laughter. "Pathetic!"

Adal bent down in pain, groaning as he rubbed the top of his foot. As he knelt underneath Pajak, Adal too began to laugh. At first, his laughter was a soft, barely audible chuckle, but soon it grew into a loud, maniacal sound.

"Whose. House?" Adal reared up and brought his reinforced fist underneath Pajak's pointed chin. The metallic crunch was followed by Pajak stumbling backward. Adal followed his momentum by lunging forward and spearing Pajak in the midsection, sending them rolling backward. Pajak's thin spider legs flailed in the air as he fought to steady himself.

Arija took the opportunity and rolled over Adal's legs, colliding with the floor and sliding over to the pile of weapons. As she reached out to grab one of her daggers, Fausto realized what she was doing, and he lunged at her. Fausto clumsily pawed at the weapons, sending Adal's metal knuckles sliding across the room. Arija slammed her shoulder into him, forcing him back as she awkwardly fumbled for her blades.

She threw herself over Fausto and was surprised when she came up holding one of her lethal blades in each hand. The look of shock and horror on her face melted away into a long, wide grin as she looked from the glistening edges of the blades in her hand to Fausto. Now the fight was fair. Fausto slowly rose from the ground looking almost like he was embarrassed to have been rolling around with a Topsider. He straightened out his shirt, eyes burning with rage as he looked down at Arija.

"Well look at that, looks like we're gonna have a little fun after all," Arija teased, bringing her blades up in a fighting stance.

"This won't be pleasant for you. I guess if that's what you mean by fun, then yes, this is going to be a blast." Fausto reached behind his back and withdrew the same blades he had fought Cog with not too long ago. Arija looked from his weapon to her own. His were longer. Arija lowered herself, feeling the weight of her body on the balls of her feet, and then sprung toward Fausto, blades ready.

Pajak wrapped one of his legs around Adal and flung him across the room. He was much stronger than Adal had anticipated and with him only having one fist that could do any damage, the fight wasn't off to a promising start. As Adal slid to a stop at the base of one pillar, his head spinning, he had the sudden urge to throw up. "Why does this keep happening to me?" Adal grunted as he bounced to the floor.

Pajak was making his way across the floor toward him, using only his thin, spider legs and Adal pushed himself to his feet, bringing his fists up as he tried to think of a plan.

"You are pathetic, Topsider! Just give it up!" Pajak demanded, sounding bored with the little tussle.

"I was just going to say the same thing to you!" Adal shouted, hoping the strength behind his words would mask the shakiness.

"Oh well, at least you still have your sense of humor. It will come in handy as I'm taking you apart piece by piece. You see, I really need you alive in order to fully understand your inner mechanisms. But don't worry, that quick wit and sharp tongue of yours will be your solace when you are in unbearable—" Pajak's words were cut off as Adal spired him to the ground.

Arija and Fausto danced around one another, taking various swipes from a distance, before leaping in, meeting blades and then pushing away. Arija was in her comfort zone as she squared off with Fausto like she'd done a million times in wrestling. The threat of death was new, but she found it to be a special kind of motivator. Her mind and body were moving in perfect unison as she remembered Fausto's fighting style from the fight with Cog on the docks.

"What's the matter? Scared to fight me because you know I have no problem killing you? Just like you didn't have a problem setting up your brother's death!" Arija yelled, trying to sound more unhinged than she actually was. Fausto seemed unbothered by her words. He merely snickered and swiped one blade at her.

Pajak lifted Adal into the air by his shirt and collar, holding him high enough that his feet dangled above the ground. Adal tried to pry Pajak's hands off him as he kicked at Pajak's chest as hard as he could.

"You can't beat me Adal, just give up and accept your fate. If you're a good little boy, maybe you'll live long enough to see me make history." Pajak laughed as Adal went limp. Taking a moment to think, Adal remembered one of Arija's wrestling moves he'd watched her use to win countless matches. He released both of Pajak's hands and grabbed him by one wrist. Turning it inward and pulling Pajak's hand toward him, Adal broke his grip and utilized the momentum to bring him down to the floor.

Pajak gasped as he was pulled to the ground and snapped one of his arachnid legs at Adal like a whip. Adal rolled out of the way just in time to see the leg strike the floor and leave a perfect gash in the metal. Adal looked at what could have been his face with his eyes wide. "Damn!" The word slipped out involuntarily, but Adal couldn't help how impressed he was.

Arija and Fausto were still squared off, neither one willing to make the first move. Every so often Fausto would fake inward, and Arija would kick at him. She would follow with a bladed strike of her own, only to have it immediately swatted aside by Fausto's longer blades.

Arija shot a look to Adal, worried at what she would find. Adal was a great fighter, but he knew nothing about wrestling or using your opponent's weight against them. She tried to make a move to get to Adal, only to be cut off by Fausto.

"Oh, we wouldn't want to spoil their fun now, would we?" Fausto teased, placing himself between the two groups. Arija scoffed at him, but inside she was terrified. Adal was repeatedly trying to punch Pajak which was basically like trying to punch your way out of a metal room. If she didn't get in there soon, Adal wouldn't last much longer.

Adal was exhausted. He didn't know how much longer he could fend Pajak off. "You hit like a . . . well . . . like whatever the hell hits soft down here." Adal fumbled his words, trying to sound like he didn't already know he was beaten. Every punch he threw missed once the extreme exhaustion set in. Now and then he managed to land a successful right hook, but even that was doing less and less damage as time went on.

"I am not sure what that was supposed to mean, but I can assure you, your protests are truly pathetic." Pajak swiped one long leg at Adal, forcing him to roll under the strike and slide across the smooth floor. Where were his knuckles?

Arija watched Adal slide across the smooth floor as she managed a parry at Fausto and threw her shoulder into his chest knocking him backward into a pillar. She took the opportunity to run toward Adal's knuckles and kick them in Adal's general direction. It was all she had time to do to help, and she gave a silent prayer that it was enough. Just as she kicked the knuckles, she glimpsed Fausto coming up behind her, and she spun with just enough time to crouch down and flip him over her shoulders.

    Adal heard the metallic grinding of the weapons sliding across the floor. He rolled sideways as his eyes found his weapon, and he crawled the few feet he needed to retrieve them. Pajak used the force of his legs to propel himself into the air and bring down his fury upon Adal. Adal got to his knuckles and slid them over his fingers just as Pajak stabbed his extended appendages into the hard floor of the hall, narrowly missing Adal's face and left shoulder. As he attempted a follow-up attack, Pajak realized his legs were wedged into the floor.

    "Well, this sort of sucks for you." Adal turned all of his wrath to Pajak, swinging wildly at the man like he was the punching bag in the school's weight room. Pajak brought his remaining legs up to defend himself against Adal's strikes, but his lack of mobility made it easy for Adal to maneuver around them.

A small smile creased Arija's face as she watched Adal beat the crap out of Pajak out of the corner of her eye. She was tiring of squaring off with Fausto, but she knew she couldn't let her guard down or he would see the weakness. Having noticed that Arija was distracted by watching Adal, Fausto jumped in and sliced a deep cut into Arija's arm. She jumped back before he could get her again, but she couldn't prevent the gasp that forced its way out of her mouth at the pain. Warm blood seeped from the wound, but Arija didn't have the time to tend to it.

Adal heard Arija's gasp and paused to see a stream of blood winding its way down Arija's arm only to pool on the floor by her feet. He took a step in her direction, wanting nothing more than to go to her and beat the living snot out of Fausto, but he knew he couldn't leave Pajak now that he finally had him cornered. Adal focused his rage on the thing in front of him and unleashed a flurry of punches on Pajak.

Adal was in the zone—nailing punch after punch on Pajak; but somehow the creature managed to wriggle his legs free, and he shot one of them toward Adal, catching him off guard. Adal jumped back, going on the defensive and trying to keep himself as far away as he could from the long appendages of his opponent. With all eight of his spider legs free, Pajak lowered himself onto his human legs and lashed out at Adal with the eight long, thin extremities. A cold, burning pain erupted in Adal's cheek as one of Pajak's limbs whipped him in the face. Adal stumbled backward into one of the pillars.

Pajak thrust another of his legs at Adal who managed to duck just as the powerful hit crashed into the pillar behind him, denting the frame and causing the metal to groan in protest. Adal slid from under Pajak's legs, not wanting to corner himself. As he backed into the room, Pajak shot another bone shattering strike at Adal. Adal dropped to the floor as a sharp pang erupted, and the room went quiet. Adal looked up at the stunned Pajak and traced the extended leg to its end. In Pajak's haste to finish Adal, he stabbed Fausto directly through the face. As Adal's eyes met Fausto's, his two blades fell to the floor, and Cog's twin slumped to the ground lifeless.

32

You Ready For This?

Arija stood, her mouth agape and her eyes moving from Fausto to Pajak. Her mother's voice crept into her mind. *Finish this.* Arija sprang into action, running under Pajak's arm. She crossed over Adal and swept her blade through the air, burying it into Pajak's thigh. The engineered knife ripped through the metal of his leg like it was flesh and Pajak screamed and doubled over in pain.

Before Pajak could strike at Arija, Adal moved in and brought his fist to the face of the creature. A dull crunch was met by a spurt of green fluid from Pajak's mouth. Arija removed her blade from his leg and buried it into Pajak's torso. He shifted sideways and fell to the floor as Adal brought another blow to Pajak's ribs. The tides of the battle had turned, and it was time the man behind the monsters fell. As Pajak hit the floor, Adal and Arija were at him with murderous intent.

Adal buried his knuckled fist into Pajak's face as an explosion rocked the hall. The pillars and walls about them reverberated and the sheer pressure of the blast brought Adal and Arija to a crouching halt. Arija brought her hands up to protect her head as small particles of debris rained down upon them.

Looking toward the source of the explosion, there was a newly formed hole in the ornate ceiling of the hall. Debris littered the ground, and as Adal and Arija glared through the strange formation, a craft drifted into view. A bright light from several spinning parts blinded Adal and Arija as they stared in awe.

Adal and Arija stepped backward and away from Pajak as the craft lowered into the room. Pajak didn't move, struggling to suck in air and too bent and broken to push himself out of the way.

Dust and debris blew about as the machine lowered to the ground and three large legs extended from beneath the craft as it set down on the smooth floor. The sides of the machine had been battered and dented, but they could still see the remnant of a faded red cross on the side of it.

"No way," Adal gasped.

"Who could be—?" Arija was interrupted as the doors slid open and a plume of steam flowed from its sides. Looking into the darkness of the open doorway, Webley thundered from the shadows battered and beaten with a bandage crudely wrapped around his head and left eye. He had similar bandages around his right arm and legs. His clothes were torn in many areas and singed off in others.

389

"Impossible!" Pajak gasped.

"Webley!" Adal and Arija shouted in unison. They couldn't believe he had survived the explosion. He made his way over toward them, a slight limp on his left side.

"Tha's enough o' tha'!" Webley bellowed as he marched over to the group. "This fightin' stops now!"

"Webley! You should be dead!" Pajak snarled, using his arachnid legs to lift himself into a standing position.

"Pajak, tha's enough from ye! This foolishness ends! I have let you continue to break my heart fer' too long! This is all my fault. I should never 'ave let this go on, but I was blinded by my love fer' ye!" Webley marched past Adal and Arija and directly over to Pajak who seemed to cower in his maker's presence.

"You never could stop me, Webley! This is my world." Pajak paused as he coughed up more green liquid. "This is my Machine. You cannot stop me. You don't have the resolve. Take your Topsiders and just le—" Pajak's words were hushed as Webley thrust his hand outward and grasped Pajak by the throat, lifting him into the air with one hand. The arrogance and pride left Pajak's face and was replaced by fear.

"The saddest day in a father's life is when he realizes his own children 'ave become monsters. Ye' became a monster long ago, but I was too weak te' see it. Not anymore. Ye' are done, Pajak. It is time te' face your defeat!" Webley glared into his son's eyes but spoke to Adal and Arija. "Ye two, get in the craft. This ain't a place fer' ye."

"Hey man, I'm not leaving you," Adal retorted, stepping toward Webley.

"Webley, you're hurt. We need to get you some attention," Arija added, looking at his poorly treated wounds.

"Not up fer' discussion! The two of ye, get in the craft NOW! I will be jus' fine." Webley's voice bore a strong presence. An edge insisted they listen to his demands.

Adal and Arija turned and slowly made their way over to the gangway of the tattered mobile aid unit. Taking a fleeting look over her shoulder as they walked up the small ramp, Arija could see that Webley still held Pajak in the air, unmoving as if they were the climax of a movie that had been paused.

As soon as Adal and Arija were inside the mobile clinic, the sliding doors slammed closed behind them. They both jumped at the sound, but their attention was immediately drawn to their new surroundings.

The craft was filled with strange machines similar to the ones they'd seen in Avani's shop. Countless shelves filled with assortments of parts ran the length of the inside of the craft on either side, and in the center was an examination chair identical to the one they had both been in the day before. At the far end, a set of steps led up to a piloting deck with two chairs for the pilot and a copilot.

There, sitting in the pilot's chair was Kip. His newsboy cap was charred on the ends, his clothing was ripped, and he had a large gash on the right side of his face, but he was alive.

"Holy shit! Kip!" Adal shouted, running to the pilot's deck with Arija close behind. Arija's heart raced and filled with joy as she saw the young Dweller alive and well. Adal and Arija wrestled over each other to wrap their arms around him.

"All right! I get it! You love me! Now let's get out of here! No time!" Kip straightened his hat and shifted the vehicle into gear. Adal took an extra moment to squeeze the kid as tightly as he could as Arija wiped a rogue tear from her face. Adal turned his head from her to fight his own tears. Kip flipped several switches and pulled on levers, not taking his eyes off the window ahead of him. Slowly, the room began to move as the craft lifted from the ground.

"Avani? Cog?" Arija asked, hopeful. Kip sat in silence. The urge to burst into tears nearly won once more, and Arija dug her nails into the palms of her hands.

"Where are we going?" Arija finally asked, thinking about Webley. "We can't just leave him here."

"Yeah, Kip. What's that all about? Don't leave the guy."

Kip ignored them for a moment and focused on getting the craft into the air. "Webley will be fine. This was his call. I'm just driving this thing. Trust me, you don't want to be here." Kip added. They were now well into the air and slowly making their way through the large hole in the ceiling. Once cleared, Adal and Arija stared out of the window at the horrific sights The Roost had to offer. Arija gasped as she saw the horrid nest of Kleinmasch stirring and expanding outward around them.

"What is this place?" Adal asked.

"The Roost. It's where the Kleinmasch live. That's why we don't want to hang around." Kip motioned out of the window. Droves of thousands of creatures marched toward the hall.

"Kip, we can't leave him in that!" Arija protested again, this time the frustration in her voice was noticeable.

"I don't have a choice. Webley wanted it like this," Kip replied as they turned and made their way through The Roost.

"Dude, this isn't you. You don't run from fights. We do this as a team. Let's get in this!" Adal replied, sitting in the copilot's seat next to Kip. "I know you want a piece of them. Think of Avani."

As Adal uttered his mother's name, Kip slammed on the brakes and brought the craft to a hover high above the floor of The Roost. He stared straight ahead for a couple minutes before bursting from his seat and flying past Arija.

"Wait, where are you going?" Arija asked as she and Adal chased Kip to the rear of the craft. As Kip reached the far end, he knelt at the base of a shelf and pressed a rivet. A distant clank was followed by several of the shelves sliding aside, exposing the open air and several harnesses that fell from the ceiling. Adal and Arija stared at Kip as he pressed a small button next to the open window which resulted in two large guns lowering from a secret panel and orienting themselves to point out the window.

"What is this?" Adal asked, tugging at one of the harnesses.

"Kip, I don't even want to know why you put this in here, but what can we do to help?" Arija asked.

"Put on the harnesses and stand behind one of the guns. I'm driving!" Kip turned and made his way

393

back to the pilot's seat. Adal and Arija looked at one another but did as they were told.

"Kip, you ready for this?" Adal asked, looking down the sights.

"Just hang on! This one is for my mum!" Kip jerked the machine back to life, and the group headed back toward the great hall, and deep into The Roost.

Arija and Adal shot at anything, and everything that moved as Kip soared back toward the hall where they had left Webley. The hall was covered by thousands of Kleinmasch climbing over each other and fighting to get inside. The scene looked like something straight out of a zombie movie, and Arija had to fight not scream as they approached.

The closer they got to the hall the more Arija wondered if they were diving toward their deaths. Even with the massive machine guns of the mobile clinic, there was no way they could kill all the Kleinmasch and get to Webley.

"Kip!" Adal yelled over the rush of wind. "Just get to Webley. We can't take them all at once like this."

Kip didn't reply, but Arija felt the shift of the mobile clinic changing direction. Soon they were so close to the mound of Kleinmasch that used to be the hall, that Arija figured she could probably reach out and slap one of the ugly faces of the spider-like creatures. The mobile clinic crashed into the horde of creatures, sending several of them off in various directions and then they were back in the hall.

Pajak was crumpled in the corner, and Webley was fighting off at least a dozen Kleinmasch, the creatures overtaking him as more and more seeped through the hole in the roof. Webley's eyes widened as he saw the ship approaching him and he kicked a group of Baeg that approached him.

Arija took a deep breath and aimed her sights on the creatures closest to Webley. Adal kept his fire on the new coming horde of Kleinmasch, doing his best to keep any more from making their way toward the Creator.

As Kip brought the craft as low to the ground as he could, Webley grabbed a Cead that was clinging to his side and threw it across the hall. He reached up and grabbed the edge of the craft as Adal dropped the gun and grabbed Webley's hand. "Go! Go! Go!" Adal yelled over his shoulder.

Kip pulled on one of the ship's leavers and the craft tilted back to almost a forty-five-degree angle. Arija held onto her weapon to stop from sliding across the ship and continued to fire at anything that moved.

A group of Gearrtha and Cead jumped at the craft, but Arija sent a barrage of bullets at them before they could latch onto Webley. Webley pulled himself onto the ship just as it broke through the wall of Kleinmasch and back into The Roost. Once they were clear of the horde, Arija dropped the machine gun and ran toward Webley.

"I'm fine. Don'cha worry 'bout me." Webley said, between panting breaths.

"What do we do now?" Kip asked as he pushed out of The Roost and into the light of the Machine.

"We go back te' my 'ouse and regroup. But first, we get Adal and Arija back to their 'ome."

Arija shot Adal a look. They couldn't leave now. Cog and Avani were dead, and there were hordes of Kleinmasch who would be looking for revenge. What would that mean for the Dwellers that lived in the Machine?

Adal intertwined his fingers around Arija's, brought her hand up to his lips, and planted a lingering kiss on the back of her hand. "Or . . . we go back to Webley's house. Whatever is left of it anyway. We can't just go back home and let the people of the Machine suffer. We come up with a new plan, and we take that spider-man looking bastard down!" Adal met Webley's eyes as he spoke.

Webley waited a moment before turning to Kip and saying, "Ye' heard the man."

The craft jerked to the side as Kip took a sharp turn, changing their direction toward Webley's home.

"You ready for this?" Adal pulled Arija to his chest, and she leaned her head on his shoulder, finally able to relax.

"Always."

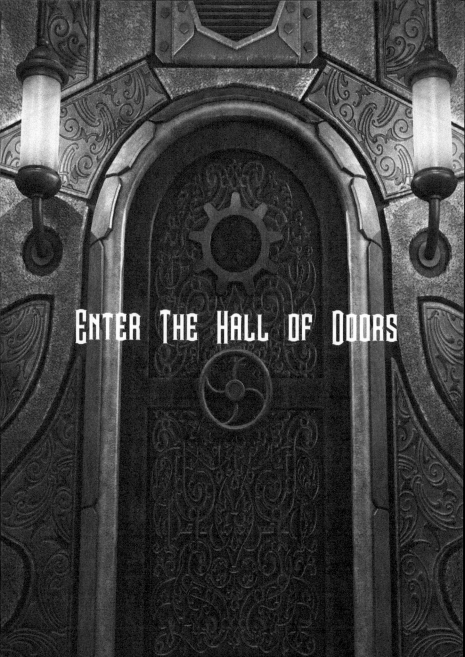

ENTER THE HALL OF DOORS

Adal and Arija loaded into the mobile clinic. Things had calmed down a little in the Machine since they'd defeated Pajak, and Webley had decided it was time to show them something important.

Neither of them had any idea where they were going and every time they questioned him, Webley would only smile at them and say, "Ye'll 'ave te' see." Then he would go back to piloting the craft. Occasionally, Adal would shoot a look to Kip in search of clues, only to have him shrug back.

Adal and Arija hadn't let Kip leave their side since Avani had died. They felt responsible for keeping him out of trouble and knew Avani wouldn't want to see him go back to living with the Desps and stealing to survive.

The craft made a sharp turn to the left, and this time, Adal slid into Arija. She placed the palm of her hand on his chest and it lingered there a long moment before she pulled it away.

"Looks are free, but you can't just be hitting on me like that, Arija," Adal flexed his chest and looked down at his pecks.

Arija scoffed, grinning wildly before clenching her fist and slamming it into his chest. Adal's face turned down in a scowl.

"Oh, big man can't take a hit?"

Adal raised one eyebrow. "I can handle anything you throw at me, little girl," he replied, trying to mend his ego.

"Oh really?" Arija asked.

"Sure enough!"

Arija grinned mischievously and grabbed Adal by the collar, pulling him close and pressing her lips against his.

In that moment, Adal's world fell away. Thoughts were replaced by the sound of blood pulsing through his veins. When Arija pulled away, he reached for her, needing to feel the warmth of her lips on his again, as if they were the only thing that could warm his guarded heart. Arija placed one cold, delicate hand on his face and then suddenly the world rushed back into view.

"Uhh . . . I . . . I . . . mean, next time warn me. Sneaking one in there on me like that," Adal stuttered nervously, clearing his throat and straightening his collar.

He cursed himself for ruining the moment, so he did the only thing he could do . . . he made it worse. "I mean, that was definitely the best kiss you've ever had, right?"

Arija rolled her eyes, doing her best to hide her smile. Adal looked at her expectantly, and she could tell he was looking for confirmation.

She couldn't help herself.

"Meh," she replied, shrugging her shoulders and turning her eyes toward the back of Webley's head.

Arija let him wait for a few minutes before she turned back toward him. After all, he deserved a little grief. He'd made her wait for ten years for this moment. He could stand a few more minutes.

When Arija decided she'd made him suffer long enough, she slid back close to him. Adal was still sitting there, mouth half open, staring at her. She let a big smile spread over her face. The first real smile she'd had in what felt like forever.

399

Adal placed his hand on her cheek. He traced the line of her jaw down to her chin then pulled her toward him into another kiss, this one soft and sweet. He wrapped his arms around her waist and planted a soft kiss on her cheek. Arija nuzzled her face into his chest just as the mobile clinic touched ground.

Webley rose from his seat and walked past the three passengers. "Well, 'ere we are!" Webley opened the hatch door and stepped outside with Adal, Arija, and Kip sliding out behind him.

They stood on another platform, deep in the Machine, but unlike most of the platforms Adal and Arija had seen, this one didn't seem to lead to anything important. At the far end of the empty platform stood a single door. The door was black and looked almost exactly like a bank vault.

Before Adal or Arija could ask any questions, Webley made his way to the door and placed one large hand on the spindle "This was somethin' tha' Cog wanted te' show ye. He helped me build this. I think tha' he'd want me te' take ye 'ere. The lock inside is always movin'. Ye' 'ave te' be able te' feel the mechanisms movin' an know just when te' pull…" Webley went back to focusing on his hands.

Just as Arija was about to ask what was behind the door, Webley yanked the handle sideways and pulled the door open.

"After ye'." Webley motioned for the group to enter.

The vault door opened into a long, narrow hallway dimly lit by dozens of Edison bulbs. At the end of the hall was another door identical to the one they had just come through. Webley squeezed past Adal and Arija with Kip pushing his way behind him.

"Wow! This place is the coolest!" Kip yelled, his words bouncing off the metallic walls.

Webley didn't need to focus to open the second door. As soon as he grabbed it he pulled, and the door popped open with a sound like a suction cup being removed.

Kip pushed past everyone and ran into the dark room. As Arija and Adal stepped through the entryway, Webley closed the door behind them, snuffing out the small stream of light from the hallway.

Arija's heart thumped in her chest. She hated feeling claustrophobic, and in the darkness of the room, she felt like the walls were closing in on her. Arija reached out a blind hand, grabbing onto Adal's arm. A distant 'clank' rang out, and in another instant, the room was lit by large bulbs that slowly grew to life.

Arija looked up at Adal who was wagging his eyebrows at her and she let go of his arm. The walls were lined with numerous tubes, pipes, coils, and all other assortments of parts that seemed to bleed to the center of the room. Arija followed the pipes with her eyes until they landed on an archway.

Webley walked from the doorway over to a large panel where Kip already stood, staring at the surface.

"What's all this?" Adal asked as he approached the panel with its dozens of knobs and switches. All of which had strange words or symbols etched into the metallic surface below them.

"What does this machine do?" Arija asked, shooting a glare at Kip as he reached past Webley to try to flip one of the switches. Kip, caught her look

401

out of the corner of his eye and pulled his arm back to his side.

"This is somethin' special tha' Cog helped me build. Ye' see, I'm a Creator, an this world isn't the first tha' I've been a part of. Travelin' back an forth was getting' exhausting over time. So, Cog helped me catalog all the worlds. This place is how I get te' them." Webley fanned his hand over the controls.

Arija's eyes bulged as she realized the strange words and symbols weren't labels, they were names. Name of other worlds.

"Wait, so you mean this place is like a portal or something? And you can go to other planets? Does Scotty know about this?" Adal joked, walking over to another panel with a row of strange necklaces hanging from it.

Webley stood in confused silence for a moment, Adal's reference lost on him. "Those are the keys! Ye' need one o' them te' get back. Ye take the chain an' spin it as fast as ye' can. If the portal is closed, it will open. If it's open, ye' jus' jump through an' no worries. Always make sure te' close the portal behind ye, though. Never know who may make their way through with ye'," Webley warned.

"How do you close—?" Arija asked when the room started to shake as the portal roared to life. Panicked, Arija shot her gaze from side to side as a bright light erupted from the center of the room and a portal opened. Arija brought her focus to Adal, but he wasn't touching anything. She then brought her gaze back to the control panel, but Kip was no longer there. She ran over to the controls and saw that one of the switches had been turned to 'on'.

"Taraveil," Arija whispered as she read the label under the switch.

"Kip don't!" Adal shouted. Kip was making his way down the side wall, sprinting for the portal.

"Let's get this party started!" Kip shouted, running into the light. "Cannonball!" he yelled as he disappeared into the vortex.

Arija turned, wide-eyed and fuming at Adal. This kid was going to get her killed. She locked eyes with Adal, then they both sprang into action. Adal grabbed two of the keys from their hooks and whistled as he tossed one to Arija. She caught it in mid-air and threw it around her neck.

"Ye' two be careful! Ye don't know what ye' are doin'!" Webley shouted at them but they were already standing in front of the portal, fingers laced around each other's.

"Just keep anything from coming back through the portal! We have to get him!" Adal called over his shoulder.

"I'm going to kill this kid!" Arija growled as she looked into the blue electric current of the active portal.

"Me first!"

"I guess the fun is just starting, huh?" Arija squeezed Adal's hand as they leaped into the light and disappeared.

THE END
FOR NOW

Thank you for reading **Webley and The World Machine.** If you enjoyed Adal and Arija's story, help other science fiction readers by leaving a review on Amazon. It can be as short as you like and will greatly help get more attention for this book.

The book may be over but the characters still have many more adventures to tell. Another adventure from the Hall of Doors will be coming out in 2018. Here are some ways you can stay updated on my upcoming books:

1. Join my Facebook Fan Page (Bowtie's Book-O-Holics): https://www.facebook.com/groups/1398062083644123/

2. Visit my website to connect with me on social media and join my mailing list: https://zachchop.com/

About Zach

Zachary is a bow tie wearing, formal vest rocking, pocket watch using, sarcastic monster of a writer. Currently residing in Orlando, Florida, he spends his days working, writing and procrastinating.

Coupled with being an award winning author of young adult fiction, Zach spends his days trying not to kill himself with lethal levels of caffeine.

Zach is the author of the Gabrielle series, a young adult fantasy with a paranormal-historical-time traveling twist (try saying that five times fast) and Webley and The World Machine, a steampunk adventure with snarky yet lovable characters.

CPSIA information can be obtained
at www.ICGtesting.com
Printed in the USA
FSHW020516061118
53566FS